Cry 'God for Harry'

═══ A NOVEL ═══

Martha Rofheart

BOOK CLUB ASSOCIATES
LONDON

This edition published 1972 by
Book Club Associates
by arrangement with Talmy, Franklin Ltd

Made and printed in Great Britain by
The Garden City Press Limited
Pixmore Avenue Letchworth
Herts SG6 1JS

Cry 'God for Harry'

The game's afoot:
Follow your spirit; and, upon this charge
Cry 'God for Harry! England and Saint George!'

WILLIAM SHAKESPEARE

To my father-in-law, Will

THE HOUSES OF LANCASTER AND TUDOR

*Plantagenet Kings
†Lancaster Kings
‡Tudor Kings

EDWARD II*

EDWARD III* (the Black Prince)

RICHARD II*

Lionel Duke of Clarence

John of Gaunt Duke of Lancaster

Edmund Duke of York

(Henry Bolingbroke) HENRY IV†

John Beaufort Earl of Somerset

HENRY V . . m(1) . . Katharine of Valois . . . . m(2) . . . . Owen Tudor

Tom · John · Humphrey

HENRY VI† m Margaret of Anjou

John Beaufort 1st Duke of Somerset

Edward Prince of Wales

Edmund Earl of Richmond . . . . m . . . . (1) Margaret Beaufort

Owen

HENRY VII‡ m Elizabeth of York

HENRY VIII‡

Contents

BOOK I

The Boy

(Told by Henry of Monmouth,
later Henry V)

Chapter 1

We are not the true kings of England, though my father wore the crown before me. I knew this, I think, from my earliest years when King Richard was our liege lord. I call to mind the words of my grandfather, John of Gaunt; I was four and had cursed the king for calling my father to battle, taking him from us for long weeks.

He stood before me, that tall old man, the famous bright fairness all gone to white by my time, like a bleached bone at the water's edge; he spoke harshly, his big hands heavy on my shoulders.

"The king is sacred to his subjects. He is king by right of line. You are second cousin to Richard, Hal, and nobly born, but your duty and your honor are his. When you are grown, you will owe him your sword, and your life, if there is need. He is the king."

I was not much taller than his knee, so he did not beat me, but held out a dish of bears' grease soap, such as poor folk wash with, and bade me take it in my mouth. It was to wash out my ugly words. To this day my stomach heaves, remembering the taste.

I lived all my days till my seventh year among the Welsh border folk in our home castle of Monmouth. These Welsh are a small dark people, for the most part, and merry, though their saints are half pagan, and they love wild tales of magic and dark blood. At my nurse's knee I heard the songs of Madoc's sword that leaped from his hand to cut down his enemies, and of Merlin, who could call the wind. Later, when I came to fight the great Owen, I never feared his witchcraft, as most men did, and I a boy only.

Monmouth lies in a gentle scoop of valley, like a shallow bowl. The people pastured their cattle in the fields around our holding, for my grandfather was a gentle master in his later days; the grass was close-cropped by the grazing beasts and lay like a green carpet right up to the foothills. In the summer the bluebells covered the ground, so thick they were that no green showed. I used to think when I was very small that in the summertime our castle turned blue also—some trick of the light perhaps, from the blue sky overhead and the deeper blue underfoot. The hills rose steeply all around. I thought that they were mountains and that giants lived in them; when it thundered you could hear them walk. My nurse told me you could see them in the lightning if you looked hard, so I never hid my head under the coverlet, in case I should miss them. I missed them anyhow, for the lightning was so quick; I know now that she said it to keep me from fearing.

All us children were born at Monmouth, I myself, Tom, John, Humphrey, and my little sisters, Blanche and Philippa. Edward, who came before me, and only lived four days, lies in the chapel courtyard beside our mother, who died when I had just turned six. Philippa was born then, the day of Mother's death, and for a time I would not look at her, poor babe, because I blamed her. She was a fair child but frail, for weeks hanging to life by a thread. Our great families do not expose girl-babies, even the puniest, preferring to use them as pawns in dynastic marriages. It is said the common country folk do abandon their weak newborns, especially females, in times of famine, and certainly I have heard them wail in the Welsh hills, my blood running cold, and even on our own moors in the night. But then famine is always with the poor, God help them.

My mother's face I always confused with that of Our Lady, whose images she much resembled. Her name was Mary, too, and she had gone early to be a nun, studying with the Poor Clares. But she was heiress to the vast de Bohun estates, and my grandfather, ambitious for his only true-born son, parleyed long and hard and got her finally. They were betrothed when she was ten, and my father, Henry of Bolingbroke, not yet fourteen. She bore her first child at fifteen, and of the seventh she died; she was twenty-three. I remember her face, long, Italianate, and very sweet, her brow high and rounded, her eyes large, with calm, full lids and eyebrows thin as pen strokes arching above. Her mouth was grave and sweet, too, but when she smiled, she was like a child, for her teeth were as small as milkteeth, with a space between the front two. All we boys take after our mother, being brown of hair and eyes, though Tom is bigger boned. The little girls have the Plantagenet fairness from our father, but paler; they are like moon maidens, delicate and cool.

I alone, of all of us, have any real memory of our mother; Tom and John recall only that she wore blue and smelled good, and Humphrey can remember nothing but the little man, made of sweet, hard dough, that she gave him once when he was teething. Blanche was a baby still, and hardly knew her anyway; our great ladies, who are forever bearing or in childbed, mostly give their children early out to suck. But I remember Mother's books, lives of the saints, exquisitely written on vellum, with pictures marvelously colored and overlaid in gold. I was not allowed to touch them, but she read to me, holding me in her lap and turning the pages. She sighed sometimes, and I think now that she missed the life of the cloister, though my father loved her well. But she was grave and bookish, spending much of her time reading. I remember her eyes were rimmed often with red, from long hours in a poor light. She was fond of romances, too, in the French tongue, and Latin songs, but these I never saw till after her death. All her books came to me then; I have them by me still.

I remember well the day she died; it was a May morning, fresh and fair. Tom and I had both been given our first hawks and were trying them out on the broad lawn in back of the kitchens. We would have falcons later, for we were of the blood royal, but these little birds were our first. I can feel still the tiny claws gripping my finger; mine was white, with a breast speckled like an egg. I called her Melusine, after the fairy in the song. Tom's hawk was black as pitch, and bigger; there was no favoritism about it—we had chosen them when they were hatched and had little more than a scant pinkish fuzz. White Will, who tended the falconry, had tied threads, blue for me and red for Tom, on each, to tell them apart.

We called it a lawn, the place where we stood, but it was bare and scruffy; we boys played there at tilting, and the dogs were let loose to roll and to scratch. White Will was there, instructing us in the hooding and loosing; he was still young, but his hair and brows were quite white. His eyes were pink and frightened me, but he was kind and gentle, and had a good smell, like leather and hay. I know now that he was born white, like some rabbits and mice.

Our father, for a rarity, was home, and not off somewhere at a tournament or at court. He came out with my mother to watch us at our hawking and to sit in the sun. He is a man they called ruddy, for kindness, I think; his hair was the color of scraped carrot and his lashes and brows reddish, too. Against them his face was the wrong color, a raw burned look. He was handsome though, but for that; he was sturdy and strong, broad in the shoulders, his legs bowed a little from much riding, like all our best knights'. He grew thick, later, and bloated with disease, and his face—but never mind. In those earliest days I thought him the finest knight in the world.

Mother was gay, happy to have him home with her; she moved awkwardly, the child heavy in her. I remember she was wearing her favorite color, blue—a dress cut very full, with hanging sleeves that touched the ground. There was a stone bench where they sat; she was laughing and feeding my father bits of marchpane. Some of her hair had slipped from its knot and was showing under her coif; my father pulled it playfully, leaning close to her. She was all rosy from the low edge of her gown up. She saw me staring and called to me, giving me a piece of the marchpane. "You spoil him, Mary," he said, frowning. "You spoil all the boys. . . ."

"Oh, Harry," she said, "don't scold . . . I will not have them by me long."

She meant that we would leave her house and go to a knight's household to be reared and trained, as all nobly born boys do when they reach a certain age. But I felt a sadness in her words then, and after, as though she had seen her fate.

Tom, from eagerness, let loose his hawk too early, and it flew to the top of a tall old oak tree and would not come down. White Will coaxed it down hours later but not before it had damaged its claws scrabbling in the high branches. Mine, Melusine, performed perfectly, spotting her prey, a gray nesting dove, and bringing it down almost at my feet. I disgraced myself; when I saw the dove, all bloody, and Melusine's beak stabbing in the entrails, I leaned over and vomited up the marchpane. Tom was sent indoors to our nurse, for a punishment, but I—Father hit me so hard on the side of the head that I fell, my teeth rattling. My mother ran and dropped heavily to her knees beside me, cradling my head; I had a glimpse of Father's face, dark red with rage, but that is all, for Mother cried out then, putting her hand to her side. There was much confusion—Father picked up my mother and carried her inside; I remember her head, limp on his shoulder, the coif fallen and all her long hair loose on his sleeve. The hanging sleeves trailed in the dust as they went. White Will helped me up, and I cried, burrowing my face into his shirt as he knelt beside me. White Will is dead now, too; such white creatures do not live long—the blood is weak. But he was a comfort then, the day of my mother's death.

I remember little of my mother's funeral, for the fever I took soon after drove it all to confusion in my mind. I recall vaguely a multitude in somber dress, or so it seemed, a chill, unseasonable wind, and the horses. The cortege was followed by great black horses, draped, too, all in black, black plumes nodding at their huge heads. One, the lead horse, shied at something in the lane, rearing high and pawing, blocking the procession. My father, where he walked behind the casket, heard the beast's high whinny, and turned, his face dark with fury. He ran back from his place, drawing his sword, and with the flat of it beat the horse to its knees. I remember its eyes, the whites rolling, the black plumes draggling in the dust, and the pitiful forefeet that scratched for a footing like a snared rabbit's. They dragged it out of the way; we heard it moaning until we turned into the chapel yard. They had to run it through later, for its neck was broken.

The house was full for some days after, with the folk that had come to pay their respects to the dead, but my father did not drink or feast with them but kept mostly to his chambers. Many were inclined to think ill of him for this, for it was against custom, offending some of his guests, but the Lady Kat said gently that it was his great grief, overcoming his courtesy, and shielded us children from his dark moods. We called her the Lady Kat to distinguish her from our real grandmother, our mother's mother. The Lady Kat was my Grandfather Gaunt's third wife, and dearly beloved. She was a commoner, born Katharine de Roet, daughter of a poor Flemish knight; she had made, in the eyes of the court, an unbelievably good marriage, above her station, and was Lady Swynford when my lord grandfather first saw her and loved her. She had been his mistress for twenty-five years, after the death of her husband, Sir Hugh, and had borne three sons to Gaunt. John of Gaunt held fast to her, through two titled marriages of state; after the death of his second, Constance, the Infanta of Spain, he persuaded the young king, Richard, his nephew, to grant him permission to marry his beautiful commoner. The young king, high-spirited and autocratic, was moved by the long and legendary romance, approving the match, and legitimizing their bastard sons, creating for them the lands and title of Beaufort. He won much disapproval among his peers for this act, for it was high-handed and without precedent, and a blatant gesture of favoritism. I knew all this later; at the time of my mother's death I knew only that the Lady Kat was lovable, and my uncles Beaufort kind, and supposed that King Richard in his wisdom loved them too.

The Duchess Katharine, Lady Kat, to her death-day wore a fabled beauty; when I was six she could stop your heart. She was more than forty then, but her age had left little mark on her, and the wild years of her love had brought her to a glow. She was all color and shine, though the court fashion was for a pallid ivory; her thick hair showed a gleam of red where it waved beneath her gauzy headdress, and her eyes were like great blue gems. She dressed in rich clothes—velvets and brocades, amber and russet colors, and bright gold yellows; against the dark castle stone she moved like a flame, her lips and cheeks lightly tinted with the Moorish paints my Grandfather Gaunt had brought from his Spanish kingdom.

My real grandmother, Mother's mother, Joan de Bohun, the Countess of Hereford, I could not love. I respected her, of course, all who walked, even my Grandfather Gaunt, did that, for she was a prideful and learned woman, with a straight back and forthright tongue. She found much fault with all us boys, except for little Humphrey, who even at three had none of the toddler's playfulness and stared as quiet and solemn as an owl. Tom and I, especially, felt often the rough edge of her tongue and even the smart on our knuckles of the great key she wore at her belt. She named us unruly and ill-mannered as puppies; I was glad to see the back of her as she rode away home. She left a fortnight after her daughter's death-day, but the Lady Kat stayed on to mother us. Our father claimed she spoiled us, whenever we were under his feet or our voices rose, but all the household loved her, and even the servants flew to do her bidding. She had a bearing at once grave and merry; she was the only grown person I ever remember who listened, truly, when children spoke; or who did not bend to us, but raised us up, as it seemed. The name of Katharine has been dear to me always, since her time.

Many of our funeral guests stayed long past their time, for they were reluctant to leave the soft air of Monmouth and journey in the dusty heat. There was plague still in London; Richard's queen, Anne, the sweet-faced Princess of Bohemia, had died of it at Sheen Castle just before my mother's death, and none knew how far afield the infection had spread. It was midsummer before our castle was quiet again. Our father grieved terribly still and could not bear to see us boys romp or laugh; Lady Kat was forever shooing us out of his sight, to spare him, and us, too, I believe. This was how I caught the strange fever that to this day comes back upon me in the hot months.

It was August, perhaps; a still day, you could see the heat shimmer in waves above the grass, all yellow now and dry. No breeze stirred the wall hangings, though all the windows were thrown open. The rushes on the floor of the great hall were changed daily, but still they rotted where they lay; the stone walls seemed to sweat. For days now we had been picking lice out of our clothes and even our hair.

There was, some distance from the castle, a little stream that came rushing down from the hills; some of the village boys had dammed it up for a swim place, and would go there to splash and play in the summer. The pages from our household went sometimes, too, coming back with their long hair dark and stuck to their cheeks with the wet. Tom and I begged to go along this day, seeing the page Rolfe, whom we knew well, setting out with some others. The Lady Kat, taking pity on us, cooped up and idle in the heat, gave us in his charge, and so we went, joyfully.

Rolfe was a big boy, looking clumsy in his page's hose, and somehow comic, with his great feet like boats in their long, pointed shoes. He was kind, though, to us younger children, as some of the others were not. This was his last year in our house; he would go back after Christmas to his father's manor, somewhere in the north, so I suppose he must have been about fifteen, perhaps. The others were younger, sons of some of the Marcher barons nearby; one of them was as fair and pretty as a girl, with fresh cheeks and hair curling onto his shoulders. I kept stealing looks at him, for I thought him as beautiful as an angel; his skin was so delicate and fine that bluish veins showed at the temples and the red flooded into his cheeks as he saw me watching. Later, at Richard's court, I saw many such, but my father liked a more robust sort about him.

We were lucky at the swim hole, for there were none of the village boys about; they must have started the haying early that year. The pages were uneasy, for they were allowed no weapons yet, only small jeweled daggers at their belt, used at table, and not much sharper than toys. There were still some rough fellows around the villages; the great Wat Tyler rebellion had left the commons bold, those that remained after the hangings and punishments, and hedge-priests still gathered the people sometimes, under cover of night. I knew little of this then, except what some of the under-nursemaids whispered to us children when we were naughty. "Old Wat will get you," they would say, or "John Ball eats bad boys." But the noble boys of our house knew more and dreaded ambush; they never went far afield without company. Rolfe told me that most of the village people hated the manor folk and jeered at the pages when they rode past; he, Rolfe, had even been hit once, by a stone, between the shoulder blades.

The little pond was very still, yellow-brown in its depths, though the stream which fed it ran green and sparkling down the rocky hill. A dark cloud of insects hovered over it; some of the boys took sticks and drove them away. Rolfe said it was too deep for Tom and me; we must wade in the shallow running brook. I untied the points of my hose; I had just learned how and liked to show off, but Tom was too young and chubby-fingered, so Rolfe did it for him. The water felt wonderful, icy and delicious against our bare legs; we shouted with shock and joy.

The pages took off all their clothes, throwing them in heaps anyhow on the bank. Their bodies, naked as fishes, gleamed white beneath their sunburned faces. They none of them could swim, but they leaped about in the water, up to their necks it was, splashing and pushing one another under. Tom and I leaned on the stones of the dam and watched them, envying.

Without their fine, slashed sleeves and bright hose, they might have been peasant boys, merry and rough. They ducked and spattered one another, but the little girlish one—I never knew his name—they tumbled and teased mercilessly. One of the biggest, with a shock of black hair on his head and some beginning, too, between his long legs, even pissed on him, grinning. Tom laughed, but I saw the bright red rush into the pretty face and his soft mouth crumple as he tried to hold back from crying. Big Rolfe clouted the other boy on the ear and put his arm about the pretty page's shoulders, leading him out of the water and talking to him gently.

It had started a new game, though, and thin streams of bright silver made arcs in the air as the boys pursued one another, yelping. Tom tried it, too, and wet his long smock. Rolfe took it off to dry, as kind as a nursemaid he was, always, for all his great size. I took off mine, too, and we began playing in the pool, just at the edge, where it was shallow. It was not so cold as the stream, or perhaps we were used to it by then; we lay down in the water, trying to float. Tom could almost do it—he was still fat, like a baby—but I went under and came up gasping. It was great fun, though, the wetness, and the nakedness, and no grown-ups about to scold; I think it was the only time in my childhood that I had been without supervision. Certainly it was the last.

It was late when we came back to the castle; I remember our shadows long on the grass and grotesquely humped at the top, for Rolfe carried Tom and me both in his arms the last bit of the way. I was so tired that the walls of the castle, reddened in the sun, danced before my eyes, and when we crossed the footbridge, the moat, dry these many hot weeks, seemed to toss like the sea. When Rolfe put me down, I retched, though there was no food in my stomach; long strings of mucus hung from my throat, gagging me. I remember little fat Tom backing away from me, his face screwed up and red, crying, "Ugly—ugly Harry!" and the Lady Kat's hand, cool on my forehead, and that is all; I must have fainted.

The days were cool again, already, before I recovered, slowly. Much was changed. My old nurse had taken my sickness and died, and a new one tended me, along with the Lady Kat. The pages had all been beaten and sent back to their fathers in disgrace, for my own father was wild with fear for my life and laid the blame to them. All except Rolfe were punished; he too had died, like the old nurse, and, hearing, I wept weak salty tears. Tom, who, for a miracle, had not taken the fever, and all my brothers and sisters had been sent away to Pleshy, to our grandmother of Hereford. I remember feeling sorry for them, under her harsh care.

My father had sent to Sheen Castle for the king's own physician, fearing the plague. When he examined me, though, and bled me, he said it was not, but a thing he called marsh fever that came in the hot months. My father forbade any of the household to go near to that swim hole and even, later, had the dam destroyed. The next year though, we heard, they dammed it up again, so little did the nobles' word go for in all the country parts.

When I was able to hear and see again, but still too weak to raise my head to feed myself, I heard my father say to the Lady Kat, "It sickens me to see my oldest puny—like his dead brother . . . he'll likely not live to see his twentieth year . . . at least Thomas proves strong. . . ."

The Lady Kat hushed him quickly and turned her head to the bed where I lay. I closed my eyes, pretending sleep, and heard her say, "But the boy Rolfe took it—took the fever—the strongest and biggest of all took it. Illness is a mystery of itself—I, as a child, survived the plague, and my sister never took it, though my father and mother both died of it. . . ."

My father laughed shortly and said, "Let's hope you're right, Madame Katharine . . . myself, I have more hopes for the other three. . . ."

It was long before I forgave my father this, but I think now I profited from his harsh words. I have ever strived to set myself above others in all sports and deeds of chivalry, practicing by the hour to master a heavy bow, for instance, or to gentle a hot-blooded horse. For all my effort, and all my achievements even, the words of praise from my father have been few. He was a hard man, and grew harder with his bitter years.

Chapter 2

I was long months recovering and forbidden by the doctor to take more exercise than to walk from bed to closestool and back again; on top of the fever, which had waned, I had growing pains, he said, and the joints were sadly weak. I think now that I was exhausted from much bleeding; it was done three times a day, and after the first weeks there was scarcely a spot on my body that did not bear the mark of the lancet. The room reeked with the smell of blood and of physics, for in the winter months the windows were barred and hangings drawn across them. Braziers were set around my bed and in the far corners of the chamber; their smoking choked the nostrils, but still there was a chill of the tomb. My eyes watered and my nose ran constantly. My bowels, too, were often loose, and the chamberpot full, when I could make my way to it quickly enough. The maids sprinkled vinegar against the smells, but there was little use; the bedclothes stank, though they were changed daily, and I lived in a revolting miasma of my own filth, like a dog in its vomit. I used to watch the maids when they thought me sleeping, grimacing and holding their noses when they came near me. I thought the plague could not be much worse; at least one might die of it.

In spite of all, I grew stronger slowly, and by Christmastime the doctor left us. We were like children let out of school, I, the Lady Kat, and my new nurse, Joan Waring. She was a young Welshwoman, widowed, and in the fullness of her strong beauty. She wrapped me about with woolen robes and propped me high against the pillows, while she and Lady Kat drew aside the hangings and threw open the windows. The air rushed in, blowing the rushlights and making me cough. Joan Waring thumped my back, holding a bowl to my mouth. "Spit it up, boy," she said. "Spit out the poison! Doctors! . . . God made the good air and put us on the earth to breathe it!"

I coughed and spit, coughed and spit; when it was over I felt empty and new, the breath filling my chest with an ease that was like a miracle. I sank back, looking about me. The room was filled with light, for there was a new fall of snow, and the sun sparkled on it. I had seen nothing but half-shapes for weeks. The Lady Kat looked frightened by her daring and a little breathless; it was morning, and her hair was undone, hanging in a thick braid down her back. Smiling at herself a little, for I was barely seven years of age, she took a linen cloth from her sleeve and bound it up in a wife-coif, hiding all its beautiful disarray. I smiled, too, for I had grown, somehow, in worldliness, in this time out of the world. She put her arms around me and whispered, "Oh, Hal, I am a wife now. . . ." I stroked her cheeks. "But your hair is so pretty," I said. "I love you, Lady." "I love you, too, my Hal. . . ."

I saw my nurse, Joan Waring, clearly, too, for the first time. She looked to me very beautiful also, or perhaps all things did, that first day of my return to life. She was a big girl, I remember, with round arms and breasts and a long throat, full and straight as a column in a church. From it her firm chin rose, cleft in the middle, at a pure angle; her head she held very high. She had the old Celtic color, high red on the cheeks, over a milky skin, with thick black brows over light eyes, and a cloud of smoky hair. She did not smile often, for, as I saw later, her teeth were crooked, though white, and one was missing at the side. Her crooked teeth pushed out her upper lip a little and made it full. I wanted to kiss that pouting lip, and, even at seven, I knew how that mouth would feel. I never did kiss it—the years were too many between us—but I regret this still.

That night I was carried on a litter, wrapped in furs, to our little chapel to hear Christ's mass. The bearers' feet crunched in the moon-bright snow, and the icy diamond air stung my cheeks. I do not remember ever being so filled with pure happiness. My father was away from home; he was at Pleshy with Tom, who had hurt himself on some new snowshoes from Sweden. I did not think of that then, though, for all the rest of our housefolk crowded the chapel to give thanks for my recovery. My Grandfather Gaunt was there, beside his lady; he had aged since I saw him last and leaned heavily upon a cane. We heard prayers for my mother's soul and for the soul of my dead brother Edward. There was a statue of the Virgin, old, very old, carved in wood and stiff-looking in the antique way. Her hands, crossed on her breast, were too small, and the artist had not known how to carve the fingers, so that they looked like sausages. The colors of her robe were faded almost away, and the gold leaf was chipped, but the face brought tears to my eyes, for I saw my mother in it. There was that over-long, sweet chin, the bald, high forehead, and the little crescent smile that I remembered well. The Lady Kat moved to my side, for she feared I might be weak still; I waved her away, whispering that I wept for my mother. I could not tell her that the Holy Mother's image had brought the thought.

During the Latin, I looked around, seeing the pages, all new, sniggering and jostling where they stood, restless and bored. I wished that I could be among them; I even smiled in their direction when the priest was not looking, but they never saw—the candlelight was too dim. It was a new priest, too, not old Father Stephen; he stumbled on the words, this one, and the pages giggled. My grandfather looked at them sternly, and they must have felt it, even in the half-dark, for they quieted. I wondered if the old Father had died, and crossed myself in his memory, just in case. As we left the chapel, the bells began, for Christ's birthday, swelling out into the frosty air. They would go on for twenty-four hours, until midnight of Christ's day. In my deep joy, my happiness at being well again, silently, within me, I could imagine that they rang for me.

When I woke, late next morning, there were gifts for me; it was just coming into custom, the exchange of gifts on the birthday of Our Saviour. Englishmen had used to do it twelve days after, when the Three Wise Men had brought their gifts to the babe. The Lady Kat said we would save some for then, too. But this day there was a giant marchpane castle, I remember, all colored bravely and with little flags at each corner, flying the colors of Lancaster and York, and King Richard's own arms, too. It was a lovely sight, but I was too tired to do more than gaze at it and nibble a tiny morsel from the back, where it did not show. My father was not there, though I had hoped against hope, secretly. But he had sent some toy knights of Saracen workmanship, cunningly wrought in ivory and inlaid with gold. I turned one over idly in my hand, thinking shame that he chose this day to be with Tom, who, after all, had only sprained an ankle at play. He does not love me, I thought; I was still weak and easily moved to petulance.

Later, though, I took great enjoyment from these little knights, spreading them across the coverlet in ranks to fight mock battles, and when I was stronger, drawing battle plans before the fire on the hearthstone with a piece of charcoal. I charted many plans of strategy this way, in my lonely play, marking them out on paper, too. When my father came finally, I saw that he was well pleased with me, remarking that I had an old head for my years.

When spring came and I was well enough to sit a horse, we all of us removed to our manor at Kenilworth. My father would not chance another summer in the Monmouth fens. I loved the place, though, for here were all my first memories, and dearest. Often, in later years, I visited the old castle, pausing in the dim little chapel to look at the old wooden statue of Our Lady and its smooth, worn face that wore my mother's smile.

Chapter 3

Kenilworth was much grander, with a high tower that commanded a view for miles around; it had new hanging tapestries from France and many carved chairs and chests, but I never loved it as I did Monmouth, perhaps because it marked, in a way, the end of my childhood days. I think of it always as a place of lessons and study. Because of my illness, I had started my studies late; little Tom could already write his name and conjugate his Latin verbs, so it seemed to me, that to catch up, I worked sad, long hours. This cannot have been so, for we hunted, too, and practiced with blunted swords. But, where Tom took his letters from Father Rhisiart—the new young priest I had seen first at the Christ's mass, who was gentle and fumbling, with slow, sweet speech and a winning manner—I had my Latin and calculus, too, from our half-uncle Henry Beaufort, who was so brilliant a scholar that he dried up the juices of my mind.

My Uncle Henry was the second son of my Grandfather Gaunt and his mistress, Lady Kat; he had early chosen the church for a career, and, even before his legitimization by King Richard, he had risen high, for a bastard. He was, in time, to rise to one of the highest positions in the land. At the time I speak of, he was barely out of his teens and already a canonical lawyer. He was as handsome as a god-figure from a pagan frieze, in a high-nosed way, and patient with me, too, though lordly. But I never loved him as dearly as my other uncles; his eyes were the iciest I ever saw and seemed to look through you to something finer beyond. He never punished me, but marked my faults down on a sheet of paper, presenting it to my father each week. If the marks against me were few, I was let off with a cut in my small allowance-monies, but more often I was beaten and sent to bed supperless, without a candle. I cannot hold it against that uncle though, for it was his duty and his task to tutor me, and he was well paid for it besides. Often and often I have been told of my good fortune; many great nobles, and princes, even, can barely hold a pen. And later, in my brief time at Oxford, I was glad of this strict training, being able to hold my own against scholars nearly twice my years.

Uncle John, Lady Kat's oldest son, was not with us often; he had his own dukedom of Somerset, with much land and many villeins to keep in order, and a wife and two small children as well. Thomas, the youngest of my uncles, I loved the most dearly. He, of all of them, it seemed to me, was most like his mother. He was tall and robust and would be fat later, but then he was only eighteen, with long legs like tree trunks and big gentle hands. He had his mother's coloring, too, the thick, reddish hair and the dark blue eyes. He was married, too, but his bride was a child still, too young for bearing. He brought her with him once, at Easter-time I think it was; she was small and shy, with hair like a mouse's fur, and thin, little mouse bones, too, but she had a voice like one of God's own angels. High and pure it was and piercingly sweet; they would sing together of an evening, one or the other playing on the lute, and it was the finest sound you might ever hear. I think it was their only love-bond, for she died soon after, never having come to womanhood.

Thomas it was who taught me to play; it has been always one of my sweetest pleasures, though my voice is thin and disappoints me. Sometimes, when I am alone (a rare pleasure), I pull the curtains of my bed close around me and strum my lute and sing soft; then it seems to be a full, sweet, bardic sound, such as I might be proud of in company. Sometimes, in my tent, on the field of battle, I do this, too, in the soft night—a childish thing, but a comfort, too.

King Richard's own poet, Geoffrey Chaucer, came to us at Kenilworth, too; his dead wife, Philippa, had been Lady Kat's sister, and they three had been close for many years. I have heard said that his Criseyde, in *Troilus and Criseyde,* was modeled on my Lady Kat, in those years, when, as Katharine Swynford, she lived in flagrant concubinage with my Grandfather Gaunt. I hardly credit this, though, for his Criseyde is false and meanly small, though beautiful. I cannot think that men of genius draw wholly on real life for their creations, for where, then, would be their gift? Surely the Arthur the bards sing has never lived but in their divers songs!

He was a merry little man, this Master Chaucer, though saddened, too, at times, by all the ugly things of life. He must have been quite old then, for the Lady Kat swears he was above thirty years when she first met him, so long ago. But he had no sign of age about him, save deep lines at the corners of his eyes and a small paunch under his monkish robes. He affected a monk look —long, girdled robes, but in velvets and brocades, and often a little skullcap, too. Sometimes he wore a kind of full bonnet, which he said was Scots; I never saw him bareheaded, but I think he was totally bald. Sometimes the headgear would slip in a high wind, but never did I see a trace of hair beneath.

The king had given him a small manor house in London, but it had been burned, along with so many others, in the great commons' rebellion, and was never replaced. So now he had no holding of his own, though King Richard had granted him ten pounds a year for life; he spent his years now in visits to those manors where he was welcome, and to the king's court, too. Many, my tutor, Uncle Henry, among them, thought Master Chaucer's work of no great account, for it was in the vulgar tongue, but Richard held him to be a poet of great sweetness and understanding. My Grandfather Gaunt left me, when he died, many manuscripts from Geoffrey's pen, for he, too, was one of Chaucer's patrons. Among them is a eulogy upon the death of his first wife, Blanche of Lancaster, who would have been my grandmother. It is a lovely and moving piece of work; one would swear that the poet had loved the lady dearly. But then that is the cunning gift of these gifted people, that semblance of feeling that is truer than the feeling itself. I would rather have had that gift than a throne. A thing no one will believe.

My father, as I have said, was away from home more than he was present, and this was true more in these four years we spent at Kenilworth than in my mother's time. We children were always told that he was "on the king's business." He was first cousin to Richard, John of Gaunt being brother to Richard's father, Edward, who had been king before him. This King Edward had been known, even after he came to the kingship, as the Black Prince. I never saw him, for he died before my time; I used to think it a dire name and that he was like the devil, but the name was taken, I learned later, from his habit of wearing shining black armor into battle and the lists. I once saw a portrait, when I was older; it shows Edward golden-fair, like Richard and all his Plantagenet race. Such is the stuff of child imaginings. But, as I say, my father was often with the king, or at his court. I knew nothing of the kingly policies then or the plottings and counter-plottings that go on about famous men, but as I put it together in after years, one such plot had been discovered, a particularly vile one, against the king's person, and those who were in it, when discovered, were most cruelly punished, and many heads rolled. King Richard, afterward, confiscated the conspirators' holdings and distributed them among his truer friends, partly as reward and partly to strengthen his kingly position. One of these was my father, whom Richard created Duke of Hereford; men dubbing him then Henry of Hereford, Lancaster, and Derby, a mort of ti-tles, and carrying great wealth with it. Another close friend to Richard, Thomas Mowbray, Earl of Nottingham, had been created Duke of Norfolk. I remember that even to us there filtered down the London commons' name for this; they called it dukitting, so Richard must indeed have scattered dukedoms like wheat.

Tom and I, and even John, were getting big enough boys now to play with the younger of the pages, and one of our favorite games was this "dukitting." It is lost now, this game, in the mists of my memory, but it had to do with spying and beheading and the like. John, being the youngest, was most often beheaded, and Tom and I, having had from infancy a natural animosity, quar-reled bitterly over our mock dukedoms. It was, I see now, a grim play, for it, in its way, presaged the bitter events which were to come.

One day in January, it must have been when I was eleven, or nearly, my father rode into the gates, all shrouded with white like ghosts they were, he and his following, for it was snowing hard. He had been gone for almost a month and had not even remem-bered to send us our Christ gifts, though the Lady Kat said they must have been lost or stolen on the way. His face was grim as death; each year since my mother's death it had grown sharper and more shut-in upon itself. Warming himself before the fire, he told a fearful tale, not even bothering to shoo us children away.

He and this Mowbray I had mentioned before, now the Duke of Norfolk, had been riding together, each with but a few men-at-arms, from Brentford to London to join the king. It was a blustery December day, Father said, so cold their hands grew stiff inside their mail, and they had to keep blowing on them to keep them live for the reins. As they crossed Brentford Bridge, shrouded in mist, Mowbray drew horse near to my father and whispered words; words of treason, my father said. I could see my father hated the man; there was a cold fury in his face. I did not know what these words were, and do not even now; no man is sure, after what turned out, for event followed awful event in the months and years that followed.

When they reached London and Richard's court, my father went straight to Richard and repeated the man Mowbray's words. Mowbray denied them flatly. Each man was of high degree, noble, and a person of knightly honor, at least thought so by the world. Richard could not, in all conscience, do other than order an open hearing. This was to be on the day of St. George, in about two months, at Windsor Castle.

I was present, and all our kin, for my father wanted witnesses of his blood, should Richard play him false. I was still enough of a child to think it high good fortune to journey so far, to lodge at court, and to see the king. I did, in truth, see Richard then, but from far away, for I was not presented, and all our party were hustled into a small keep-room over the Great Gate when, at nightfall, we arrived. Grandfather Gaunt and the Beaufort uncles had ridden ahead with my father and were lodged somewhere within the castle, but we children were kept, boys and all, humiliatingly, with the women. Tom raged at the king, and I, too, found it hard to forgive, for we were cramped, and without water to wash, and our only food was cold meats, with weak, thin beer. Even so, excitement bore me up, for I could not but think that on the morrow my father must prevail, and gloriously, and that Richard would beg our pardons and call it all a sad mistake.

It was a brave pageant next day; I had not seen the like in my time, for we lived simply at home, for all our wealth of family. It was a fair day, I remember, but windy. I wore for the first time a long mantle, clasped at the left shoulder with a gold brooch which bore the Monmouth arms; it was blue, over a green houppelande and hose, the Lancaster colors. The cloak kept flapping in the high wind and wrapping me about, and I had much to do to keep it seemly. I felt, as children do, that all eyes were on me, when none could care, and all were watching the empty throne, far away across the castle grounds, for a glimpse of the king himself. There was a high scaffolding, built just for the occasion, to seat the nobles and high of the court. It went clear around three sides and was draped most gloriously with the king's own colors, and the supports were crusted with gold leaf. The lords and ladies, bright as jackdaws in their fine clothes, chattered and laughed the whole time; one would have thought they were at a play with mummers and clowns, instead of the highest law court of the land. Some of the ladies still wore the silly horned headdress from Bohemia in the dead queen's honor; it was the ugliest fashion I ever can recall and made them look like painted cows. I was glad my own Lady Kat wore a simple Cathay silk caul, though for sure nothing could have made a cow of her.

It was long waiting, there in the stands; in the field below, the heralds' horses pawed the ground. Then a ripple went over all the crowd, as of wheat bending in the breeze, and someone, my lady probably, tugged me to my knees. It was the king. They said he loved homage and the show of worship; it must have been a full minute that he stood, watching us all kneeling there. I raised my head a little and stole a look; the wind caught my bonnet, blowing it off my head. I grabbed for it and missed, falling against Tom. We both straightened quickly, but I saw Richard turn toward us, and, trembling, I fancied I could feel his kingly frown.

When he gave the signal to rise, I could not take my eyes off him; even so far away, one could see that he was encrusted stiff with jewels, like an image in a rich cathedral. So thick they were that no color of his clothes showed beneath, though I had heard, always, that he wore cloth of gold. His hair and beard, too, were gold, and shone in the afternoon sun, with an Eastern pomade, men said, that cost ten shillings the ounce. The points of his shoes were so long that they turned up nigh to his knees and were fastened somewhere, by ribbons, to his high hose. My own new shoes were pointed, and twice as long as my foot, so that it was hard to walk without stumbling; I could not imagine how Richard could move at all. It is a fashion that has since gone out of style, I thank dear Jesus; conceive, if you will, of such gauds on the march!

I gave over marveling at the king's looks, for the trumpets sounded then, and a herald, wearing our colors, rode forward from the field to stand before the king. His horse, too, was richly caparisoned with our own Bolingbroke arms, and wore a mantle that reached the ground. We heard his voice, rich and ringing, trained to reach a thousand ears. "My sovereign Lord, Richard of Bordeaux and England, most puissant ruler of this realm, I salute you in the name of Henry of Lancaster, Duke of Hereford and Earl of Derby, called Bolingbroke. This lord says, and I also for him, that Thomas Mowbray, Duke of Norfolk, is a false traitor to your royal majesty and the whole kingdom! Further, Lord Henry charges that said Norfolk received eight thousand nobles for the payment of the garrison at Calais, which sum he kept for himself, witnessed by Lord Henry. Further, said Norfolk has been the cause of all the treasons against your Kingly Person in the past eighteen years. Finally, Lord Henry proposes to prove this with his, Henry's, body against that of Norfolk in lawful combat in the lists." The herald wheeled his horse and rode back to the Lancaster party.

Then another herald rode forth, bearing the crimson and silver of Norfolk, who declared that everything said against his master was false and a slanderous lie, that the duke—but here were cries from the stand of "Louder—speak up!" and the man's voice was drowned out. Out rode another knight, all in crimson too. The stands buzzed like a hive of bees when a stick has been thrust into it. I heard "Mowbray . . . the duke!" and looked hard at this man, the enemy to my father. He was bareheaded, and never did I see a face so bedeviled with anger. My own father could not hold a rushlight to it, and him I have seen often in a black fury. Mowbray's voice too, was like a clarion, hoarse and loud; after the curtesie-trained heralds he bellowed like a bull, and some of the ladies tittered. The king held up his hand, glittering with rings, for silence, and we heard Mowbray shout, sputtering, that Lancaster was a vile dung-thrower, and worse, that he, Mowbray, had used his monies properly, in all good faith, for the king, and that never, never did he plot against him. He beseeched the king to allow him combat against this false accuser. Richard stood, all eyes upon him, saying nothing. Then Mowbray, that poor choleric creature, wild with the waiting, pulled his horse, pawing, into the air and rode to where my father stood. He dismounted, his armor clanking beneath his robe of state, and grabbed the reins of my father's charger. After that, all happened so fast I could not see rightly, but I think my father jumped from his horse to close with him, and the two were pulled apart by those who stood there. Richard spoke then, or shouted rather. "Peace! . . . I command you . . . Peace!" His voice was high as a woman's but piercing, and the thin vowel sound of "Peace" shocked like a shriek. I saw my father then, still held by two knights, pull off his gauntlet and hurl it. It did not fall, as in knightly practice, at the man's feet, but hit him full in the face. Even from our place in the stands we could see the blood run from Mowbray's nose, where the jeweled cuff had caught him.

Richard stood a moment, watching, then turned and resumed his throne, taking from a courtier nearby a goblet—wine perhaps or mead—from which he drank. The stands were silent then; the only sound was the neighing of the frightened horses, loud in the still moment. Richard beckoned his own herald to him, a man almost as bejeweled as himself, and sat leaning over the parapet talking with him low. Then, with a sudden flurry, he rose, waved his flashing hand in a languid half-gesture to the crowd, turned on his heel, and left, followed by half the stands, his court.

There was more silence, with shufflings and murmuring and high, nervous laughter, while Richard's herald wrote something on a long sheet. Then, standing, he advanced to the space before the throne.

"Good people," he read. "Lords of London and Peers of the Court, our most puissant King Richard, Monarch of England and Heir to Bordeaux and the French lands, announces his decision. These dissenting nobles, Lancaster and Norfolk, dukes created by His Grace, and subject to his will, will place body against body in the lists, fighting to the death. The place of combat will be Coventry, in the tourney field, and the time, in this year of Our Lord, will be September, the sixteenth day. May right go with the victor . . . Good people, your king bids you go in peace!"

Tom, beside me, shouted for joy and clapped his hands, but the beautiful voice of the herald rang in my head like a mourning bell, for I was old enough by then to know fear.

Chapter 4

All that September our kin rode to us, through the ripening wheat, for the combat trial would be at Gosford Green, outside Coventry, just twenty miles away from our castle. Kenilworth, though a massive place, was crowded to bursting, and some of the men-at-arms had to bed down in the courtyard. Each of our family traveled in state, with a large retinue of followers; Lady Kat was busy from sunup to setting, just seeing to the feeding of such a multitude. I remember her in her shift, her bare arms still round and pretty, laughing as she took over the churn from a dairy maid, or in the big kitchen, flushed from the ovens, all floury to the elbows as she kneaded dough for honey cakes. Once I backed away quietly, coming upon my Grandfather Gaunt, his white beard nuzzling into her nape as he stood behind her in the counting house, his big, veined hands on her breasts. I had thought him too old by far for such play. Most of our fine ladies, in their home manors, could turn to and make such delicacies as marchpane, or they might candy the big chestnuts from their own trees, but his Katrin, as he called her, had been reared as a lay pupil in a poor convent and had learned all the homely arts. Some of the duchesses spoke hard of her for this, as for her beauty and her low birth, but I never saw her take offense, even at flagrant sneers; she had the long love-faith of the highest noble in the land, next to the king, and wished for no more. In those days I was sure God would send me such a one as her, for in the minstrels' songs there are so many ladies of great heart and soul, and passion too. I have had many women, but only one I ever met was anything near to Lady Kat, and she was taken from me.

All my mother's kin came, those I had not seen since her funeral; my Grandmother Joan came, that harsh old lady, straight as a poplar—we called her Granny Gallow-post, but not to her face—and with her her daughter, our Aunt Eleanor. We boys had a name for her, too; we called her the Purse. She had a mouth small and tight, with little wrinkles all around it, and no lips at all; when it shut, one could imagine the drawstrings pulling it tight. She was very rich, too, in her own right, and had married wealth as well. She wore the latest fashions, no matter how ugly, and her thin face was caked with paint from Paris; she had an unpleasant odor, too, like mutton, I thought. My father said she used a perfume from the Eastern lands that was made from the spleen of a great fish, but this I could not credit. No one liked her; she had plagued my father with lawsuits before my mother's death, and after, too, trying to get her hands on my mother's inheritance. She had some trumped-up case that my mother had forfeited her share by having been a novice nun; it could never hold water and was thrown out of the law courts time and again, but there was much coldness between her and Father. I could not fathom why she had come for the combat-trial, seeing this was so; Father said she came to gloat, in case he was killed, and to grab what pickings there might be after; it was a grisly thought and frightened me.

My uncles Beaufort came, too; Uncle Thomas from London, where he said that in the taverns there, the odds on my father were two to one against Mowbray. My blood ran cold to think of men putting their wagers on my father's head as cold as upon a cockfight or a Shrove Tuesday football match. Father laughed, though, and took great heart from it; he had been practicing with lance and spear all that summer, and his muscles were like bands of iron.

Father had been close to us all that time of waiting and even at moments almost tender. He gave us horses of our own that summer, Tom and me, and John and little Humphrey had ponies brought from Scotland, sweet-faced little beasts with long manes and tails that almost reached the ground. We had lances, too, and shields; mine was emblazoned with our emblem of antelopes, the Lancaster arms, and Tom cried because he could not have them, too. "I am only eleven months younger than Hal, but he gets everything!" My father took him onto his knee and spoke gravely for once; I think he must have had a qualm or two about the contest and wanted things made clear to us boys, in case. "Hal is older, though it be by so little, and that means he will inherit all the titles. You will have lands and manors in your own right, when I am gone, and John and Humphrey, too, but Hal is the first-born. . . ." He punched Tom gently in the jaw, a play blow, with his great fist, and went on. "Think, too, Tom—who is it that we beat when you are both in wrong, when you are both to blame?" Tom's sobs sank into soft hiccups, and his face brightened. "Why, Hal," he said, laughing. "Hal is our whipping boy!" My father did not laugh with him but said gravely, "It is because he *is* the heir that he is used so ill . . . he must learn strength and fortitude, and to take all responsibilities . . . he must bear the fortunes of our house, and so must have hard shoulders . . . you would not grudge him a little show of arms—for all he has suffered? It seems but fair, little Tom. . . ." And he laughed, hugging him. He did not hug me, but, as he looked at me, I fancied I saw a look such as he might give a man grown, and my throat swelled with pride, so that I had to swallow the ready tears. My father had never spoken so before; I thought it made up somewhat for the hard blows he had given me from my earliest remembrance. Still, in my bed that night, I wept softly into my pillow; if only he had held me, too, in his arms, or touched me only with that same tender fist he made for Tom!

On the combat day, my father left before sunup, and fully half the household with him; only us children and the guest children were left behind, with the Lady Kat and our Grandmother Joan. Those ladies might have gone too, for Joan Waring and all the maidservants were at hand to tend the younger babes, but Lady Kat had a soft and squeamish heart and never liked even to watch a mock tourney, far less this trial to the death, and our ramrod of a Granny had her own firm ideas about the matter. She went about the house muttering; I heard "barbaric," and, with scorn, "Sweet Richard!" I asked her what she meant, for in my great unease I had forgotten my fear of her. She glared at me, as if this day's work had been all my doing, and said, "Boy, listen well—the day will come when this custom will be outlawed, this death combat . . . It is fit for beasts only or bog-savages that leap around a bonfire naked and painted . . . It proves nothing, only that one hog is bigger than another or that one wolf has more teeth!" I could not love her for likening my father to a hog, or a wolf even, but there was sense in her words. If Mowbray dies, I thought, my father will then be proclaimed right and all his treason-accusing true, but all Mowbray's kin will hate us Lancasters to the end of time, and so it will go the other way also. I could not think it through though, for my thoughts were on my father's peril, and in my head the scene was vivid and awful, no matter how I tried to shake it out, of my father lying dead and broken on the fading grass of Gosford Green, while the people gawked between the rails and jostled one another for the sight.

Even, I thought, if Father is unhorsed only and thrown upon the ground, it will count in the tally against him, and when it is over, if both are left alive, the loser in points will go to the headsman's block. The Lady Kat saw me, where I lurked in corners and drummed my fingers upon the window, and bent to me, saying, "Hal, will you not go out into the sunshine . . . I hear Tom and the others playing. It will ease your mind. . . ."

I went out into the courtyard. All of the children were there, except the littlest, playing at trial-by-combat. Even the little girls, my sisters, and the other small damsels sat, playing at great ladies, with silken barbettes pilfered from their mothers' chests covering their hair, giggling and shouting, while Tom and one of the younger pages galloped their horses and thrust out their lances. Little Humphrey sat, solemn and haughty, among the baby countesses, wearing a paper crown. I could not stay to watch, for just then my stomach gave a great heave, and I thought my insides would come out at both ends. I ran, my hand over my mouth, around the kitchen garden to the midden heap, where we boys often went to make water when we were caught short out of doors. There I squatted, among the garbage, vomiting and purging until I was empty and weak, while the helpless tears ran down my face. Small wonder, I thought, that Father called me puny; none other of the children are taken this way. "Dear Jesus," I vowed, still squatting, "I promise to hold my bowels if you will save my father this day . . . Sweet Jesus, save my father!" It is a vow I was never able to keep; later I learned that the hardiest of knights are afflicted in this way often and often, before battle, so perhaps it was simply that I was older than Tom and the others and my insides more aware.

When I could move, I crept around the outer bailey, so none could see, and climbed the great tower. I had done it before, but then it had seemed easy. There were no handholds in the rounded stone walls, and the circling stairs made me dizzy, after my weakness in the midden, but when I reached the top I was glad. The air up there was fresh and stinging, where the wind blew from the north, and I could see far, far, along the road to Gosford Green. I do not know how long I stood there, straining my eyes into the distance, before I saw a great cloud of dust far away on the road, and moving slowly nearer. I clutched the bars of the little high window until my hands went clammy and I had to wipe them on my hose; the iron was rusty and left long red-brown smudges. I thought, even through my fear, of the scolding I would get from Grandmother, or the knuckle-whack, perhaps.

As I watched, a small dust-cloud separated from the larger one, and a party of riders galloped up the road and across the drawbridge. I pulled myself up by the bars, my muscles straining, for the window was high, so that I could see down into the court-yard below. The riders had dismounted and were pulling off their helms; I saw my Grandfather Gaunt's thin white hair, and beside him the carrot-red of my father, flattened by his head-piece. My heart, or something there in my chest, turned right over, and I turned and flew down those treacherous stone steps; my feet, I swear, never touched them, so light with joy they were.

Though I was fast, Father had come into the great hall before me; when I saw his face, I stopped in my tracks. I could read no triumph there; his eyes were as grim as death. He saw me staring and shook himself a little, like a dog that has lain too long by the fire. He rubbed his face all over with his big hand, massaging the welt on his forehead that the helm had left and running his fingers through his hair so that it stood on end like a cockscomb. Then he gave a great sigh, looked at me as if he did not see me, and said shortly, "We did not fight." Then, turning on his heel, he went out of the room to an inner chamber somewhere, his armor clanking in the silence.

The little group of us stood like stone for a moment; I saw my grandmother's face, anger beginning to creep on it, and behind her, in the doorway, the Lady Kat, round-eyed. My Grandfather Gaunt waved them away and sank wearily onto a carved bench before the fireplace. The fire was all but out, I remember, but he held out his hands to it as if it flamed steadily. They shook; he reached up and unclasped the pin at his shoulder, letting his cloak fall to the floor, staring all the while at the charred log in the hearthplace. Finally, he waved the men-at-arms away and beckoned me to him, saying we were not to be disturbed. I never dared speak but waited still.

He said, finally, not looking at me, "You see your father un-hurt, Henry?"

"Yes, my lord."

"The king would not let them fight . . . The earl marshal had thrown down the Lancaster gage, and your father had set spurs, even, to his horse—Richard flung his scepter out onto the field and stopped them. . . ." I saw his face and dared not answer.

He had turned to me, and it seemed I had never really looked at my grandsire before. It was the same face, all bold lines, and full of a harsh pride, but I saw something else. Something old, old, and infinitely weary; the eyes had a thousand years in them. He spoke as though he spoke to the wall, or to himself perhaps. "These twenty years I have served Richard—setting the kingdom above my own interests or my sons' . . . For twenty years I watched them, my son and my nephew, grow to manhood . . . I have watched . . . and I have known, inside myself, but putting the thought aside, that these two—these cousins—might well destroy one another . . . it has begun." He still sat on, staring at nothing. I still dared not speak; I heard, from far away, my brothers and sisters, clamoring still, in the courtyard. They had not even heard my father's party ride up.

After a long moment, the old duke said, "This day your father is banished from the kingdom for ten years."

"Oh, sire—" I cried, the words catching in my throat.

He nodded. "The king himself pronounced punishment."

I felt something flare in me, and hot, angry water smarted behind my eyes.

"The king is unjust," I cried. "The king is cruel!"

"He is the king," said my grandfather heavily.

"But—ten years!" I was still young; it seemed a lifetime. "I shall be a man grown before I see him again . . . I shall be twenty-one!"

"They are at least both alive . . ." said my grandfather. "Be thankful, Harry, you are not Mowbray's son . . . Mowbray is banished for life."

I could not take comfort in a stranger's woe; it seemed to me as though my father might as well have been laid beside my mother in her grave. "Oh, sire," I whispered, very low. "I do not think that I can bear it. . . ."

He drew me to him, his arm about my shoulders; it was a rare gesture—he was not an affectionate man. "Poor little boy," he said. "Poor Harry . . . Take heart . . . your father will come back to you. . . ."

I sobbed. "But, sire—all those years—I will not know him. . . ."

He held me from him, looking full into my eyes. "You will be twenty-one, Harry . . . and you think the world has ended for you. Look at me, his father . . . I am fifty-eight, Harry, and have lived hard and fought hard all my days . . . Do you think I will live to see my son come back to me?"

I looked at him then and stopped my crying, reading in his face the full import of those long ten years. I laid my cheek against his, awkwardly. As I turned away, I saw two thin tracks, pearly, like snail traces, marking his face.

Chapter 5

I had thought to spend all my hours with Father in the little time that was left, but in truth I saw him only once again, the day of his leavetaking. He had scant days to set all his vast estates in order, barely a month, and his holdings were scattered over all England so that he traveled the whole time, picking stewards he could trust to manage his manors while he was gone or calling upon kinsmen to aid him in his trouble. I know he gave much thought of where to put us, his children, into whose keeping to give us, and a score of lesser things. I knew this, but in my heart I felt that, had it been I, I would have found means to spend this last little space with those I loved. But let it go; we are different men.

My Grandfather Gaunt, after that day when he spoke to me his heart, on the day of my father's hard punishment, seemed to grow closer to me and wished me by him at all times. Father planned to send us three oldest—myself, Tom, and John—to Pleshy, to our Grandmother Joan; it was the greatest stronghold in the realm, or nearly, so he had reason, for all men have enemies. Grandfather, though, asked to have me in his keeping, swearing to protect my person and my inheritance with his life, if need should come. Little Humphrey and my sisters, Philippa and Blanche, were sent to Sir Hugh Waterton and his lady at a place called Eton Tregos; Sir Hugh was an old and trusted comrade-at-arms and was in my father's debt besides, so he felt they could be safe there. Kenilworth he would close except for its fortress, keeping men there to safeguard it.

We all were busy, in that household, packing our personal things, deciding what favorite game or toy or even garment to take and which to leave behind, for it was impossible to move everything. My mother's books I took with me, for they were precious, not just as relics, but worth a king's ransom, too, Grandfather said, for their age and perfect workmanship; we needed two sumpter mules for them alone. At the last minute I took my play warriors, given to me that Christmas long ago at Monmouth, hiding them in my clothing chest under my smallclothes; Tom would have laughed, I know, for he never kept anything longer than a few months at the most, and all his toys were broken and useless after a little. I myself, from earliest childhood, have set great store on beautiful things or things that were wrought with care and love; I even took with me a belt, too small already, that my sister Blanche had stitched for my last birthday; the threads had been picked out many times and done over, for she was only six then. But who knew when I would see her again; it might be years. The Lady Kat called me her little peddler, but lovingly, and only in my ear; I could see she understood. The fact was, when my grandfather saw our train, as we set out for his castle of Leicester, his eyebrows went high and his lips twitched in the wintry smile; it was as though we traveled with forty kings across the world. He said nothing though; he knew that I got it from him. All his manors were filled with treasures to the bursting; some even were kept in storerooms only, there being no place to display them. I looked my last on Kenilworth, not thinking to feel sadness, for I had not been happy there, as at Monmouth; as we rode out though, I did feel an ache, somewhere inside. So must a young tree feel when it is transplanted; I have had many such uprootings, and I have felt them all, in one degree or another.

In the last days of the month—it was October—my father rode to Eton Tregos, and then to Pleshy, to make his farewells to all his scattered children, coming on the very last day of all to me, where I stayed with Grandfather at Leicester Castle. It was a raw day, for the month was nearing its end; all the leaves had fallen already, and the land looked bleak and colorless, waiting for winter; it was winter in my heart, too, and my grandfather called me to him as we heard my father ride in. "You are not to cry, now, Harry—your father has enough to bear. I know you strong beneath, with a will and a soul like steel, but your father's thoughts never run deep, and tears to him are womanish and not fit for his oldest son and heir. You must show him a strong outside, so he can take faith in you along with him in his exile. . . ." He held me in his arms for a moment, whispering. "We two know him well—this son of mine . . . he is brave as a lion, but a simple man. Try to be as he wishes to see you. . . ." God help me, I understood his words that day, and beneath them, too. I saw my father clear that day; it was perhaps the only time.

He came in, my father, walking heavily in his mail, for he rode with only a few attendants. His face was whiter than I had seen it before, and a few brown redhead's freckles stood out strongly on it; I had not noticed before that there was gray in his ruddy beard. He spoke with me about the care of my horse and the feeding of my hawks, talking at length about saddles and the proper tightening of the girths, and such small things I knew already, until, it seemed, he ran down, and sat looking at me, pulling at his knuckles till they cracked. The Lady Kat ran in then, weeping, and threw herself at his feet. He patted her head awkwardly, where it lay in his lap, his face softening like a child's. I had not thought him to be fond of her, but then I remembered. He had been raised motherless, too, like me, and the Lady Kat had been his governess when he was little. I felt my throat working and turned away, feeling in my pocket-pouch for my gift of parting. It was a St. Anthony's medal, a charm against travel. He took it, laughing, and seemed to throw off his torpor.

"By Christ's nails," he cried, "I'll need it, boy!" It was his favorite oath. He stood up, then, looking almost happy to be gone. He put his hands on my shoulders; I saw he had to reach above his chest to do it, for I had grown fast that summer. "Well, Hal," he said; it was the women's name for me, and I never remember him using it before. "Hal, be strong . . . the hopes of Lancaster rest on you now . . . don't forget your father. . . ."

I bit my lip hard, for my mouth was working in grief. "No, Father, never. Never will I forget you." He did not embrace me even then, but he gave my shoulders, where he held them, a hard squeeze that took my breath, and turned to go.

I fumbled for a word, shifting where I stood. "Maybe," I said, "maybe the king will let me come to you . . . in a year or two, when I am bigger . . . maybe he'll let me come to you—in France or wherever you are. . . ."

"The king—" he said, low in his throat, a strangled sound. I looked and saw his face, alive with hate.

My grandfather put out his hand. "Henry," he said, "I would not have you go from these shores in anger. . . ."

"By God," cried my father. "Am I a saint? What do you ask of me . . . to love Richard for this?"

Gaunt said, "Remember that our land is full of rebellion and unrest—hate between you and Richard can be England's death. . . ."

"God must help England then," said my father. "I think that no man was ever used so treacherously as my cousin the king has used me. You do not know all. . . ." His face cleared, and he knelt before his father. "Your blessing, sire. . . ." My grandfather raised him to his feet. "My love goes with you, Harry, and my faith . . . I have Richard's promise," he said. "If I die before you return, your inheritance will be safe. . . ."

"You'll have many years yet, Father," said the son, in that hearty way men speak when they speak of such things. "God keep you all," he said. "And now I must go or I will miss ship. . . ."

We watched him ride across the drawbridge and onto the London road, and watched till there was no longer a speck on the horizon to show. When we went back through the castle door, the halls seemed to echo with our footfalls, and the rooms seemed empty all that day, though there were servants always about, and minstrels, too, at table. I never wept for my father then, though now he was gone, I could have; it was a thing too grim for tears, or perhaps my manhood showed early, just for that day.

Chapter 6

That February my grandfather lay dying. He knew no one, not even the Lady Kat, his dearest love. He lay as in a swoon; the doctors could not rouse him—even their lancets he did not seem to feel. King Richard had sent his physician, too, as soon as the news had reached him; this John of Gaunt had always been his favorite uncle. But it seemed he was beyond the arts of men. We all had seen him stricken, it seemed by the hand of God.

It had been his habit, before retiring, to play, in the long winter evenings, a game of chess with me; he had spent much time teaching me the game, those months after my father rode to his banishment. We were all gathered in the great hall, for a huge fire raged at each end of it, and only the very center was cold. Our bedchambers were like the tomb, for it was a bitter winter, and we delayed our bed-going longer and longer, drinking sweet wine from Lorraine that was warmed by the fire.

Lady Kat had set up a large loom against one wall and worked there with Joan Waring. This Joan was no longer needed as a nurse for me, I was rising eleven and not anxious to be seen by women in my smallclothes, but she was a clever young woman who could turn her hand to many things, and the Lady Kat valued her and kept her on. Grandfather and I sat close to the hearth, at a little table, one of his treasures, a pretty thing from the Eastern lands, all inlaid with ivory and gold, with the squares all marked in gems. He had just won the game, as usual, and was reaching down to the wine flagon at his feet, for he was always cold, even in his furred robe, though my cheeks were flushed from the fire and the sweat trickled down my side beneath my clothes. I heard a sound, like a groan cut off short, and looked at him. He was frozen there, his hand stretched down to the hearth, and tipped sidewise in his chair, like a chess-piece that has not been set down properly. His face looked surprised; his eyes stared. Slowly, slowly, while I watched in my own frozen horror, he toppled off the chair, his head falling right into the ashes. I jumped up then, calling out for help, and tried to drag him free from the hearth. A servant ran in, and another, to help me, and between us we moved him to a cleared place on the floor. Lady Kat knelt beside him, cradling his head, and Joan Waring ran for his valet, William Malbon, a man grown gray in his service. Malbon came, hurrying on his old, stiff legs, his face twisted with concern and love. He gave orders swiftly, taking charge, like a man half his age, calling for a litter and furs to wrap him about. Even so, it took all of us to straighten his limbs in seemly fashion; they were like logs. We could not close his staring eyes; they stayed that way, turned up to the ceiling, all the while we shifted him onto the litter and piled him with rugs of fur. His white hair was charred on top where the little flames had licked it before we could drag him away. The Lady Kat walked beside the litter, wringing her hands and moaning, like a small animal caught in a trap in the woods, Joan Waring beside her, bearing her up and making soothing sounds.

He lay this way, like stone, for eight days; my half-uncles were sent for, but he never knew them, though they kept vigil night after night beside his bed. He never knew me either, or his beloved wife, though toward the end his eyes lost their stare and followed us about; they were the only parts of him that moved, until the last. It was twilight, on the eighth day; supper had been brought to hall, but we all lingered by his bed, his three bastard sons, his mistress-wife, and I, his first grandson. I saw the fingers of his right hand move and clutch my Lady Kat's arm; she made a sign to Joan Waring, who ran for the bowl and wafer, ready for days. There was no need to call a priest, for Gaunt's middle son, my tutor, and another Henry, like father and me, had just been ordained. He made the sign of the cross above his father, wet his lips with wine, and touched the wafer to them, murmuring low in Latin. As though he heeded the words, my grandfather's eyes grew keen again with the light of reason; he moved his head a little on the pillow. Lady Kat took his feebly working fingers, and his eyes rested on her. A little almost-smile flitted across his face, a ghost-thing, but plain to see. His mouth worked, and we leaned close to hear. I thought he said "Henry" twice, but could not be sure; it was scarcely a whisper. Then, clearly, he said the word "England . . ." closed the eyes, so long wide, and we knew him dead. I heard a sob and, surprised, knew it for my own. As I looked, two thin trickles of blood ran from his nose. The Lady

Kat wiped them away with her hanging sleeve and bent and kissed him tenderly on the lips. When she straightened up, and I saw his face, I thought he looked young, as I had never seen him, his skin waxen-pale, and all the deep lines wiped out. He had turned a yellow color by morning, but till they sealed him in his tomb he wore that look of youth; I saw how men had called him once the most beautiful noble in the land.

We gave him a quiet funeral, for the Lady Kat said he had wanted it, though all his days had been spent in pomp and splendor; the ground was frozen hard, and the horses' hooves rang sharply against it as we bore the catafalque to the great vault. My uncles had ordered a larger-than-life effigy; it was nearly finished. One of the finest stoneworkers in the world had been commissioned for it—a Fleming; I have forgotten his name. It was clear he knew his business, though; even in its first rough state, one could see the look of my Grandfather Gaunt. The man must have known him in his prime.

The Lady Kat changed after his death; she still had a look of beauty, but the color had gone out of it. In her mourning black, she looked bluish-white, like milk when the cream is skimmed off the top; there were two broad white wings in her red hair, at the temples. I spoke of it, for it was not unattractive, and she answered that the dyeing of it was too great a chore, now that he was gone. I had never known that she used any arts to keep her looks; I was still a boy and very green. Also, I think she suffered from what our old monk poets called "accidie," a kind of sickness of the soul, where nothing has meaning, and one day goes by like another, in an endless string.

She called me to her one day, just two weeks after we had laid my grandfather in his tomb, and said she wished to retire to a convent in the spring. Joan Waring would go with her, for they had grown very close, for servant and mistress, and there they would live out their days. I wept, for I was never shamed before that sweet lady, and she took my head between her hands, raising it to look into my eyes, and saying, "Oh, Hal, it will be better so, for you also . . . a boy cannot live all his youth with women. We'll send you to Pleshy, to be with your brothers. Your lady grandmother—already she has asked for you."

I smiled, even through my tears, and said, "Granny Gallowspost? I had rather go to jail. . . ."

"Oh, Hal, you are unkind. . . ." But the Lady Katharine's lip twitched, for all her words; she had never heard the nickname before. I did not doubt she understood its meaning well either, for often and often I had heard my Grandmother Joan rail at her for some fault as if she were a child or stare her through when her finery seemed too bold.

Still, though I did not relish my gran's harsh rule, I began to think of Tom and John, too, and all the boy's ways we would share there at Pleshy. It was surrounded by dense forest, almost untouched, and the hunting would be fine; a river ran beside the land, too, full of trout, our steward said. Besides, I had not seen my brothers for near five months. They neither of them had come for Grandfather's funeral, being just over the measles, and still weak. So, all in all, I looked forward to the move.

Lady Kat was busy for days, snipping off the jewels from her gowns and robes and unwinding the gold braid trimmings. All these she would take to the convent with her, for it was the poor one she had lived in as a girl, and would welcome all that could be converted into monies, having gone without so long. The fur she left on everything, for, as she said, the poor would need its warmth; I thought of our village women, with their broad, flat faces and matted hair, their lice and their filth that they wore from one year to the next, and smiled to think of them going about in her beautiful gauds. Everything was going to our poor, except for her black garments, which she would wear to the end of her days, and one fine court gown, in case she should be summoned from retirement by the king. Though her hair seemed to me even whiter, and growing more so each day, she hummed as she worked, and some of her color had crept back into her cheeks, but delicately, like the last blush on a rose before the petals fall. I think she looked forward to her convent, though she had never shown much taste for religion; perhaps she thought to see some of those others she had known there long ago. I asked her once, and she answered yes, many of the novices had remained on as nuns and could not be so very old, just her own age. Though, of course, she added with a hint of her old self, smiling, her age was greater than I knew. She looked a girl again as she said it, though I never saw that look upon her again. Her finest jewels she kept for us children and her own sons; Blanche, who I think was her favorite of the little girls, got the great betrothal sapphire of Lancaster, one of the most perfect in the whole realm, and in the world, as far as I might know. She gave me a small ring, too, and her harp; it had been a gift from her Master of Gaunt long ago, when she had been governess to his children, and he had first seen her and loved her. It was a beautiful thing, very old, of Italian work, and much worn, for she had practiced faithfully, though never had she learned to play very well. "Perhaps you will have better luck, Hal, with it . . . the strings always cut my fingers, I never got the knack." It was a heavy thing, and big, so I could not take it then; years later, after her death, I sent for it; the strings which had hurt her hands were all rotted by then and had to be replaced. I thought of her mortality then, and her own sweet rotting bones, and thought of these days of my childhood, her goodness, and my boy's love for her, and I wept as I handled it. It will seem I weep often, for a man-creature, but it is in secret always, and no eyes see my weakness.

It was the day before I was to ride to Pleshy; four men-at-arms were to ride with me and stay there, too, part of the household, and all my gear was packed and ready to be loaded on the mules. I went outside the castle, for it was one of those fine days you get sometimes in March, without a wind, and with a hint of the spring to come in the air. I walked through the gardens and saw that the first crocuses were out, though a thin frost still lay like a glaze over the ground. The walls of stone enclosed the garden like a monastery wall, but above the stone was a kind of gallery fashioned of wood, going right around. Set in the blackening oak, old now and weathered, gleamed in gold and silver the emblazoned arms of the Plantagenets, of Lancaster, of Derby, and of Chester. I had been deep in thought, saying my inward farewells to this place, as I had to two other homes before, when I heard a splintering noise above my head. I looked up and saw soldiers, in chain mail, hacking at the blazoned work. I did not recognize any of their faces; they were none of ours, I was sure, and I called out to them, angry. "What are you doing?" I cried. "Come down from there, before I call the steward and his bailiffs!"

One of them, just above me, got the tip of his lance under a blazon and wrenched outward, levering it from the wood with a loud, sickening crack. He stood on a ladder and dropped the blazon to the ground. I saw red and ran over and pulled the ladder from under his feet, so that he fell, his mail clanking loud on the flagstones. He clambered to his feet; he was not hurt, but very angry, and reached for his dagger.

"Let be," called another. "It is Derby's whelp!" This man climbed down from the wall and stood looking at me.

"What are you doing?" I cried, still wild. "Those are my father's arms!" Then my head cleared a little, and I saw his badge of the White Hart on the mail over his breast, Richard's insignia.

I must have turned pale then or showed something of what I felt, for his face softened a little, and he said, in a rough sort of kindness, "Best go in to your lady grandmother, hinny." He spoke in a northern speech-sound; I could hardly follow it and stared at him still. Joan Waring came out then, her face all red and the cords standing out in her neck. She took me about the shoulders and shouted at the soldiers in Welsh, so that they laughed, not understanding the tongue, which for sure has a barbarous pitch to ears that have not heard it before. She stormed at them a while until she saw one of them make an obscene gesture, known even to me, then she spat at them, calling them, in English, pigs and whoresons, and their king, too. It was treason she was uttering, but in truth she was so pretty in her fury that they liked her for it, and I heard one of them say, "What a wife on a cold night," and shake his fingers as if they burned, a gap-toothed grin splitting his face.

She bent to me. "You are to go inside now, Lord Hal, to the lady. . . ." I saw that under her wild words, her eyes swam bright with tears.

I had heard nothing, where I had walked in the walled garden; I had heard no horses, or the gate creaking open, but there were strangers in the hall, men, richly dressed, that I had not seen before. My grandfather's steward, a man named Walter Hungerford, who had served him for many years, sat at a trestle table which had been set up at one end of the room. His rent books were in front of him, I recognized them from our arms and their size; I had seen them often, even sometimes practicing my sums with them. He hunched over them with a quill and inkstand, marking figures on each sheet. One of the strange men stood behind him, scanning each page as it was turned. He was splendidly garbed in the king's colors, his sleeves lined with fur, and a large blue jewel gleamed in one earlobe; I gawked, for I had not before seen such a fashion on a man. He must have felt my eyes, for he turned and looked me up and down; I felt, obscurely, that now I knew what Joan Waring meant when she complained to the lady of some rude man-at-arms that he "skinned her of her shift." For this man's eyes held a strange interest, with contempt under, and dwelt upon my hosed legs, where they met my short surcoat. His face gave me the creeps, though it had a pinched sort of comeliness; he toyed all the while with a little jeweled dagger. His eyes slid from me, and he pressed the dagger point into Hungerford's back, lightly, between the shoulder blades. "Get on with it, man!"

I burst out to my lady, who stood helpless, clasping and unclasping her hands, "They are pulling down my father's livery from the walls!"

A little spasm went over her face, but she spoke calmly. "They are following the king's orders," she said. "The king is taking your father's holdings in forfeit. All that he thought to inherit—" And her voice broke, like a lute string that has snapped.

"But my father cannot live—" I cried. "How can he come back with all his inheritance gone?"

"Oh, Hal," she said, very low, "your father will not come back . . ." I stared at her. "He'll not come back again . . . the king has banished him for life."

At this I broke. I had thought myself wild-angry, but now I knew; this must be the blackest day of my life. I burst into a storm of weeping. I heard the peacock stranger snort in disgust, and my lady clutched me hard and knelt beside me, but I could not stop. Joan Waring ran in, too, and spoke soft words in Welsh to soothe me. It seems I was out of my wits. Then he of the earring walked over to me, cold-eyed, and slapped me smartly across the face. It was like a bucket of icy water; I froze. With all my beatings I had never been hit in the face. The Lady Kat stood up, smoothing her gown; I had never in my days seen her angry. "Who are you, sirrah," she said in a voice like drops of poison, "that you dare touch a Lancaster?"

He bowed and smiled thinly. "Sir William Bagot, at your service, Lady." She almost gasped, though she made no sound. All the world, even I, knew him for Richard's minion. I felt myself blush, for these things were new to me still, and I felt shame at my knowledge before the women.

"I only tapped him lightly," he said. "It is the best way to deal with hysterics . . . Would you have him rolling on the floor in a fit? Besides," he said, drawling the words, "he is no longer a Lancaster, as you know. He is nothing, now, but the king's creature. His father Derby has seen to that." He turned away, as if bored, back to the rent-book business, and Lady Kat drew me to her again, sitting down beside me on the carved bench where my grandfather was stricken weeks ago.

"Hal," she said, and there was no more a tremor in her face, "Hal, my poor Hal—there's no cause for such tears. Listen— Richard has always held me in his favor . . . when you are fifteen, we'll go to him—I'll go down on my knees to him, he'll not refuse me, for my dead lord's sake—we'll go down on our knees and beg him . . . beg leave for you to go to your father in France or wherever he is . . . you and he can travel Europe together . . . go on crusade, maybe . . . see Jerusalem and the holy places . . . sail together in the great fast ships from Genoa. It will be so—I promise you. . . ."

"He'll want Tom with him, too," I said, choking. "And John . . . he'll want to see all his children. . . ."

"All—all of you shall go—I'll beg the king's mercy . . . I promise, my sweet Hal . . . you'll see. The king is good, I knew him as a boy. . . ."

I burst out again. "How can he be good—when he uses my father so? How can he make my father wander about the world, away from home, until he dies . . . Oh, Lady," I said, low, "the king will break my father's heart."

Behind me I heard Bagot make an impatient sound and close the rent-book with a snap. "My Lady," he said, "we have not all the time in the world. Will you prepare the boy and let us get to our journey?"

My eyes must have grown round as marbles this one day, for again I stared.

The Lady Kat sat silent a moment, then spoke, slowly. "The king has summoned you, Hal. You are to go to him in London." I felt an unknown dread, and she must have read it on my face, for she said gently, "Oh, Hal, there is nothing to fear. You are to be under Richard's care and protection, that is all. You are his little cousin, and he wants to know you." She spoke for my ears alone, saying, "Oh, Hal, do you think the king would send his own great friend to fetch you if he meant you any harm?"

I was still in panic, and I cried, beside myself, "No—no—I won't go!"

"Oh, by the cross," said Bagot, annoyed. "I am here to carry out the king's commands, not to argue with little boys. Prepare him, my Lady, and quickly. He is permitted one servant, and baggage that will be contained on one mule. Make haste; it is a long ride to the city, and there is a masque tomorrow night in which Richard himself appears . . . if I miss it he will have my head." I looked up, fearing, and saw that he jested. He smiled again his thin-lipped smile, and I saw it, in a sort, a look of kindness, or pity, perhaps.

I rose, mastering my voice. "Sir, have I time to change? I would not go to the king in my oldest clothes."

I saw this pleased him, but he only said, "Be quick, then." As I left the hall, I heard the Lady Kat ordering wine and cold meats and ale for the soldiers; I heard her, also, call for old William Malbon, my grandfather's faithful valet, to go with me and be my man-servant. Joan Waring followed me out, sobbing loud. For this last time, I suffered her to help me dress, for my fingers trembled on the points, and besides, I knew I would never see her again in this world.

Chapter 7

We came to London in good time, by late afternoon the next day. I saw it in wonder, for it stretched clear to Tyburn, and we rode past field after field, with cottages close to the road, as I had never seen them, miles before we had come to the gates of the city itself. I had made friends with one of the soldiers, he who had spoken to me in the garden and laughed at Joan's Welsh. The first night, when I was ready to drop from weariness, before we came to an inn, he had taken me up before him on his own horse, leading mine, and I had fallen asleep against his sweaty shirt; under the sweat was a smell of hay and horse, and as I nodded off, it seemed I was again in the arms of White Will, who had held me close on my mother's death-day, long ago.

This soldier—he was an archer—spoke, pointing to a wide road on our left; I had grown used to his brogue now and understood his words; he was from Northumberland, where the Percys ruled, richer than kings. He said, "Look you, lad . . . yonder— the road that leads to Westminster where all the kings are crowned."

"But I thought King Richard lived there," I said.

"Sometimes," he answered, "but he has many castles, as many as we have fingers between us, and more. Just now, he is lodging in the Tower."

We came to a broad street which he said was called The Strand, and there the city itself began. I had never seen its like. It was noisy and crowded, smelly with a thousand things I could not identify, its streets filled with booths, gaily colored, full of wonderful things to eat or wear. Everywhere there were swinging signs, spelling out the shops and even the houses where folk had their various trades. There were signs for all these crafts—pictures and symbols—but I did not know them yet; they were like letters of Greek to me. Apprentices bawled out the wares of their masters' shops, standing in the doorways, and holding out marvelous things—combs with jewels set in (after, I learned they were made of glass); great silver loving cups, fake, too, I learned, but finely glittering; rolls of silks and brocades; jars of cinnamon and other spices I did not know. Over all was a heavenly smell of new-baked bread. My new friend, the archer—Wat was his name, like the dead rebel—leaned down to a bake-wife and tossed her a coin. She held up to us two pale-brown loaves, still steaming from the oven; she was fat and wore a red petticoat above bare feet. He pinched her cheek and took the loaves. "Who is the pretty lad?" she shouted. "Not yours, I'll be bound, you toothless wonder!"

He laughed in high good humor and shook his head. "Nay, lass—this be the king's own nephew, come to see the sights . . ."

"Go on," she said, unbelieving. We rode on. The bread was wonderful, crisp and chewy, hot almost to burn our hands.

I had heard my grandfather say often that poverty lay upon our land like a filthy cloak, but here it was masked, certainly; everyone seemed to buy, and money flowed from hand to hand. The streets throbbed with all sorts of people—great ladies, even, though Wat said they were just expensive whores; my eyes popped at one, a beauty, not much older than I myself, but dressed all in silver and gold, a ring on every finger. She wore no head-coif, and her black hair hung down her back, curled into a thousand ringlets. She would not smile for us; I was a boy and my companion-at-horse a common soldier, but she curtsied low to Sir William, who rode behind. "Little good you'll get from him, poor lassie," I heard Wat mutter as we passed.

There were cassocked friars, too, their tonsured head showing sunburn, and black-gowned clerks and hooded scriveners; aldermen in their scarlet, and guild-men in their guild-livery. Wat knew them all; he had been two years in London. To me, the city was like a great fair; I fell in love with it then, and I have never fallen out.

By the time we came to the Tower, it was twilight, and they were lighting the torches. At this time of year, night falls fast, and so I saw little as I was led through the winding halls and up dim stairs to the White Tower bedchamber where I would be lodged. William Malbon was with me; I looked at his face in the rush-light and saw him weary to the bone. He was an old man, of course, and not used to long rides on horseback. We stood in the bedchamber where they had brought us; our guide had dumped my gear in the middle of the floor, on a carpet, rich-looking, and with many intricate designs in red hues. The wall hangings were rich, too, and new, and the room was very large. "Am I to go to bed now," I said, "without seeing the king? I thought he would greet me; we are cousins."

Someone laughed from a doorway; I caught a whiff of the closestool before the door was shut. "There are so many cousins here. . . ." And he laughed again. It was a boy, about my size, but very fair and flaxen; even his eyebrows and his lashes were blond. He had a pale and sickly look, but haughty, too. He frowned a little, looking at me. "I know you," he said, and snapped his fingers, thinking. I saw his serving man, in a dim corner, emptying a bowl of water into a large ewer. The man was poorly clad, his livery patched at knees and elbows; the boy, too, wore a robe, or bedgown, the fur moth-eaten, and the velvet rubbed away in spots. There was something sad and faded about them both, and my skin crawled a little with a wordless fear. The boy said, snapping his fingers again, "I forget the name—" His man answered, "It is Lord Henry of Lancaster," he said. "He will share your bed at present, being under the king's protection, like yourself."

The boy laughed again; I wondered if he was an idiot. "I am a cousin, too—yours also. I am Duke Humphrey of Gloucester . . . do you have to use the closestool?" He was no idiot; he had seen me as I stood, moving from one foot to another, to hold my water in. I nodded. He pointed to the door he had come out from. "It stinks in there; there is no window . . . you can leave the door open if you like," he said, kindly. "I will hold my ears. . . ."

When I came back, he was in the great bed, with the coverlet pulled up to his chin. As Malbon helped me to undress, the boy said, suddenly, "You have beautiful clothes . . . so new. . . ." It had a wistful sound.

"I do not much care for such things," I said. "But I have many more—there was not room to bring them."

"Be sure you will never see them again," he said. "They have stolen all of mine. . . ."

"Who?" I asked, startled.

"Oh, some of the others," said the boy, airily. I thought about this, getting into my nightshirt in silence and creeping into the bed beside him. He moved over, but taking most of the coverings with him; Malbon put my fur bedgown over me, tucking it all around. Humphrey waved his hand at his man in a lordly fashion, telling him to blow out the candles and leave us. Malbon, too, went with him, bidding me sleep well.

"Where will they sleep?" I whispered.

"Oh, outside, somewhere. I think there is a dressing room . . ."

All our folk had been taught to take care of our servants' welfare; I could not think how he had been brought up, this Duke Humphrey, and resolved to find out how Malbon was faring as soon as morning came. I spoke again, softly; the strange room, darkened now, with only the firelight flickering on the shadows, made me feel wary. "I had thought," I said, "to see the king . . . do we always go to bed so early here? I have been used to sit up a little. . . ."

His voice grew sly, somehow. "Oh, that's because there is a masque tonight. They never let us stay on a masque night. They say it is not for boys. . . ."

"Do they have whores there?" I asked, eager to show off my little knowledge.

He laughed again. "Of a sort," he said. He was silent for a little, and we watched the glow of the fire on the stone-arched windows, and the ironwork sconces black against them. Then he said, in a sad little voice, "You are pretty, Lord Henry. Richard will like you for it . . . He said once that I looked like a rabbit. . . ." I remembered his two big teeth at the front and pushed the thought away for its unkindness.

"You are golden-fair," I said. "Like the king's own self. . . . Maybe," I said, feeling very bold, "maybe the king is jealous. . . ."

"Oh, no," said Humphrey. "We are all of us here Plantagenet, all fair—he is used to that . . ." His voice trailed away, and I thought he had gone to sleep. But he asked suddenly, "How old are you, Henry?" I answered that I was eleven.

"You are too big for eleven," he said in a smug sort of way. "I am fourteen."

"I expect it has to do with my forebears," I said. "My grandfather was passing tall . . . my mother, too, for a woman. . . ."

"Is your mother dead then?" he asked.

"Yes."

"Mine, too," he said. "She died eighteen months ago—and so

you are Derby's son," he said. "And a pauper, too, since Richard has taken all your inheritance and banished him forever."

"How do you know this?" I was astonished. "I only knew it yesterday, myself!"

"The court is all gossip," he said. "Everybody knows everything. There are no secrets . . . though there are things that are only whispered . . . things about Richard. . . ." He lowered his voice even more. "I hate him," he said, hissing into my ear. "He murdered my father."

"Murdered him?" I repeated, stupidly, my hair crawling on my scalp.

"Sh-h-h," he said, putting his hand over my mouth. "Listen," he whispered. "It was in Calais Castle. Mowbray's men did it."

"Mowbray—but my father—"

"Yes—your father—he knew about it, found out somehow. He was there at Calais . . ." He was still for a moment; I thought I heard him sob under his breath. "Get all the way under the covers," he said, "and I'll tell you. . . ." We pulled them over our heads and lifted our knees to make a sort of tent; I remembered that Tom and I used to do this long ago, at Monmouth, talking our boys' secrets, when we were supposed to be asleep. But this was headier stuff. The boy went on, whispering low; his breath smelled of mint—he must have been chewing it earlier, to clean his teeth. "The king always hated my father; he put him under arrest as one of the lords appellant and locked him up in Calais, in the donjon there. Mowbray was in charge of Calais garrison. Richard told him to see that my father never came out." He drew a long shuddering breath. "Mowbray's men held a feather pillow to my father's face so that he could not cry out for help. And that was how he died, strangling, with Mowbray watching till it was done. It would take a long time," he said, his voice shaking. "I tried it myself one time with a pillow . . . I would rather have the ax. . . ."

I could not take it in. I said so. "Such a thing—it could not be. . . ."

"Oh, don't be a fool-baby," he hissed, angry. "What do you think your father accused Mowbray of on Brentford Bridge? What do you think he said to the king?"

I was silent, my thoughts running around in circles.

"No one dares to say it, but everyone guesses. Why was your

father sent away? Because Mowbray was the king's man, and when he named Mowbray a murderer he named the king, too."

"But," I said, my mind fumbling for reason, "your father was the king's uncle, like my Grandfather Gaunt. The king would not murder his own uncle."

"Why not?" said Humphrey. "He'd murder anybody to keep his throne. All kings would. My mother said it. She said all kings wade knee-deep in blood."

I felt stifled myself suddenly and threw down the coverlet from my face. I still could not take it in; the whole thing was so different from all I had read of kings and great people in high places. But was it yet? I remembered Arthur's story, all romance-hung, but with Mordred in it, too, who betrayed his own father and plotted his death. And the Danish king, long ago, who killed his brother to lie with his brother's wife. Under the rippling notes and beauteous words of the songs were the terror and the blood, the avarice and the shame.

"Have some mint leaves," said Humphrey suddenly. "They're dried, but if you chew them a while they get soft. I stole them from Richard's own pouch," he added proudly.

I took what he offered; its sharp and pungent taste spread through my mouth. I remembered where I had thought to be to-night—at Pleshy, with my brothers, and my grandmother, who, though harsh, had surely made no one die of it. And I thought of the Lady Kat, whom I would probably never see again. I must have made a sound, though I tried not to, for my cousin Humphrey said, "You can lean on my shoulder if you want to cry. Myself, I never do it anymore, though I used to, at first." I did not move or speak. "Oh, well, never mind—I expect you'll do it anyway, after I'm asleep. . . . But you'll soon get used to it here; they have a lot of banquets, and hunting, too, sometimes. . . . I wouldn't mind, except for all the tutors . . . and then Richard never gives me any pocket money. . . ."

Chapter 8

I did not see the king next day. Humphrey said, with that laugh that seemed a part of him, that Richard slept the full clock round after a masque. I could not help liking Humphrey, though many of the tales he told I thought he made up in his own head; he was old-seeming, in some ways, for fourteen, though I was a half inch the taller. He knew no games or knightly exercises and could barely sit a horse; likewise, he was lazy at his studies and had, indeed, no accomplishments that I could see. But he knew all the gossip of Richard and his court; when he pointed out this one or that at table that first day, I grew uncomfortable, thinking of whose bed each was in or out of, according to his whispers. By the next day, though, we had grown to be good friends, for we were the youngest boys there. I had more suits than I needed, and he had only one out-of-fashion wine-colored outfit, much worn and beginning to smell moldy; I bade him take one of mine, in yellow velvet, which I did not much like. He could not credit his ears and cried, "But it is like new! I cannot take your best!" I answered that it had a wine stain on it, near the waist, which was true, and that I hated it besides. He was full of delight and put it on right away; when he had buckled his wide leather belt, only a tiny speck of the stain showed. He strutted like a peacock, and, truth to tell, it transformed him, for the color brought a glow of gold to his fairness, and the hose, which were striped around with orange, showed off his straight, slender legs. "You must have something in return," he cried, and rummaged in his trinket chest. "Here," he said, "have this." It was a little knife for meat, ivory-handled, with a real blade made of steel. I had never yet had one, only a bone blade that was never sharp enough, so I was much pleased, and we were quits. So we strolled out, arm in arm, to explore the Tower, he bright as a butterfly in his saffron, and I with the little meat-dagger fastened conspicuously to my belt.

"I'll take you to see the lions, if you like," he said in a bored way.

"Lions!" I cried. "There are lions here—in the castle?"

"In the Lion Tower. They're nothing much to look at—their fur is mangy and they only walk around, and throw up, sometimes."

"Throw up?" I said.

"The damsels feed them sweetmeats, though they have been bidden not to. Girls are stupid. Lions should have meat only." What damsels? I thought, for I had seen none, only great ladies, all old, to my eyes. And then I remembered Richard's new queen, who would, of course, have ladies about her. This marriage of the king's, four years ago, after Queen Anne died, had been a little scandal in the realm; even the serving folk talked shame of it. For Richard had married a six-year-old princess of France; it would be many years before he could get an heir on her, and he had no children either from Queen Anne. Richard was young yet, of course, but kings are expected to breed heirs or their subjects talk.

Duke Humphrey knew his way about the place well and was friends with all the guards, so we passed into the Lion Tower without any questions, though there were soldiers all about; at one corner a little knot of them threw dice and did not even look up as we went by. There were stairs inside, leading up to a kind of narrow gallery or platform that ran all around. Below was a pit, where the lions lived. There were only two, and they were asleep; only kind of tawny-gray humps showed in the straw, and I was disappointed. We made noises to attract their attention, whistling and banging on the railing, but they never roused. There was a partition in the pit, though, with three other beasts, tawny-gold, too, and spotted all over with dark marks. They looked like big kitchen cats, though their faces were broader; Humphrey said they were the famous leopards sent by the emperor long ago to Henry II. I began to count in my head, looking my disbelief, and he said, "Not the same ones, silly. What do you take me for? But—there are always leopards kept here since that time; they symbolize the arms of England." I watched them for a time; they padded silently in the straw or lay down to scratch their fleas. One began to wash itself all over, like our tabby at home in Kenilworth, twisting its head right around to lick the back of its neck, and using its wetted paw to wipe its face. It was truly rather boring after a while, as Humphrey had said, and the smell was rank and caught in the nostrils, so we turned to go. "There is another one," he said, "through here." And he led me through a small door into a little chamber cut into the wall. There was a cage there, filling the room, its bars as thick as a man's arm, and padlocked. Behind it paced a beautiful creature, black as coal, another cat, but bigger, and heavier in the shoulders. It was a leopard, too, but rarer, Humphrey said, from Egypt; the Baron of Glendourdy had brought it back for Richard. He was the most traveled man in the realm, Humphrey said, and Richard's great good friend; nothing nasty, he added, seeing a funny look in my eye. Only that Richard called him the most civilized man of the age and loved to converse with him, for Richard valued fine talk. It was the first I had heard of this great baron but not the last; men mostly called him Owen Glendower in my time. He was a Welshman, and we nearly lost England to him; but then I paid little heed to the name, watching the fabled beast in the cage.

It never stopped but paced endlessly back and forth, two strides, and turn, and two back, and turn, and so on, its muscles rippling like waves under the silky black of its coat. Its face was pure savage and took my breath away; under its shelf of brow, I saw, with a little shock, that its eyes were bright yellow, the iris pleated with amber. I had never seen anything so beautiful or so noble. I felt pity for it, too, in its raging, insistent walk; it must have thought, poor marvelous thing, that it could walk the bars away.

As we came down to the foot of the stairs, we heard a noise along the hall, like a hundred birds twittering, one voice above the rest, sharp and high, talking at great speed. A group of lords and ladies flowed out into the broad hall, like water when it spreads out from a stream; the ladies wore tall headdresses and had no eyebrows—they were plucked clean away—a new fashion; and the men, richly dressed, laughed too loud. At their head, like a spearpoint, went a gorgeous young man, all in gold like a walking gem; his ringed fingers were long and slender, his narrow hands waved about as he talked, never still. I had seen him only from far away, in the stands at my father's trial, but it could be no one else; this was Richard of Bordeaux. Humphrey had fallen to his knees, and I knelt quickly, too, my new dagger, improperly fastened, making a clatter where it fell on the flags.

Richard stopped; I felt his stare and raised my eyes a little. The face I saw above me, under its gilt circlet, was surely the most beautiful in the world. It looked as though it were carved of some precious substance, not flesh; I remembered that Humphrey had whispered that Richard wore some thin paste, made of an Eastern plant, to color it. He looked sun-kissed all over, indeed; I saw that under the gold and jeweled trim, his suit was yellow, and felt, beside me, Humphrey trembling. Richard reached out one long hand and raised me gently.

"You are our cousin Lancaster," he said. "I see your mother's face, when first she came to court . . . Very lucky you are, my pretty boy, that you do not sport a carrot top!" He looked about him, waiting, delicately. The men laughed, emptily, and a twitter rose from the ladies. I felt the hot blood rush to my cheeks and my hands make fists. His eyes were bright blue and very keen; he smiled. "You have your father's cock spirit, though, I see. . . ." Again the foolish laughter rose. He whirled suddenly, like one of his own big cats. "Let be!" he said, and the words were like two drops of ice. "We are cousins, close, Red Derby and I . . . he is worth a thousand such as you. . . ." He stood still for a moment, turning back to me while I struggled to master my feelings, so mixed as they were. Richard waved a languid hand, not even looking behind. "Leave us," he said. Behind him the lords and ladies, silent as mice, backed away through the doorway; the last two lords collided. We heard a tiny sound, cloth ripping; a sword hilt must have caught somewhere. Richard laughed. It was the first I had seen of his swift changes; a faint tremor washed over me—I knew him dangerous.

Humphrey had risen, too, and was edging toward the door. Richard whirled. "I have not given you leave," he said. "Stay, little yellow bird. . . ."

Humphrey fell again to his knees; they cracked, sharply, and I winced. "You think me cruel, cousin?" asked Richard, looking at me.

"No, sire," I said, lowering my eyes.

"You have such long lashes. . . ." Richard said, smiling faintly. I could not think where to look. "Come," he said, his long fingers cupping my chin. "Let us have the kiss of peace." And he stooped and kissed me, full on the lips. His mouth was as cool as marble. He turned again to Humphrey. "You may rise, sir-rah. . . ." He looked him coolly up and down. "The effect is good," he said. "Never had I thought to see you so near to hand-some . . . but who gave you leave to ape your king?"

"Oh, sire," I burst out, "it is my fault . . . I gave him the suit! His own was falling into rags and smelled, too—he had no other . . . and I have so many! The color does not become me either . . . and he gave me this knife, too, in return. . . ." Richard still stood, looking a way I could not read. I took my courage in my two hands, or in my mouth rather. It must be all or nothing, with this king, I thought. After all, he cannot kill me for it. "Sire," I said, "we could not know you chose to wear this color on this day—be fair. You are the king. My grandfather told me, of all others, kings must be fair. It is their duty."

I saw the crimson mount from beneath his jeweled collar, up under the paint. His eyes were cold. I shook inside but gave him stare for stare, though I had to tilt my head back to do it. It was a long moment; I do not think I drew breath. The color faded slowly from his face; he shifted his weight to one hip, threw back his head, and laughed. His laughter was rich and deep, unlike his voice. "You are bold, fair cousin," he said. "I like you well. . . ." And he made a fist, playfully striking me with it on the jaw, as my father had done once to Tom, while I watched. "Maybe I should have a list made, posting my attire for each week—would you have that? It would give my stewards something to do. . . ." I laughed, too, then, seeing the joke.

"You have a good eye, though, cousin Harry . . . you have made our Humphrey bloom." He looked at Humphrey. "Which of us is the fairer in the color, do you think?"

"Oh, sire," I said, earnestly, "I think there is no fairer man on this earth than you . . . except my Grandfather Gaunt, maybe, when he was young. . . ."

He gave a little pleased smile but said mildly, putting his arm about my shoulders, "You know how to flatter, Harry. . . ." I opened my mouth to protest, but he waved my words away. "Let be, sweet cousin . . . I know you honest. You please me well . . . But let us get to this problem of Humphrey . . . why has he no clothes?"

"Oh, sire, they have stolen them. . . ."

He frowned. "Who is 'they'?"

Humphrey swallowed, audibly. "I do not know, sire . . . but they have been missing since I came here. . . ."

"So long?" said Richard. "Well, cousin, we shall see to it . . . you shall have others. I like pretty boys about me, not raga-muffins . . . you please me, too, today, Humphrey. Come—you, too, shall have the kiss of peace."

And he bent to him but kissed him on the forehead only.

I spoke again, quickly, before he had lost this mood. "Also, sire, he has no pocket money . . . In truth, I have none either . . . except two nobles from the Lion-Heart's time . . . I was saving them for their great age. . . ."

"You shall both have monies," he said. "Come—follow me . . . be quick, I shall not always feel so generous. . . ."

He led us, holding onto both our wrists, like leading little dogs, to a small chamber where a scribe sat; he dictated to him low. When he had finished, he handed us each a paper. Mine set forth, that by the munificence of my lord, the king, Richard of Bordeaux, I would receive, while my father was in exile, the sum of five hundred pounds each year. I gasped. "Oh, sire," I cried. "It is too much! What shall I do with it?"

He looked amused. "You will have servants to tip—and your man's wages . . . besides, your clothes you will outgrow soon, by the look of you . . . and then, there will be presents—for fair ladies, later. . . ." He looked sly.

"I do not much care for girls," I said, "except my sisters."

"Boys do not," he said, laughing, "at your age." But I saw my answer pleased him, and that also he enjoyed being generous. He turned to Humphrey. "And you, cousin," he asked, "can you buy clothes to suit you now?"

Humphrey's eyes brimmed with tears; he could not speak but grabbed the king's hand and kissed it. Richard patted his shoulder. "Remind me, Humphrey—I have some earrings that would suit you well. They are too small for me, but they are topaz . . ." He took Humphrey's earlobe, giving it a little pinch. "We will have to pierce these. . . ."

"Oh—" said Humphrey, looking scared.

"It does not hurt. . . ." said Richard. "I would not hurt boys. . . ."

"Sire," I said, "may I send to Kenilworth for my play warriors? It is not that I need toys, but I like to plan campaigns with them . . . and they are very fine-made, too . . . I had not time to bring them when I came. . . ."

"Anything," he said, with an airy wave of his hand. "I will lend you a man . . . But mind you keep all your boy-stuffs in your own chamber . . . I cannot bear clutter. . . ."

"Oh, sire—thank you!"

"You may call me Cousin Richard," he said, "when we are private . . . have you met my little queen, Harry? She is most fair, with lashes longer than your own, and just your age. . . ."

"Oh, no, Cousin," I said, a little cross, "she is a full year younger!"

"Oh," he said, laughing that rich laugh that differed so from all the rest of his person. "Oh, for sure—a year is such a great time when you are young. . . ." He looked, on a sudden, tired, and in the light that slanted through the latticed window I saw, around his eyes, tiny fine lines against the smooth skin of his face. And, I remembered, he was thirty-two.

Chapter 9

I still did not see the little queen; I learned she had the measles and was still in quarantine. I said to Richard that she could come out, as Humphrey and I had had the sickness already, along with our other cousins and most of the pages. They did not call themselves pages here, but squires, or gentlemen-at-livery, or some such fancy titles, but they were still green boys, like ours at home, not much older than myself.

But Richard laughed, fisting me again in that way of play that I rather liked, and saying, "But I have not had that same pox yet; would you have your king laid low like a schoolboy? Besides," he said, "I thought you had no great liking for girls. . . ."

"Well, but I have never yet seen a French person," I answered. "And I can speak the tongue a little." In truth I was curious; a little jealous, too, for all our cousins spoke of this girl as though she were sent straight from heaven.

"Well," said Richard, "you will have your fill of them, Harry —all her damsels are from the French court and chatter like magpies, but faster—except for one, that is Welsh--Owen's by-blow. . . ."

"Owen?" I asked.

"The great Owen ap Griffith, of Glendower . . . he is in France now, my envoy—no doubt between Isabeau's legs. . . ." I stared in shock, for Isabeau was the queen of all the French, and I had not thought Richard would say such a thing of royalty, being royal himself. "You know little, fair cousin," said he, ruffling my hair. "I would not have you grow into a prig—you may as well know now—she is the whore of the world. . . ."

I swallowed; I had been brought up by women mostly, after all, who stopped their talk when I came in the door. "They say, though, that she is beautiful . . . Queen Isabeau." I tried to speak as a man who knew the world.

"If you like them fat," said Richard, making a face. "She rubbed against me all the while the bishop said my marriage lines . . ." He laughed. "He was half blind and thought she was the bride . . . I wish our Owen joy of her—by now it will be like screwing a bucket . . ."

I stared again, and Richard threw back his golden head, roaring loud; we were seated on a little bench alone, but the hall was filled with ladies, and I blushed like a flame. "Still," he said, wiping away his tears of laughter on his sleeve-lace, "Owen will manage well . . . he knows all manner of magic, herbs and the like . . . and besides they say half Wales is his get . . ."

"Do you think, Cousin Richard," I said, whispering, "that the little queen knows . . . ?"

"Isabelle?" he said, raising his eyebrows high. "How can she not? Isabeau had Orléans in her bedchamber where all the little girls slept too. Sure they could not have snored through it all!"

"Orléans—the duke," I thought. "Her own brother-in-law!" I saw in truth that I had been brought up monkishly. But then my father had been so often away . . .

I still did not dare mention my father to the king, but in my heart I felt that Richard liked me, and someday might listen if I begged a favor of him. I crossed my fingers, wishing.

There were not so many cousins about the court as Humphrey had said that first night; only two, besides ourselves, that were true-born. There were plenty of bastards, but richly dressed and in no way slighted, and some girl-cousins too. Of the two true-born boys, they were men really, I liked one on sight and did not like the other. Our cousin Edward of York reminded me a little of my uncle Thomas Beaufort; he was fairer, sandy of hair and not red, but he had the same face in a way, full and fleshy, with an expression of good will and mildness, and besides he played sweetly on the lute and sang too. The other cousin, his brother, was Richard of Cambridge; they were both sons of the Duke of York, but very different. This Cambridge was a haughty creature, very vain, and dressed as richly as Bagot or the king. He had that fair look, too, which is always called Plantagenet, I discovered, as though no others had a right to it. (Actually, most of the true English are fair; the peasantry especially, since they have little other than Saxon blood and date back to before the Normans came. The Celts are another story still, and an older race, even.) I guess you would call him handsome, except that he lisped terribly and worked his eyebrows all the time as he talked; I thought he looked like a freak at a fair, in his laces and silks, with rouged cheeks and hair always crimped from the irons. Humphrey said he and William Bagot had been rivals for the king's favors, not so long ago, and Bagot had won, so Cambridge was forever taking it out on everyone else about him. I had learned by now to take Humphrey's stories with a grain of salt, but it might well have been true. He and Bagot certainly had no love for each other. Myself, I would not give a fig for either, though Bagot did not lisp. At first I had thought it a full lie, thinking of incest, and that the king was Cambridge's own first cousin; but then, in the dark of our bedroom, I blushed again, remembering they were men.

I was not unhappy, the contrary, rather, for there was so much that was new here, and much to occupy me besides. I was not even homesick, though I thought, once in a while, of the Lady Kat in her convent, and even, when poor Malbon was clumsy, of Joan Waring. I spoke once of the lady to Richard, and his face lit; such a woman, he said, if she had been younger—and then he broke off. But he said one day he would send for her, command her to court from her nunnery for a little; perhaps she would even stay.

Two weeks went by, and it was April, and true to itself, raining. One day, the most dismal, I was left alone, for the king had gone, with much of the court, too, to visit at a manor in the south, where the fishing was good, for it was Lent. Humphrey and I had been left, I know not why, perhaps because they would have masques there, too. But Humphrey had waked with a runny nose and hot cheeks and could not get out of bed. While his man tended him, I wandered about the Tower, looking for something to do. I liked often to be alone, when I could not, but this day I was restless and could find nothing to amuse myself with. We boys knew all the men-at-arms well, for we roamed pretty much at will, except in the women's quarters, so no one even noticed me. Richard's men-at-arms were always lazy, also, and chosen mainly for their looks, so they lounged about in corners, gaming and gossiping, for the most part.

I had been often to the Lion Tower—there was no novelty— but I liked still to watch the black panther-beast, so I went there again. On this day, though, so gloomy and dark, he saddened me with his fruitless pacing and his look of blunted fury, and I turned to leave. I heard light voices on the stair and stepped back into the shadows. A group of girls flitted past me in light dresses, like nymphs on some antique vase; their perfume almost knocked me over, for the air was close and full of the lion smell, too. One passed so close that her full breast rubbed against my shoulder, for she was tall; she turned to stare and said something, in French it was, I suppose, though I did not know the language as well as I thought, for she spoke very fast. They all came clustering around me then, and I dropped to one knee, while they chattered, laughing and pointing as though they had never seen a boy before. They were the queen's damsels, certainly; she must be let out from her sickroom.

I spoke carefully in French, what I had been taught, "Bonger," it came out, for I had seen it written always, and they laughed like blue jays and stood watching me with bright eyes. I tried again. "Moy," I said, pointing at my chest. "Moy, Henry— Henry Lancaster. . . ." I was mouthing loud, as you do to foreigners, and getting red to boot. They kept on laughing, and I began to get angry and think I could never, never like girls, when one of them, the full-breasted one, took my hand, and raised me up. "It is Henry of Lancaster," she said to the others in perfect English. They nodded and twittered again in French, all speaking at once. It was like a little hell full of birds, and I covered my ears. I saw they were all pointing to themselves and saying names, their own, I guess, but I could not hear one for the other. Full-breast spoke to me kindly; she had a full, high-cheeked face, too. "They mostly can understand English, if it is spoken slow . . . they cannot speak it much yet. I am Morgause—or, you might say, Morgan. . . ."

"Morgan le Fay!" I cried, delighted. "You are the Welsh one!"

"You have Welsh?" she asked, her eyes alight.

"I was brought up in Monmouth and spoke it always when I was little."

"I am Morgan ab Owen," she said.

"Morgan, daughter of Owen," I translated.

She laughed, delighted. "You shall have a kiss for that!" And, taking my face between her hands, she kissed me sweetly, while all the others giggled.

They all kissed me then, stroking my arms and hands and making me feel foolish, and like that boy in Greece, Heracles' friend, whom the nymphs dragged down in the pool to drown. For they were truly dressed that way; I learned later it was a fashion Richard set for them, his own invention and fancy, and very charming, too, for they were all very young and, except for Morgan, slender as water-reeds. They wore soft, pale colors, barely tinted, in some floating stuff that you could see through; I was embarrassed when I looked at Morgan, though I liked it, too.

"Which is the queen?" I whispered, taking her hand.

"Come," she said. "It is the black beast she loves best; he eats from her hand."

She led me into the room with the cage, leaving the others. A girl stood there, her hand thrust in through the bars; the fierce black panther was licking her fingers, his yellow eyes closed in ecstasy. "Sh-h-h," said Morgan, putting her finger to her lips. We watched, scarcely breathing, while the little queen took more marchpane from her girdle-pouch and fed it to him. He ate delicately, nibbling like a kitten. *"C'est tout,"* she said, and for a miracle I understood it; of course she held out her palms, empty, so it was easy. She stood yet a moment; the panther lay down on his side and yawned, showing a wicked array of teeth. He covered his face then, with his paws, and slept, as cats do, all at once.

She turned and looked at me. She wore white, filmy like the others, but girdled in black velvet; there was a fine veil over her face, which blurred her features a little, though one could see they were fine. I wondered if she had had the smallpox; actually I had had no blemish from my measles. She raised it, though, to look at me, and I saw her skin was clear. She smiled a little smile, grave and sweet; I loved her from that instant. I cannot describe her well, perhaps because I felt something for her, and it clouded my perception, or perhaps it was that I knew her such a short while. I think her face was not girlish, but a little stern, its lines all straight and neat but tender of expression. Her hair was in a sort of black velvet net, but it was a soft, fine light brown; her eyes were gray.

Morgan spoke to her quickly, in French; I heard the words, "de Lancaster." The queen pointed to herself, "Isabelle," she said, holding out her hand. I took it and held it, staring stupidly. She said my name, pronouncing it "Awnree." It sounded prettier than the English, and I smiled. She raised her hand to my lips; I had forgotten my manners as I gawked. I fell to one knee and kissed her hand. She touched me lightly on the head, then took my hair and with a little tug pulled me to my feet, giggling. I lost my stricken awe of her then, for she sounded like the rest of the girls, only quieter. And that was my meeting with my queen.

All that time while the court was away and Humphrey's cold mending I spent with the little queen and her damsels. Richard had given her the best apartments in the Tower; they were airy and large, with many windows and wide doors that opened out onto the gardens. They soon lost their language-shyness with me; I found they spoke English right well, if Frenchly. The queen and Morgan had Latin, too, so we could all understand one another well. Sometimes, when it was fine, they would all come into the tiltyard to watch us practice with our swords and lances. The pages had more training years than I and did well, but I did better; it was like a sickness with me always that I must be first at everything that I turned my hand to, so that I would work in secret and alone. At my Latin and sums, no one cared, for very few would knot their brains with such things, deeming them unmanly. I cannot fool myself, though, that older boys could like me well for beating them at tilting or at tennis. Often I caught a black look from one or the other of them, and would have to go out of my way another time to defer to them, asking their advice in some matter of arms or the like, pretending in a way that my winnings were an accident.

So many of us noble boys had like names, such as Henry or Richard or Edward, the little French girls would be all confused. Morgan, who had a pretty wit, gave us nicknames, such as Richard Longshanks, a boy taller than all the others and very thin, or Edward Shockhead, who had a stubborn cowlick which would not stay combed. She called me Harry Long-Twist, at which all the older pages laughed, and I got red as new brick, for I was beginning, here at court, to take all the dirty meanings. She frowned though and said she meant nothing of the sort, for I was a little boy yet; she pointed out how my face was long and leaned, she said, to one side. I was angry with her after, till she let me cuddle her in a dark corner of the garden and pinch her in places, too; she whispered, laughing, that in time the other meaning would be true, too, and so I forgave her. All the boys were after Morgan, for she was the biggest, and I would see them staring at her nipples showing through the thin stuff of her dress, but she never, that I could see, went apart with any of them, except that once with me, or even wrestled on the chamber floor, giggling and pretending to learn the art, as so many of the other girls did. We had music, too, and dancing; many of us knew lute music, and some the guitar, too, though it was new to me, and I never got the hang of it then. One girl, Yolande, with great dark eyes, Saracen-slit at birth to make them even larger, had a kind of guitar, round, with a very long neck—I forget its name—on which she used to play melancholy airs with a rough and haunting sound; she was from Navarre, in the south, and even her French was strange. We held a little court there, of our own, while Richard was away. And so we whiled away some of our days; Humphrey was up from his bed now, too, though he still sniffled, and chewed garlic against the infection, so that all the damsels held their noses when he came near. The week of Good Friday Richard came back to celebrate the Easter and attend mass in his own chapel.

It was a fair, sunny day for once, and not raining, though the grass was wet from an early shower. All of us young people were in the garden; some of the boys and girls were playing blindman's buff; for once none were rolling on the ground in the wrestling game, though the girls, some of them, had their skirts kilted high for running. I was sitting with the queen and two others—I forget who; she was trying to place my fingers on the guitar strings. Her fine brown hair hung down beside her cheeks; there was a high, fresh wind, and it blew bits of her hair into my mouth. I spat them out, laughing. We heard a voice from the wide doorway, that high, emperor voice of Richard.

"What, Lancaster, would you steal my queen?"

"Sire!" I cried and fell to my knees. The little queen, always so decorous, leaped up then and ran to throw herself into his arms. He laughed and picked her up, covering her face with kisses. "How is it with my little Flowerface?" I looked agape, for I had thought it no more than a marriage of state; but it was plain that Richard loved her well in his way. He walked about the gardens with her, easy and gay, quipping with the pages and twitching the girls' dresses down and wagging his finger at them. They shrieked with laughter and ran to kiss him, too. He looked at me. "Get up, you great booby," he said, "and come give us a cousin-kiss, too." I jumped up from my knees then and ran to him, where he whirled me around, and planted a kiss on each cheek, in the French fashion. "I swear by God's boots you have grown, boy!"

"Oh, sire—it is just three weeks!" But I was pleased. Never had my father acted so toward me or looked with such liking on me.

Richard put an arm about each of our shoulders, his Isabelle's and mine. "Shall we walk a little—I am stiff from horse. . . ." He admired the flowers that grew there—the little Isabelle knew all their names, in French, Latin, and English—and he plucked a small stalk of white lilies, like little bells, and tucked it in her untidy hair.

"Lily of the valley," she said, laughing, and its French name, too, but I have forgot.

"We will have a fine Easter . . . I have brought back some jugglers and dancing girls and thirty new cooks for pastry. . . ." She clapped her hands; she was more of a child than I knew. "And then," said Richard, with a high gay humor, "then, I am off to the Irish wars!"

Her little, stern, marble face crumpled into soft flesh; she cried, "Oh, no, my Lord . . . Oh, no . . . you will be killed!" And she broke then into a torrent of French.

Richard laughed and gathered her into his arms. "Never, my sweetling . . . I do not mean to give them a chance . . . come, dry your eyes . . . they are getting all red. . . ."

He held her head to his chest and spoke to me over. "You, Harry—would you like to go to war with me?"

"Oh, sire," I cried, wild with joy. I, too, was more of a child than I knew.

Chapter 10

On Easter day, to celebrate Christ risen and the end of the Lenten fasting, there was a magnificent banquet: I have never seen its like before or since. There were oxen in the hundreds, roasted whole, and stuffed with geese and spices, suckling pigs, candied, and filled with fruit, and all manner of other foods, including a marvelous pie, huge, out of which, when cut, there flew a miracle of live doves. Of course, that was not for eating, but to show the pastry cook's art; I still cannot think how it was done, though Humphrey, sitting next to me, said the top crust was put on just before, of course, and baked separately. This cousin of mine, though slow at his studies, was shrewd in ways most people would not bother thinking of; I still am not sure, anyway, that he was right, for it steamed clear to the roof as it was brought to table. There were huge ices, too, depicting Richard's White Hart symbol, and a red-colored one, like a dragon, in honor of the guest of Wales. It melted, though, as it was set before him, so that its shape was blurred, and I saw the Welshman, at Richard's right hand, laugh and draw his hand across his throat as if he jested at his doom. Richard banged his fist, making the dishes jump, and drew down his brows, but the man put his arm familiarly across the king's shoulders and whispered in his ear, so that the king laughed. I do not know, of course, what he said, but I heard afterward that he saved the poor ice sculptor's neck.

We sat with the pages and the queen's maids above the great saltcellar, for we were all noble, but there were so many above us, to take precedent, that a sea of white napery separated us from the king. He sat with little Isabelle on his left and the stranger on the other side. For a wonder, Morgan sat beside this man, instead of with the rest of us; I whispered to Humphrey that this must be Owen Glendower, back from France, for I had heard Richard say that Morgan was his natural daughter. Humphrey argued, as usual, for he always wanted to be first with any news, and said no, the man must be an Irish king, there were so many of them.

"But we are going to war against the Irish," I said, thinking to settle it.

"No matter," he answered airily. "Only some are rebels . . . this is one of the friendly ones." I pointed out, coldly, that the ice had been dragon-shaped, if melting, and red to boot, and that the lordly stranger wore a great red dragon emblazoned all over the front of his surcoat; the red dragon has been the symbol of Wales since the time of Uther Pendragon and of Arthur. Humphrey, of course, knew little of heraldry, never dipping his nose into a book if he could avoid it. He subsided, muttering that all men knew the Welsh were small and dark. I stopped arguing and craned my neck to get a look, though, for sure, I had not to move it overmuch, for the man was head and shoulders taller than any other. Richard, beside him, looked like a boy, and he was middling tall himself. Whoever he is, I thought, he looks like King Arthur, or rather, as I imagined Arthur to have been. He wore his hair long, right to the shoulders, and straight, in the antique fashion, middle parted; his beard, too, was forked in the middle and trimmed neatly into two perfect points, like all the old paintings. Beard and hair both were the color of deep tarnished gold, or like a lion's mane, and around his brow was a thin circlet of some dark metal. He was older than Richard, but not by much; he had an ageless look. Even at this distance I knew I would never see again a face of such pure pride. He is a Brython, I said to myself, out of the old songs, of that race that was here long before any Celt, even, set foot on these shores.

I was so busy with my musings that I did not hear the silence that fell when the musicians stopped or feel the pages' eyes; Humphrey nudged me hard. "It is your turn," he hissed, "to pour the wine." I jumped to my feet, nearly tripping over my robe, for we were all dressed to the teeth, and grabbed up the great pitcher. Richard held the bottom of the pitcher as I poured for him, to steady it; his blue eyes glinted at me, laughing. Putting one arm about my waist where I stood, he said, "I saw you gawk, fair cousin, at our guest . . . you were, perhaps, bewitched?" And a great roar of laughter went up from the lords who sat near, making my face go hot with shame.

"Softly, Dickon," said the stranger, hunching his wide shoulders and cackling in the voice of an old crone, "or your English will burn my poor bones. . . ." I stared, holding the pitcher; the man's face, even, was transformed, and an old, old woman looked out of it, a toothless hag, for an instant, and then was gone. The laughter came again, for the man certainly had magic, of the mummer's sort, at any rate.

Richard looked keenly at him, not smiling now. "Not in my time," he said. "Not in my time, my Owen, will you burn. . . ." I saw there was much real love between them, of a manly sort, and more, a measuring of each, and a surety.

"Have I not a fair lad here?" said Richard, his arm still around me. "My young cousin Hal. . . ."

"Very fair," said Owen, for of course it was he, and I was right for once. "I have seen faces like his in Sicily . . . or painted on old Etruscan walls. . . ." I saw his eyes, deep-set under high cheekbones; they were the color of his hair, yellow amber like the panther-beast in the cage. "But take your hand from him, Dickon . . . he is too young to be your play-maiden. . . ." He said this last very low, so that no one around heard him, and I waited for Richard's anger. It never came though; it seemed this Owen could say all he pleased.

Richard merely smiled and shrugged, giving me a little push away. "It is not that," I heard him say as I went. "It is that I wish he were *my* son. . . ." They spoke low together then, and I could not hear. But passing behind them later to fill the glasses on the left, I heard Glendower say, "I saw Derby in France . . ." and then, something like "some powerful friends . . . dangerous. . . ."

Richard clapped his hands then and said loudly, "No more, Hal, for the damsels . . . I do not want them puking all down their new gowns . . . and it is their bedtime, too, and the pages'. . . . Off with you, my pretty," he said, smacking his little queen loudly on the lips. And so we all went, grumbling, to our chambers, feeling we were missing everything.

I would have liked to have eavesdropped more talk of my father; I had not thought of him in weeks, and my guilt rode me, like a demon.

Humphrey had eaten too much and had too much wine, too. He vomited several times during the night; I could hear him in the water closet as I lay awake, thinking.

Dawn was beginning to send gray fingers through our latticed window; Humphrey climbed into bed, white and shaken from his last spasm. He saw I was still awake and asked, curiously, "Are you sick, too? By Christ, there is surely nothing left in *me!*"

"No," I said, "not that. But I am thinking. . . ." And in a rare mood of confidence, I said, "And praying. . . ."

"Praying!" he exclaimed. "All night? What for?"

I felt foolish, but I said, "Praying for my father . . . that he— that a miracle will happen, and he will come back, some-how. . . ."

Even in his weakness, Humphrey sat up from the pillow; I could see his mouth had fallen open in surprise, for the light was stronger already. "Sweet Jesus," he said, "you are the greenest of the green boys from the country. Haven't you yet figured out why you are here? You are Richard's hostage, his guarantee . . . in case your father gets up to anything over there in France or wherever . . . If once your father sets foot in England, forget your prayers . . . Richard will have your head."

I did not say what Richard's words had been, that he wanted me for a son, nor mentioned that scrap of talk I heard, disquiet-ing, about my father's dangerous companions. My thoughts whirled this way and that; I heard Humphrey snore, for all his sick feelings, before I fell, at last, into a brief, troubled sleep.

Chapter 11

In May we set out for Ireland. We went from Tower Wharf by barge; all the damsels were crowded at St. Thomas' Gate to bid us good-bye, except for Morgan, or Morgause Owain, as the queen and all her ladies called her, in the French way. Morgause had gone back to Wales with her father to live in his great new manor house there, with Owen's youngest legitimate daughter, Catherine, under the care of the half-English wife whom Welshmen called the Argyllwyddes. Morg, as I always thought of her, had bade me farewell with tears in her eyes and a great wild kiss, which surprised me, for I always had thought of her as a maiden of light, jesting spirit. I was surprised, also, to see how much I missed her, after.

Richard traveled in great style, as I guess he did always, but it seemed foolish to me to go to war in such a manner. Humphrey, whose company I had had to beg for from the king, he being so poor in the use of arms, said it would be no real war but just a sop to the commons, who loved conquest. There were minstrels, embroiderers, body servants, and as many as three hundred cooks, truly! To say nothing of all the baggage, horses, hounds, caged birds, and more that I cannot remember even. There were a hundred barges, so it took us most of a day to get started.

Isabelle had no eyes for me at all, but clung to Richard, weeping bitterly, until finally he had to bid her ladies take her inside. He went in the first barge with his favorite, William Bagot, both dressed as though for a court ball. They had to be carried on board, on account of their pointed shoes and their sleeves, which hung, sweeping the ground.

Humphrey and I rode far behind, in a barge with the horses, and some men-at-arms. The poor animals were afraid and neighed piteously the whole of the way downriver.

At the North Sea we changed to sail, and Humphrey was sick. I truly think that this cousin of mine ailed mysteriously, for he had always a queasy stomach and his nose ran most of the time, whenever the wind changed; also, his breath came hard from his

chest in certain seasons. So it was not just seasickness. Many of
the men-at-arms suffered from this; they looked so wretched that
I thanked sweet Jesus I was a good sailor, for they say it is something that cannot be controlled, but is a gift from God only.

There was no great fighting in Ireland; we lodged in splendor
at Dublin Castle and had lessons from tutors, and studying, just
as though we were at home. I say home, for in so short a time I
came to look upon my life with Richard as my homelife, odd to
say. But then he was ever kind and affectionate to me; I was
never beaten either or even spoken to in harshness. My father
would have thought me spoiled, indeed.

There were skirmishes, it is true, where soldiers would go out
against some of the rebel Irish chieftains; usually, though, they
would return without trophies and sometimes without even a
sight of the enemy. The land was so strange to us English,
shrouded in mist, and with treacherous bogs underfoot, the
harrying tribes seemed to melt away. I asked Richard why he did
not get some guides from the friendly Irish we lived among, for
they sure must know the land, and then it was *their* holdings
which were being plundered and laid low, so it seemed to have
sense in it. He looked at me quizzically, stroking his little golden
beard, and said, "It is perhaps a thought. . . . You are a canny
lad, my Hal. . . ." I felt it strange that he had not thought of it
himself, and he must have read my feelings, as he could so often,
for he said, musingly, "Oh, Hal . . . I am a peaceful prince. I
have no love for war. . . . My people do not love me for it either." He sat a moment, thinking, with a sad look, of a sort, on
his face. "Look you, Hal . . . we have been at peace with the
French all my reign, where we have had nothing but raids from
them on our shores these many years before. The Welsh, too, love
me, and the Scots. . . . For more than ten years none of our
young men have died in battle, and the women all have husbands and do not crowd the brothels of the cities . . . even here,
in Ireland, there is no great shakes of trouble, a few petty chiefs
from the peat bogs, who are always about, like outlaws, living off
the land, and what they can pilfer. I came here only to satisfy the
Parliament, and the lords and commons . . . it seems they cannot bear a peace-minded king."

I thought of what my Grandfather Gaunt had said, that Richard had beggared the land with his lavishness and waste, his

pomp and splendor, but I dared not speak. Again he read me, though, for he said, "Do you think that war is not expensive?. . . . Then you have never seen it. . . . In my father's time, and him all men loved, there was famine so heavy on the land that the starving people fought over rats and vermin and killed one another for a cat's carcass. . . . He was the great victor of Crécy, and the commons went wild with joy at the sight of him when he rode abroad. Yet still, beneath the surface, there was hatred for all the nobles, and the commons rose, after he died, and I was king . . . I was only fourteen . . . but I was brave, then, too— perhaps you will not believe it . . . I rode out to face them, alone. . . ."

"I know, sire," I said, eagerly, "and they loved you and hailed you as their young savior. I have heard it. . . ."

"They were brave men," said Richard, "those peasants, Wat and the rest . . . never let men tell you other . . . They had their greatness. John Ball, who died so horribly—I think he was a saint truly. . . . I tried to give those men what they wanted, but I had so many about me, so many bullies . . . and I was young. . . . I could not prevail, for they had the charter of rule, Thomas, my uncle of Woodstock. . . ." His face, so mild, looked almost as black as my father's for a moment. My skin crawled; it was Humphrey's father, murdered, as he had told me, who was that Uncle Thomas. Richard's face cleared, and he went on. "Perhaps if your grandfather, my uncle of Gaunt, had been there. . . . But he was in Spain, struggling for his Spanish kingdom . . . and so the commons lost all. . . . But they will win, someday, Hal . . . they will win—not in my time or yours—but all rules change, and give way to other needs. . . . I have tried to give them a little . . . peace, and some small, piddling laws of benefit . . . but they do not love me for it. . . . They begrudge me, even, my little vanities. . . ." And, at this, his voice grew pettish, and he tossed his head peevishly, like a woman. I was silent, for I knew him wrong . . . and right, too, under. . . . He was a man of many parts and not easy to understand, especially for a boy. But with all his faults, I had grown, in this short time, to love him well.

I was not happy though to see no fighting, and begged to be let go with the soldiers. I was a boy, after all, and forgot much that Richard had said to me, wanting to try my arts of battle. He gave in to me and let me go on some of the forays, but I held arms only for the knights, and never even saw a barbarian, or a bog even.

It is a long story, so I will not tell it all, but part only. I had brought with me my play warriors and spent much time, at night, moving them about in battle positions and studying, though Humphrey laughed. I had made friends, too, with some of the younger Irish squires and had a map drawn for me of the lands about that place. There was a stream along one side where there was sometimes fighting, but in the mists the Irish outlaws would ever slip away, before they could be caught. We lost some men that way, too, from arrows coming out of nowhere and spears thrown, too. I surmised the Irish enemies had a ford-place and so crossed, before we could ever meet with them, after they slew a few of ours. So we figured, studying the map and moving the soldier pieces about, that we could force them to a deep place they could not ford and so hem them about and win.

There were ten of us English boys, and about twice as many Irish, anxious to get our taste of war, and fretting, and we were all in on it. Now the barbarians always made their forays at dawn when the mists were thickest. We plotted to sneak away in the night, before any called us back or saw us even, and lie in wait for the enemy's dawn raid in this place. I did not want Humphrey to come, for I was afraid for his life—he had so little skill—but he insisted, so I made him promise to carry the extra arms only.

I thought then that I would never forget it, it being my first time of fighting, ever, but I have forgot all the same. There have been so many others. It worked, my plan, that is all I really know, and we were all knighted for it in the end. Now I can just remember that loose-boweled feeling, waiting; lying on our bellies in the bog, our fronts all muddy, while the sky grew faintly gray. I know an arrow whizzed past me where I lay, making a sound louder than I could have ever thought, and I saw dim shapes and whispered, "Come on!" We jumped to our feet, yelling, and forced them into deep water and so won them, almost all. I killed my first man that day, and that I remember well. I could not see him clearly till he was upon me, where I waded out after them. He rose up before me, all dripping, with a spear turned toward my belly. I had thrown mine already but thrust downward with my sword; it went between his eyes and came out in back, above his bronze collar. He looked surprised and sank back into the water. When I pulled out the sword, a great gush of the man's blood came with it, making the water red all about.

We dragged the dead ashore; there were more than thirty, so each of us had had his kill. My spear, too, was in one, but I could not count that, for I had thrown blindly. When we brought the dead back to the castle, I threw that man over Humphrey's saddle, for his claim, though I knew he had not loosed a weapon. Our horses had not been blooded before and screamed and neighed in terror all the way back; if any others of the barbarians had been about, it would have been our death, but we were lucky, like first-time players at dice.

Richard was like some old nursemaid, railing at us and wringing his hands; "Sweet Jesus," he kept crying, "you might have all been killed! What would your mothers say . . . they would have my neck. . . ." I had a long scratch down my arm, maybe from the arrow I heard go past, or maybe I scratched it later on my enemy's rough-made collar, but he went wild over it, as though it were something dreadful; it did not hurt even. I felt a fool among the other boys, with the physician tut-tutting and salving me and binding up my arm from wrist to shoulder, while Richard hovered, scolding.

He knighted me after, though, along with all our ten English boys who had been with me. It was, after all, about the only bloodshed in those Irish wars. There was a banquet to celebrate, and Richard, all dressed in state and crowned with his best gold crown, touched us each lightly on the shoulder with his jeweled sword that had never seen battle. I was first and cannot remember his words. I thought, like all the old tales, he had said, "Arise, fair Knight!" But that is not the way it went.

We had with us in our company a Frenchman, by name Créton, a noble, but I forget his rank. He was more minstrel than soldier and wrote down much of what happened. I have it by me still, though the man himself is long dead; it is in fair metrical verse and courtly French, so his words are not probably exact but flowered-up, as the French do. But he quotes Richard, and I have his writings before me, "My Fair Cousin, henceforth be gallant and bold, for unless you conquer you will have little name for valor." Thinking upon it now, I wonder if he meant it as a satire, in part, after he had complained to me that day of his subjects' lack-love for him. I do not know, and anyway, I misdoubt the Frenchman's words somewhat, for in that same poem he describes me as "a fair and handsome young bachelor." I was just rising twelve!

Chapter 12

Just three days after my knighting I had dressed for the evening meal, buckling on my sword, which as new-made knight I had leave to wear; there was a scratch at my door, and when I bade them enter, it was a petty clerk of Richard's, a man whose face I barely knew. He addressed me without title, saying, in a too-loud voice, "You are to keep to your room; the king commands it!" He turned without ceremony, twitching his heavy clerk's gown, and went out. It was the first time I had been spoken to as less than a great-grandson of a king; this man, in particular, had always fawned upon me, praising my letters and the like. I was astonished.

The door opened a crack then, and Humphrey came in, sideways, like a sneak-thief. "What ails you?" I said. His face was white as tallow.

"I would not be in your shoes," he said. "No, not for all the treasure of the Saracens. Richard is wild and hurling things about, cursing Derby and swearing vengeance. . . . He has left table and bid everyone be gone, too, so that we simply grabbed what was on our plates and fled. It is maybe all we will get tonight. . . ."

He drew from under his surcoat some greasy drumsticks wrapped in a napkin, a small round cheese, and a comb of honey, dripping. "I am not hungry," I said. "What do you think it means?" In spite of my efforts, my voice cracked; it had been doing that lately. The first time it happened, Richard had jested that he must lock up the Irish maidens.

Humphrey sat on the bed, heavily, still holding the food. "Here, give me that stuff," I said. "You are messing the whole place."

"I do not know," said Humphrey, "except that it has to do with you. . . ."

We stared at each other, not daring to guess. I do not know how long we sat there, while the light ebbed and the room grew dim. Neither of our body servants were about, and we were

afraid to shout for them, so we lit the candles ourselves, spilling
the wax over our fingers. When the latch of the door lifted, we
jumped as if it were a thunderclap.

It was our cousin Edward of Aumerle; he, too, came in sidling,
as if the fiends were after him. He shut the door, too, behind him,
and slid the bolt. Coming close to me, he said, softly, "Listen,
Harry . . . your father has landed at Ravenspur four days ago
with six men. . . ." My God, he is dead now, I thought.

"What happened, Cousin?" My throat was dry, and the words
croaked.

He put his hand on my shoulder. "*He* is safe . . . and more."
His mild face wore a look of fear. "We hear that Northumberland, with Harry Percy, too, and Willoughby and Greystock
have all ridden to join him. It is revolt . . . they are marching
westward across Yorkshire to your father's duchies to take them
back from the king. . . . By now they may easily have twenty
thousand men. . . . They are joined all along their way by other
nobles, discontent. . . . God knows where it will end. . . ."

Humphrey sank back upon the bed, sobbing loud. "Oh, before
Jesus, Harry . . . he will kill you now. . . . Richard will kill
you. . . ."

Our cousin shook him roughly. "Be still!" He turned to me.
"Come, follow me. The king wishes to talk with you."

Humphrey, quiet now, looked up at me with horror. "Oh,
Harry," he said, very low, "for sure your father hates you. . . ."

"No," I said, and my voice seemed to come from far away to
my own ears. "No," I said again, "he is only coming to get back
his inheritance that was seized. . . ."

"But you are hostage for him. . . ." His words trailed off, and
he looked at me in horror, as though I were a corpse already.

"Peace now, Humphrey!" exclaimed our cousin, more sharply.
He looked at me. "Take off your sword," he said. "It looks
bad. . . ."

Richard was in his own chamber, where I had never been before. It was lit by torchlight only; his face was like a white mask
in the gloom. Bagot and some other lords were with him; we had
heard Richard's voice, railing, thin with hysteria, as we came
along the hall. But he was quiet now. He snapped his fingers at
his attendants, his eyes on me. They left, slinking like ferrets.
"You, also," said Richard, with the ghost of a smile, his eyes

slewing around to our cousin, where he stood, his face set in apprehension. "I will not behead him just yet. . . ."

I heard the door close behind Aumerle and fell to my knees. "Oh, sire," I said. I do not know what I said. It is long ago. I have looked it up in the Frenchman's chronicle-poem; he was not there, of course, but this is what I read. I have read it other places, too. "In truth, my gracious king and lord, I am sincerely grieved by these tidings, and, as I conceive, you are fully assured of my innocence in this proceeding of my father." What prig or imbecile could have uttered such words at such a time? I probably said nothing but knelt there, shaking. Richard raised me up and seated me beside him on the state bed. "My Hal—I cannot think your father loves you. . . . I, for sure, would never leave my son to a great king's mercy while I ran wild, my heart black with revolt and gathering armies at my back. . . . Unless, of course, he thinks me, perhaps, a soft woman-ninny. Which, for sure, I see I am . . . for I will not hurt you, Hal . . . I read your misery well . . . and besides, I have much love for you. Never have I known a fairer, finer youth. . . . Oh, Hal," he said, softly, and his white face streamed with tears, "my Hal . . . I would have made you my heir. . . ." I fell to sobbing then, too, and flung my arms around him wildly, for all he was my king. It was my huge relief, I guess, that snapped the string. And then, I loved Richard, too. I had forgot, in that moment, all the injustice he had done my father. So powerful are sweet embraces and fair words, especially to the lonely young.

"What will you do to my father?" I whispered, finally.

Richard laughed a small laugh, hollow-sounding. "It is the other way around, I fear. . . ." Then he straightened up and stood. "We will have to fight," he said. "And God, I pray, will be with the victor."

He kissed me tenderly, then, on both my cheeks, embracing me, and saying he would send me away and out of it. To the Castle of Trim he would send me, and Humphrey, too, to be under the care of the Lady Ulster there, while the civil war raged.

We rode to Ulster next day, Humphrey and I, he marveling that I was in my whole skin, and I sunk deep in thought. I did not pay great heed to his complaints on the journey, for he was always either too cold or too hot, or his saddle too small or too big, and such like moanings; I was used to it. In truth, it was a hot ride, for summer comes early in those parts, and we never stopped to rest but to change horses only.

When we reached Ulster and the Castle of Trim, he had to be lifted from his saddle, burning with fever, and by the morning he was dead. The chroniclers would have it that he was poisoned by Richard, but that could not be; we two had eaten all the same foods. Besides it made no sense, for if he would poison any, surely it would have been me, though I am sure he would not have done that either.

My heart was almost bursting, though, with grief for my first good friend and cousin and with worry for my father and Richard, too. It seemed to me that I was torn between those two men who fought.

We buried Humphrey there at Ulster on a bright green day, the Lady of Ulster and I. She was a sweet, kind lady, and much moved by my grief. She had masses said for Humphrey's soul, paid for out of her own pocket, for my allowance I had not liked to ask for from Richard, though it was due.

As for Richard, him I never saw again in this world.

BOOK II

The Enemy

*(Told by Morgan ab Owen, natural
daughter of Owen Glendower)*

Chapter 1

When I first came back to Wales, to live in my father's house, I had thought I'd queen it a bit over the other girls there, because of having spent so much time at the French court. But this was impossible, I saw from the first; all the maidens of Owen's house, even the lowborn ones, speak French nearly as well as I do myself, though their accents are comical. Also, they are very learned, with as many tutors as boys have in other places; Owen's ideas are all very modern, in spite of his dressing in his own fashion, with an antique air. That is simply his whim; he likes to pose as a king-hero out of the old Welsh legends. At first you think it is strange and forbidding, but after you know him it is endearing rather; you can see that he likes to act, to play parts the way children do.

For instance, at the French court, where he was a sort of ambassador for Richard, he was the most courtly creature you could imagine. He trimmed his hair and shaved his beard and wore the latest fashions, the very short tunic that shows the leg all the way up the thigh, and the huge slashed sleeves; the French all thought he was the most polished courtier in the world. And then when I went to England in Isabelle's train I heard him called the Welsh magician. It seems he dressed up as Merlin once, in flowing robes and a cone-shaped long hat—like those you will see in old pictures—and put on a show at court, looking into a crystal ball and making strange passes with his hands, speaking gibberish as if it were a magic language. He pretended to call the wind, like old Merlin, too, but it seems he had noticed that a storm was brewing, and so it came, and the big wind came with it, as if at his command. He and Richard had a good laugh over it afterward, but the whole thing got about, and tales were told of it, and so the people think he really knows magic. Here in Wales he goes about bearded, with the old bronze crown of Prince Madoc on (it looks like a thin metal string) and wearing the ancient sword of Eliseg, that is only half as long as a modern one, and made of iron; it could not cut through butter. But the Welsh people, especially the hill folk, think he is Arthur, come again. I do not say this about him to talk slightingly of him but simply to explain; I have a great love for him, and gratitude, too. It is not all bastards who are treated the way Owen treats us. Also, I am certain that he knows more about every subject that there is under the sun than any other man living; there can be no question of that once you have heard him speak at any length.

I was in France so long, and England after, that I had forgotten what Wales looked like. Owen had taken me to France when I was only three years old, to get me away from my mother. I will have to explain this; Mother was Lowry ferch Morgan, ferch Lowry, ferch Morgan, and so on, supposedly back to the first Morgan, that I am named after who was the one of Arthur's time. That is, of course, ridiculous, but here they will believe anything. Anyway, Mother was the last prophetess of Dinas Brân; Dinas Brân is an old, old stronghold, and looks it, too. It is supposed to date back to the first settlers of Wales, who came from some place in Greece, crossing over the ocean on foot on a continent that sank long ago into the sea. I think it is really silly, but Owen says not to say that sort of thing here. The prophetess thing is supposed to be hereditary and handed down from mother to daughter, and *that* is supposed to go back to when Wales was a matriarchy, meaning ruled by women. I guess it might have been so once, but it is certainly a misty dream by now, to say the least. Anyhow the prophetesses lived there, in Dinas Brân, sort of like queens, and had maidens, like nuns a bit, and they all worshiped Saint Derfel, who used to be a god before the Christians came, and also, some old goddess called Epona. And they would come out once every year, in the spring, I guess, and bless the crops and cut a poor little lamb's throat over the ground to make it fertile (it used to be a human sacrifice, Owen says, but that makes me shudder to contemplate—things are bad enough as they are everywhere, with executions and wars) and then they would dabble their fingers in the poor thing's blood and prophesy. And *then* they—the prophetesses, I mean—would bed with the Chosen One, and the daughter would be the next prophetess! (I don't know what they did if it turned out to be a boy; strangle it, I guess.) I mean you can't imagine such things going on in modern times. But it did, up until I was born, Owen being the Chosen One at that time. I asked him how he could

have gone along with that kind of thing—it is so pagan, really—
but he just laughed and said my mother was very beautiful.
(There must have been a good many beauties around a little earlier, because there are quite a few children running around the
palace that look like Owen. He is what they call a lusty man, or
used to be, at any rate.) But Owen put a stop to the whole thing
by stealing me; he broke the chain, as it were. He stole me when
I was a little baby, and Mother kept plotting to get me back, and
finally he took me out of the country. Mother was so enraged and
grief-stricken that she killed herself; she was found hanging by an
old girdle, which the people insisted was Princess Myfanwy's
which would make it about a thousand years old and too rotten
to do the job. But Owen says, though they are a wonderful people, you cannot talk sense to the Welsh. I sound awfully mean
and disrespectful about Mother, but, after all, I didn't know her
at all. And I certainly wouldn't have wanted to be a priestess or
whatever it was. And afterward, all the little nuns ran away and
became whores at the Tassel Inn, where all the English border
soldiers stay. Owen says they were quite wanton anyway, really,
and not a bit like Christian nuns.

When I first saw Glyndyvrdwy Llyys, where we live now, I was
astonished. And that is the last time I will call it that; I was just
trying to show off. It took me a morning to figure out how to spell
it in English. From now on it will be simply Glendower House.
You really couldn't call it a castle—it is so different. Owen de-
signed it himself, drawing plans and supervising everything. Now
every castle or great manor I have ever seen is made of stone, and
always, also, looks more like a fortress, with hardly any windows,
except arrow-slit openings. But this Llyys, or mansion house, of
Owen's is wood! It is true that there is stone under, but all you
can see is wood, smoothed and polished so that it looks almost
like ivory, except that it is very dark. Owen had it brought by
ship all the way from Cathay; the Genoese make such trips often
—they have very fast, strong ships. Owen went on the first trip to
pick out the trees; the wood is called teak and is very hard, and
will probably never wear out. It is a very difficult palace to describe, Owen's, being so different, but I will try. All around the
whole thing is a wall, not very high, of this teak wood, too, over
stone, and inside there are lots and lots of buildings; dwellings,
barns, stables, storehouses, and everything you can think of, al-

most like a city. Except that it is all low, just one story high. Only the main house, in the middle, has two stories; the top story is all for the women, and is where we live. The downstairs of this building is one huge hall, with a big chimney, built of bricks, in the middle. It is square-built, and there is a hearth on each side, so there are four fireplaces, which do a good job of heating, better than anywhere else I've been. The upstairs is divided into four main rooms, each having a fireplace, as the chimney continues on up. There are screens to divide all these rooms into any shape you might want or to provide privacy; it is complicated but works very well. There are covered walkways leading to other buildings, where the men of our family sleep, and all the buildings around have men and soldiers, minstrels and bards, servants and visitors staying in them. There are no fortifications, except that there are hundreds of men-at-arms and guards right there. Owen does not like to live in a fort, he says; life should be more gracious than that. He says it is built on the lines of a Homeric palace, that is, like very ancient Greece and how their kings lived. Homer was a great bard of that time, and you can still read him; it has been handed down. There are descriptions of palaces in his poems, and that is how Owen found out about them. But, of course, everything depends on being rich and having a great many retainers because otherwise the place would not be able to be defended.

Owen says the Greek palaces were all open, with many windows, porticoes, wide doors, and openings in the roofs, too; of course, it was very mild there and even hot most of the time, so he couldn't follow that exactly. But we do have a lot more light than most manor houses, only all the openings are glazed. Our girls' sleeping place is open to the sky, with a glass roof, for instance, which is wonderful, sometimes, if you are wakeful and can look up at the stars, and drop off to sleep, counting them. Elliw, one of the maidens who live here, hates this, though, and says she feels exposed, though I have told her only eagles can see her. But she always goes about fully robed, and we have put a canopy over her bed; so she feels comfortable. She is an odd little creature, anyway, I think; she is the daughter of Rhys Dhu, a kinsmen of Owen's, but a wild hill chieftain, so she has spent much of her early life in caves, which may explain part of it.

We girls, and there are a lot of us, live all together under the

Lady Margaret's rule; she is a most fair, though portly woman, Owen's wife. The people call her the Argyllwyddes, a sort of title. It is old Welsh, which nobody understands anymore, though all the bards pretend to. Some say it means the Englishwoman; I can hardly credit that, for she cannot have more than an eighth of English blood. Her father was Sir John Hanmer, a wealthy border lord; the family is very old, so maybe, far back, there is English, but the Welsh would count it, for they are fiercely patriotic. I speak as though I am not Welsh myself, but that is because I have spent so much time elsewhere, and also, Owen himself holds that there is little difference between men, even Saracen or Jew. By the way, he says not to say that word, Jew, for it is a sort of epithet among Christian peoples; he says they are Israelites and should have their correct title. He says that even the peoples of Cathay, who are very different to look at, with eyes that are unlidded and slanting upward, and broad, flat faces, and the Africans, who are *black* in color, are much the same as the rest of us, having different customs only. *Black* is a hard thing to believe, but I know that he does not lie.

Anyway, as I started to say, we maidens live all together; there is plenty of room, so we do not argue too much. First, there is Catherine, Owen's youngest daughter; she is the Lady Margaret's child, too, so is the only legitimate one of us. She is a year younger than I am, just the age of Richard's queen. People would have it that all us girls are Owen's, but that is not true. Only Efa and I are his without doubt, besides Catherine. Efa is a nun's daughter, from the convent at Valle Crucis; her mother died giving birth. Efa herself says she is Saint Derfel's, but everybody knows that is not true, unless he was the image of Owen. We three, his daughters, all look much like him, with tawny hair and cat-colored eyes. We are all very tall, too, like him; I used to be too fat, but I have lost that flesh now and am slender as the others, except that I have too much up top in front. Lady Margaret makes me wear a sort of binder-cloth; she says it is more seemly.

Then there is Elliw, that I mentioned before, and two daughters of Tudor ap Griffith, Owen's brother, named Gwynneth and Gwenllian; they are twins and very beautiful, with dark, rosy skins and black eyes. They are bastards, too, though, got on some Celtic princess from the hills; they all call themselves princesses, those hill women, but the daughters are sweet maidens. They are sixteen already and marriageable, but Owen will have to dower them handsomely on account of their birth. The other damsels are of low birth and could be either Owen's or Tudor's, or one of the bards'; their mothers, though, are serving maids here. The girls' names are Olwen, Sibli, Megolin, and Modry, and they are not treated any differently from the rest of us; of course, they cannot hope to marry well, that is all. Megolin, though, wants to be a nun. So, after I have counted, I see we are ten. We all have tutors and women who teach us sewing and weaving; we take harp lessons from the bards, besides. In fact, we are always very busy and do not play very much, but it is pleasant here.

Owen has six acknowledged sons, four bastards and two trueborn. The only one I have met so far is Meredith, the youngest, who is about two years older than I; they have all been studying at Oxford Town, for Wales has no university, though Owen would like to found one. Meredith was the last to go, so I met him when I came here, almost three years ago. He, again, is like us, resembling Owen; he is fine-boned, though, and much fairer of hair, getting his coloring from the Lady Margaret. I cannot remember him all that well, of course, because I saw little of him, really; he is coming home though, almost any minute now, with all the others, and heaven only knows how many more, students all. There has been an uprising there at Oxford; as a matter of fact, there have been a few, and all the Welsh are coming home, spoiling for a fight, and even some English with them. It seems there is a real coil there, and indeed all over in other parts, too, of England, on account of the new king and his unjust laws. They are even burning people alive there! It is too gruesome to think on, but Owen says, looking grim, that it is just beginning.

Poor, sweet Richard is dead, and un-kinged, too, and Red Bolingbroke is crowned. Strange to think that little Harry Long-Twist is now the crowned Prince of Wales! One awful thing after another has been happening over there in England; these last years have been humming with news like a beehive, even here, where we get it late. Owen must have had wind of some events to come when he fetched me from the court two years and more ago. He had just come back from France then, after all, where Henry of Bolingbroke was plotting in his exile. It is a long story, and astonishing and sad, too, so I will say it all as briefly as possible. Henry of Lancaster, that is, Bolingbroke, as he is sometimes called, little Harry's father, though banished by Richard, was still able, in exile, to get the ear of other nobles discontented with Richard's rule. When he landed in England, more than three-quarters of the nobles, with all their retainers, flocked to his banner; he won the revolt and routed poor Richard, who was never warlike anyway. He forced Richard, who was by then his prisoner, to abdicate the throne; he did not do what most people expected, place the Mortimer heir, who is the closest blood claimant, on the throne, but took the crown for himself, saying that all men begged for his kingship, and so he was forced to it. Such a thing happened long ago, said Owen, in Rome, when Julius Caesar made himself emperor by the "will of the people." Owen says this is nonsense, of course, in both cases. As a matter of fact, Owen rode to Richard's succor but had not time to get men enough up from Wales to do any good. And so all was lost. Richard died in Pontefract Castle prison, some say starved to death; murder is whispered, too. Owen says we will never know the right of it. At any rate, a body was shown, in all pomp, or rather, the head only, the whole being sealed away in a lead casket, to satisfy the people that he was dead, and not from violence, for the head bore no marks. Even so, many say that it was not Richard at all, but another man, his double, called Richard Maudelyne, and that Richard is safe in Scotland somewhere. I privately think this cannot be, for I knew that man Maudelyne at court, and he was not so very like to Richard as all that. After all, though Catherine and I are sisters, and look a bit similar, no one would mistake us, in truth. Griffith, my oldest brother, saw the casket in London, and holds that it was Richard, without doubt; he says, however that a starved creature would show the marks of that, too, so one can tell from his letters that he, Griffith, at least, thinks that Richard was killed somehow; he even names the murderer, one Piers Exton. Owen says this is hearsay but says, also, that Red Bolingbroke could not afford to let him live— Richard, I mean. It is all very complicated and politically mixed up; there have already been plots against the new king's life, and his son's, too. I am glad that Harry did not die; he was near death from poisoning, it is said.

I am so sorry for Harry; it is easy to imagine how he must feel now. Richard was more of a father to him than ever that grim man who is now king. That man used to beat him with a whip! I myself have seen the old scars on his back, long healed, and he was only eleven when I knew him. Also, it is not Red Bolingbroke's doing that he even *has* a son-heir, but Richard's mercy only; he was hostage there, after all, when his horrible father got up to all his tricks! I hate him well, though I have never met him. Owen would say this is wrong, but I guess it is my mother coming out in me.

They say that young Harry was drugged at his coronation, when he was made Prince of Wales (an empty title, if there ever was one, for that is what all men call Owen, in fact). They say he would not do his father's bidding and that he ran at him with a sword, the one Richard gave him at his knighting; they say, also, that he accused his father of Richard's murder and was sent off to Oxford to escape his father's wrath. (Who sent him, I wonder. None of it makes good sense; Owen says all gossip must be taken with a grain of salt.) We will learn more, of course, when my brothers come back from there.

I keep calling him little Harry. He was shorter than I when I knew him at Richard's court, but I have stopped growing now (I hope), and perhaps he has not; we are the same age to a month. Of course, Owen being six feet and a half, we are all giants around here, which scares me sometimes; I would not like to attain such a height as that, with all my suitors looking up at me! I liked Harry well, the best of all the lads at court; he is the handsomest, to my mind, of any, though his face does lean a little to one side, and is long and narrow. His color is like some of the Lombards I saw at the French court, dark of hair and eyes, with strong-marked brows like birds' wings, tilting up and outward, and lips the color of watered wine. I think of him when I read of the young Alexander, the Greek boy who conquered practically all the world long ago and was beautiful, too, they say; Harry always would beat the other boys at play tourney or feats of strength, even those older and bigger, although he never bragged. Catherine says I am half in love with him, but that is silly; we were just children then. Catherine is very romantic, always falling in love and out, sometimes with people she has never even seen; I suppose she thinks all girls behave her way. Anyway, I am anxious to hear news of Harry; Meredith, I know, has the same master at Oxford there, so will know it all.

I have spoken of all the many men-at-arms we have living here at the Llyys; Owen has never been a warrior, truly, though long ago he did serve in the Scottish and Irish wars with King Richard. But these defenders of ours are needed now, for there are constant skirmishes between Owen's men and the retainers of Lord Grey of Ruthin. Now this lord is English, a borderer, and has been seizing lands which belong by hereditary right to Owen, that is, to us. Grey has also sent them over the countryside, burning and pillaging, raping our women and capturing villages. Not a day goes by but what there is not some new tale of woe or some complaint from the people hereabouts. They look to Owen for protection and also for revenge, though by Welsh law he is not their true lord. It does not work here exactly as it does in other places, like England or France. Here the people are not unfree but hold their lands by rent or purchase. In England, though, they are serfs and can own nothing, but are bound to this lord or that. I am not well versed in law of any sort, but Owen has explained it a little. Wales has had no king or ruler, really, since Prince Llewelyn lost a great battle with Edward I of England. Owen is the highest noble of the land right now, though he has not the title and actually owes allegiance to England's king. Now, in Richard's time, all these lands were granted to my father, but since the revolt and the new king, old Cess-pit Grey has grabbed a lot of them by force, and although Owen has appealed to Red Bolingbroke for justice, and a hearing in law, nothing has happened, except that Grey's men get bolder and bolder, and are devastating the countryside. So, actually there is nothing for it but that Owen must send out men, too, to fight against Grey's marauders. So what happens now, is that whole villages change hands; first they are Welsh and then English, and vice versa. Only, in the meantime, innocent blood is shed, and the poor people suffer; it is a silly situation. Owen says all wars are, even the huge ones that lay waste a whole nation; he says this is just how wars start, small, like what is happening here. But, though Owen is a man of peace, if he cannot get justice from the new king, he must fight; he cannot allow those under his protection to be butchered, or his own heirs to be beggared.

Efa, who is a strange girl, finds all this exciting; she watches for the men when they come home at nightfall and listens for the cries of their bereaved women, for always there are some who do not return. The rest of us are saddened, and frightened a little; the bards sing dirges each night now at hall, and the Lady Margaret sends us girls to bring death gifts to the widows. We are suddenly in the midst of tragedy; it is even becoming commonplace. Life here has always been so pastoral and sweet, if a little boring.

I have not spoken much yet of the bards. They are Owen's great enthusiasm, though he has many others, of course. I privately think, from the design of his house, and from these same bards, that Owen is re-creating, insofar as is possible, in his own life, the ways of ancient Greece. There are many musicians here, who play songs of their own composing, on the lute and the mandol, and even the lyre, which is not a popular instrument anywhere else. Owen treats them like honored guests, giving them fine clothes and feasting them, but they are guests who never go home. I think they have no homes, in truth, but will live here always. All large manor households have visiting ministrels, jugglers, too, sometimes; they are as common as the rain from heaven. But here they are part of our life; I think, once they come avisiting, they just do not leave, and so there is a whole large building where they live, with a great platform in front; in fine weather it is like a fair, one show after another.

The true bards are another story; they are, in a way, storytellers, except that they sing the stories and play the harp. There are several of those, too, but they live with the house-kin. They are all of them wonderfully talented and can make you weep to hear them; but there are two, I think, who must be the greatest poets in the world (it is hard to explain; the harp sound is as a background only, to the words, though the harp, too, can break your heart). One of the great ones is Griffith Lloyd, a man about Owen's age, but with no hair on his head, or even, Efa says, anywhere (she is always spying on the men in the bathhouse). His skin is like a baby's, pink and white, except for his fingertips, which are hard and brown like horn, from plucking at the strings; his feet, too, have calloused soles an inch thick, for he goes barefoot always, like a friar. He has a huge, craggy head, like a dome, and deep eyesockets under bald shelves of brow; his eyes look out at you as from caves—they are so blue the breath catches at their beauty. His face, indeed, is like a face carved into a mountainside, so large and stern the features, but for those flower eyes. He, like Owen, has a great reputation for getting bastards, but they are not so easily spotted from a hairless father. Some of the girls think Sibli is his because she can play any instrument without even studying and has a lively imagination as well. Privately I do not think so; she is tiny and dark as a Moor, with eyes as black as raisins. There is so much talk always about who is son or daughter of whom around here; it is comical in a way. That is because Owen is forever adopting all the likeliest lads and girls; he cannot resist the glimmerings of intelligence wherever he finds it. He says we must stop this speculating about birth; Owen swears that he has found in hovels, among filth, the long fingers and delicate features that are supposed to be a mark of noble blood and, conversely, among nobles the grossness and thickheadedness of the peasant. But then Owen is not like other men, and holds with none of their common beliefs. He does not even believe in God, though I am almost afraid to write it down. (Since I have not been struck dead, he is probably right.) He says man has wondered always about the riddles that be in nature and the marvels that he cannot understand, and so has invented gods. All men have done this, he says, time out of mind, and always will, and they are all the same gods, too, but with different names. I hope he does not say these things away from home, for they are burning people for saying much less, in England, with that old hawk, Arundel, watching! And he is archbishop! I hate him, too, although I have never seen him.

Anyway, that bard, Griffith Lloyd, is Owen's own bard, sometimes setting Owen's words to music and usually composing all sorts of songs to the honor of our house. Richard had a favorite poet, who sometimes lived at court, but he was not musical and wrote verses only; his name was Master Chaucer, and Owen says he was born out of his time and is far ahead of all of us. And they say Red Bolingbroke has a fool, like the Spanish kings, always about him, to make jokes. I suppose he cannot think of anything funny by himself. These fools, or jesters as they are called, are usually dwarfs, or born misshapen, so Richard, who loved beauty, never had one. But I remember, at the French court, though it was long ago, that the queen, Isabeau, had a little pet lady, no higher than a three-year-old, that she used to dress up like a doll and carry around! All the princesses hated this little creature, for she had beautiful clothes and jewels, and they had

none but made-over rags and one state dress between them. No
wonder the first two were so happy to be married off, even to old
men! But anyhow, Owen has a bard, instead of these other kind
of protégés. (That is a French word, but I don't know how to say
it in English.)

There is another bard, too, a very old, old man; Catherine says
he is over a hundred, but she is not always sensible. At any rate,
Iolo Goch—that is his name—is a very ancient man. He can no
longer sing, really, for he has no teeth in his head, and his voice,
too, is thin with age, but his playing would make a stone weep.
He does not play often, for it wears him dreadfully, and afterward he looks like death, gray and stark. He will play tonight, in
hall, Efa says; she always knows everything that is going on—she
is everywhere at once, that one. But something like that must be
true, for the Lady Margaret has bidden all us girls to dress in our
second-best gowns, and no jerkins or hose either. Of course, we
do not often come to meat in our riding wear, anyhow, except for
Catherine, who hates skirts.

I must explain something which will sound peculiar to those in
other places. All us maidens wear page's gear when we ride
among them or in sight of the men-at-arms; Owen says it is more
sensible and more seemly, too, on horseback, for our skirts blow
up around our waists otherwise. Richard's first queen, Anne of
Bohemia, a lady, of course, I never saw, used to ride a sort of
lady-saddle, on which she sat sidewise and not astride. They have
these saddles where she came from, but they have not caught on
much yet in England, and here we have none at all. I cannot
imagine how one would not fall off.

But anyhow, there is a dreadful coil upstairs here because of
this fancying-up; Efa has accused Sibli of stealing her furred surcoat, and Sibli has scratched her face, so she will look a pretty
sight. It serves her right though—Efa—she is always doing such
things; most like she has left it in the pages' house or the minstrels'. Lady Margaret says she will not need it anyway, for the
hall will be warm with all the crowd. This really makes me curious; who is coming, besides the usual company? Which is big
enough, in fact. I think I will wear my saffron if Catherine is not
wearing that color; it is my favorite, though the velvet is rubbed
a little at the elbows. I will turn it back, though, to show the lining, a nice red, and no one will notice. I wish there were time to
wash my hair, but Lady Margaret says not.

Chapter 2

There was so much stress upstairs that I thought we would not ever get to our places at table; besides the quarrel between Efa and Sibli, the twins Gwynneth and Gwenllian went about sobbing and sulking because the Argyllwyddes would not allow them to dress alike, which they do usually, and no one can tell them apart. There was a kind of queer feeling in the air, as happens sometimes before a storm, although the skies were clear; our hair crackled as it was brushed, and quick angry words rose all about. We are usually at accord here; it was most strange. Catherine, who had planned, also, to wear her saffron, was snappish, in reverse, insisting that she would not wear the color and I must. I then said no, she must be the one to go in yellow, and so it went between us, until the Argyllwyddes reproved us for our silliness and forbade the color to either. So it turned out that I wore purple and Catherine green, by command, and, these being each our most unloved gowns, we exchanged looks of annoyance, making faces behind the Lady Margaret's back, and giggling. In truth I would not have her job, poor lady! But then, I never will, in all likelihood, for that I am not true-born, and so will not ever become so respected a matron. Little Elliw, who never quarrels, and is always like a scared rabbit, began to cry because of all the strife about and had to be comforted by nurse like a baby. Nurse favors her and slipped her a sweetmeat, so all the rest of us clamored for one, too; it was dreadful! We were like a lot of bad children. And the youngest of us, even, is old enough, truly, to bear a babe, had we lived in the ancient days! So the Lady Margaret reminded us, scolding; she is not usually so severe, but, as I say, the very air crackled, and she, too, was perhaps affected. Finally, Efa and Sibli were forbidden hall completely and told they must eat upstairs with nurse, so after, all the rest of us were quiet and seemly, to escape the same fate. I do not feel so very sorry for those two anyway; they will simply wait till the harping and drinking begin and slip in among the pages. They will be punished all over again for it, but then Efa, in particular, would always rather be hanged for a wolf than a sheep. Nurse says she will come to no good end. Nurse is a very old woman; she was serving maid to the Lady Margaret's mother and then nurse to the lady, and now all of us; no one can remember what her given name is; she says one name sometimes and then another, so she probably does not even know herself! She pretends to be very crotchety, but all us girls can get around her; she spoils us dreadfully. She is very lewd, too, as the old women sometimes are, and the tales she tells us at bedtime, after the Argyllwyddes has gone to her chamber, have made my face flame, even in the dark. By heaven, when I give up my maidenhead, I shall be at no loss how to go about it! To hear her tell it, one could think our old nurse had had more beddings than ever Helen of Troy even! But Efa says all old women boast like that, even the nuns at Valle Crucis.

At the last minute, Catherine and I have made everyone wait while we go to the water closet; giggling, she loosens my breastbinder, while I stuff her front, which is still small, with a silk cloth, which makes her look suddenly grown-up.

When we reached hall, the whole world and his brother seemed to be in it. There were men standing in groups in the middle by the hearths and squatting in twos and threes in corners, and there were two extra trestle tables set up at the far end. The chimneys were not drawing well, and there was much blue smoke in the room; my eyes watered, and I could not at first make out who the newcomers were, but, by my side, Catherine gave a wild cry and dashed into the midst of a group of youths, all in riding hose. I hung back a little, with Elliw, who was always shy, for I did not know them. All the other girls rushed after Catherine, though, and there was much hugging and kissing and cries of delight. I could not be so thickheaded as not to guess that they were her brothers, and mine, too, in fact, so I stretched my neck to pick out Meredith. I found him soon, for he stood a little apart, with two others. Even from where I stood I could see that the whole mort of them were dusty as scarecrows; they must have just that moment ridden in. I greeted Meredith with the kiss of welcome, and he returned it, on both cheeks, in the French manner, calling me *belle soeur*, in compliment to my court days. One of his companions was a dark youth, like a gypsy, with a beaky nose, and a look of gawky pride; he was called a cousin, but some removed, of Owen's, half-Norman, Rhisiart by name. I was not sure yet whether I liked him. The other was a young man of great self-possession, with a round, smooth countenance, and a smile of extraordinary sweetness; I did not catch his name, for introductions flowed all around me by then, all my new-met brothers speaking at once. They had, all of them, that elusive look of Owen that he stamps on all his get, though they were all unlike, really, except for size. Big young men they were, all, of shades of fairness from flaxen to brown. I felt I must wait to sort out all their names. They were just come from Oxford, as we had expected, with others, too, almost they would make an army among them. Which explained why the hall was so crowded. It was warm, too, with the breath of so many heating up the air, and all the fires going. One of the fireplaces smoked still, though some of the serving men were trying to wave the smoke back and up the flue where it belonged. Catherine coughed, and Meredith thumped her on the back; out flew an edge of the silk stuffing from her bosom. The dark Rhisiart stared, Catherine blushed and fumbled, and I saw the Argyllwyddes frown. Oh-oh, I thought, we are in for it now; she will notice my front, too. But Owen himself came up then, to embrace his sons and make all welcome, and so a diversion was created, thank the Holy Mother.

I was much surprised to hear Owen's words to the young round-face. "A hearty welcome, sir," he said. "And great congratulations to you. It is not often we are honored by such a celebrity"—who could he be, I wondered, listening for Owen's next words—"to confound Arundel and all his inquisitors—no mean feat. I shall expect you in the Saracen Room tonight . . . come with Meredith, after all this . . ." and Owen waved his hand at the company. He brought forward the Lady Margaret. "My dear, may I present Sir Walter Brut, from Oxford, too, and lately of Hereford . . . ? My Lady wife, sir. . . ."

I saw Lady Margaret's neck begin to come out in red blotches, a thing that never happened except when she was angered. "I am honored, sir," she said, holding out her hand. "It is good to know that cruel upstart Arundel thwarted for once. . . . I should like to see him beaten to his knees and stripped of all his powers. . . ." Her voice rose as I had never heard it, and I stood, amazed.

Owen smiled, patting her arm. "Women are ever the most bloodthirsty. . . . My Lady is more Lollard than any in these parts—even, it might be, than you, yourself, sir. . . ." And then it all came together in my mind, making sense, and I knew the name. For even here, so far away, we had heard of the famous trial for heresy of this same Walter Brut, and how he was acquitted, by virtue of his clerkly knowledge and his nimble tongue. He was the only accused Lollard yet to escape the stake. And here he was! I looked at him again, marveling. He had, in truth, such an open, frank manner, so harmless a look . . . I shuddered again to think of the flames. . . .

For the last thirty or forty years, maybe before, there have been Lollards all through the isles of Britain, particularly in England, where Master Wycliffe preached and taught. I do not know precisely how to define the term Lollard; Owen says it is from old Saxon and means "tares," another archaic word, which means "seeds," so it has come to mean in truly orthodox clergy's minds, "dangerous weeds sown by the devil." This is Owen's explanation, not mine; I personally think a Lollard is just sort of anyone who thinks for himself, especially about religion. Mostly they are believers in the Englishing of the Bible, so that the poor and uneducated, who need the word of God, can get it without going to the priests, who might have their own reasons for withholding certain passages. Then, too, they do not believe that the consecrated wafer and wine do actually become the body and blood of Christ, but is a spiritualization only. And other things, too, all kinds of dissension, in fact. King Richard was half a Lollard himself, and the new king's father, John of Gaunt, was a supporter of Master Wycliffe, and even granted him monies for the finishing of the English Bible, but Red Bolingbroke is somehow thick as thieves with Archbishop Arundel, who is now his chancellor, and there is dreadful persecution in England now, and the Lollards preach in secret or not at all. The new archbishop has even obtained an edict from the Pope to support it! It is named *De Heretico Comburendo,* and, of course, means, *Concerning the Burning of Heretics.* Which means that Lollardy, which used to be just a sign of reason, is now considered heresy, and those found guilty may be burned alive! People say that one out of every three persons in England is Lollard, so it can turn into a holocaust, Owen says. The universities at Oxford are seething with dissent; they are all Lollards and rebels, even, there. Great numbers of them have been flocking into Wales for the past two years; there are teachers in all the taverns and preaching at every hedge-corner. The worst of it is, says Owen, that old Red Bolingbroke does not even do this persecuting because he believes in orthodoxy or is pious, but for reasons of policy only. He is pushing for the support of the clergy and the established wealthy, who, of course, do not want to see any changes.

I heard Owen say to Master Brut, "Forgive me if I put you just below the dais. . . . There are two gentleman of the clergy present, and they must be honored at table, and I fear you might be uncomfortable in their presence. . . ." And the Lollard answered that he liked nothing better than to sit among the lowly, for, after all, did not our Saviour love them best. . . . Owen laughed loud then, putting his arm about the man, and saying, "It is easy to see how you confounded your questioners, sir . . . but you will not have such very lowly company as all that, for I have placed our new cousin, Rhisiart, next you, and his young Oxford friends. . . ." I looked carefully at this Master Brut and decided that he had the face of a homely angel, if there might be such a thing. Certainly the contrast between this man and our "clergy" guests is remarkable. Father Domitius has the face of a satyr, dark and evil, with red, moist lips, and eyes that strip the serving maids of their bodices. I have seen him pinch them, too, under their skirts, when he thinks no one sees. The other, Father Simon, is a Cistercian, and a mild little man, but fat as a pig from rich pastries, and with grease stains all over his habit. Not all the clergy are like them, of course; there are some saints, even among them, but it is fellows like these that give the orders their bad names.

The Argyllwyddes came among us then and herded all us maidens like sheep to our places. We sit apart from the men and pour our own wine; it is as if she thought we might be seduced by the pages as they passed the pitchers! I find that I call her the Lady Margaret when I like her, and the Argyllwyddes when she annoys me, for it is, indeed, a foolish-sounding title. She is a good lady, though, and kind, mostly; it is true that the men get drunken quickly, and there are fights often.

And so we sat, all panting and bright-eyed with our unaccustomed company, looking over the young men, and giggling among ourselves. Catherine whispered to me that she has never yet seen a young man to please her so much as our new cousin.

She thinks he looks like Roland, in the song. I have said she is romantic. He watched her, too, whenever she turned away; when their glances meet it will be a lightning bolt. Catherine looked very pretty; we had earlier darkened her fair eyebrows with chimney-soot—they are her only flaw. There are darkening dyes to be had somewhere, but we have not been able to get hold of any around here, though we all rub beet juice on our cheeks when it is in season. I had brought back all kinds of paints and perfumes from Richard's court, but they have run out long ago, with all of us using them, and the Argyllwyddes will not let us buy any from the peddlers. It is not fair, really; she uses something herself on her hair. It is too bright, and sometimes there is a line of gray showing at the roots. I suppose she is right, and we do not need such things, but they are fun to play with on a dull day, after lessons.

At least, though, we were unattended by nurse, or any other, and were also raised on a little dais of our own, so we could watch everything with ease, and not have to eat dishes we disliked or water our wine down to nothing. I, in fact, could eat no food at all; I was far too excited. I kept watching Meredith, who fascinated me. He had a sad face, old for his years, but fine-boned, and with a kind of shine upon it; there is a little hook to his nose, and his mouth is too large; otherwise he would be as woman-pretty as poor Richard. He looked at me too, his lips curving, often and often, and I felt he saw me as fair. What a pity he is my half-brother; I am in worse case than Catherine, who is looking to fall in love with a cousin only! Of course, we have all read of those ancient peoples of Egypt and Crete who were ruled by brother and sister espoused in their cradles. But those days are gone forever, and even distant kinships are frowned upon in unions. Owen says it is best, for close marriages thin the blood-stock after a time, as in cattle, and make idiots, or worse.

The speeches began, but we listened with half an ear; they are dull and rambling as a rule. Besides, Catherine, who cannot spell, was trying to compose a note to that eagle-nosed Rhisiart, and she had all the words down wrong, and I had to help her. We are allowed visitors in our solar upstairs by day, and she wanted to make sure of his company tomorrow. For sure, he will come anyway; all the young men will come—it is a courtesy.

The voices from the dais rose and fell, rose and fell. First one and then another, and all, in the main, in Welsh, and about Welsh freedom and English oppression; Owen sat like a statue— he has these fits sometimes of seeming to be somewhere else, his eye looking through at some other thing. They do not last long but are frightening somehow. Beside him is the Argyllwyddes, in a robe made of little white skins of ermine, with sleeves of gold cloth. She is stout, and I wager she is sweating under it all, while Owen wears a thin linen tunic, with bare legs. On Owen's other side is his oldest son, Griffith, whom I never had before seen. He is unlike Meredith or any of the others, much stockier of build, and with a face that looks like a clerk's, small and tight. Catherine, who had abandoned her writing, nudged me and began to giggle. "Look at that great booby," she said. "He is wearing the belt of Eliseg—around his neck!" The belt of Eliseg, like the crown of Madoc on Owen's brow, is a hereditary honor to the wearer. It is the oldest son's privilege to wear it; I suppose the Argyllwyddes made Griffith do it, to please Owen, on this night, with all his sons around him. I whispered to Catherine that maybe our brother thought it was a gorget, for the neck, and she whispered back that it would not probably fit around his waist, as he takes after their mother, a thing I would not dare to say. We began to giggle helplessly then, and the Argyllwyddes, who misses little, began to frown; even Owen turned his head slowly in our direction, like a sleepwalker. Oh-oh, I thought, here we go up to our chamber in disgrace, but choking with laughter all the same, when there came a horrible commotion from the courtyard, where the peasant folk had assembled to hear the bard. They were shouting loud, the deep notes of men gruff and wild, and rising above it the shrill thin women's voices.

The doors of the hall were flung open and a great group of soldiers burst in, dragging someone across the flags. I heard, "An Englishman . . . A spy . . . a Ruthin spy!" We all stood up, but we could see nothing. It was like a pack of dogs worrying a fox. I saw Meredith run up to the dais and take his father by the shoulder. Owen shook himself a little and rose, holding up a hand.

"Silence!" he cried. "Stand back!" The soldier crowd flowed backwards, tripping in their haste, leaving a circle where a man knelt, gripping another by the throat.

"Mother of God," whispered Catherine. "It is Rhys the Savage!"

I had never seen either of them before. The man she called Savage was indeed the wildest-looking creature in the world; one might even believe he belonged to that old race that is said to have occupied the earth before man. He was thick and squat and wore a skin of some wild animal around his middle, and was naked above but hairy. Hair grew down, too, low on his forehead and down his backbone; his mouth jutted forward, the teeth showing like fangs. He knelt over the other, a knife in hand. From where we stood, we could see the man was bound and helpless, blood running already down his face; he was dressed in the jerkin and hose of an English archer. Voices rose all around, and from the yard the women loudest of all. "Kill him! Kill the English pig! To the fire with him!"

The company sat or stood, frozen, like a scene in a masque, Owen with his hand still upraised. On a sudden, Walter Brut, the Lollard, broke from his place at table and ran to the men on the floor. "My Lord Owen," he cried, ringingly, "this man has an immortal soul! He must be heard!"

Rhys the Savage gave a murderous sound, more like a growl than a word, and raised his knife. The voices rose again. "He will not speak! Throw him into the fire!"

Owen's voice thundered where he stood. "Rhys Gethin! Hold!" And he spoke other words, in Welsh, too fast for my understanding. "Speak, man! Where are you from?"

"Speak, speak!" howled the mob, inside and out the hall.

The bound man, loosed by the Savage for a second, struggled a little ways up from the floor. I saw his face clearly, white as chalk, with runnels of blood upon it.

"God save King Harry!" cried the Englishman. "God save Lancaster—and to hell with. . . ." but his words ended in a long-drawn death cry, for Rhys the Savage did not hold his hand.

There was a hush of horror upon the hall; then, over the whole assembled crowd came shriek after shriek in a woman's voice, rending the air. It came from the courtyard outside and went on and on, piteous and wild, until it stopped suddenly, in the middle of a wail, as if sliced by a sword. Again there was silence.

Quiet, cool, like drops of rain, fell Owen's words, as he faced the killer. "You shall answer to this blood, Rhys Gethin. In court of law, beast that you are, you shall answer. . . ." He made a sign with his hand to the soldiery. "Bind him . . . and take him away." His voice sounded weary, with the weariness, I thought, for I am fanciful, of an old and sickened god.

As they dragged the brutish creature from the hall; he broke from his captors and ran toward Owen. Oh, my God, I thought, Owen is lost, for he carries no weapon. But this Rhys Gethin flung himself at his feet, grabbing at the hem of Owen's tunic and kissing it. "Kill me . . . Kill me. . . ." he said in a broken sort of Welsh. "Do what you will with me, Prince . . . but save Wales only!"

"Save Wales! Save Wales!" rang through the hall, from a hundred voices. "Hail Owen, Prince of Powys! Hail Owen, the rightful Prince of Wales! Saint Derfel for Owen and the Red Dragon! Owen and Wales! Owen and Wales forever!"

Owen looked long on the figure at his feet, slobbering at his gown. He stood for a long moment, still as a stone; then, stooping, he raised him up, kissing the filthy creature on his matted head. "My son, my son . . . poor animal . . . poor, poor creature of God. . . ." And the tears stood in Prince Owen's eyes, glittering in the flickering firelight. "Go to your prison, my poor son . . . bear him kindly. . . ." And he made sign to the men-at-arms, who took the Savage away.

All was confusion in hall. Owen sank down onto his seat on the dais, his head in his hands. The Lady Margaret left his side and, quickly, for all her great size, went to the end of table, where the bard, Griffith Lloyd, sat, whispering in his ear. I saw the other Griffith, the belt of Eliseg still hanging askew about his neck, standing foolishly by his father, struck dumb. The Lollard knelt beside the dead Englishman; he had torn his fine gown into strips to wipe the face clean of blood and hide the gaping wound in the throat. I saw him take, then, the small cross he wore at his belt and place it between the dead man's hands, crossed now on his breast. There was a goblet of wine overturned on the floor, and blood and wine mingled, reddening the strewn rushes of the hearth and staining the remnants of Sir Walter's gown. It was a scene of antique horror; only Cassandra was missing, though I felt her words within me like a doom.

Chapter 3

There was harp-playing all that sad evening, but it was the bard Griffith Lloyd, and not the ancient Iolo Goch, who would not leave his chamber after the violence below stairs. We were all herded to our quarters, too; little Elliw had fainted clean away, and Meredith carried her up the stairs, handing her to nurse, who cuddled her as if she were a baby; I think, though, that she was already come around in Meredith's arms, for I saw a little gleam under her eyelids and a flickering, too. It must be pleasant to be carried so; I fear, alas, it will never be my fate, though, unless the man be a giant, which Meredith is not.

We could hear the harping from the hall, haunting and wild; old dirges, and one new one that the bard improvised, more beautiful than all the rest. We could hear only scattered words though—there was so much commotion in our apartments alone. But Griffith, our brother, came to us soon, to tell the news. He is the Lady Margaret's favorite, one can tell, for we can seldom welcome young men when the lamps are lit. He said that Owen had forbidden any war songs and was trying to clear the hall gradually. Already the great doors had been closed, and men sent to disperse the folk in the courtyard.

Efa was furious that she had missed all the excitement and made us all sick with her blood-greed; how old was the Englishman, where was he wounded and in which parts, how far did the blood spurt, how far did the knife go in, and so on. Elliw turned quite green and had to be put to bed, shut away behind her curtains and with her canopy over. It is difficult to fathom Efa; Catherine says she is fey; privately I think it is worse than that. Why should there not be minds that are ill, as bodies are? It is a strange thing; though she is my half-sister, I do not like her. She is the only one of the maidens I have no feeling for; even Sibli, who is forever trying to fondle me, does not really annoy. One just must avoid her embraces, that is all.

Griffith, I said, looked like a clerk; he speaks like one, too, long-winded and precise. Meredith had to remind him that he was expected to join Owen, with some of the other young men, in the Saracen Room. (This is simply a large chamber furnished with Eastern treasures, costly carpets, and beautiful, rare wall hangings.) We have never been there, we girls, for some of the hangings portray scenes which the Argyllwyddes considers too lively for our maidenly senses. Naturally, we have imagined all sorts of things, obscenities, even, but Iago, one of the nicer of the pages, says it is simply a lot of naked women lying about seductively. So that, I conceive, it is much like the books of Eastern workmanship that Catherine and I found in an old sea chest. We both of us thought the women were too fat.

Griffith told us that the two holy fathers, who were at hall, have left in a huff because Owen allowed the Englishman's body to be put into our private chapel; they argued that he was a Lancaster dog and should be thrown on the dung heap. Owen did not answer, but gave them escort for the ride back to the cloister. He has made two more enemies, I guess; some of the clergy call Owen a heathen already, though many and many a night they fill their bellies at his table. I wish, myself, that they would go over to the English; they are cut of the same cloth as old flame-crazy Arundel, anyway.

The hall was emptied slowly, and the last strains of the harping died on the air. We were all in our shifts and locked in for the night; Catherine and I shared a bed—we were waiting to hear nurse snore, so we could talk. There came a light scratch at the door, and then another, and we heard nurse grumble and the clink of keys. There was no moon, but the ceiling was open to the sky, and by the light of the stars we could see that the serving maids were bringing something in, something like a body, long and still.

Catherine and I sat up, and all over the chamber we could hear rustlings; no one was asleep. After the maids came the Lady Margaret, with a candle; in its light we saw her fingers pressed to her lips. "Sh-h-h . . ." she whispered. "It is a very sick woman. . . ."

Sick, indeed, she looked, in the flickering light; I would almost have thought her dead. The twins rose quickly and got other candles to light from the lady's, and Catherine and I fetched the great rushlight from the mantel. All the maidens were up now, except Elliw, and she was peeping from between her curtains.

The lady took a wet cloth from one of the serving girls and sponged off the blood from the face; they had laid her on my bed, which was the only one empty, I having been in Catherine's. I saw with a certain squeamishness that she was a very dirty wench, besides soaking blood into my coverings. I pushed the thought away, for it was not that of a gentlewoman, and held the light for the Lady Margaret. The woman—she was really not a great deal older than we, twenty, perhaps—had several gashes on her forehead, and a great wound in her arm; blood kept flowing from it, though the lady had wadded cotton against it. Her clothes were all filthy and mostly torn away; she looked as though wild dogs had been at her. There was, too, a huge bruise already purpling on one cheek, under her eye. The lady turned to the serving maid, making a gesture. "Quick—fetch the Israelite!"

"I'll go!" cried Efa. "I know where he is . . . he's with Owen in the Saracen Room. . . ." And she darted out between the serving women, before anyone could stop her, running down the hall in her shift. I saw the lady bite her lips and frown; Efa would pay for this. It crossed my mind that maybe the lady might even send her away, with all the young men home; though she has spent most of her days here, Efa is as wild as a fox-bitch from the forest. I stopped thinking about her though, for the girl on the bed began moaning and moving her head from side to side. Her hair, if it had been washed, was pale as flax, long and very straight. It was hard to tell what her face might look like—it was so beaten and swollen—but her body was very fair, with firm, rounded limbs, and white skin. She was sturdier of build than any of us maidens here but still comely.

We heard Efa running back, her bare feet slapping the flags, quick and loud in the quiet house, and behind her the dragging limp of the Israelite. When she slipped in through the door, I saw her face was flushed and near to laughter, her reddish curls all tumbled about her face. Her shift had slipped off one shoulder, too, exposing a breast; oh-oh, I thought, glancing at the Argyllwyddes. But she had not seen and had risen to speak to the physician. He was just coming down the corridor, Nathan ben Arran, Owen's friend and doctor. Owen had brought him back from one of his Eastern trips long ago; no one can remember when he was not here in the household. I think that no one yet, under his care, has ever died; he has great skill, far beyond any of our own people. Catherine and I take lessons from him, too, for we are the cleverest in such things, but we do not study doctoring but just some theory only.

He dropped to his knees, quickly for a lame man, and bent his head to the girl's heart. Then he straightened up and rummaged in his big box, which Iago, the page, had brought, taking out a wound-up length of cloth. This he bound tightly, very tightly, about the girl's arm, a few inches above the bleeding gash. He explained as he worked. "This is to stop the flow of blood . . . her heartbeat is strong but very rapid. . . ." And he handed Catherine a twist of paper, telling her to empty the powder in it into a little wine. When he put the doctored wine to the girl's lips, she made a face, though her eyes were closed still; the stuff must have been bitter. He tipped her head back, forcing the potion down. "She will sleep now," he said. "It is poppy juice . . . in a little while she will feel nothing, and I can get to the dressing of this nasty wound. He swabbed around it gently; she gave a little moan. "Not yet . . . who is the maid? I have not seen her before. . . ."

Catherine and I spoke at once, saying that we did not know, that no one knew. The Lady Margaret stopped us, saying, "They found her in the courtyard, after the people had been driven away . . . the women had beaten her and cut her with knives . . . we think she is from the castle at Ruthin. . . ."

"I think she is the woman of that young Englishman—" said Efa, in her important little way; she was not even in hall but still she knows everything. Perhaps she is a witch. As a matter of fact, this proved to be the case, not Efa being a witch, of course, but the girl being the lover of the dead Englishman. We found all this out later, when she came around and could talk; it was she whose shrieks we had heard from the courtyard after Rhys the Savage had used his dagger.

The girl (she said she believed she was about eighteen, though she looked somewhat older) was from the castle at Ruthin, as we had thought. Her name was Alice, and she had the surname Oxerd, in the English fashion, according to the occupation of the family. So this meant that she was a byremaid, or cattle girl, someone who worked in the stables. This was why she was so dirty, aside from the women having thrown her to the ground.

Anyway, Alice had followed her man here to Glendower House; he had been sent to spy, and she feared for him. When she cried out at his death, the women knew that she was English, too, and beat her cruelly, kicking and slashing at her with knives. The men-at-arms had finally dragged them off her, but she looked dead to them, and if the Lollard, Master Brut, had not intervened, she would have been laid on the cold stones beside her dead lover.

We did not find this out all at once but in pieces only; Alice wept continually as soon as she woke from the poppy drug. She was in dread of all of us, too, and screamed if any came near her; Nathan, the doctor, said she was in a state of shock and remembered nothing. Master Brut said she had miscarried of a babe, too; it looked to have been about six months inside her. He buried it just outside our burying ground; the priests would not allow it in hallowed ground, for that it was English and not shriven either, never having lived. Master Brut says there is nothing in the Scriptures that condemns a babe unborn to the flames of hell, or to limbo either, which is what some of the orders believe. He says all creatures, when they die, rest in the lap of the Saviour, even felons and madmen, even murderers, even the louse cracked between our fingers, and not humans only. He says all life is sacred to Jesus; Master Brut is very religious.

We held the funeral services for the dead Englishman, burying him beside the babe. There was no priest who would officiate, so Nathan, the Israelite, read some Hebrew words over him, and Master Brut some Latin. Owen translated into Welsh, and both of the eulogies were very beautiful, especially the Hebrew, which was by an ancient king and poet named David, which is a Welsh name, also, strangely enough; it had to do with green pastures and valleys and the infinite comfort of God. It made me think of our land here, Wales, which we mostly call Cymry, and Catherine and I both wept. The Ruthin girl was still not well and did not attend.

She mended slowly, poor thing, her face turning all the shades of the rainbow before it finally looked human again. She is not ill-favored, but I fancy there is a sly, unpleasant look about her; the Lady Margaret says she has been badly used and is wary of people and surly. Certainly if the stories she tells are true at all, I cannot blame her. She says that she was ravished over and over again by both the Lord Grey and his son, on her wedding night, so that when her husband had his turn she was near to dead from the rapings, and they could not bed for a week. It is hard to credit, but the Greys are known in these parts for their wickedness, and besides, such things are said to be an English custom, brought over by the Normans. They burned her mother, also, Alice said, for a witch. The strange thing is that Alice said she *was* a witch and could work evil. She herself boasted that she has learned much of it, too; Efa is with her a lot, whispering, for she is very curious about such things.

Alice is very ignorant, of course, and cannot read or write; as she recovers, the Lady Margaret is having lessons given to her, just sewing and a little spinning, for the moment, but she does well, for a person who has never done anything except tend cattle. The Lollard has asked permission to visit her and read from the Scriptures; he says it will comfort her for the loss of her man, and the babe, too.

She was horrible about the babe and said she did not care if it burned; she did not know whose it was anyway, on account of the things done to her by the Grey men. Master Walter spoke gently to her but said such thoughts were wrong, for all creatures have the right alike to immortality. She has come to look forward to his visits, preening herself, and listening to him in all meekness, and she does not with anyone else.

Owen says that the teachings of Jesus have always gone down best with the very poor and the ignorant; that is how, he says, the whole religion started, among the slave population of Rome. Also, he says, it appealed to the barbaric tribes that Rome conquered here, in Britain, and in Gaul, and other places, long ago, and so has spread over half the world. But Owen says that so much evil has been wrought over this religion, just like the burnings that are happening today, which are all on account of some small point of doctrine. He says to look at all the holy wars, the Crusades in Jerusalem, and the devastation there which went on for centuries and is even now going on, in a smaller way. Just two centuries ago a whole nation was wiped out—and they were Christians themselves—by other Christians! He means the Albigensians, who had the Cathar religion, just differing a little from the established church, and they were all burned, by the hundreds!

I asked him if that had not been so, too, with the old pagans, and he said it was lost in the mists of time, but that he did not think so; they were all much alike, he said, with simple gods drawn from nature, and not much of abstract thought to argue about.

Evil has certainly been done, I see that, but the Lollard, for instance, is a true believer in Jesus, and one can see that he is not in any way evil but almost, I think, a saint. Owen says there are many such but doubts that they can weigh very heavily in the scales against the prevailing horror. Owen, though he says these things, is not a pagan either, as many people imagine, but a thinker only. I once heard poor King Richard say that Owen was a man ahead of his times. I believe that Owen would be ahead of whatever times he lived in; that is the kind of man he is.

It is true, though, that religion is the cause of much strife; even here in the castle there are arguments and shoutings among all the young men, particularly those who have come from Oxford. They are mostly Lollard, but even among themselves they disagree; they will talk a point until it makes your head swim. Meredith told me that once, oh, centuries ago, in Paris, where the greatest minds of that time studied, scholars argued for weeks and months over how many angels might dance upon the head of a pin! It is hard to credit, but some of these discussions around here are just as silly. And all over nothing, as I privately think, for I cannot help agreeing with Owen. I do not voice this though, for even though women are given much freedom in Wales, no one would allow us to speak of doctrine. There is a woman in France, Christine de Pisan, who is much respected as a poet thinker, but she is a very orthodox believer and almost a mystic; I have read her works and do not count them as very much. It is like applauding a dog who has learned to walk on his hind legs or a bird whose clipped tongue can imitate speech.

Many of the young Oxford men are extremely rebellious to the new king, spitting and cursing at his name; most of them, too, are fiercely Welsh, and are all for war with England. There are a few commoners among them, too, those who studied under Owen's grants, and they want to bring about another peasants' revolt. There is unrest all about, that is certain, but this castle is a hotbed of seething ideas. Owen does not speak but listens merely, showing courtesy to all.

Every day the young men visit in the maidens' quarters, or we ride abroad together, if it is fine, and there have been no skirmishes roundabout; indeed, since the slaying of the Ruthin spy, there has been little fighting and no reprisals from Lord Grey. I had expected it to be the other way around. The Lady Margaret fears that it is but a calm before the storm. In the meantime, though, we are enjoying ourselves greatly, for it is nearly summer, and green everywhere, with all the little flowers abloom upon the hillsides, and the winding streams leaping down into the valleys.

We mostly ride in groups, but there is some pairing off. The twins, Gwynneth and Gwenllian, have found themselves two brothers, imagine it—big, laughing boys from Ireland, with flame-red hair cropped around their ears in the new fashion. They are spoiling for a fight, and there is not enough going on in their own country, so they have come to offer their swords to Owen and Wales. I could see Owen's lip twitch as he heard them swear fealty, but he spoke gravely to them and thanked them most kindly.

Many of the young men have their hair cut in this way; it is a fad started by Harry Percy, he they call Hotspur; he is the biggest hero in all England, and even though he is allied with their enemy of Lancaster, even the dissenters copy him. In fact, they mostly refuse to believe that he will stay pro-Lancaster, but will come over in time to Owen.

I privately do not care very much for the look of this hairstyle; it is as though a pot were set on the head and scissors cut around the pot edges. Below, all is shaven, just the opposite of the monks' tonsure. They call it the helm cut, to fit under a helmet easily; you can see they are all afire to go to war! Owen, I think, still hopes to avoid it; the talk is that he has sent peace envoys even to Bolingbroke, but as yet there has been no answer. Meanwhile, he sits at hall like a broody eagle, at the high seat, listening but not speaking often.

As I have said, there is some pairing off between us young folk; besides the twins, Catherine has got her Rhisiart, and they go about hand-in-hand when the lady is not watching. No good can come of it, of course, for he is not noble, and she is the only legitimate daughter of the highest prince of the land. Owen has other daughters by the Argyllwyddes, four of them, but they are much older, children of their youthful days, and all are married off in high places; I have never met them—they are scattered all over Wales.

Walter Brut spends most of his time with Alice, the Ruthin girl; he is teaching her his Scriptures, and she has almost lost her sullen look. Indeed, now that she is clean and in seemly dress, she is very fair, in a large, white, Saxon way. She does not ride with us though or go outside the castle; the lady is afraid the sight of her will provoke more battles with the Ruthin people. So they two, Alice and the Lollard, sit in corners, talking in whispers of the Bible, and cuddling, too, I suspect. Alice is not a wanton, like Efa, but I have seen the look in her eyes as she gazes at Walter, a look of hunger, truly; it cannot all be greed for knowledge!

As for myself, there are none to my taste here, though I like all my newfound brothers, except Griffith, perhaps; he is so prim. I know all the names now, of course; there is David, and Rhys, Tudor, and Evan. They are all for a great war for Wales, and all wear the helm cut, but they are gentle under, one can see. They talk of battles with eyes that are friendly as hounds!

Meredith is still my favorite; we are much alike, I think, and can talk of anything. He has told me all sorts of tales about Harry, the king's son, for he was at Oxford, too, Harry. Most people call him Hal, says Meredith, and he is much liked, even by those who hate his father well. They studied together, Meredith and Hal, under the famous master of law, Sir John Oldcastle, and much admire this man. This amazes me, for Oldcastle is the most famous Lollard in the whole realm, and Hal's father so orthodox. But Meredith says that Hal does not agree well with his father anyway and speaks out against the persecutions and burnings, though he, Hal, is not a Lollard either. The strangest thing is that Hal has a name for tumbling all the wenches in the countryside—he cannot be turned fourteen! Meredith says I must not call him little Harry anymore, for he has grown to be a half-head taller than Meredith himself, and I have myself to raise my eyes a little to Meredith. This gives me pleasure to think on, silly though it is, when we are almost enemies now, Hal and I, on account of our fathers. Even so, when I think of Hal sporting with all those girls, I feel the blood mount to my face and have to turn my head away so that my brothers will not see. It is most strange.

Chapter 4

I can never forget the night of Iolo Goch's death, for in a way it marked the true start of the war; also it happened on Midsummer Eve, when all the fires were lit all over Wales. The two things go together, as you will see. There had been skirmishes before, and scattered fighting in our northern parts, between Grey's men and ours, but Owen thought for a long time to avoid a full-scale conflict. This was not to be.

I have said the bard was very ancient; he had been around so long indeed that one began to think of him as more than mortal. Even Owen, I believe, did not realize that he was dying. He had been ailing since the night in early spring when the Ruthin spy had been murdered; Nathan ben Arran ministered to him daily, but even he could not save him—his days were running out.

He lived among the house kin, Iolo Goch, for he was Owen's great friend. There was no harping in the hall, even on guest nights, for the music disturbed him strangely; Griffith Lloyd's great harp hung on the wall behind him where he sat at meat, and every night he waxed the strings and polished the wood, for it was like a part of him, that harp.

We had lit our own fire that Midsummer Eve, on the mound outside the walls. It is an ancient custom, from long before the Christian days, this lighting of the Midsummer fires; no one can remember exactly what it means. It celebrates the summer and the yield of the earth, I suppose; Owen says, again, it probably started with sacrifices to propitiate the Mother Goddess, and so is even older than Britain itself. They do not do this firing in England much nowadays, but Wales is full, still, of the old traditions, and ridden with superstition.

Our fire was burning true, the flames leaping into the air as soon as the late sun went down. We had all come out to watch, the house folk and all the soldiery and company. It is a fine sight, a bonfire, especially when you know that no one suffers in the flames. (Perhaps that is why they do not observe the custom anymore in English towns.) The fire was high, right at the top of the mound, so that it could be seen for miles around. This mound is not just a hill, but something made by men, long ago. Owen says there are many of them all over Wales; they date from Druidic times, or before, and are thought to be burying places of the Old People. The Great Mound at Mathrafal was struck by lightning, years ago, when Owen was a boy; the whole hill was split asunder, and bones were strewn all about. Owen went to see—even then he was as curious as a cat; he says the bones were small as children's and bent in a posture like the child inside the womb. It was a thought that made me shudder, for I could not help thinking of child sacrifice, but Owen says no, the Old People were a smaller race than we are, that is all. The heads of arrows were found, too, at Mathrafal, and broken pieces of pottery, and even jewels, blackened by time. Owen says that meant these folk believed in an afterlife, too, and buried their possessions with them for use in the other world. Owen says often that when he has time he will dig up our mound here, and study what he finds; it is a pity he does not have nine lives, like a cat, also!

Our fire burned bravely, and we watched for a while, as people will, drawn by the flames' patterns. We young folk stood on the wall, holding one another for balance, and looked at the horizon for the other fires. One by one, roundabout, they sprang up, far away; we counted nine in all before we went back to hall.

It is a lovely moment, that time of the first lighting of the fires of Midsummer; something full and rare about it—the heart seems to burst with rapture, and laughter bubbles in the throat. This was all shattered, though, when we went back indoors, for a strange hush had fallen there, all the company was silent; two dogs snapped in a corner, fighting over a bit of meat on the floor. Someone shooed them out, and we could hear a strange whistling sound. There was a little knot of people at one end of the hall, bending over something. As we drew near, we saw it was a litter set down on the ground.

The bard, Iolo Goch lay on it, his wasted body barely raising the coverings. The whistling sounds were coming from him, as he labored to speak. Owen bent over him like a son, trying to understand, his face drawn in concern and pity. The old man heaved himself up on his elbows with a mighty effort, straining the muscles in his throat, his eyes staring wildly. He was so tiny and withered, he might himself have been one of the Old People of the mounds. His head seemed no bigger than a fist; it was crowned with a nimbus of white ringlets, soft as cotton. On his upper lip there was a mustache, long and drooping; the sparse hairs of it were bright red, like copper. Once the hair of his head had been red, too; it was how he had come by his name, Iolo the Red. We girls had always thought he dyed the hairs of his upper lip, but it could not be, now, on his day of dying. Those thin red hairs, gleaming in the firelight, seemed to draw into them all the life that was left in him, but for the staring eyes and the reedy whistle that came out of his throat. It was plain that he was trying to speak, but no one could hear his words under the desperate gusty breaths that came out of him. All over the hall the people crept close—soldiers, archers, servants, guests, and pages—all crowding around the dying man. Many fell to their knees. There was the soft sound of women weeping and the harsher sound of the soldiers sobbing; he was the most beloved figure in these parts.

Owen was on his knees now, too, his head close to the old bard's lips. There was a look of awful strain on his face as he tried to understand the sighing, bubbling breaths, and a terrible flashing of angry impatience in Iolo's eyes; over all there was, always, that dreadful, high whistling, louder now.

Walter Brut was at Owen's side, holding a plain wooden cross; the bard pushed it away angrily; he was a true heathen, proud and contemptuous, and blasphemous, too, in his time. Walter said to Owen, "Perhaps, sir, the other bard might understand him . . . ?"

Owen signed to Griffith Lloyd, who pushed through the crowd and fell to his knees beside the litter; the big man, bald as a mountain, bent his huge head to kiss one of the knotty, wisened hands of the dying poet; then he, too, brought his ear close to the old lips. He listened long, while the whole company fell quiet. The ancient bard was louder now, frantic, but the series of sounds were meaningless, the whistle shrilling now in a heart-rending way. Finally Griffith Lloyd straightened up, shaking his head.

The poet on the litter made a sign then, gesturing the people back; there was a listening look on his face. As the crowd fell back, I heard someone whisper, "He is calling on Derfel!" I heard, too, Walter's reproving words, "He is praying. . . ." The bard did not seem to hear anything about him; as I said, he looked to be listening to some sound within himself. I saw that Owen stood very still beside him, with big, unnoticed tears running down his face. As we watched, Iolo Goch seemed to relax suddenly, his passionate tension dropping away. He sank back, and Owen knelt to support him. The bard accepted his support with a faint nod, and even something like a smile. For a long moment he lay there, in Owen's arms, not moving. "Jesus receive him!" I heard the Lollard murmur softly.

I, too, thought the end had come, but the terrible whistling sound continued and the eyes still stared. Suddenly, he made a slight movement, looking, as I thought, toward me. But Elliw, beside me, started forward. I remembered that she was the poet's kinswoman, on her dead mother's side, and that she had been raised to the sound of his voice from infancy. He must have been, I thought, trying to get it straight, her great-great-uncle.

She, too, bent over the old man, her slight figure bearing him up, taking Owen's place. I remember she wore white; her cloudy brown hair was tied back with a ribbon and fell loosely to her waist. I heard her voice, small but clear. "What do you say, Uncle Iolo? Say it again, slower! Whisper it—whisper it, Uncle Iolo . . . I can hear you. . . ." And her head bent very close to his lips.

Owen raised his hand for silence, but there was no need. The entire hall was silent as death. It was easy to see that this was the great poet's last chance to be understood. We all held our breaths, waiting.

And she did understand him, though how she did it was a mystery. It was, I thought afterward, her instinct in making him whisper, perhaps. I was astonished at Elliw's calm; she had always been such a timorous thing, as jumpy as a deer or a rabbit. But this night she sat straight and listened and repeated clearly, in a voice that didn't even tremble, all his whispered words.

I heard a little page somewhere behind me struggling not to cough, and there was a muffled sneeze from the end of the hall, but except for that every word Elliw said fell like a smooth stone into the silence.

"He says he willed someone to come," she said. "*Me* to come," she corrected herself. "He says you must all swear on the belt of Eliseg to be Owen's men against the English. He says September the"—she paused then, and we could see her bend lower, frowning in concentration, trying to catch the word—"September the fifteenth—no, the sixteenth—the sixteenth . . . you must all come here and proclaim Owen the Prince of Wales. . . . He says on Saint Matthew's Day we must—"

She broke off. We could see that the old poet, light as he was, had become too heavy for her as his body slumped against her. Then in almost a cry she repeated the single word, "Ruthin," and sank sideways beneath his weight. That word, "Ruthin," the name of Grey's stronghold, must have been the last word uttered on earth by Iolo, for he never stirred again, and his staring eyes looked now at the ceiling.

Meredith ran forward and gathered up Elliw in his arms, for she had fainted. As he left, carrying her, we could see that the front of her white gown was all marked with Iolo's blood, where it had gushed from his mouth as he died. I saw the Lady Margaret speak to Alice, and the girl followed the two to our upstairs chamber. Even in the shock and turmoil of events I found myself marking the Argyllwyddes' circumspection. Never, never must a maiden be alone with a man where there is a bed nearby!

Owen still stood above the bard, his face all wet with tears, like a statue of grief. He took off his purple short-mantle and, kneeling, laid it tenderly over the wasted form. The dragon of Wales was embroidered on it in gold, and I had the sudden fancy that Wales itself lay there under it, lifeless.

There was a little pause; then from a knot of men Owen's son Evan came forward, followed by his brothers. He advanced to the foot of the litter. "I swear by the belt of Eliseg—"

I heard Rhisiart's voice, sharp and clerkly. "Where is the belt . . . ?" he asked. I thought suddenly, no one had seen it except around Griffith's neck when we laughed at him that first night.

Everyone turned to Griffith, who looked bemused. The Argyllwyddes came close to him, speaking low; he shook his head. Oh, the booby, I thought, he has lost it! It was a strange scene, Owen, unmoving, in the midst of all the bustle, silent while the voices rose all about.

Suddenly Efa pushed past me. "I know where it is—the bard has it! It is in the bards' chamber! Hanging on the wall!"

Which bard, I said to myself, and how does she know? That one is a puzzle, Efa! But we turned to look at the bard Griffith

Lloyd, and he nodded; there were tears, too, on his face. Someone ran for the belt.

There was a great surge of motion in the hall, and a sound of
many feet, as all the company lined up to take the oath. There
were two Cistercian monks here tonight; they pushed forward
importantly, so as to be first. The Cistercians are the most Welsh
of all the clergy, and fiercely patriotic. I knew one of them by
sight, Father Ambrosius; I saw that his eyes shone with excitement. There were both of them large, burly men, in rough wad-
mal habits, more soldier than churchman. At their girdles they
wore short swords; I saw no sign of bead or crucifix, and their
tonsures were growing out, making their heads look very odd.

Through all this Owen stood, unseeing; someone thrust the
belt into his hands. He looked down at it, from far away, as if it
were a snake he held. Slowly I saw the understanding come into
his eyes; he gave a little sigh as of regret and turned to the waiting crowd. Briefly he raised the belt aloft; there was a ragged
cheer, and then, very strong, the cry, "Owen, Prince of Wales!
Wales and Owen!"

Father Ambrosius advanced to the foot of what was now the
bier, and his deep, rich voice, trained to intone the Latin ritual,
rose above the hubbub. "I swear by the Belt of Eliseg to be true
man and liege servant to the puissant Prince Owen ap Griffith
Fychan as long as my breath shall last!" The second monk
echoed his words, each touching the sacred relic in Owen's
hands. It looked, in truth, a sorry thing, an old rag of leather,
moldy and black from all the swearing done already in its name,
but no one but me seemed to see it in this way, and many even
raised it to their lips as they made their vows.

The noise in the hall was now so wild that it hurt the ears, but
Owen did not raise a hand to quiet it; he seemed to be in one of
his "fits," as I think of them, where he is not *there*, but somewhere
inside himself. The world flows about him like water around a
rock in midstream; it is strange and chilling but does not last
long. I remembered that Rhisiart had asked me about it, saying
that it made him shiver to see him so. Just then I heard Rhisiart's
name. Someone shouted, "Make him swear! Make the little
Hereford calf swear . . . make him give a kick at his king!" I had
a glimpse of Rhisiart's face white with strain. He was liege sub-

ject to King Henry, and to swear would be arrant treason and his life forfeit.

"Make the damned Lollard swear, Prince Owen!" cried another voice. "See how a heretic dog takes an honest Christian oath!"

At these words Walter came forward boldly, with a smile. He placed his hand, not on the belt, but on the hilt of Owen's sword; the other hand he placed tenderly over the dead man's heart, as he repeated the words of the oath. At this touch, Owen roused, looking down at the hand on his sword. When he saw who it was, a faint smile crossed his lips. "You, too, Master Brut?" I had seen before that there was much accord between them.

"I swear, too," said the Lollard, "on the risen Christ, the Saviour of all."

Owen, roused from his trance now, saw Rhisiart where he stood, hesitating.

"Make the cousin from Hereford swear!" the same voice called again.

"No need for any of my family to swear," said Owen, with careless dignity, though most of his sons had sworn already. "Besides," he said gravely, "we may need our cousin to represent us at Lancaster's court, as he is a lawyer. It would be a mistake to narrow his freedom by oaths and vows." He finished easily. Then he raised his head, looking all about. "But it would be a great comfort to me, and all my family, too, if everyone here tonight will vow with me, by Our Lady of Valle Crucis and Saint Derfel of Endyrnion, that we will seek the king's justice for Wales and—"

He was interrupted by a thunder of voices and a savage clatter of arms, as every hand and every weapon was raised in the air.

One voice rose above the others, guttural and wild. "Saint Derfel for Wales! Saint Derfel for Wales!" I saw, at the far end, the hairy creature, Rhys Gethin, standing in his chains, and wondered how he had got out of his prison and into hall. But other voices took up the cry, and not only the hall but the very palace seemed to rock and sway to the shout that arose, "Saint Derfel for Wales! Saint Derfel for Owen Glendower! Saint Derfel for Owen and Wales!"

Owen stepped lightly up onto a trestle table, raising his hands for silence. "And now," he said, "the Lady Margaret and I have only to tell you that there will be mead and wine in hall till midnight. Griffith Lloyd ap Dafydd ab Einion will sing to you . . . he will sing of the dead and the living—of our wrongs and of our hopes. He will sing the glory of Iolo Goch, our dead friend . . . he will sing of the rise and fall of Dinas Brân . . . He will sing of the great King Eliseg of our house upon whose belt you have sworn. . . ." And as he spoke, there was a movement of relaxation all over the hall, men began to sink to their places by the fire, their weapons clattering softly as they settled. I saw the men-at-arms leave, and the great gate outside being opened, as the guard was relieved. Owen stepped down then; taking a goblet of wine, he stood over the bier where the dead bard lay, muttering Welsh words low. He took, then, a long drink and, dipping his fingers into the goblet, sprinkled the body. It was some old ritual, I suspect, or maybe some private communication of his own, but it is such doings that give Owen a reputation for trafficking in magic. He made a sign, then, to some servants, to take the body into chapel. He stood there, for a while, sunk in thought, sipping the wine.

I saw, sitting alone by the fire, my stepbrother Griffith, staring gloomily into the flames. All about him was excitement and chatter, but he sat on, rubbing first one shin and then another, as he felt the heat scorching him.

I felt myself alone, too, for Catherine was at her Rhisiart's side, and all the maidens had drifted off; I would have gone to Griffith, but he made no sign, though he saw me watching, only turned back and went on gazing into the heart of the flames. I felt shy and foreign, suddenly, among all this Welshness; the singing had started, and the songs of the Cymry fell, haunting and wild, on the air. I would have gone to my chamber, but a touch came on my arm. It was Meredith, and I smiled at him gratefully. "How is Elliw?" I asked, for I knew he had been with her above-stairs.

"She is sleeping soundly now—we gave her a potion . . . the whole thing is a great shock to her, of course. . . ."

"She is such a little goose, usually—" I began.

"She is a very brave girl," Meredith said quietly.

Oh-oh, I thought, another love-struck one. But I said no more and pointed to Griffith. "He has not sworn either," said Meredith. "I was upstairs, so could not come forward . . . but Father noticed Griffith, I think."

"But Owen said our family need not swear," I began.

"That was the reason—before anyone could call shame on his eldest. . . . Griffith is angry about the oath, I think. He never liked Iolo and thinks Father was bewitched in a way. . . . Griffith has no heart for music or poetry. He thinks the bards are all half mad." He gave a little smile and looked at me in an impish kind of way. "I daresay he's right, too. . . ."

I nodded, smiling too. "It is the madness of genius," I said.

Meredith went on, more soberly. "Griffith will go along with whatever is decided, but he thinks it's silly to break with the king just because of Grey. He hates all this Welshness and superstition and oath-taking . . . But Father feels—and I think he's right— that if Wales is ever liberated, it'll be through madmen and bards, through hotheads and firebrands, through Derfelites and patriots, rather than through the counsels of the prudent. . . ."

Rhisiart had come up then with Catherine, and he broke in eagerly. "But wouldn't it be wiser to wait?" he said. "Will Owen really let them proclaim him on September the sixteenth? What was that all about?" He looked more than ever like a young eagle, with his dark face flushed and his eyes shining.

Meredith obviously did not trust the English part of him, for he brushed the question aside and said merely, with a vague wave of his hand, "Oh, Father will wait for another sign, I suppose. . . ." But I had seen Owen's face when Iolo named the date, and I knew he took it seriously. Rhisiart's thin lips drew in at Meredith's withdrawal; one could almost see his feathers wilt.

Catherine, noticing this, said quickly, "Come, let's go out on the wall and look at the fires. . . . It's still Midsummer Night. . . ."

It had grown a little chill; there were no stars, and the night was very black. We giggled as we felt for holds in the smooth wall. When we stood on top of it, a strong wind blew in our faces. "It feels as though September had come already," said Meredith softly in my ear; I shivered, and he put his arm about my shoulders as we stood staring at the fires.

"How many did you count before?" I whispered softly, watching.

"Nine," he answered, very quiet. I went over them again in

my head—seven, eight, nine—and, to the left, a tenth, larger, a wall of flame, blowing in great tongues to the west.

Meredith's arm tightened on my shoulder. "Valle Crucis," he said. "It's Valle Crucis . . . the English are burning Valle Crucis. . . ."

We four turned frightened faces toward one another in the dark. "Yes," Meredith said slowly. "I think September the sixteenth has come. . . ."

Chapter 5

Since the burning of Valle Crucis, Glendower House has been overflowing with clergy. Some were killed when the English attacked the monastery, and a few died in the flames, but most of them were saved. Of the nuns, not one remains; there is no trace of them, so it is believed they were all captured. It is a very wicked thing the English did, for the monastery was without defenses, and all the people were helpless against the marauders. Already, though, they have begun to pay for it.

When we sighted the Valle Crucis fire on Midsummer Night, Owen rode swiftly to its defense, with all his sons and a great company of armed followers. No one of our side was wounded, even, but the English suffered great losses, for those that remained were taken by surprise. Owen took some captives, too, among them Lord Grey and his son. They are in the donjon keep, awaiting ransom from old Bolingbroke. I would not be in their shoes, for Owen has asked an enormous sum for them, and everybody knows the stinginess of the new king. Owen will not put them to death, but they do not know that, of course; it is satisfying to think of them lying there, underground, in discomfort and terror, after what they have done. I have never been vengeful or bloodthirsty, but jail is too good for these devilish men. Alice goes every day to look through the bars and taunt them, calling them all manner of filthy names. In a way, one cannot blame her, seeing how she has suffered at their hands, but it is not the act of a gentlewoman. *That* she is not, of course, but Walter says it is not the act of a Christian either. He reproaches her constantly, quoting Scripture, but for once she will not listen.

I saw these men, the father and son, when they were brought in that first morning. One could almost feel sorry for them; they were in a dreadful state. Covered with mud they were, their clothes all tattered and torn and their armor stripped away; the older one stumbled as he walked, for blood kept running down into his eyes from a great cut on his brow. All the women shouted insults at them, and threw stones and garbage, for they are objects of great hate among the peasantry roundabout. They have ever been oppressors of the people, in the English way, but lately they have done worse—rapings, as with Alice, and slaughter and plunder, too. Strange, that one cannot read their wickedness in their faces; they just looked wretched and sick and conquered. The father is even well favored, though the son looks somewhat like a frog. Old Grey, I saw, did everything he could to protect his boy, trying to shield him from the women's blows. It is strange to think of such a monster knowing love, but Owen says such feelings are instinctive to most things that live, even rats.

As I said, one can hardly walk about without bumping into a monk, and they are busy throughout the whole place, gathering men to them at corners, and exhorting them in the name of all that is holy to go to war. These same monks call it a Welsh crusade, and the Derfelites want to bring back all the old customs, while the students and Lollards want political and religious freedom and the peasantry want a revolt against all nobility. It is said that more and more students, Lollards, and just discontented serfs are crossing over into Wales, all ready to fight beside Owen. Owen, in the meantime, is playing a waiting game. I think he still hopes for some kind of peace terms from the king.

There is a constant stream of visitors: high officials, prophets, and foreign dignitaries. He is closeted away with somebody or the other every night. There have been Frenchmen from the Valois king, and from Burgundy, too. Burgundy is like another king, there in France. I do not know much, but Meredith says Owen will not enter into real battle with Bolingbroke without help from France. Personally, I think we are at war already, though Owen will not admit it and will make no move except for reprisals.

Last night there was an envoy from the Pope at Rome. (There are two Popes, one in Avignon, which is really pretty silly, when you come to think of it.) Anyway, this man, an Italian, very small, and swarthy, and sly-looking, pretended to have an important message for Owen from his master, and all the while, he carried another for the usurper Bolingbroke in a pouch beneath his shirt! One of the pages found it while the man was bathing. Owen was very angry and sent the man on to Bolingbroke, with another demand for the Greys' ransom, twice again what he had first asked; the sum, he said, went up with each delay.

The sixteenth of September has come and gone, and true to

old Iolo's memory, Owen was proclaimed Prince of Wales, not only here, but in other places all over Wales. They say there is now no stronghold in the country that is not with Owen, except for Nannau, in the south, where Hywele Sele is lord. This Hywele Sele is a near kinsman of Owen's, too, but he has always been an enemy and pro-Lancaster. No one knows why they are enemies, but it is some old quarrel of their youth; one can see that Owen hates the man; it is in his eyes whenever Nannau is mentioned.

About a month after the proclamation, in October it was, and the days still beautiful but growing cooler, a great group of us young folk rode out along the road to Mathrafal. Halfway there, there is a beautiful woods, dense with all sorts of growth, the kind of place where you can almost see Arthur and Merlin. I had been there once before, in the spring of the year, but truly it is said to be a wondrous sight in autumn, with all the leaves changing color and blazing against the sky. We were all looking forward to it; we had taken hampers of food and ale and were planning a whole day's outing.

It was a glorious day, diamond-clear, with a little wind from the north whipping into our cheeks and making them tingle. I wore a leather jerkin, dyed green, with a dragon, our arms, embroidered on the front. It is the mate to Catherine's; Owen had them made for us when I first came here. There is a shirt under, to match, and hose of a darker hue. There is a picking out of scarlet and gold threads on the dragon, so we are quite gay. All the damsels but Alice are in hose, so that we look like pages, except for our hair, which we wear braided, for neatness while we ride. Catherine, though, is riding amongst all her brothers; she will not come near to poor Rhisiart. I am sorry for him; he looks like a broody eaglet, hunched on his mount, an old piebald thing that he has had since he learned to ride. Catherine had come upon him, where he cuddled with Efa in a dark passage abovestairs; she did not tell the Argyllwyddes, but she will not speak to him either; Catherine is not forgiving. I have told her that he is not to blame, a man would have to be made of stone when Efa comes rubbing against him; there is not one, I warrant, that she has not dallied with, including the old minstrels and her own brothers even. But Catherine rides ahead, and Rhisiart is sunk in gloom.

The road to Mathrafal is straight and smooth as though cut by a knife. It was made by the Romans long ago and has only fallen away in spots here and there. It runs between thickets of trees and bushes, all gold and red, and in places our horses' feet go ankle-deep in the bright leaves that have fallen already. The birds make a small savage music all about, those that have not yet flown off to their winter homes. We have to look hard to find them though, for they are colored like the leaves; now and then one flits across under our noses. It is all pretty and magical, the scene, except for Rhisiart sulking.

I tried to cheer him, humming an old rhyme that has to do with birds, but the only words I could remember were far from heartening. Surprisingly, though, he raised his head, interest lively in his face. "What is that song?" he asked. "I had a Welsh nurse . . . she used to sing it to me when I was no higher than her knee—"

"I have forgot the words," I said, laughing, "except the part at the end, and it is passing sad. . . ."

"Sing it!"

I began softly: "Woe for us! Woe for us! The embers are dead./The Birds of Rhiannon are all flown away,/Beauty has gone with the Blessed Head./We are left to the sword and the wind and the clay!"

A voice joined in behind me, solemn as a dirge, repeating the verse. It was the Lollard, Master Walter, who had ridden up with his Alice. There was a glow on his face as though he listened to an angel; I am not so good a singer as that, but I held back the merry quip that rose to my lips, watching his countenance. We four, even Alice, who is not any part Welsh, rode in silence for a while, thinking on the old lament. I thought of the fall of the Old Kingdom and the turmoil in modern Wales and shuddered to imagine what might be the outcome of this present conflict. Beside me, Rhisiart said, "A goose has walked over your grave!" He spoke lightly, and I saw his mood had lifted.

"I do not know the saying. . . ." I said.

"Oh, it is English . . . they always say it when someone shivers. . . ."

"It is Latin, too," said Walter. "I have read something like it in Pliny."

They fell to talking of language sources and such, their scholars' minds kindling. By and by Walter began to point out the
birds to Alice, naming their Latin names, and some, too, that
have Greek ones. I know enough of both tongues for that, so we
all began vying with one another to flaunt our knowledge. Except for Alice, of course, who has no learning. She did not mind
though and repeated the words haltingly after us, like a child at
its nurse's knee. We were very merry and lagged along on our
mounts, letting them nibble at will among the grasses by the side
of the road. I noticed, somewhere in the back of my mind, that
all the other riders had passed us, even the men-at-arms who
were bringing up the rear. I looked ahead, seeing the road
stretching empty before us.

There was a sharp rise ahead, where the road bridged a good-
sized stream; we could not see over it and had lost sight of our
companions.

"We ought to catch up—" I said, spurring my horse. We all
fell silent then and pushed our horses on. The bridge still climbed
before us, rounding over the stream, so that we had no sight, still,
of those ahead, but I caught a gleam, too bright for water, beneath, and gave a little cry, pointing. A head, helmeted, came
into view; a horseman, mounted and in armor, rode up from the
bank of the stream under the bridge. Another followed and another, and then they were upon us, too many to count.

"They are of Lancaster!" cried Rhisiart, wheeling his horse.
The poor animal, unused to any sudden move, rose on his hind
feet, pawing the air and neighing in terror. All our horses took
fright, too, and behaved like unbroken colts. I am a good horse-
woman, but even I could not get sense into my mount, though I
pulled at his head with all my strength. The men surrounded us,
their swords drawn.

"We are unarmed!" cried the Lollard.

"Would you draw sword on ladies?" shouted Rhisiart, his Norman face dark red in rage.

"This one is no lady"—one of the men guffawed, pointing to
Alice—"it is the Greys' whore. . . ."

At this Alice opened her mouth and screamed shrilly, as she
had done that night when Rhys Gethin had slain her lover. I
reached over and grabbed her arm, my fingers biting into her

flesh to quiet her. "Sh-h-h—" I hissed into her ear. "We are too few—the others will hear you and ride back, and we will all be captured, or worse. . . ."

By now Rhisiart's horse had stopped thrashing about, and he, too, had forced back his first quick anger. He spoke haughtily, with that high-nosed Norman look that cows all the English. "Where is your captain? I will not parley with men-at-arms!" He looked so imperious that they fell back a little, muttering, parting their ranks. A big, burly man came riding forward then, dressed in light mail, and with his head bare. He drew no sword, and his face had a good-natured look about it, for all he wore the Lancaster colors.

"I am Denis Burnell," he said, "constable of Dinas Brân. I am at your service, Lady Catherine," he went on, turning to me. I opened my mouth to correct him, but Rhisiart, beside me, gave me such a kick on the ankle that I went pale. I stole a look at him and saw him frown warningly. The man Burnell continued. "I am come to bring you back to the castle, in the king's name. You must stand as hostages for the Greys till your worthy father sees fit to release them." There was a hint of irony in his last words, and a faint smile played about his lips, but he maintained his courteous attitude. Rhisiart spoke up, still arrogant. "I will stand hostage gladly, and I can speak for Sir Walter too, I trust—but I must beg you to let these ladies go! It is against the laws of chivalry to hold women. . . ."

"They will suffer no hurt, I promise you," Burnell said with dignity. "But stay they must . . . they will lodge in the Ladies' Tower, the Lady Catherine and her serving wench." His words had a final ring, and his face lost its look of good humor.

"I am a citizen of Hereford," said Rhisiart, "and liege subject to King Henry. I am at present acting-secretary to my kinsman, Baron Owen—"

"I have heard of you, sirrah," said Denis Burnell shortly. Rhisiart subsided, with a chastened look. I saw that he suffered embarrassment before me and did not look at him just then.

"Permit me to escort you, Lady," said Burnell, bowing gravely in his saddle. It was the first time I had been addressed as a fully grown gentlewoman; it flustered me, and I nodded my head, without words. He led the way, back down where he had come from. I followed, seeing that the streambed was dry and made, indeed, a passable road, cutting to the west. We did not even have to lower our heads as we passed under the bridge, it rose so high.

They put no restraint upon us, letting us ride as we would, so we kept together, talking low among ourselves. There were soldiers all about, before and behind; it was useless to attempt to free ourselves. Burnell rode some little way ahead, out of earshot.

Rhisiart said, looking wise, "Let them think you Catherine; it will give us better bargaining power. As for me, I shall make much of being close kinsman to Owen—"

I thought wryly, What difference will any of this make if the English mean mischief? We are in their power. But Walter said, surprisingly, and nodded, "You are right . . . the more value they place upon us, the more care they will take. Me, they will have heard of, no doubt. But, as I have already been acquitted of heresy, they cannot, with any fairness, bring me to trial again. It is Alice I fear for—" As she made a sudden move, he laid a hand on her arm, saying, "Look—I shall say she is my wife, Mistress Brut of Clyde . . . I am a knight; it will give her standing. Besides," he went on, "it is what I wish, if she will have me. . . ."

I stole a look at Alice; her face was very white, and there were tears on it; she was too moved to speak.

"Will you have me, Mistress Alice?" asked the Lollard, smiling. "It is no great bargain—I am a confessed heretic. . . ."

She nodded dumbly. "I would be whatever you are, Wat. . . . Let them burn me, too!"

He raised her hand to his lips. "So be it then . . . but no talk of burning. The English do not burn women—"

"My mother," she said stubbornly, "they burned my mother!"

"Your mother," he said, with a sweet reasonableness, "your mother was an avowed witch." And, so saying, he made the sign against the evil eye, the two middle fingers folded in, and the forefinger and little finger held stiffly outward. I was aghast. I have seen the soldiers and the peasants make just such a sign against Walter himself!

Rhisiart had been watching them curiously; I think he wondered at the Lollard's choice—he has the Norman snobbery. He snapped his fingers suddenly.

"I can marry you!" he said. "I am a clerk-at-law!" But then, as suddenly, his face fell. "We have not the two witnesses though. . . ."

"No matter," said Walter. "It is a fine idea . . . we can perhaps find them—there at Dinas Brân." I could not imagine what he thought to find there, in the enemy camp, but I said nothing and fell to thinking of our plight.

None of us spoke for a little: I think we were all a bit afraid; I know I was. I was surprised to see Walter ride boldly forward to Burnell and seek converse with him. We watched them talking, it seemed quite amiably. Beside me, Rhisiart bit his lip; he was most likely chagrined that the Lollard had shown so bravely, while he rode along with girls.

Walter came back presently, a smile on his face. "They are taking us to Dinas Brân," he said. Well, we all have surmised that, I thought, a trifle acidly, but I said nothing. "The Percys are there, with some other English lords, all of them close to the king, and not unsympathetic to our cause. We may yet thank the heavens for this happenstance . . . we may perhaps be emissaries of peace even. . . ."

"Hotspur!" cried Rhisiart, his dark features lighting up. Ah, I thought, even our little scholar-clerk is not armored against the magic of Hotspur's fame. He is the idol of all the youth of Britain.

"They say the young prince is with him, learning the arts of war," said Rhisiart. "He, too, has much respect for Owen . . . at Oxford he had many friends among the Welsh. . . ."

"Among our Lollard brothers, too," said Walter. "Oldcastle was his master. . . ." They both brightened visibly, while my heart, unaccountably, began to beat very hard.

Chapter 6

The first sight of Dinas Brân is enough to shake the heart, especially coming upon it as the sun waned and seeing it dark and wild against a blood-red sky, as we did that day of our capture.

The castle stands upon a high crag and can be seen for miles around. Even so, none of us had ever glimpsed it, for it had long been an English stronghold. We all four fell silent, gazing at it, and even the rough talk of the border soldiers died down, though perhaps they were just weary. They had, after all, ridden both ways that day.

Dinas Brân is the oldest fortress in Wales, getting its name from Brân the Blessed, who lived long, long ago, before written history, and only the old songs tell of him. He was a hero-king, a giant, so it is said. And indeed, the castle looks as though it were flung up by giants in a time beyond thinking on; even its ruination seems to have been done by giants, hurling thunderbolts. Its roofline is jagged and savage against the sky, its windows like blinded eyes, red where the setting sun pours through.

It broods above a gentle, rolling countryside; we had long since come out of the roadbed of the stream and journeyed along a winding trail beside a tiny brook where late flowers still bloomed among the reeds. The way seemed endless, always the fortress high above us; it looked inaccessible. I glanced at Rhisiart, beside me; his face looked gray and exhausted. I saw that it was covered with grime and dust, streaked where he had wiped away the sweat. We must all look like that, I thought, with some dismay, and pulled my linen smallcloth from under my jerkin. The Argyllwyddes made these—I think they were her own invention; they were for spitting into or blowing the nose and were very useful. I had a little flask, too, at my belt, and I tipped some water onto the cloth, and so made shift to wash my face, in a sort, pinching at my cheeks, too, to bring the color up. I saw Rhisiart look at me curiously and offered him the use of what was left in the flask. He took it and, throwing back his head, swallowed it down. He handed it back to me, saying, "How do we get up there, do you think?" and squinted at the blazing sky. "It looks deserted, too . . . Do you think they will feed us up there?"

I, too, was hungry; we had had nothing at midday but some black bread and cheese and a strip of some dried meat, too tough to chew, soldiers' rations. I thought longingly of the delicate meal we had packed, cold partridge stuffed with herbs, wine, too, and small white loaves fresh from the oven. Surely, they will not starve us, I thought; we are hostages, after all, not prisoners. But a cold feeling went through me just the same; who could tell with the English?

There was a soft whimper behind me, and Alice whispered, "Oh, Mistress Morgan, I am sore afeared. . . ."

"Hush," said Walter, putting his arm about her shoulders. "Have courage. We are in the Saviour's hands . . . and she is the Lady Catherine—remember? And remember, too, you are Mistress Brut, wife of Sir Walter Brut of Clyde in Hereford!"

I prayed that she would remember, for her own sake, though, for myself, I did not too much care for this "Catherine" masquerade, though I knew our captors might well honor more Owen's legitimate heiress. If indeed, they knew anything at all of honor. I felt a little creeping of fear and tried to push it down. I pushed down the thought of Harry, too, telling myself he would have forgotten me for sure, anyway, after all the time that had passed.

We had begun the ascent of the hill now; the road did not wind, as I had imagined it must but went straight upward, a steep incline. I looked again at the massive ruin above; how, in Derfel's name, had they ever dragged up the huge stones to build the place? My back ached as I thought of the poor slaves who must have done it. And I thought, too, of the common folk, still almost enslaved in England, and here, too, if truth were told. Will they gain really if Owen is victorious?

"It's a real Welsh fortress," said Rhisiart, looking up. "Built before Edward's time, probably in the time of Bad John. . . ."

I shook my head. "Oh, no," I said. "It is much older than that, older than the Caesars. . . ."

The Lollard said slowly, "Its foundations are older . . . it has been built upon an older site—many times rebuilt, perhaps. . . . I have heard that it was first a hill-city, before it was a fortress at all. . . ."

"All that is hearsay—" began Rhisiart hotly, and they were

off! By Our Lady, I thought, these fellows will argue at a word! It is the very pulse of life to them! I reached behind me and took the reins of Alice's mount.

"Come, Mistress Alice," I said, "let us climb this together. We shall rehearse our new selves—myself a true-born princess, and you my waiting woman, and a lady-wife!" And so it came to pass that I rode into the place of my birth, and into the torn pages of Welsh history alike, beside a Saxon byremaid!

There was, at the summit, a huge gate, obviously of recent building, made of some hard wood; as it swung open I heard a creak of pulleys and knew it was very modern. It was as thick as a man's body and wide enough for six horses abreast. The pass-word sounded like "Owen whoreson," which did not reassure me. Though the great gate was new, the walls were from some much earlier time, like the rest of the castle; they, too, had fallen into ruin and had not been repaired. I remember thinking, why take so much trouble over this fine new gate when all a challenger need do is storm the walls? In places, indeed, they were completely fallen away, and mounds of rubble stood in their place. There were not so many defenders, either, I noted, scarce half again the number who rode with us.

It was much darker inside the walls than out, and true to the Lancaster reputation for stinginess, there were very few lanterns or torches, though twilight was upon us, and the sun almost gone. I blinked, and my horse stumbled.

"This way, milady," said Denis Burnell, who had materialized suddenly before me out of the gloom. I followed him, holding Alice's hand across the backs of our mounts. I felt, rather than saw, that there was grass underfoot; we must be in the courtyard. It was vast enough to contain hundreds of tents, it seemed, though it was empty now.

My eyes grew slowly accustomed to the dimness, and I could see quite well. The place, besides having been damaged in battle, had so fallen into neglect that many of the upper chambers had sunk into the courtyard, leaving only the lower rooms; one had to pick a way through piles of stones and rubble to get to these. Burnell explained that only the Ladies' Tower, and some rooms close to the outer wall were habitable; the great hall, he said, was in use, though accommodations were crude, but the chapel, the library, and the little court were shattered out of all recognition.

As he pointed them out, I could see, among the heaps of stones, some that still showed their ancient carvings and moldings, barbaric and intricate of design.

A light burned in the entrance to the Ladies' Tower, where he was leading us. As we drew near, I saw it was held by a girl no older than myself but oddly dressed and smelling of some Eastern scent, heavy and pungent.

"This is the Lady Catherine and her serving woman, Mistress Alice," the constable said, as he helped us to dismount. "They are to lodge in the tower tonight. . . ."

The girl shook her head solemnly. Her eyes were very large, as you will see sometimes on a doe, with that same frightened look. "No coverings," she said.

"Coverings will be sent." He spoke impatiently. To me, he said, "I will send a page to bring you to the dining hall presently . . . Till then, Catherine ap Glendourdy. . . ."

I could not help laughing, as I corrected him. "Ab Owen it is . . . I could not very well be the daughter of 'two streams'!" That is what "Glendower" or "Glendourdy," as he called it, means in Welsh. As we spoke, I saw that the lamp-bearer crossed herself with her free hand. She beckoned to us then and led the way up the winding stairs. I saw, following her, that the curving walls had huge cracks in them, enough to let in daylight, had it not been almost dark. But the flame of the lamp she held blew in the gusty drafts and all but went out; the stones of the stairs were deathly cold, too—I could feel them through my leather shoes. I saw then, with a little shock, that the feet of our guide were bare beneath a full skirt of some heavy, dark red stuff. The soles of her feet were dyed the same dull red, and there were twin bracelets around her ankles, gold-colored, and shaped like little snakes. What manner of place is this, I thought and caught myself up, remembering the dim tales of the ladies of this very tower, of whom my own mother had been one. Was I born here, too, in this tower?

We climbed up and up, winding at every step; it could not have been very high, but I was panting a little at the top, and Alice too; the rigors of the day had tired us.

We came out into a round room, surprisingly large and comfortable, with wall hangings and cushioned seats and fur rugs beneath our feet, lit by rushlights in sconces set into the wall.

I turned to the strange girl. "Why did you cross yourself just now!"

"Owen," she said, "Owen—you said his name . . . he has the dark magic. . . ."

"That's ridiculous!" I said. "He's no more a magician than you are!"

"Oh," she said, nodding and smiling, "I know a little, too . . . from the Lady. . . ." I saw that her large eyes were stupid really, and her mouth hung open and was too wet. I wondered if she was feeble-minded, seeing that she crossed herself again. "The Lady will want to see you," she said. "I'll tell her you're here. . . ." And she left the place by another door, bewilderingly.

I stared at Alice. "What lady is this?" I wondered aloud. Alice only shrugged; I think she was reassured by the looks of the place, half-expecting to be put into a cell-keep or worse. I saw a chest with washing things laid out, and a comb and bottles, and above it a mirror hanging. It was made of an old shield, silvered, and curiously wrought; the design bordering it was a snake motif again, hundreds of little serpents writhing, with forked tongues. It brought to my mind the Medusa monster, who turned men to stone, and for a moment I, too, almost made the cross sign; then I remembered that Medusa's *hair* was made of snakes, and that she was mythical, anyway. I looked in it, seeing myself all nose, for its front was curved to turn aside weapons, but not so bad, otherwise, as I had feared. My hair was coming undone, that was all. I picked up the comb; it, too, was crowned by a snake's head.

There came a kicking then, at the door where we had entered, and two young boys, in page's clothes, came in, their arms laden. The taller carried a large caldron, steaming and smelling of lavender. "Where am I to put it?" he asked, huffing and puffing. "Where is Angharrad?" he asked, looking about him.

"Is that her name . . . the barefoot one?" I said, smiling at him. He was a pretty youth, curly-haired, with his shoulders broadening already, though his voice still cracked.

"You don't miss much, do you? . . . Yes, that's the one, Angharrad. She waits on the lady. She's the only girl in the tower . . . till now." He set the pot in the middle of a fine embroidered rug, where it slopped over, making a dark stain. "You must be

Catherine . . . the Lady Catherine, that is. . . . You have that
funny yellowish hair. I am Lawnslot." He finished proudly.

"Oh," I said, "from Arthur's time?" Such cock-robin boys always bring out some mischief in me.

"Well," said he, not abashed, "I am descended from him. . . .
And this is Madoc," he said, gesturing toward his companion.

"A good name, too," I said, "though not of such ancient lineage."

A look of sweet bafflement crossed his face; I saw it was no use
teasing him, so I said, "This is my waiting woman, a lady of
Clyde, Mistress Alice—"

"Oh, we know who *she* is! Grey's—" At my look, he said hast-
ily, "Oh, we won't tell—we are Owen's men." Which made me
want to smile again, but I kept my face straight and said only,
"How did you know?"

"Well, it is simply deduction," he said, airily. "Everybody
knows the Argyllwyddes took her to live among the daughters,
and she could not be any of *them*. . . ."

The little one spoke then; he, too, had set down his burden of
bedding next to the water. "We are going to run away and join
Owen's army . . . we have already stolen the swords!" He could
not have been, I thought, more than ten.

"But who are you? Do you live here in Dinas Brân?"

"We are the sons of some nuns that used to live here," the
older boy said. "They broke their vows and ran away with some
soldiers, so the Lady kept us here, to live among the sisters. . . .
They have all run away by now, except for Angharrad."

"Angharrad, too, is a nun?" I asked, looking skeptical.

"Well . . . in a way. It is a very ancient order."

I'll wager it is, my boy, I thought; you have it somewhat gar-
bled. But I said nothing, except, "Who is the Lady?"

"Oh," said the young one, in his light, childish voice. "She is
old, so old . . . a hundred, maybe. . . ."

"She is the Lady," said the other. "That's what everyone calls
her . . . she is the"—he lowered his voice—"she is the high
priestess. She has always been here. . . ."

Always. I thought, wondering, thinking of my mother. But the
boy Lawnslot went on; he was one of those, I learned, who never
stop. "They have given you Myfanwy's Bower, I see," he said,
nodding sagely. "Right below this window is where they staked

him out, her bard lover, night after night, forcing her to watch.
. . . They say, at midnight, when it is the full of the moon, you
can hear his cries still."

"Then I am glad the moon is dark," I said sharply.

"There is another ghost, too," said the little Madoc, and his
face was alive with interest. "The Hanging Lady . . . right there
she hanged herself, after Owen left her. . . ." And he pointed to
a beam in the ceiling, where, true enough, a great spikenail pro-
truded.

"The Lady Lowry, that was, before my time," put in the other,
talking one. "Mad with grief they say she was. She did it with
Myfanwy's belt. It broke, but she died anyway." A shiver went
through me, for it was my mother he spoke of. I do not credit
ghosts, but I knew in the dark my mind would see her there,
above me, long and limp, toes pointed to the floor. I resolved to
keep a light burning all night, just in case.

"Aren't you going to wash?" asked Lawnslot. "The water will
be getting cold, and it was monstrous heavy to carry, all this way
up. . . ."

"I am not in the habit of washing in public," I said pointedly.

"Oh," he said, unabashed, "we will sit on the steps outside . . .
though Angharrad lets us watch . . . she doesn't do it very often,
though. . . ."

I held the door open as they passed through and closed it behind the two boys, catching Alice's eye and laughing. "It is a
strange household, for sure, mistress," she said.

We were trying to guess a way to pour from the heavy can into
some smaller bowl, that we might wash each in her own private
water-store, when Angharrad came back, still bearing her lamp,
to lead us to the lady of the tower. I saw she had need of that
light, for there were none lit in the corridors where we went.
There was a heavy, gravelike odor, too, from those cold walls,
rotten and sweetish. At the end of the first passage was a heavy
door; it took all three of us to pull it open, and I wondered how
she managed it alone at other times. Clearly the way was known
to her. As the door swung shut, it gave a sighing, sobbing sound,
which echoed all up and down as we proceeded. Alice pushed
close to me and I felt her tremble. I am not such a strong creature myself, but, being a gentlewoman, I had to bear myself with
the look, at least, of courage. She could not see me, so I took her

hand firmly and said, "That echo should be seen to . . . windows ought to be cut, too. The air is foul."

Angharrad turned, the whites of her eyes in the feeble lamplight glowing like marsh-fire. "Oh, no," she said, "no echo. It is Myfanwy sobbing." We waited a moment; the sound grew softer and died away, as echoes do. Truly the poor girl was ignorant.

We came to another door, as heavy as the first; it opened onto a chamber that must have been the mate to the one where we had been lodged, Myfanwy's, for it too was circular; the passage must have connected double towers, probably above some ruined hall. The room we entered, though, was very warm, stifling, and reeked of incense like a church on a saint's day. Indeed, though it was dim, I could make out several holy images: a Jesus, hanging, his features contorted with agony, the running blood looking as though it had been painted yesterday and still wet; a Saint Benedict bristling with arrows, carved by the same rude hand; and a delicate and graceful figure of the Virgin, of some Eastern workmanship, her robe picked out in gold. There was Derfel, too, on his horse, with his Derfel-bride flung over his saddle, painted on a cloth which hung in a doorway; he was depicted as a Christian knight, except for his horned helmet.

I could not see the Lady of the tower at first; she sat as still as any of her images. She was on a low divan, swathed around and around with draperies of that same dull red stuff the girl wore, shapeless as a bundle; her head, too, was covered in an old-fashioned wimple, but I could see by her face that she was very old, as old as the ancient bard, Iolo Goch, had been, perhaps. She was all wrinkles, and her eyes had a blue film over them. She stretched out a skinny hand, like a bird claw, and fastened it on my wrist, drawing me to her.

"I cannot see well, child—come closer. . . ." She spoke in Old Welsh, so that I missed some of her words, but her voice was surprisingly full and rich, with a music in it.

She brought up her hand and touched my face, moving along its bones and hollows as if to memorize them; her touch was dry and cool, mortal. "It is the Owen-face . . . a sun-child . . . all the moon-girls are dead and gone . . . long gone. . . ." Her voice rose in a sort of wail; I knew then she was mad with the weight of her years and wandering in her wits, and a pity crawled in me. "Yes . . . you are his daughter . . . my daugh-

ters he has driven away, yes, and granddaughters, too. . . .
Prince Owen . . . but men must go where the fates lead
them. . . ." She took her old hand away then and bowed her
head onto her chest. She stayed thus for a long while, it seemed.

I heard Angharrad whisper, "She is looking into the future
. . . she is seeing your future. . . ." I stirred uneasily, the hair
crawling on my scalp as I watched that still figure.

When the voice came again, it came without movement, and
the old one did not raise her head; it had a hollow sound. "The
English one I cannot see . . . flames only I see . . . flames
. . . but the Owen-child will know pain . . . and sorrow too
deep for tears . . . and the bright wings of love . . . and ruin
. . . Owen will bring you to ruin. . . ." I knew it for the gibberish of the addled, but still a cold wind touched me in that heated
chamber. I wanted to leave that presence, but there was a numb-
ness on me and I stared still. She was silent then for a time; presently her body began to shudder, and low, sobbing breaths came
from her. She lifted her head, looking at me as though her filmed
old eyes could see, and said, "Go now, Owen's daughter, and all
the saints walk with you!" She cackled suddenly, like the crone
that she was, and her voice lost all its luster, "It is all that they
have left me . . . Lord Griffith made Christians of us, and there
are no good gods left and no goddesses either . . . and Owen
broke all my altars even and took my daughters. . . . Only Angharrad is left—a good girl but without the wit to remember a little prayer . . . go, go—all of you. . . ." And she waved her hand
at us in vague dismissal. As we left, I saw that her head had sunk
again onto her breast.

We traversed again that dark passage behind Angharrad's
lamp; cold as the grave it was after that hot and fetid chamber,
and echoing its soft sighs behind us. When we reached the Myfanwy room, I saw that Alice was deathly pale, her forehead
beaded with sweat. She moved close to me, whispering, "Oh,
mistress, she saw flames for me! Like my mother—"

"Hush," I said, "you are no witch. . . . It is only an old mad-
woman, with nothing to occupy her, and no thoughts at all, and
lonely. . . ."

"Oh, no, mistress—she has the second sight for true . . . her
eyes were all covered with cataracts, and yet she knew I was
there. . . ."

"Don't be foolish," I said, briskly, "Angharrad will have told her of us, of course." And I took up the comb and brought it crackling through my hair, though I saw in the mirror that my eyes had a look of fright.

Chapter 7

The great hall of Dinas Brân had fallen into so ruinous a state that if it had been raining, it could not have been used at all. There were great jagged holes in its roof, and indeed I saw several wild birds flying about among the stone arches high overhead. The one advantage was that the huge clouds of smoke could find their way out without choking everyone to death; there were many fires burning and no chimneys, but vents only. Men sprawled on the benches with their drunken heads down among puddles of wine, and there was no smell of roasting meats; along one whole side of the hall the tables had been fastened back to the wall (they were the old-fashioned kind that hung when not in use) and the trestles taken away. Holy Mother, I said to myself, we are not to be fed—I was quite empty now, almost sick from it, and from my apprehension.

I was still in my hose and Alice in her riding dress when Lawnslot fetched us; there were beautiful clothes from a century ago in the press above-stairs, but they were unaired and smelled of must and that same Eastern scent that hung about the Ladies' Tower. Angharrad did not come to the hall with us; Lawnslot whispered that she never left the tower.

I caught sight of Rhisiart and Walter standing irresolutely in another doorway and hurried joyfully toward them. There was much noise and confusion; I could hear a lute playing softly under. There was not much more light here than upstairs; the dark shadows menaced along the walls and disappeared into the pitch-black upper reaches.

I saw that Rhisiart was scowling. "No one has come to give us greeting," he said. "And the soldiers are all drunken and filthy . . . no servants about—"

"And no food, either, it seems," said I.

A voice spoke, at my elbow; in the darkness I almost jumped. It was Constable Burnell. "They are setting up a clean table for you over there," he said, pointing. "The dogs are finishing the

last of the venison, but there is partridge and a good hare pasty
. . . Lord Percy himself has gone to see to your torches."

True to his word, I saw soldiers carrying in a fresh-scrubbed
table and two long benches, and setting them up against a dark
far wall. Another set two torches in their sconces, and by the light
I saw the wall was hung with a tattered and faded hanging; it
looked like a scene of ancient battle, with horses' manes tossing
and horned helmets and long spears.

The scowl had not left Rhisiart's face. "Lord Constable," he
said, "I must protest for the lady . . . for my cousin Catherine—" And he lowered his voice. "There are whores here. . . ."

"Quite right, sir," said another voice, "quite right . . . and I
agree it is an insult—but I fear my men would revolt if I sent
them away. . . . The soldiers have been long away from
home. . . ." I turned to see a squarish man in a loose-fitting
furred surcoat. He had the blackest eyes I ever saw, and the
whitest linen. His shirt was carelessly worn, open at the throat,
and the laces dangling, but it was dazzlingly clean. His cheeks,
too, looked fresh-barbered, the shaven skin beneath his helm cut
showing pale against his weathered neck. His had a blunt, cleft
chin, and his nose was flattened from some battle blow; it was a
face crude-cut but with a speaking charm. Indeed, the whole
man shed a kind of glow about him like a fire. This, I thought,
could be no other than the fabled Hotspur, the Lord Percy, even
as I heard Burnell pronounce his name. It was easy to see how he
had beglamored the youth of a nation.

"I give you greeting, Catherine ab Owen. . . ." He smiled
into my eyes, for we were of a height; I had thought he would be
a tall man. His voice had the soft burr of the North Country and
something else, some hesitation or impediment that gave earnest-
ness to his speech. I was myself beglamored, for though he was a
man of many flaws—even his teeth all crooked—yet I warmed to
him as if he were a very Apollo. I saw Rhisiart go red, too, with
pleasure, as the great warrior shook his head. "Will you be
seated, Lady Catherine?" And he led me to the bench against
the wall. Alice he did not even glance at; the Percys thought
themselves finer than kings. This was a flaw I could not like, for
it is not the way of the truly royal, and bespeaks ignorance to
boot. But Walter drew Alice apart, whispering fondly into her
ear.

The fowl was brought, and a pasty, and good white bread, only a little stale, and wine and beer, too. We ate like starving peasants, only nodding as the Percy pointed out this one or that. He sat across the board, toying with a goblet of pale wine, looking out over the company.

"That is a kinsman of yours, I believe—" He indicated a burly, redheaded man in his middle years, in light mail. "Hywele Sele . . . but he is not for Owen—he flies the Lancaster flag. . . ." I looked at the man closely then, remembering that this was Owen's avowed enemy. He seemed intent on a little game of his own; at his feet a soldier lay sprawled, fast asleep. Hywele Sele held a long goose feather to the man's nose, gently twitching it back and forth. At each touch of the feather, the soldier sneezed but did not wake, which sent his tormenter into spasms of raucous laughter. It seemed a childish occupation to me, but I suppose he, too, was drunk. In truth, most of the hall seemed the worse for the free-flowing mead, and many snored, insensible.

I was curious, too, about the whores, for I had never seen any. They did not look much different, that I could see, from court ladies, except that their heads were uncovered and their gowns, for the most part, made of shoddier stuff. But they, too, had the new fashion of shaven eyebrows and hairline; I have always thought it a strange, bald look. They were thickly painted, too; one could see it clear across the room. One had a head of black hair reaching to her waist, crimped from the irons; I wondered how long it had taken to achieve. She was seated on somebody's lap; it must have been the lute player we had heard earlier, for we saw the fellow dribble what was left in his goblet down her bosom and tumble her off onto the floor. She only smiled, though, and blew a kiss to him as he took up his lute and began to finger it idly.

"The prince will want to greet you, lady," said Hotspur, rising and making his way to the lutist. So there was little Harry! I had not known him, of course, from the distance, and his back was toward us, too. Hotspur bent to his ear and spoke. He looked toward us, and then back to the girl on the floor at his feet, who was just pulling herself up, holding onto the table; I saw with a little surprise that she was drunk, too. I had never seen a woman so. Still seated, Harry gave her a playful kick in the rear, which nearly tumbled her over again. It was a disgraceful tableau; I stole a look at Rhisiart beside me and saw that his Norman face was set hard, like a rock.

Walter reached over, touching his arm. "Gently, lad," he said, with a smile, "it is only a camp-follower. . . ."

Harry was coming toward us now with Hotspur. I let out my breath, which I had been holding, as I saw that he walked easily and in a straight line. I do not know why, but I could not have borne it if he had been like all the rest. I watched him, marveling; he was more of a man, at fourteen, than any of my brothers, though slenderly made. He had none of the colt about him but moved with a quick compact grace; as he came closer I saw the little Harry again, the long face, leaning a little to one side, the skin clear and pale, a fine, smooth brow. But three years had made a big change; I wondered if I, too, had aged to womanhood. He looked at me full, and I saw something leap behind his eyes. I rose, all confused, and made a low court bow, my head down. I heard Hotspur, "The Lady Catherine ab Owen, Baron Glendower's daughter . . . His Highness, Henry of Lancaster and Monmouth, the Prince of Wales. . . ."

Harry took my hand, raising me up, and drawing me a little apart, speaking low, "You are not Catherine, though, sweetheart—"

"And you are not the Prince of Wales," I hissed under my breath, "for my father is!"

"Touché!" he said, smiling, and clapping a hand to his heart; it was a term from the new art of fencing. His French was still poor though, and I told him so. "Do they have no tutors at all at Bolingbroke's court?"

"That's my Morgan!" he whispered, laughing, and raising my hand to his lips. "Come, sit apart with me and talk a little . . . it has been so long. . . ."

"You have not forgot me then?" I asked.

"How could I? You are the first girl I ever kissed. . . ."

"But not the last, I wager!" I spoke a little sharply; I had forgot that he was heir to England, if unlawfully, and that I was hostage in the enemy camp.

"You were the sweetest though . . ." I felt his breath against my cheek, stirring the hair, and blushed; I did not know where to look.

"You were not dressed so when I last saw you," he said, looking down at my legs in their hose.

"It is my riding gear . . . all of us dress this way—all of the maidens of Owen's house—"

"But not the Saxon heifer?" he said, with a glance toward Alice.

"You noticed her then?" I asked. "I had thought you had eyes only for me. . . ."

"I notice all women . . . but she *is* a heifer."

He thought to please the woman in me, but I had tired of the game. "She is a poor girl, much abused, that we brought back to life," I said.

"I know her story." He said it shortly, annoyed.

"*That* you do not, sirrah!" I answered angrily, and rose. "Or the wrong side of it only—"

He caught my hand, holding it hard.

"Let go of me, little Harry!" I saw his eyes change, but he did not loose his grip. I was all red from the neck up; I have that kind of skin. All the eyes were on me, too, from the rest of the table, though they could not hear our words.

"I am not so little anymore," Harry said. "And you will sit! . . . would you shame me before them all?"

"You are master here," I said gracelessly, and sat again.

He gave a short laugh. "I am not master anywhere . . . but I am sorry I offended you. . . ."

"And I am sorry, too, for my anger—"

"Yet how do you know"—and he spoke with a sweet reasonableness—"how do you know the girl's story is the true one?"

"It cannot be otherwise," I said. "All Wales knows the Ruthin men are brutes."

"All the peasantry of Wales, perhaps . . . you champion them, like Owen. . . . They say your father's followers are armed with pick and shovel—"

"Maybe you will find it otherwise when first you come to face him," I answered, quiet now.

"Maybe," he said, with that same mildness. "I faced him once —at Richard's table, where he sat in the high seat. I thought him then more god than man. . . ." His face was shut in thought. He spoke again, slowly. "It is not such a bad thing to be, I think—

the commons' champion . . . my father feels otherwise—he has
cast his lot with other dice. . . ."

We were silent then, for a little. I looked down at the board,
feeling his stare, tracing with my finger some initials cut in the
wood and a lopsided heart, black with age. He spoke, still looking at me.

"Is she so very like you, then . . . Catherine?"

"Not to mistake us, no," I answered. "We were dressed alike
. . . and she had ridden on ahead . . . No, we resemble Owen,
both, but she is fairer of hair, and I am taller. It was our cousin
Rhisiart who thought up this playact—I do not much relish it,
myself . . ."

"No, it is best," he said. "They will let us be together now . . .
there is talk of my father asking Catherine's hand for me. . . ."

I felt my heart give a great leap, and my breath came short.
"It would make for peace . . ." I said, not trusting myself to say
more.

"I would not wish it," he said, "except if she be your twin in all
things. . . ."

I glanced sharply at him, fearing to see his lips curving in that
mocking way they had done earlier, but he was grave, and not
even looking at me but into space. Almost one might have
thought him sad. "They have been busy already on my behalf,
my father's advisers . . . so far none will have me. The first they
asked for was Richard's Isabelle . . . he was not two weeks in his
grave. They had hoped, with it, to sweeten France. She refused
. . . and chose exile instead. . . ."

"Exile—" I said. "Where is she then?"

"She is in Scotland—well, and safe, I hope. . . . They tell me
nothing. . . ."

I sensed the hurt child and more, under his words, and put out
my hand to touch his. "Oh, Harry . . ." I whispered.

"It is true," he said. "The whole country knew of Richard's
death before I had any word—and I asked for him every day
. . . he was my friend. . . ."

"I know. . . ."

"After—it was many nights before I slept . . . and even then,
my dreams—" He broke off; control sat on his face like a mask,
ugly to see on one so young. I thought then that all of his aging
had been done in one short span of time.

"You think, then . . ." I said slowly, not wanting to finish.

He looked full into my eyes. "I do not know what to think . . . my father speaks shortly to me, if at all. And even if I dared ask him, I fear the answer. Humphrey said—he was a boy at Richard's court—"

"I remember him," I said softly.

"He said that all kings wade knee-deep in blood. . . ."

"It seems to me that all *men* do, also—" I said, thinking to ease him, and remembering all the wars and crusades that have gone on time out of mind, and the private killings, too. He looked at me strangely, and I saw he did not take my meaning.

"I had rather the clean blood of battle . . ." he said. His statement had the taint, to my ears, of old piety, and I said so.

"It is still blood," I said, "and men die from its spilling—"

"Oh, my old friend—don't quarrel with me over words. . . ." He took my hand, and his face changed, losing its look of gravity. "You are too beautiful for that . . . and then, too, women always hate wars, while men love fighting—it is the way of the world."

"It is a way that should be changed," I said hotly. "And we are not man and woman either, but boy and girl only—with private thoughts, still—and not yet set in a mold. . . ."

"You are right, Morgan," he said mildly. "I am surprised sometimes when I think how few years I have . . . I seem to have lived so long. . . ." His face, with its long sweetness, was very sad then, and the woman's heart in me melted all at once; it was there, after all, no matter how much I denied it. I think now that I loved him already, though I did not know it.

I have forgotten what else we said then. I know we talked a while still, apart from the others, and that later we joined them.

Rhisiart was surly and looked at me in a way I did not like. I saw he had no love for the prince, or some jealousy, perhaps; Rhisiart has no feel for class, or, rather, he thinks himself at the top of all society in spite of his low birth. It would be a good trait if he admitted all men to be somewhat equal, which he does not. Also, he acted in a proprietary way toward me, as though in truth I were his Catherine. As if I could stop the prince's attentions, in any case!

Walter Brut, on the other hand, showed much respect and admiration for Harry, drawing him out and even hanging on his words. He hoped, I think, to win him to the Lollard side. The prince had been present at his heresy trial, and the two talked eagerly. The prince, though, thinks Lollardy is for the elect only, not for the commons, treating it as a separation of doctrinal thought, whereas Walter wants the New Learning, as he calls it, to be the sustenance and hope of the lowly. Harry, though, is horrified at the burnings and would like to see Arundel out of power. He would have his father appoint his Beaufort cousin, another Henry, to Arundel's post, and said so openly, though Hotspur frowned. Hotspur is, one can see, his guardian, here in the Welsh Marches, though a lenient one. He has a son just Harry's age but does not treat him like one, but like a young companion-at-arms. One can see that the prince adores him and looks up to him in all things.

The prince played for us, too, on his lute. (There were no bards, or minstrels, either, with their forces—a thing that seemed strange to me.) And he played more than passing well, too, as he does all things he turns his hand to. He would not sing though— he said he had no voice—but the Percy did, and gladly. I thought privately that he, too, had no voice, being accustomed to those great singers who take their living from it. But he sang pleasantly, carrying the tunes and putting us all in a light mood.

Harry struck up a sweet air, new to me, called "Greensleeves." It was in compliment to me, he said, for I wore green, but Hotspur stopped him, saying it was a song for a light woman. Harry answered that so many love songs were but changed the tune.

"This one," he said, "is the loveliest of all, written by Master Abelard to Héloïse . . . she was no light-of-love, for they both took holy orders later. . . ." It was lovely indeed, and in my ear, softly, Harry sang it too. I remember it still, though it is years ago. ". . . Come death unrelenting . . . with quiet breath consenting . . . I go forth unrepenting . . . Content, content, content . . . that ever such delight were to me lent. . . ."

Chapter 8

I never heard Myfanwy sob again, for we were not resummoned to that strange presence in the other tower room, nor was I troubled by visions of the "hanging lady" in the night. I slept soundly, fatigued by the long ride and by the late supper and the wine. I did not even dream of Harry, though I fell asleep on thoughts of him.

Hotspur, after informing me next day that he was sending envoys to Owen to treat of our ransoming, disappeared. Harry said there was good hunting in the woods around those parts, and he was an active man, Hotspur. He was gone most of the day. We young people—Harry, too—were left to our own devices; it was a day I remembered long among the barren years that followed.

Harry and I had much to do to lose Rhisiart but lose him we did for the best part of the morning. (Later, Rhisiart was to confess that he looked to protect my virtue, knowing the prince's reputation!) We walked about the ruined walls of the old fortress; struck with a still magic they were in the early sunlight of that October. We sat for a while on a marble bench that must have been Roman, till its chill struck through to us, and we must walk again, and we talked. He told me sweet secret things of his childhood at Monmouth, which he loved and still longed for; I told him of my life, too, as mixed up as his own. He only half-believed the story of my mother and the priestess cult; I could see he thought it another of the tales cut out of whole cloth that went around constantly about Owen. He showed much interest, though, in the French court, the Queen Isabeau and the little princesses, dirty and wild as street urchins they were then, and the poor neglected madman, the king. I was only repeating stories I had heard really, and some small dim memories, for I had been five when I left in Isabelle's train for the English court. I said, though, to tease him, "There are more princesses left for you, Harry, if Isabelle would not have you. They were very dirty, though their hair curled naturally, a wonder to behold . . . in fact, my father's spies say there is yet another born only this year, called Katharine, like my sister—though they spell it with a *k* . . . it may be her hair will curl, too. . . ."

"I want no princesses," he said, bringing a piece of my hair to his lips, "though her hair be ever so curling. Yours is beautiful— straight as rain—and amber-colored in the sun. . . ."

Later the others came out to join us, with the two little pages, Lawnslot and Madoc. These last were all eyes for the prince and followed him about like puppies. The littlest one, Madoc, sidled up to me and whispered, "Lady, we are still for Owen—never fear! It is just that they name him—the prince—the finest jouster in the realm—and he so young! He has unseated Hotspur even!"

And Lawnslot, too, whispered eagerly, "For tennis, too, they call him a wonder. We have nets and balls within— but I fear there is no match here for him. . . ."

"Do you hear, Harry?" I said. "You are a tennis champion, it seems! I know something of the game, though I am a girl. Will you play me?"

"We have no rackets though," said the little one, his face falling.

"Never mind," said Harry, laughing. "I have three in my luggage pack. It is a present my father always remembers to send . . . Sometimes I think it is all he imagines I can do—play at balls. . . . I have had one each saint's day since I was seven, even when they came late. I will play you," he said to me, "but I warn you, I will win. . . ."

"Do not be too sure of that," I answered. I was wild and light that day, as though wine ran in my veins. He was right though; I am a good player, but I was no match for him. When it was over I was beaten roundly and sank to the ground, panting.

"You are good, though, for a girl," Harry said handsomely. "Though never have I played a girl before. Girls do not play tennis in England."

"This is not England," I said sharply, "however much your father seeks to make it so. . . ."

He sank down, too, then, beside me on the grass and said, as if idly, "At Monmouth, in the grave-place there, where my mother lies, there are flowers growing . . . it is a little garden only, planted by my mother's hands, long ago, when she was alive. There is a rose there, deep yellow, and amber at its heart. . . . It was so beautiful; when I was very small, I reached out to pluck it from its stem. I have a scar still, here on my palm. . . ."

"All roses have thorns—" I said, but hanging my head.

"Let us invent one that does not," he said, softly, for my ear only. "We are not enemies, my Morgan . . . and I did not plot out my father's ways. . . ."

We were silent then for a little, watching the others. Rhisiart and Walter were playing, the Lollard like some of the girls at home, serving the ball with an underhand thrust, though he was quick to return. Rhisiart played as he did all things, fiercely, as though upon it life depended. He was almost good enough for Harry, but not quite. As we watched, the Percy rode through the gates, a huge deer slung over his mount. He sent it away with his man-at-arms and, throwing off his mantle, flung himself down beside us.

"You will play me, my Lord!" cried Harry. "You have promised now for months—and the net is all set up . . . you cannot refuse!"

"Ah," said Hotspur, lying back upon the grass, "what stakes will you put up—I do not play for no gain. . . ."

"What you will," said Harry, his eyes shining. "I will pay you when next I have my allowance—if it be that I lose, that is. . . ."

"Get along with you, lad—you'll never see such . . . no more than the rest of us do—" He finished under his breath. "No—I'll not play . . . I am winded from the hunt. . . ."

"Oh, please, Hotspur—" Harry chewed his lip, thinking. "I will put up Mercury—against your silver gauntlets if I win!"

"Your new black charger? What will you do for a horse then?"

"I will ride the old roan—but I will not lose. . . ."

Several of the soldiers came over to watch when they saw Hotspur take up racket, for he had much skill and was beloved of his men besides. He played in a careless fashion at first, not taking off his surcoat, thinking to win easily. After a while, he saw he was held and began to press harder, raking the court with short, fierce strokes. Harry could not match his strength or the hard spin he put upon the ball.

Hotspur won the first set, and they stood for a moment, resting. I went up to Harry and said, "He has you the way he is playing

—try your volleys very high, for the far side . . . he is not over-tall."

Harry saw it was sense and aimed his drives high so that Hotspur had to jump for them, and his own strikes began to fall short. He grew angry and red and at last took off his surcoat, throwing it hard to the sidelines. I could see that he feared he might be shamed by a boy, with all his men watching, for by now a crowd had come up to lay bets. Harry won the next set, making all even, and the last set they played as grimly as if it were a battle. Hotspur's face was reddening now almost to purple, though his shots were true, but Harry was white and spent-looking. The Percy's last shot was just inside, a tricky return, and everyone cheered. Harry returned it though, smashing it to the court behind Hotspur. I thought it fell inside, and the page Lawnslot, mad with excitement, screamed, "My lord the prince has won!"

The Percy glared at him. "Are you blind, boy? It fell outside."

"My Lord," said Lawnslot staunchly, "I thought it fell true."

"It did not!" shouted Hotspur. "There is a shadow on the court—it moved in the wind. . . ."

The prince walked over to Hotspur; I could see he was tired almost to falling. "I will have my groom bring Mercury to your stall. . . ."

The Percy was amiable now that he had won, putting an arm about Harry's shoulders. "I thought for a moment that you had me," he said. "It was as close as ever anyone has come. . . ."

"I will win one day," said Harry, smiling but serious under.

Most of the castle was there by now, and I heard Denis Burnell say, speaking to Hotspur, "He put up a good fight to the last . . . surely you do not mean to take his horse?"

"It's what I played for," said the Percy.

The prince, beside me, touched my elbow. "Come with me to the stables—I want to take my farewell. . . ."

"Your horse?" I asked.

He looked shy, suddenly. "I have a great love for animals. . . ." I saw that he breathed heavily still, and myself went slowly, as if it pleased me to do so.

He laughed. "I am not so worn by this small conflict as that. It is true my chest pains me at times. . . . They say it is the fever I took as a child, and that I will outgrow it. . . . But it has passed now—we can go at a more likely pace."

The horse was a great, shining black creature, a noble beast. I could see it would be hard to part with him. Myself, I have never had such a horse; my own little mare is lively and good-natured. I asked where she was stabled, but he did not know. He took from his pocket two lumps of sugar, giving one to me; I saw he was a boy still, in truth, with his pockets full of all manner of oddments, for some marbles fell out, too, and an old, petrified beetle skeleton. When he had fed the horse, I held up my palm with the sugar on it. The charger took it delicately, its wide lips like velvet against my skin. He pawed the floor of his stall after and bowed his beautiful head, acknowledging the gift. I laughed aloud, delighted.

"You like him?" asked Harry, all aglow, looking at me. "A pity he is no longer mine—I would have given him to you for a love token. . . ."

"*That* you would not!" I cried, shaking my head. "Only—now I will never know—"

"I would have given him . . . I would give anything—when I see you laugh. . . . Your face goes all up at the corners as if someone pulled the strings."

I laughed again; it was so absurd.

"Walk with me a little—here in the soft dark," he whispered. In truth the stable was a sweet place in a way, warm and shadowy, smelling of hay and horse, with little rustlings and whisperings of leather and hides, and now and then a low horse snuffle or a high whinny, more like a sigh. There was a shaft of outside light, golden, slanting through the broad door-place, and a pile of fresh straw in a far corner. He drew me down upon it and kissed me. I had never known kissing before, in truth, though we all played at it now and then, carelessly. Kisses like wine, the poets sing. I do not know, but it was sweet, so sweet. For fourteen, he knew many secrets. I doubt now that I should have risen up a maid but for the canvas drawers the Argyllwyddes had made for all us girls, that he could not find the closure for. He was angry at first, but, after, he laughed, saying it would be a pity to force a noble damsel. I laughed, too, and said with some chagrin that it would not have needed force, but fled from out of there anyway while my heart was still almost whole. In daylight I saw myself ruined by the straw, all rumpled and covered with chaff that I could not pick off. I made a face, saying, "Harry—shame! My jerkin will do, when it is brushed, but the rest of me! My hose are in a sorry state . . . and all will guess something of this . . . I have none other. . . ."

"I will send you some scarlet hose—I have outgrown them—and a shirt, all gay with ruffling, worn once only. It will fit you," he said, with a measuring look, "for it shrank after, when it was laundered." And taking hold of all my hair in his fist, he gathered it up behind. "When we have cut your hair, you can be my page—"

I slapped at his hand, teasing too, and so we parted, gay, and I ran up to my tower room, thankful to meet no one on the stairs.

Chapter 9

It was a fair, fine white shirt he sent, and the scarlet of the hose only a little faded from much washing; I felt pleasure in their freshness. Never had I thought, though, to wear boy's gear so many hours in a row. I was beginning to find it most comfortable, and might do credit as a Ganymede if ever I were at court again and masque-playing the fashion.

Though this second night we came early to hall, before the first meat course had gone around, yet we found many of the soldiery far gone in their cups already. I thought, in faith, that the whole Lancaster force was rotten-ripe to fall, if this was the measure of its defenders; I was going over in my mind my reports to Owen— when we should be safe back home.

This time, we were led to the high table, where Denis Burnell sat with his lady, a thin, dark magpie creature, richly dressed. I learned later she was a London tanner's daughter only, so that explained why Alice sat with us there too, making all even, so to speak. There were some lords there, too, beside the Percy, that I had not seen before, Le Despenser and de la Pole. Harry was late, slipping in next to me when the pasty was brought in, smelling strong of rosewater and dressed fancily, though all in black. His tunic was rich velvet, embroidered in silver, and he wore a short cloak, flung back to show its lining of silver, too.

"Are they crowning you tonight?" I whispered meanly, and he pinched me under the table.

"You have the shirt on backwards," he said.

I sought a place to pinch him in return, but his boy's muscles were too hard, so raked my fingernails, none too gently, against his leg. I think that Hotspur saw, for he wagged his finger at me, grinning, and I grew all hot. And so we giggled and played the fool through all the speeches, while most of the company swilled. They were dull speeches truly, with no cheering, and no songs such as we have at home, and concerned taxation and boundaries mostly, I think, though Hotspur drew up a list of monies due him that was to go to the king. All present huzzahed at that, so I gathered that Lancaster owed them all. The prince simply shrugged and said, *"Mea non culpa,"* at which all laughed.

There were a good many Cistercian monks about; I recognized them from their habits, thinking shame of them, for it is a Welsh order, owing allegiance to Owen. There were a group of minstrels, too, at one end of the hall, near the entrance, some bards, even, among them. I noticed they did not stick together, as such folk do usually, but roamed about the room, listening and looking curiously at the fallen drunkards and the dicing soldiers. I caught sight, too, of that Hywele Sele whom I had seen last evening. Again he played a kind of small torture on his attendant henchman, who was already snoring among the rushes. I looked more closely at this man, too, seeing him swarthy and, it seemed, small, though he was lying down; he was covered, even to his hands, with thick black hair. "Who is that fellow?" I asked Harry and pointed.

"Davy Gam, he is called, though that is a kind of nickname . . . I do not know his true name—but he is your father's blackest enemy, to hear him talk."

"He is black, anyway," I said, wrinkling up my nose.

"Do not be so nice, my pretty," he said, laughing. "He is only halfway to an ape . . . and he is a loyal Lancaster. . . ."

"I'll warrant," I said. "I can read it all over him—"

"Be careful, girl—I will have you up for treason. . . ." In truth, Harry took his father's cause most lightly; I think that he still, at that time, thought all this strife would be settled shortly, without much shedding of blood.

We watched the Lord of Nannau, swaying a little, laboriously take a smoldering splinter from the fire and hold it to the sole of Davy Gam's thin leather boot; he would hold it there, very still, till the heat penetrated somewhat to the insensible figure, then the foot would draw up, as if involuntarily and curl against the other calf, though the man did not wake. This gave Hywele Sele much glee, and he would heat the brand again and apply it to the other foot till the process was repeated; I thought it the occupation of a backward boy, rather than a man of responsible nature. I saw that one of the bard minstrels was struck by this pantomime, too, and stood watching from some little distance. I looked again at this man; there was somewhat familiar about him, but I could not put my mind upon it. It was perhaps his calling and his dress, like so many at home, but there was something else, too. Though his long beard was white, and his face, where it showed under his minstrel's hood, looked brown as parchment, yet he stood tall, taller than any in that hall. As he saw me watching, he bent his back, turning and reaching his hands out to the fire. Just another poor begging bard, I thought, with no voice left and little music to his strings.

The food was plentiful, but something greasy, and I had no knife to cut my meat. Harry cut it up for me and fed me morsels from his hand; we made a merry thing of it, I pretending to be his pet dog, and making sounds like little barks and lickings. Rhisiart, three places down, wore a look of disgust, so haughty-Norman that we two were sent off into giggles anew. Truly some spirit of foolery had entered us this night! Harry said, attempting to ape Hotspur's North Country speech, "Hinny—thee has a'most the mumming-genius of thy wold fader—" which dissolved me anew, for it so lacked ear. I replied, he, for sure, took after his own dullard dad, who must have, as I had heard, ever a paid fool about to do his mimicry for him. "Oh, aye," he said, sober for a moment and something sad, I thought. "The sun will set in the east before ever poor Hercules may imitate any man . . . though he is an agile mountebank, for sure. . . ."

I was curious and thought to ask him more but saw something which made me reach out for his hand, to enjoin him to silence. The Lord of Nannau had left off his play-torment and let fall the smoking brand, while he stared at the tall stranger bard. This man stood now at full height again, and as my eyes went to his face, I felt a queer shock go through me. At the same time, Harry's fingers came down tight over my hand. "It is . . . yes, look . . . it is. . . ."

"Owen . . ." I whispered. The white beard had slipped an inch below his chin, and the gleam of gold showed under. The two kinsmen stared, like figures in a masque that have lost their words, while the whole company sat oblivious, and we two, Harry and I, watched as if a spell were on us. From the tail of my eye, I saw that Davy Gam's short bow lay beside him on the floor; the Lord of Nannau fitted arrow to it, took aim, and let fly. My cry came a beat before, and Owen, for it was he, moved to one side. The arrow went through his shoulder, pinning his mantle, and sticking out on the other side. I saw his face quiver with the sudden pain, but he threw back his mantle, drew his bow, fitted the arrow, still with that awful barb through his shoulder and, seemingly without taking aim, shot the man Hywele Sele in the throat. He fell to the floor without a sound, blood pumping in an arc from the vein.

It was an awful tableau, still without sound, except for scattered snoring and the rattle of dice; Hotspur half-rose from his seat but was stopped by Owen's voice, as he stood there, calmly fitting another arrow to the short bow in his right hand. "The first man who makes a move will get my next arrow! The Lord of Nannau lies dead, for his hand shook, and mine did not—nor will! Behind me are my henchmen . . . ready at a word. . . ." And, unbelievably they were, all that force of Cistercians and minstrel men, too, with cloaks flung back and arrows poised. Owen gave an impatient shake of his head, not taking his eyes off the company, and the hood fell back, showing his tawny hair and the iron circlet of Eliseg at his brow. He looked a calm and angry Zeus, ready to loose a thunderbolt.

"I am come for my hostages! If they tell me all is well, we will go in peace—for now. If they have been harmed in any way . . . I have an army at the foot of the hill, a thousand strong, and we will fire this castle. . . ."

No man there had weapon to hand, and none moved. Beside me I heard Harry's voice, clear in the hush. "My lord prince— you may kill me where I sit, for I am unarmed, but I will yet take my farewell of this, my old friend. . . ." And, rising, he pulled me to my feet also. The pointing arrow in Owen's hand shifted, its shaft toward us, and a gasp went up from the table—Alice, maybe, or Burnell's lady. "A kiss will not harm her," said Harry, and, taking me in his arms, he kissed me tenderly and long. Then, taking me by the hand, he led me boldly up to where Owen stood, the arrow never swerving from him all the while.

Right up to arm's length from Owen he led me, giving my father stare for stare. Then he turned me to him, holding me by the shoulders, and said, "I can plight you my heart's troth only, but this will seal it. . . ." And he drew off a ring, slipping it onto my finger in the sight of all. It was a great emerald, my birthstone, though he could not know, circled around most cunningly with a wreath of the little blue flowers that are called forget-me-nots, in sapphire chips. "It is the Lancaster colors. . . ." I whispered.

"Yes," he said, "it was my Grandfather Gaunt's first gift to the Lady Kat, his dearest love—when they were both unfree and could not come together. She gave it me before she died. . . ."

While Owen's arrow stayed upon him, and the men behind aimed at all the company, at the ready, the prince led out each hostage in turn, treating Alice with as much courtesy as if she had been a great lady, till we all stood beside my father. Slowly, deliberately, the fighting monks closed in around us. Owen raised his voice to fill the hall. "Men of Nannau!" he cried. "You are leaderless now—and Welshmen all! I ask you only to think where your heart lies . . . I want no rioting here . . . and my hostages must get safe away . . . but later—we will muster in Glendower valley, under the flag of the red dragon, that was Arthur's. . . ." He finished quietly. "Arthur and his cause bring you to the right!"

He made a sign then with his head and eyes, and his men came in closer. Harry kissed me once again and whispered in my ear, "Forget me not, Morgan. . . ." He bowed then, low, to Owen, and dropped to one knee. "Great prince of the Cymry," he said in Welsh, "take your hostages and go in peace. . . . None will follow, I pledge my word!" None would follow anyway, after the warning Owen had given, but it was a brave speech anyway, and Harry, as I was to learn later, always doted on ceremony and high words.

I saw, as we left the hall, that the hairy fellow, Davy Gam, awake now, cradled his dead master of Nannau in his arms, sobbing and cursing.

There was a pile of longbows stacked beside the door, and many spears leaned against the wall. Several of our men gathered them up on the way; they were well trained already, I thought.

I had imagined we would go over the ruined wall, but the great gate stood open, with its guards fallen, dead maybe, and a man of ours, his monk's robe girded up, keeping watch. We made our way down the hill, slithering and sliding in the loose earth and gravel, for we did not use the road. There were men there, too, though not near the thousand Owen had boasted, with horses pilfered from the stables. Someone helped me to mount, very high it seemed; it was dark there in the shadow of the castle —I could not see my white sleeve even. But when we had ridden a little ways and were onto the flat plain, I saw by the light of the sickle moon and the stars that the mount under me was Mercury; I recognized the bridle and bit, with the arms of Lancaster set in, and the initial *H*. Hotspur had not had time to change them for his own. I said as much to Owen, who rode beside me.

"It is not all you have had of that young cockerel, it seems. . . . Has he had kisses only from you?"

"That is all, Father . . . but yet—we agree well. . . ."

"I doubt it not. . . . He is a bonny lad—and brave, too. . . ." I heard him chuckle in the dark. "He had no surety I *would* not let fly at him—yet of all the company, only he defied me. . . ."

We rode in silence for a little, each with his own thoughts; then Owen said heavily, "I would not see him debauch you, my Morgan. . . . He has the name of it—for all his tender years. . . ."

"We have jested a little . . . and he has sung me songs . . . that is all. We were friends when we were children, and he lodging at the Tower. . . ."

"Aye—I remember . . . poor Richard loved him well."

I said then, "The Baron of Nannau—will they cry vengeance for him, do you think?"

"I know not," he said, slowly. "He drew first . . . and I care not either. It is the end to an old feud." We did not speak then for a while, I feeling he had somewhat more to say and waiting for it.

Owen sighed, and I looked sharply at him but could not read his face in the near-dark. "I have not spoken of this to any . . . but long ago, when we were boys still, he did me a great grievance, this my kinsman. We had been used to winter in the south at a manor of ours there, close it was to Nannau, also. . . . There was a damsel there, not noble, but of decent yeoman stock—her father was our seneschal, having lost an arm in the Scottish wars —she was beautiful as an angel, I thought, and holy, too. She meant to go to the nuns at Aberystwyth when she reached the age; my father had dowered her—he had much fondness for that family. She had a real vocation; no one questioned it. She and I—we had played together like sister and brother all our young years—we were very close, though she was not noble. . . . I desired her greatly that last winter, for I was turned old enough then—but I would not have touched her, for that she was promised to God and was my dear friend besides. That baron who lies dead . . . Hywele Sele . . . he saw her one day and took her— whether with her consent or not, I do not know—but carelessly, as though she were a doxy, and left her after without a thought. When she found herself with child, she threw herself into the millrace. . . ." He rode on; I could feel his anger, almost it was a solid thing around him that you could touch. "The wheel was turning, though it was full night, for the miller was a Latin scholar by day. . . . She was crushed against it. It was not a pretty death. . . ."

"Oh, Father," I said, groping for his hand on the reins. I had no words, but my heart swelled for that shy and feeling youth that he had been.

"What was her name?" I asked, after a bit.

"It was the reign of the Black Prince, Edward, when the Welsh were loyal Englishmen. All the maidens then were named after his queen, the fair Maid of Kent, as men called her—Joan. My Joan was called so, also."

"The Lord of Nannau had a black heart," I said. "I'm glad you killed him."

"It is nonetheless another sin to lie heavy on me. . . ."

"The Lollards say," I ventured timidly, "that Jesus forgives all sins—even the blackest—"

"No—that is too easy. . . . There is that within a man that—" He broke off. "Morgan . . . *you* forgive me! Forgive me," he said, very low, "forgive me the sin of your birth. . . ."

I was straightway seized by a great unease; noblemen do not, nor other men either, speak so. I could form no words.

I said, and forced a little laugh, "Oh, sir—I have nothing to forgive, for I would not be here beside you had you not fathered me!"

"You are a good lass to turn the thought so merrily—but I would that you were true-born. . . ."

"That I would not," I answered, meaning it. "For I would be the Argyllwyddes' daughter then—and though I esteem that lady greatly, still I think she could not have made me. . . ."

He laughed then, too, saying, "Well . . . that she could not, poor Margaret . . . and it is done now. . . ."

Walter Brut had been riding apart from us, so as not to over- hear our words, for he had much delicacy in such matters; when he felt us silent, he came near, saying, "My Lord Owen, that arrow ought to come out—"

"You are right, young sir—every time this beast goes over a rut in the road, it stabs again! Over the rise of the next hill, we will stop. There is a goodly moss that grows there by the second stream. The doctors will not have it so, but that moss has healing properties. All the old women knew of it, time out of mind. . . ."

When we came to the spot, he called a halt. His shoulder must have pained him greatly, for he had to be helped from the saddle.

"You, Cousin," he called to Rhisiart, "take a lantern—under that oak tree is a growth of fine moss—gather all you can and bring it back here . . . You, Walter, will you be my surgeon? You must take a sharp knife and cut off the barb, and then pull hard and straight as you can so as to keep the wound clean. It is in the flesh only; a few inches another way and I would be done for." He looked at me; in the lantern light I saw his face strained and white, though he smiled. "We have not even a petticoat to bind up the place."

"Father," I said, "this shirt I wear is clean and soft. I will tear it from below the jerkin, where it does not show . . . it is overlong anyway. . . ."

And so it came to pass that the English prince's linen bound up his enemy's wound over the moss medicine, and the place healed cleanly.

The torn shirt and the hose I laid away in my clothespress; when we fled Glendower House, at the war's worsening, I had to leave them behind. The black stallion Mercury, though, I kept by me always, currying him mostly with my own hands; and the ring I never took off. It was not much to go on, but it was all I had, save for Harry's parting words. Those I told over to myself night after night in my bed through all those long, hard years.

Chapter 10

I never thought to find myself a maid still at twenty-one, though in truth I am a married lady. It is the strange fortunes of war. For we have been at war all this time; I can hardly remember life before it anymore.

After Owen redeemed us four, his hostages, an uneasy truce ruled for a time. The Greys' ransoms were paid, but they had to raise the sum from their own estates. Harry's father would give nothing; they were beggared. Our manor at Glendower House was in constant threat of burning and siege, and many of its defenders were out aforaging or sent to quell some border lord, so Owen feared for us who were living there. In the deep fastnesses of Snowdon Mountain, he found an ancient, ruined fortress and rebuilt it, making it almost impregnable. In the spring of that year, we all removed there, our whole household. I was sorry to go, for it was very gloomy; one could never once forget there that a war was awaging.

We had much company there though, at first, for more and more Welsh students fled there to us for sanctuary, as it were, and to give their swords to the Welsh cause. The little pages from Dinas Brân were among them, with their stolen arms, and they became the pets of all us damsels. We spoiled them sinfully, Lawnslot with the curly hair and the younger Madoc, until that Lawnslot got Owen with child, and they had to marry. It was a disgraceful match, for she was almost nineteen, and a foot taller, but she swore the babe was his, and he did not deny it (though privately I thought that he was bragging only).

Many such odd matches happened during those war years. Walter Brut was true to his word and married Alice; he taught her to read the New Scripture for herself, and they were happy enough, though childless, in the first years of their union. And Efa, that wild girl-thing, ran away with Rhys Gethin, the Savage, and fought beside him in his hills, like another of the same. Actually, in spite of his brute looks and his deeds of terror, he became, in time, one of Owen's most trusted captains, waging his own untrammeled kind of warfare in the dark mountains where he was born; he was the terror of the English borderers, burning and laying waste wherever he appeared. I should not have liked to see him coming at me out of the dark! Though I suppose Efa did not mind; she must have loved him, in some strange way. When he was killed later, and his mangled body borne in on a shield, she took his sword and fell upon it, to keep him company.

The twins, Gwynneth and Gwenllian, wedded their Irish redheads, but they were both killed early, leaving fatherless babes. Modry and Megolin, she who wanted to be a nun, were captured in a raid and, we heard, were made into camp harlots by the English soldiers; I shudder to think of it, for they were delicately bred. The Argyllwyddes ran out of hair dye, and her hair all turned white; she looked an old woman and unhappy, and her flesh hung on her, for she worried it away. Catherine has been happy, in a sort. But I am running ahead of my story.

I do this often now, mixing things up, like some old dotard who cannot remember yesterday but can count the dishes on his fifth birthday feast-table. But that, perhaps, is understandable, the state we are all come to lately.

I will try to set it all down in order, though it is hard to sort out. The year after we moved to Snowdon Mountain was the year of the great comet that blazed across the sky and that all Wales called Owen's Star. In England, too, it struck fear in enemy hearts, and no armies marched against us while it stayed. It was indeed an awesome sight. I remember we all rushed out on the grim ramparts to watch it when it first appeared. It was a freezing cold night in February, though no snow fell; our nostrils were all caked with our frozen breath, and our hands numb. The sky was blue-black, and, in the northwest, against it, that vast body of flame, trailing a huge, fiery train of lesser stars, like a swarm of burning insects. It was as bright, too, as noon, dimming the torches, and illuminating the mountain around about. The bard improvised a song that first night, of its glory, and its portent to Wales, and the soldiers all shouted victory for Owen, but he himself sat deep in thought, his tankard full before him and untouched. "It is," he said finally, to those of us who sat beside him, "no prophecy for me, no augury, but some mystery of the firmament, a star dying—or being born. . . . Someday astronomers will predict these things. . . ." Owen had a fine room at

Glendower House, all roofed with glass, and in it instruments for
star-watching he had brought back from the Eastern lands,
where they have much knowledge of such things; it is all destroyed by now, no doubt, along with the rest of that manor. The
rumor of that chamber got about among the ignorant folk, and
they deemed it a warlock's chamber, where magic was worked,
but Owen studied the stars there and charted their courses on
great sheets of parchment.

The great comet lasted in the sky some three weeks; by the end
of March it had disappeared. The weather, though, never
warmed up, as it does usually, and snow lay on the mountain
throughout the month of May; the peaks, even, were still snow-
capped in July. It was the worst year of cold any man could remember. The fortress was drafty, too, and we all had frostbitten
fingers and noses that ran when we came near a fire. It was a
great year of victory though for Wales, and the comet seemed
truly to have foretold it.

That spring Hotspur came over to us with his father, the Earl
of Northumberland, and his uncle, Thomas of Percy. They made
a treaty with Scotland, too, where they had just defeated the
great Douglas, so we had many allies, all with their followers in
the thousands. Owen took all the large cities, even into South
Wales, and all men felt victory was sure. At the great battle of
Bryn Glas, the Welsh archers hired by the English army turned
their arrows on their masters, and turned the tide for Owen. It
was in that battle that Lord Edmund Mortimer was captured,
which led to a great change in our lives, Catherine's and mine, at
least.

This lord was close to the English throne; his nephew was that
Mortimer who was the rightful heir and whom Harry's father
had imprisoned when he usurped the kingdom. He had been all
these years in the Tower, in captivity. Mortimer, too, was brother
to Hotspur's lady-wife, so he was with us really, underneath, for
all these reasons. Also, I think he fell under Owen's spell, as some
impressionable young men do. He was a fair young man, something frail in looks, but with straight neat features to his face. His
only flaw was a too-short upper lip, which gave him a prettiness
more suited to a girl.

He was treated more as an honored guest than a prisoner,
spending much time with all the household, and Catherine in

particular. Catherine had fallen out of love with Rhisiart as though he had never been, and when Mortimer asked for her hand from Owen, she needed no urging but consented. I said long ago that she fell in and out of love easily. It was a good match though, for it brought Owen's house close to the rightful English heirs; there was much of policy in it, of course, though I think Owen would never have forced it if she had been unwilling. At least, I thought, he is not marrying her to Harry!

Rhisiart took the news of the betrothal badly, going about in his black clerk's gown and sitting glum at meat. But after they were married, his spirits seemed to lift; I guessed he judged it hopeless then. The couple conceived right away, and Catherine bore her first child a bare nine months after the wedding day. It was a boy, and they called it Edmund, too. So there was a Welsh heir now among the closest claimants to the English throne!

Harry was wounded in the battle of Shrewsbury, where Hotspur died, and where the other Percys were taken captive. At first report (for we have spies in all the English camps) they had it that he had lost an eye, and I wept for days. Later, though, it was confirmed that it was a flesh wound only, at the temple; he fell ill of it though, for it festered, and he was abed for weeks. They say he fought bravely, going back into battle after the wounding and turning the tide. It was our first defeat, though Owen's army did not join them, for the river was in flood, and they could not get through. It was a big setback nonetheless, though, for all our allies were scattered after. Both the elder Percys were put to death, horribly, with quartering and beheading; I took comfort that Harry could have had no part in it, being so sick. They were handled as traitors, their remains displayed to the sight of all, as trophies and warnings, too. Poor Hotspur was given honorable burial for his past great reputation. After, though, that same reputation dishonored him, for the whole country refused to believe he was dead, and reports flew around that he had been seen, true to his nickname, spurring hot for the north. Lancaster could not afford to let his bones rest, for such rumors are dangerous to an unsteady throne, and so he was dug up and his body dismembered; the head was stuck up on London Bridge, and other parts elsewhere, I forget the places. It is a grisly thought—that proud, bold man!

For long, though, the war seemed to be going our way, in spite of the Shrewsbury disappointment. Owen took town after town and fort after fort. Prophecies were made, wild and ringing, by a man dressed up like Merlin, in a tall cone-shaped hat and long robes covered with cabalistic signs. He looked a freak to me, with his toothless mouth that distorted all his words, but the whole company was much impressed; I have forgot his name.

He said that Wales would have two Parliaments (which came true, for Owen called them together that same year). He said also that a maid in armor would lead a nation to victory and anoint a king at his crowning. This was interpreted by many to point the way to one of us damsels (whom they had all seen riding in boys' gear) leading Owen to the throne of England. An armorer in Aberystwyth even went so far as to make a silver armor, small enough for a girl and present it to Owen "for his warmaiden"! Owen shook his head though and laughed a little. He said he could not feel to take a maid to battle, her tender flesh bruised by the metal. Also, he said, he did not seek the English throne or even the Welsh, but justice only for Wales and the people. His enemies ever rejected this and called him, in derision, King Owen. The old seer said also that a Tudor of Mona would sit upon the English throne and found a dynasty. "I cannot fathom that prophecy," said Owen privately. "There was only little Efa, who is of Mona, but illegitimate, and she is dead now . . . and another, Owen Tudor, a distant kinsman of mine. But he is far away, at the French court, and is only petty nobility, without wealth or power." At any rate the seer foretold also that the Lancasters would plunge England into a war that would last a hundred years before it was done. Which would seem to me to cancel out all the other prophecies.

Later, Owen made a treaty with the French, who gave him men and even cannons, and many more towns were taken and hopes ran high. We removed again, though, for the Argyllwyddes feared another winter on Snowdon. We went to Harlech Castle, which has one whole side to the sea and stands on a high hill besides. It is the strongest castle in Wales, they say. It is pleasanter, certainly, for the seaward side is all open, with many windows and balconies, and the breeze from the sea is westering and never cruel. Catherine's two other children were born here—a boy and girl. With these three and the twins' babes, and Olwen's, we have six children among us who know nothing but war!

Meredith was wounded, it was thought mortally, in a minor battle in a town I cannot recall. He recovered, though, for Elliw nursed him lovingly for months. He has lost the use of an arm, though, and limps badly, too. But at least he will not have to fight again. After a long time he consented to marry Elliw, who loves him dearly. I think he loves her too, but he will not give her children. He says he will not bring a child into a world as ugly and war-torn as this. He has changed greatly since his long recovering; he thinks Owen should give up the quarrel and surrender. I am of his mind, too, but Owen says he cannot now, he is committed to too much, to the good of Wales, and to the hope of the peasantry. He is right, of course, and in honor he cannot fail them, but, oh, it is a weary struggle. With all our victories, and even with the French to help, we have still not won, and Lancaster keeps coming back still in new places. Owen says it is the boy he fears, meaning Harry. Reports are that Harry is the real warrior there now; indeed, his father has left him lately in full command; they say he is ill almost unto death, the king.

On the eve of the battle of Usk, Owen called me to him, saying that he feared greatly to leave me always without a protector and asked if I would not wed with Rhisiart. He had hoped, he said, to find a nobler match for me but says that he esteems Rhisiart greatly, though he is a penniless man, and in any case I have a fine dower. I was taken aback, for Rhisiart had said nothing to me, only spoke for me to Owen; perhaps it is the Norman way. I do not love him, and indeed I think for him, too, I will always be second best. We agree well though, and in a kind of reasonableness and weary, too, I consented. We were married in the little chapel here at noon, with Owen reading the services, for none of the priests are left among us. They left for battle an hour later, Owen going with a large host to push forward over the English border, and Rhisiart, with all the brothers that are left, to Usk. I have not seen him since.

He was captured in that battle, and Walter Brut with him; I know not if he lives. Owen's brother Tudor was killed that day, and Griffith, his oldest son. Griffith was the Argyllwyddes' favorite, and she will not be comforted and blames Owen. She says he took the safer course and left her son to die. It is cruel and untrue, but she is nearly mad with grief.

We will all go mad, truly, I think, those of us that are left. We have been under siege here at Harlech for nearly eight months. There is only Meredith left among the men; the Lord Mortimer, Catherine's husband, was in command, but he died the second month. It looked like the plague, and we buried him quickly to escape the contagion; he was unshriven, but none of us here are very religious anymore. I keep remembering what Walter said, the Lollard—that all men, all living things, when they die, rest in the lap of Jesus. Since Mortimer, there have been more than twenty plague-deaths, all buried in a common grave; among them were Catherine's two youngest, she has only the little Edmund left. Though they are buried all, there is still a plague-stench. It clings to our clothes and hair even; whatever we eat seems to taste of it.

This last does not matter, for we have almost nothing to eat in any case. All the dogs and horses have been eaten; Mercury went early, I could not refuse, to save human lives. I hope if Harry hears he will forgive me. They say he is outside the walls, commanding the siege. I one time went up on the wall to look, but could not see him among the multitude below.

The Argyllwyddes died last night, poor lady, about the hour of vespers. We none of us would eat the rat stew she made, flavored with leeks. Meredith told her rats cannot be eaten, for they carry contagion, but she was crazed, I think, and scolded us for refusing cooking from her own hands, like some silly proud housewife. She died from that, I am sure, for she ate it as eagerly as if it were fine venison. It is dreadful to think on; she has the plague-look too, all black about the face and the tongue protruding. There are none to bury her; we are all too weak. I watch Meredith move, slowly, as if he walked under water, and know that I am the same. Catherine cannot walk at all, but lies in her own filth. She does not make a sound, but little Edmund moans constantly and calls for water. There is none left. Our lips are horribly cracked and our voices croak; we are walking skeletons besides. I am wearing my jerkin and hose now, for I fear the men outside if we fall into their hands. I hacked my hair off with an old kitchen-knife last week; it is a rough job but perhaps will make me look like a page and save me from raping. The others of us women have not that much energy, most of them just lie about. Truly, I cannot think who would want to ravish us, for we are all subhuman by now, but they say that soldiers are desperate.

Meredith says we must surrender, or we will surely all die, even if Owen's troops get through to us tomorrow. By then it will be too late. Catherine is the only other one with authority, and she is unconscious. I nod my head, for I cannot get a sound from my parched throat. Maybe Harry, if he is outside there, will save me from the soldiers . . . maybe he will even give me water . . . Oh, Harry—for a little drop of water. . . .

BOOK III

The Father

*(Told by Sir Hercules,
the king's fool)*

Chapter 1

I am called the king's fool, or jester, some say. I have never jested in my life, even before I became what I am. As a small child I did not grow as my brothers and sisters did; I was puny and weak, like the runt of a litter. Had my mother not begged for my life, I should surely have been exposed on the bare craggy outcroppings of Navarre, where I was born.

As it was, I grew a little; when I was eight, I had the stature of a healthy two-year-old. I was not deformed and, I think, not ugly then, though none of us had ever looked into a mirror. We were twelve children there, I the youngest, on our few small, near-barren acres. I can remember very little of my brothers and sisters, save that they hit me and threw stones, spitting, for they feared my oddity. I was much alone, with whatever thoughts I had. I did not know then that I was clever, but clever I must have been. I could make songs in my head and sing words to them, too, and I could coax music out of the simplest reed pipe. My mother protected me, saving scraps from her own plate, for my food was always stolen by my biggest brothers. When she died, I almost starved, until my father sold me.

You do not think children are sold in this year of grace, 1409? I assure you it is true still, as it was then, not so many years ago. You have only to go to the remoter provinces, where famine lies heavy on the land; human beings cannot live on air. My father got a silver piece for me, more than he had ever held in his hand before. I do not blame him. Neither do I remember him with love, for I did not know its face. My mother may have loved me; she sometimes laid a pitying hand lingeringly on my hair; I know she never held me in her arms as she did those other, large children that were hers, too.

I was bought by a group of strolling mountebanks; they were not unkind folk, easygoing and generous, too, when they had the wherewithal. They fed me well, on wine and lean meats mostly, for they did not want me to grow. They trained me, too; by the time I was ten I could turn three somersaults in the air and come down on a shoulder, and I knew every song in their repertoire, besides my own. The people laughed and applauded me in every market town; I was known as the Little Flea. My success was assured, and I grew to love their laughter; it was a good life for a little creature.

Then, alas, when I reached thirteen, I began to grow. I filled out, and my arms and legs lengthened. I reached the height I am now, about that of a ten-year-old boy, and there I stopped. I was still small, but I was no longer the Little Flea. Indeed, I was no longer of any use, for a clever ten-year-old is no novelty. At the next large market town, I was sold again.

They wept, those player-folk, for their hearts are given easily, and they made me parting gifts—sweetmeats and little trinkets. I wept, too, for I feared the large man who had paid over the money; his hand, as he felt my muscles, had been rough and heavy, though his clothes were fine.

I had done right to fear, for what came after was nightmare. You would not believe, indeed, but that my face is here before you, living proof that I do not lie.

My new masters were another kind of player, and of a higher sort; they were mummers, and played in real plays, with story and action, each taking one part. The plays themselves are all much alike; the big part is for the "good man" who is beset by devils and triumphs in the end; that part, though, is dull and cloddish, for there is nothing in it to laugh at. The real star parts are for the imps of Satan, who can do anything they like to be funny and entertaining, before the course of the play vanquishes them, and they are led off in chains, back to hell. These parts are taken by all manner of folk, so long as they be ugly or deformed, because people like to laugh at such unfortunates. The new play-people had seen me perform and knew me talented; I needed a real deformity to play an imp, aside from my small stature.

I was too old by then, nearly fourteen, to cripple by iron braces on my back, for my bones had set, and they could not break my legs, for then I would lose my mobility.

They have skilled surgeons from the East to do what was done on me, and poppy drugs to dull the pain; it is outlawed, to be sure, for the practice is going out, and the operation must be done in secret. I have seen older mountebanks with nostrils split like felons or eyes that bulged hugely from slitting; there are many such freaks of the knife still about. On me they carved a laugh! It is more of a grin, really, for the lips are removed, and the teeth exposed right round to the back jaw. I needed no skill on the stage after that, for the crowd roared at first sight of me, though it cut down my effectiveness as a singer, for the words whistle without the lips to form them. I have only looked into a mirror once; I saw fine, curling, brown hair on a broad brow, and eyes, brown, too, and intelligent as a spaniel's, and below— well, you have seen.

I was, in my time, the greatest of the imps; folk flocked to see me at each saint's day; in the courts, too, they paid much money for my services. I saw none of it, of course, except for my board and keep, and got little satisfaction from my work either. I do not know now, truly, why I took such pains to be at the top of my profession, for the laugh that greeted my first appearance never ceased to stab at my heart. But always I would give them more, and they loved me, my audiences, in their way. I was envied, too, by my fellows, especially the younger ones. Many times I have heard a childish voice beg to "have a laugh made, like Hercules!" This you will hardly credit, but it is a strange profession.

My name, Hercules, came from the first imp I played. Often the imps were called for pagan gods, to discredit them. The name stuck, because of my small size, and the paradox of it. I was famous throughout Navarre. The duke there paid such a price for me that the company all went into retirement and lived on the proceeds. And that was how I came to court.

He was a good man, the duke, and kind, though the Lady Joanna, his daughter, used to pinch me cruelly whenever she was out of temper. He gave me to her when she went into Brittany to marry there, though I begged to stay with him in Navarre. He said she needed some lightness about her, for she was to wed the old Breton duke, a man much older than her father himself.

He was not too old to give her children though, that duke, and they mellowed her somewhat. Two daughters and four sons she had of him, and much loving courtesy. He was a wise and gentle man, the Duke of Brittany, and I wept when he died, though none saw.

When the new-made King of England sued for my widowed duchess' hand, she looked upon him with favor, for he had been at the Breton court during his exile, a handsome, ruddy fellow.

She sent me to him as earnest of her intent; a princely gift, for my name was known throughout Europe. My fame did not keep them from shipping me chained in a cage like a monkey though. I was sick all the way across the channel.

My first sight of my new master, King Henry IV of England, put me near to swooning; I had need of all my mummer's art to keep the leap of recoil from my eyes. He was clad all in armor, though the day was hot, and he sat at meat indoors; his hands were bandaged clear up the forearm, the fingers swollen like sausages. His face—well, in a sort, it was worse than mine. His high handsomeness was gone, and ulcerous sores covered it, where there were not dead scabs clinging; his hair, too, had scabby sores under it and was mostly gray, with here and there a gleam of brassy red like a mocking ghost-light. He spoke heavily, too, his voice limping. The illness which ravaged him has no name, for the doctors pronounce it a mystery. By some it is called Saint Anthony's Fire—others name it ergot; I have even heard leprosy whispered. Ho-ho, I thought, my fine lady, will you bed with this? For I had not much love for the Duchess Joanna.

He spake me civilly though, commanding a sample of my art then and there, to amuse his sons, who sat with him, all but the eldest, then on an early campaign in Wales. I had not much stomach for it, being still sick from the sea, but I sang and capered, giving of my best, for it is my trade. The young boys, lively as jackdaws, beat their hands together and drummed their heels, laughing and shouting, and all the company cheered. When I had finished, the king tossed me a little purse of velvet, embroidered with pearls and heavy with coin. "What say you, He Who Laughs?" said the monarch, without a smile. "Will you wear my livery?"

"I had as lief stay in my own," I answered, for I wore always a red imp suit, with horns and pitchforked tail; I had several of them, of all cloths and weights, gifts from my first duke. And I added, low, for license is my trade, too, and I saw sardony in his blue eyes, "If it please you—King of Scabs!" I bowed low, waiting. And it came, his laughter, rich and loud, filling the hall. He laughed till the tears ran down among his boils and ulcers, and the whole company sat, uneasy and mystified, for none had heard our exchange.

"A doughty fellow you are indeed, sirrah! Well, well—you will

wear my Lancaster badge over your heart, anyway—so that all
men know us for brothers . . . I like you well, little brother . . ."
And he tossed me another purse, larger than the first, before he
stalked from the room, clanking in his armor.

That was my first encounter with the man who, I think, is
loved by none but me. We are, as the Lombards say, *simpatico*.
Poor big and little brother!

The sons of Lancaster I studied well, finding them all different
under their like comely faces; Tom is careless and something
rough of tongue, and has little thought for anything but hunting
and hawks, John is quiet, and Humphrey sly. The eldest, the
young Henry, I did not see till he was called back for his father's
wedding.

The Lady Joanna had been warned of her groom's skin affliction, for she wore a gauze veil to escape contagion. She had not, I
think, been told how long this affliction had lain upon him, near
nine months now, or the havoc it had wrought with his visage, for
I heard behind her face-veil a gasp when her eyes met his. The
Prince Henry heard, too, and when he bent to kiss her hand, his
eyes were hostile. He turned away and, as if idly, but clear
enough, said to Tom, who stood behind him, "Is our new stepmother a blackamoor then, that she hides her face?" Tom
laughed, in his thoughtless way, and I saw my master frown.
They quarrel much among themselves, this family, even to the
little girls, but they are a clannish lot and do not like outsiders. I
saw the lady-queen would have her hands full with this brood,
besides the calamity of the new husband's health; almost I could
have pitied her. Indeed, it is six years now since she first came to
England, and the prince treats her still with no more than cool
courtesy.

He is another cut of cloth from his brothers, though all share
the warm brown coloring they are said to have got from their
mother. He has a long and oval-shaped face, very still, like a
beast ready to spring. Though he is a scant year older than Tom,
he bore himself like a man, while Tom was a very boy. I saw the
prince that day lean and hard as a veteran fighter, though he
had been then only months in the Welsh marches. They said,
though, that he had ever excelled at all sports and at jousting;
men named him the finest athlete in the realm. They named him
other, too; he had a taste for wine, and women, too, already, at

fifteen. The Tavern Prince, they called him, and laughed. The Lancasters are not popular rulers; my master was named usurper still behind his back and plotted against, though Richard, whom he deposed, was a weakling and beggared the country. But then, I heard my first duke say once that England had ever hated her kings.

The young prince was not all fighter and roisterer. He had much love of learning and wrote a fine hand. His Latin, too, was better than mine, though my Navarrese master had me taught by a scholar. He did not laugh at my antics, this prince, though he applauded with the others and gifted me handsomely; I sensed he found my carven mask hard to look upon. He would take my lute, though, with a will, and play upon it with some skill. Songs of his own making he would play; they are good, though not so good as my own. He has been much away, during these years, fighting the Welsh. Each time he returned he was taller and leaner and harder, too, with a stiller face. There is a scar, also, at his temple, star-shaped, like a third eye, that he got at the battle of Shrewsbury.

This Shrewsbury fight was the first loss the Welsh suffered; before, all had gone their way. Father and son both fought in this battle, though; after, the king's sickness kept him abed a good part of the time. Young Henry brought home from camp an Oxford physician, who had tended him for a fever after his wound. He set great store by this man, for he was skilled in all the newer practices. He brought him to his father, who lay suffering from a gnawing pain in his vitals; he was dizzy, too, and often vomited blackish blood. Nicholas Colnet was the doctor's name; he was closeted for some hours with the sick man. He did not bleed him, for he held it did no good but only weakened. When he came out, his face was very long. "I think," he said, slowly, "that it is not leprosy. I think it is not contagious, either, for none close to him have taken it, not even his lady-wife, or the maids who handle his slops . . . I think it is a disease of the ancients, that eats away tissue as it runs its course. They called it the Crab, for its persistent gnawing. . . . There is no cure." He looked up, seeing the prince's face white and shocked. "He may yet live long . . . he must rest. This illness abates sometimes, and the patient will seem better—but then it gnaws again . . . and in the end. . . ."

He laid his hand on the prince's shoulder. "But the end is not yet. . . ."

The prince swallowed and spoke falteringly. "His face—will it not mend?"

"It is the same thing gnawing at his outside," answered Colnet. "His body is worse eaten under his clothes. We can do no more than lay soft cloths for protection . . . there is no pain though, from the sores . . . and I will give him a drug for the other."

When the Queen Joanna heard there was no contagion, she left off the wearing of her face-veil; I saw her cheeks were plumper and the flesh beginning to sag, though her eyes are black and shining still, and her looks pretty, in a swarthy way. I think she does not share the king's bed, even when he is up and about and home from the wars; I think he dreads her disgust and so forbears. But she suffers from it, for she has naught to occupy her days either. She has taken to eating largely and sitting long at table over the wine. She wears new dresses every day and changes her style of hair often; I can see that her stepsons think her frivolous and silly. She has about her, too, many Breton ladies that dabble in herb lore and even sorcery, in a small way. She is forever making new pastes for the king's face, usually from such loathsome ingredients as toad's blood and bat excrement; he wears them to please her. Some days his face is all white and stiff with a powdery concoction; other days it may be a green color and shiny. She giggles with her women over love philters, too, and they make eyes, all, at whoever is about the court. The days of the Courts of Love are going out, when every lady had swains who swore to love her in all purity and obey her every command; this world is too modern now for that. The Lady Joanna, though, would like to have them back, for she is bored.

I have not said much about Lollardy, which is another disease that eats at my king. There is none abroad, in parts where I have lived, but in England they say one out of every three is Lollard, and the war in Wales is, in somewise, being fought over it, for the Baron Glendower much favors this sect, and many who love the New Learning have flocked to his standard. Myself, I cannot care one way or the other, for religion does not make good sense to me, as you can understand. What God would have made me unlike my fellows or allowed men to work bestiality upon me for profit? And yet folk are dying in the flames in the name of God, and fighting on the field too!

My master, though, is not a thoughtful man and is much swayed by his crafty archbishop besides. I think he seeks, by his persecution of heretics, to ease his own sins. Archbishop Arundel is a high-born prelate, elder kinsman by marriage to King Henry; he has been given much power in the realm. Though he is a man of God, he has a face of pure evil, the lines bitter and deep and the eyes hooded as a falcon's. When I attend my master by Arundel's side, for sure the three of us could consume the poor heretic with plain fear, without the aid of fire! That man of God, Arundel, has sworn to make all heretics "hop headless" and "fry faggots"; he has a grisly, monkish humor.

I have witnessed one such burning, and I wish never to see another. There was a certain tailor of Evesham, his name was John Badby, if I remember right. He had refused to accept the theory of transubstantiation. This is a point of doctrine on which all the Lollards agree, though they argue among themselves on others. This is also one of the basic laws of the True Church, so he was sentenced to die at the stake, and was turned over, as is the custom, to the secular arm. There had been no such executions in that part of the country before, and the authorities were uncertain of procedure. Thinking to deal mercifully, they had fashioned a wooden cask, large enough to hold a man, and they put him inside, with the faggots heaped under. They had considered he would die there inside, with his agonies unseen; they had forgot that wood burns faster.

The king was there, and Arundel, and the prince was commanded to attend, as a lesson; he had many friends among these heretics, at Oxford and in the taverns of London, where they teach, defying the law. As for myself, my master, at this time, was in the habit of taking me with him everywhere, as one might bring a pet dog. I saw the prince pale as porridge under his campaign-weathered face, and a muscle beside his mouth twitched visibly. He carried a sheaf of papers, rolled up.

The marketplace was gay, hung with the Lancaster colors, and the arms of Holy Church, and crowded with folk, all dressed in their holiday best, and jostling one another for the first places. Vendors threaded between them, selling smoked eels. A little breeze carried their smell, pungent and oily. The king sat under a small tent, blue and white, raised from the crowd by several wooden steps. It was a rare day for England, diamond-bright, with a hint of frost in the air.

The prince spoke to his father. "Sire, give me leave to speak with the prisoner—"

The king gestured. "It is for your lord archbishop to give. . . ."

Arundel half-turned, his face malevolent under that gaudy canopy. He shrugged a little. "It is out of my hands. You must seek the secular arm."

Below us sat the mayor, the sheriff, and whatever dignitaries the town possessed. The prince went down the steps and spoke to them, low. They answered, and I heard his voice rise, a little shrill as I had never heard it, "But the man must have a chance to recant! It is the law!"

The prince came up the steps again, turning to his uncle, Henry Beaufort, "Sire, they have sealed the cask with lead—I cannot speak with the man—"

Beaufort rose. "This is a miscarriage of justice, Your Majesty — The man must have a chance to recant—to save his soul. . . ."

"Quiet, boy—" said the archbishop. "They are lighting the faggots!" He leaned forward in his seat.

The first small flames licked up, while the whole crowd fell silent. Suddenly the cask burst into flames like a torch. As the wood burned away quickly, for a mere second the hoops remained, white-hot, then fell to the ground, leaving the prisoner standing in his chains and penitent's robe.

The prince ran to the mayor again, in his excitement grabbing at the man's robe, so that it came away in his hands. We could not hear his words for the yelling of the crowd, blooded now. But we saw soon that the prisoner had his chains struck off and was brought to the prince. There was a little hush, for this was an unusual proceeding. The prince unrolled his sheaf of papers, holding them up to the doomed man's sight. "Look—look—here is what you must say . . . I had it from Walter Brut, who escaped the stake . . . the bread and wine become the body and blood of Christ in a *spiritual* sense . . . it remains bread . . . but *more* than bread . . . do you hear? *More* than bread. . . ." We saw him strained, his hand shaking where it held the papers. The man thus brought forward was all blackened by the smoke already, and some of his hair singed away, but his swollen lips curved in a little smile; we saw that he was past middle age. It was plain that he took the prince for a student only, for his dress was sober and he bore no arms.

"Master Scholar," the tailor said, "you waste breath . . . the bread is bread only, and the wine . . . it remains thus . . . Our Saviour has no need of miracles . . . it remains bread. . . ."

What followed is too dreadful to tell. They bound the man again, relighting the faggots; he began to sing, in a high, reedy voice, a hymn I did not know. The Cardinal Beaufort led the prince back to his seat. I heard him say, "Father, I have served you well these last years in Wales—give me leave to go from here. . . ."

"You will stay," said my master, heavily; the prince fell to his knees, as did Beaufort. The flames leaped up again, hiding the tailor from view, but we heard the singing change to a long drawn-out howl of animal agony, and a horrible stench of burning filled the air.

They have since, I heard, in these executions, employed the sweet young voices of choirboys to drown out the victim, but these were early days still. He screamed horribly until the end.

"Bring your head up, Harry," hissed his father. "Do not shame Lancaster before the whole realm. . . ." The prince stared ahead then, stiff as a statue. And I . . . whenever a drop of candle wax falls on my hand, I think of these poor wretches in the flames. The smell of smoked eels, also, ever turns my stomach, and I have not eaten them since that day.

Chapter 2

The rebellion in Wales, after seven long years, is now well-nigh put down, though there are scattered skirmishes even now. Glendower looked often to be winning, for he had, at the end, the help of the French king, Charles of Valois, men and cannon, too. He had penetrated all the way into our English shires of Hereford and Monmouth, but at the end the French help was withdrawn, and so the English came to victory after great losses. Much of the countryside is left in waste, though it is said that in Wales the destruction is even greater. Glendower has slipped the noose, though, and cannot be found, though most of his family has been killed or captured; they say he is hiding in his own dark hills and will come again at the call of his countrymen, but they are ever superstitious, the Welsh. The nobles that followed him are punished with death or imprisonment and their lands confiscated, though there is not much left in that waste for Lancaster; war does little for the victor either, as my first duke said. Glendower's peasant army is decimated, their hopes of betterment gone, and men say the Lollards are all flown, too. I know for a fact, though, that many hide here in our London taverns. Never would I give any away though, for I would not be party to such cruelty as I saw once done.

My master, the king, has grown overpious; he had not before paid more than lip service to his God. Some say he fears his own death, seeing its marks on his ailing body, and is consumed by great remorse; I know not. For sure, he pardons none, neither Welsh nor English of the traitors; they have all suffered horribly. The commons do not love him; they hail his son, the prince, though, as he rides past them, deeming him the great young savior of their land. Much hostility had grown of late between these two Henrys, father and son. The father resents that the people show their love for the youthful hero, and the son chafes under the strict controls put upon him and the poorness of his purse, too, for the king owes him for his duties in Wales and has not paid, and withholds his allowance, too. It is true that young

Henry often goes short; I have loaned him monies myself, for the
king is generous to his fool. He is in debt, too, to all his attendant
nobles, though all they have comes from him in the first place.
He keeps, when he is home, a fine house of his own though. It is
called Coldharbour, a fair mansion in the Chepe, belonging to
Sir William Poultney. It is laid all about with fine fruit trees, enclosed in green lawns, walled with brick, and with one garden-
end open to the Thames. The prince could not have afforded it,
but Sir William owed him favor for saving his Hereford lands
from Glendower, and asked no more rent than a rose on Midsummer's Day. It is a pretty conceit, that. Sir William was one of
the lords dead Richard had about him; they were all effete and
fanciful. He is an honored guest in his own house, with the pick
of all Henry's helm-cut train, so all is even. It is, though, a dwell-
ing of great charm and sweetness; I have spent much time there
myself, my services borrowed while my kingly master lay ill and
the prince entertained. It was there, to that mansion in the
Chepe, that Henry brought the girl men called the Welsh Har-
lot, or, some said, Owen's whore.

This last, certainly, is not true; she is the daughter of Glendower, out of wedlock, from some well-born Welsh lady. She herself, too, I have found to be a lady of true and noble heart, with a
fine learning and wit besides. But men will ever speak ill of those
in high places.

It was after the siege of Harlech Castle, in Wales, which lasted
many months. It was the last stronghold there to fall, and there
were not many survivors at the end. By this time Prince Henry
was sole commander in the Welsh parts, so all the garrison fell to
him. He rode by slow stages to England with his prisoners in his
train, for they were all ill unto death. Meredith, son of Owen,
and Catherine, Glendower's daughter, he brought, her with her
son by Mortimer, who is perished. They are the last of Owen's
line, it is believed, besides the girl who became Henry's mistress.
There was Meredith's wife, too, and some ladies of Owen's court,
with their babes. They were all lodged in the Tower, prisoners of
the crown, but were given gentle care and nursing, by the
prince's orders.

Couriers had ridden ahead to bring the news of the victory and
Henry's arrival, and my master, for once not too ill to keep to his
bed, awaited his son in the Coldharbour house. I think he had

expected to see the spoils of war in chains behind Harry's horse; for sure he did not know of the Welsh girl at all.

We sat, my master and I, for I was much beside him then, watching the iron gates on Chepe and listening for sounds of the prince's return. He took us by surprise, for he came by barge, up the Thames, with but a few of his personal guard beside him. He strode in, giving his father short greeting; his face was set in hard lines. He bore a burden in his arms, all wrapped about in furs, for it was November and chill. This shapeless bundle he carried past us, not stopping, into his own upstairs chamber, calling for serving maids as he went. I saw amazement sit upon his father's ravaged features and some affront, too, so said nothing; I never wished to draw the Lancaster wrath.

When the prince returned, after some minutes, he answered, to his father's query, that all the prisoners he had lodged in the Tower, bringing them there by the same barge he had come off from through his own gate. "For they are too ill," he said, "to travel by litter. The Lady Catherine, and her little son, too, look to have the plague . . ." A ghost of a smile curved his lips as he saw his father cross himself with a shaking hand; he knew his sire's fear of the plague-death. "Morgan I have brought here, to my own house . . . she is not sick but weak only and half-starved still . . . though I have fed her with my own hand. . . ."

"Another doxy!" shouted the father, his boils purpling with choler. "You have little need of more—to soil the name of Lancaster!"

The prince looked at him in his still way and said, in an even voice, "She is no doxy, Father . . . but an old friend I knew at Richard's court when I was hostage there. . . . I met her again when the tables were turned, and she was hostage—to us. *Her* father claimed her, coming himself into the enemy camp . . . he men call the Baron Glendourdy. He took her out of our hands, with three others, hostage too—and none had courage to say him nay. . . ."

There was a little silence, and then King Henry said, quiet now also, "Ah, yes, Hal—you ever admired more your enemies than your true blood! It was Richard first—you raised sword to me over him, young as you were . . . and the traitor Hotspur, too, him you loved well. Men say now that it is by the prince's hand that yon whoreson Owen slipped through our lines!"

I saw that small muscle twitch again in the prince's jaw, but he did not move, else, but said, still very quiet, "I think you know, sire, my loyalty is not in question . . . my sword, and my heart, too, has been yours, in all these battle years . . . Little profit have I had from it either. . . ." A bitter note had crept into his voice; it has been there, under, in all his encounters with his father in these last years.

The king, stung by the prince's words, for he knew his own stinginess for a byword in the streets, said curtly, "You will have monies from me this week, in part payment toward what is owed. . . ."

"It can wait, Father—I spoke in anger . . . I know the realm is poor. I would have the doctor Colnet back for a little though . . . it might be he can save Catherine and the little Edmund. And I would have you give courteous greeting to my Morgan . . . I have not asked many favors of you, sire. . . ."

The king sat, frowning. "She is bastard surely?"

"Your father of Gaunt had many bastards . . . they sit now among the highest in the land. . . ."

After a moment the king made a weary gesture, shrugging a little.

"You may bring her to me here, then, Hal . . . but she may not come to court . . . I will not have Owen's whelp at court. . . ."

Prince Henry smiled thinly, an old look on a young face. "She is not fit for court, in any case . . . I hope, indeed, that her legs can hold her up. . . ." He made as if to go, then turned. "Thank you, Father."

The prince was gone for some moments. My master stared into the fire, fingering his dried-up scabs. He laughed suddenly, a harsh sound. "Will she faint at sight of us, little brother?"

I laughed too; it was not so farfetched a thought. "I remember," I said, "a lady at the court of Brittany. She was with child and miscarried after the play. The duke allowed no pregnant women at performances after that. The child was not marked though. . . . That lady, after her churching, gave ten gold pieces to Our Lady's chapel. . . ."

"Let us hope this one is not pregnant then," said the king in wry manner.

"Is she not a maid then?"

"I have heard that Owen married off all his daughters during these years, even those base-born ones . . . I think she is a wedded woman or mayhap a widow. . . ."

It looked, though, no such who came to us then. I would have sworn, indeed, that a boy looked out from under that cropped hair. It was a starveling boy, to be sure; the bones pushed through her skin, sharp-pointed, and her face was whiter than skimmed milk, the veins showing blue at the temples. Like a wraith she walked, too, and insubstantial, but walk she did, and her eyes were steady. It must have cost her great control to look upon the pair of us in her weakened state, but her face showed nothing as she bowed before the king.

The prince bent over her tenderly, raising her up. "Father, I have given her page's livery. Her own clothes were all rags—and dirty, too. . . ."

"Dirty!" She looked at the prince sidewise, her mouth curving in woeful merriment. "They could stand alone!" She laughed, a small bright sound. "It may be they are walking about up there in your chamber, Harry—lonely for the creature who inhabited them so long!"

The prince laughed then, too, as I had never heard him, loud and free. I saw that he looked upon this wretched scarecrow as if she were the fairest lady in the realm, his face all lit as with a thousand candles. Truly he loves this lady, I thought; perhaps she is a witch, like her namesake.

The king spoke. "Think you your father of Glendower is alive still?"

"Sire," said Morgan, "all Wales believes it. . . ."

"Where would he hide, do you think?"

She spoke slowly. "He has manors and holdings all over Wales. Though they are burned or confiscated, still those folk round in parts near would give him shelter, and none the wiser . . . I do not know." She looked up at him where she had knelt before him, a fey look through her lashes, very Welsh. "And if I knew— I could not tell. . . . Would you have *your* daughters lead Owen to you—if it were the other way around?"

The king almost smiled, though it hurt his face, opening the sore places, and was not his habit lately; her answer had pleased him, for the words were fair spoken and the thought bold.

"Your tongue wags almost as free as my fool's, mistress," spoke the king. "You have not met, I think, Sir Hercules—there is not his like in Wales—" A look, almost of mischief, flitted over his bloated features. "Will you not give my fool the kiss of courtesy?"

I heard the prince's breath hiss in his throat and felt my own face redden.

She stood looking down at me for a moment, her face grave. "I am something tall, Master, I am sorry for it," she said and, stooping, laid a cool kiss on my forehead, "but I give you greeting."

The breath caught in my throat for a moment; I had not before felt the touch of a woman's lips. I summoned strength then, after, and gave her all I had to give, rocking back on my heels and pretending to peer up, up into the clouds, squinting. "You are a very giantess, Mistress"—I bowed low, my hand over my heart—"like the rest of this naughty world. . . ."

She laughed again, low and sweet, delight in her face. "You are a fine mime, sir. I like you well. . . ."

"He can dance, and tumble, too, our little brother," said the king. "And his voice is passing sweet. . . ."

"You sing, too, sir? Like a bard?"

"Like a bird, Lady!" I cried, rolling my eyes to heaven, as in rapture. When I saw her smile again, I flapped my arms, running about the room and leaping high. It is a dancer's trick, the legs spread in such a way the body seems to soar for a second. She clapped her hands, swaying.

"Oh, Harry—I never thought to laugh again!" She turned to the prince, he taking her hands.

The king rose, his armor making a harsh and grating sound where the edges rubbed. "You are too thin, Lady, to laugh . . . you will break." Never had I heard him jest before; the joke creaked, but still it was something. "We must put back on your bones some of the meat we have starved off—"

"Oh, sire," she said, "I am always hungry—and yet the food will not stay down—"

"You must eat a very little only—but every hour . . ."

She looked at him questioningly. "Do you speak true . . . ?"

He nodded. "We had a Greek doctor when I was on crusade. There were many cases of siege stomach."

And so the king went on, like a very lecturer, explaining the uses of broth and watered wine, taken in mouthfuls frequently to replace the lost body moisture, and so forth, I have forgot the rest. But she listened attentively, though it was plain she was near to dropping, and she thanked him at the end.

She said then, clasping her hands in front of her and with an air of entreaty, "Oh, sire, do not be offended—but—for your face—there is a certain moss with rare fine healing properties . . . my father swore by it for all wounds and raw places. It would heal your face quick and clean. Many times I have seen it work, even with the plague-boils. I could gather it for you. I recognize it well. . . ."

He shook his head. "Oh, no, Mistress, I have had enough of liniments and such from my lady-wife. Some itch and some burn, and all smell evilly. No more!" He made to take leave but turned. "It was a kind thought all the same, child. . . ."

We left them then, she seeming to swoon a little into the prince's arms, and he catching her up most tenderly.

After, in the king's own apartments, he sat musing while I fingered my lute; a string was faulting and had to be replaced.

He spoke suddenly. "I thought to find a wild beauty—Owen was a man right goodly and fair. She is like a mangy yellow cat, and yet she is a . . . beckoning sort, for all her sad looks. . . ."

"I think, master," I said, trying my lute softly, "that her lack of comeliness is but a temporary thing . . . what would you, after eight months of siege?"

Chapter 3

I did not see the Lady Morgan of Wales for some time after, or the prince either; he had taken her to his own castle of Monmouth, ever his favorite, to keep Christ's mass in the country. Whether it was the regular small sups of broth and wine or the winter-frosted air or just time itself, which has ever a soft touch on the young, I know not; but magic was wrought there. When next I saw the lady, she was like a great golden topaz.

The king keeping to his bed after a bout of his recurrent malady, I was summoned to Prince Henry's house for the last great festival before Lent, to entertain the company. I traveled by barge with the musicians, to avoid the streets filled with all manner of ruffians and cutthroats on this night. As we rounded the bend that led to the mansion of Coldharbour, I took one look behind me whence I had come. The king's residence was dark except for one rushlight burning beside my sick master's bed; his queen was in the north with all her ladies. Almost I wished to go back, for my heart ached for the lonely sick creature there, lying in his own abominations. It was a bootless thought, for he liked none about him when he lay in such wise, preferring to suffer unseen. I turned forward again, seeing on the water the brilliant reflection of thousands of candles from the prince's house. It was a sad contrast, and I fell to musing of youth and age, vigor and weakness, joy and pain, till we drew up to the landing stage.

The whole house blazed with light, and young evergreen branches were hung all about, their odor, faint, resinous, in the air. In the dining hall, a musicians' gallery had been newly erected and under it a place cleared for dancing; fires burned at each end, the green logs crackling.

It was a small company; the prince's brothers and but a few intimates. Tom was there with the laughing, dark-eyed girl who was the mother of his bastard son. Tom had just passed his twentieth birthday and looked younger, yet he had been wedded for full two years. His wife was Margaret Holland, widow of his uncle John of Beaufort; she was older than he and plain—he saw her but seldom. He had married her for the great Beaufort inheritance, but it was tied up and untouchable, by her husband's will, and the Lancaster greed thus thwarted. The prince, it was said, had deemed it a right good joke on Tom; the brothers had ever been at odds, since boyhood. Tom had now the title of Duke of Clarence, and fine manors of his own, with a wing to himself in his father's palace. He was already three-quarters flown with wine, his face flushed and his doublet stained. He sat between the Lady Morgan and his own doxy; he did not seem to note much difference between them, for he pawed at first one, then the other. I saw the prince, frowning, leave his place by Morgan's side and speak to his brother, leading the pair to a low dais away from the table, where Tom collapsed, laughing, and his lady curled up on the floor, her head on his knees.

The other young sons of the king were there, too, bright-eyed in the candle blaze, John talking with one of the musicians, and Humphrey at a small table with the mansion's owner, Sir William Poultney. This man I eyed curiously, when he did not see, for, though not young, he was got up like a fair maiden. His locks fell curling onto his shoulders, a style that has gone out among men, and his brows plucked into a thin, high arch. His voice, too, when I heard it, was something high and thin, and his clothes were peacock fine. There were two others at that table, playing at cards; I recognized Lord Scrope, another of the same cut of cloth, for he had been often at court. Even from a little distance I could see that young Humphrey teased these half-men mercilessly, his narrow eyes alive with malice. It was plain they were flattered by the Lancaster attention, preening themselves and tittering, waving their hands about; they were born courtiers.

At the prince's table, besides Morgan, there was the poet Hoccleve and Geoffrey Chaucer's son Tom. Lewis Allen was with them, too, he that kept the famous inn in the Vintry. This was not a true inn but a fair manor where lads of noble birth stayed as guests, though they paid for their keep. Lewis Allen was a small, dark Welshman, his estates impoverished by the wars, though he had remained neutral. This manor of his furnished him now with his only livelihood; he exacted his rents gracefully and kept a fine staff and table. London property was sky-high; even young men rich in lands outside could not afford houses of their own here, and Master Allen fared well and was even becoming famous, for the poets and Latinists made their homes with him, too, when they were in London.

We had much fine entertainment that night, beside my own; the musicians had learned some Welsh songs in compliment to Morgan, and the poets read from their latest works. After, there was dancing, and I could rest and eat my supper.

I watched the Lady Morgan where she danced with the prince; it was a marvelous fine change in this lady. Her hacked-off hair had grown somewhat, and the mass of it in the back was caught up in a pearled net, a fashion I had not seen before. The lady, indeed, made her own fashion, for she wore her own strongly marked brows and no paint on her cheeks; it was a startling look at first, but pleasant. She had put on flesh, too, but pleasingly, and was narrow-waisted and tall. Her saffron gown she had made herself, for Prince Henry had no money for needle-women. It was a good velvet though, supple and glowing, and the cut was simple and fine, with no trim except a scarlet lining to the sleeves. She wore no jewels, only one large ring in the Lancaster colors, made of emeralds and sapphires, but needed none, her beauty itself clear cut and jewel-like, once one had become used to it. The prince did not leave her side and seemed, indeed, to hang on her words; I had never seen him so.

Many of the company danced, but much merriment was afoot, for the space was small, and the dancers jostled one another as they trod the wider measures. There were not enough lady partners to go around, and Sir William paired with Lord Scrope, though that might have happened anyway, considering the temperament of those gentlemen. Tom sprawled still on his low couch, his lady with him, laughing and teasing.

At a lull in the music, when the dancers' feet were still, and they stood panting and flushed, her voice rose, berating Tom in fun.

"Tom—Tom—you are a villain . . . you promised me a net of pearls like Morgan's! I will have no no's, either!" And she took the ends of her silken girdle, beating him softly with it about the face and neck.

"Let be!" he cried. "You tickle!" And he turned over, burying his face into the pillow. "I have no monies either . . . Harry is the only rich one hereabouts, as any can see. . . ."

Morgan called out from where she stood and pulled off the

pretty thing from her head, letting the yellow hair tumble as it would. "Here . . . have mine, Frances. I can make another in an afternoon. They are not real pearls anyway—but French paste. . . . For fourpence, you may buy a trunkload!"

"I will lend you the fourpence," cried the prince, "for just this morning I borrowed a whole shilling from my cook!"

"Netting pearls is an easy thing, too," said Morgan, standing over the couple. "Alice, even, can do it well—and she dislikes needlework and does it only for a penance. . . ."

At this the woman Alice looked up from some seam she was sewing and smiled; I thought it a shame she did not do so more often. This was another survivor of the Harlech siege; Morgan had begged Harry to bring her from the Tower where she was kept, for she had been Morgan's tirewoman for some seven years. She went always in black, though she was young yet, or a drab brown, with her hair hidden under a tight white coif, like a very nun; at her waist there hung a plain wooden crucifix. The prison pallor was still on her face, and it was puffy, as though she slept ill, but her features were well made and pleasing. There had been tales of this woman, how her mother had been burned as a witch, and she herself been a very wanton among all the soldiers of Grey, and had been converted to the New Learning, and was as meek and pious now as a holy anchorite. Some truth there must have been, for she was the widow of Walter Brut of Hereford, a famous Lollard, and for sure his teachings must have rubbed off on her. Morgan, it was plain, had much affection for this woman, treating her more as friend than servant.

Morgan went on, a remembering look on her face, "Do you mind, Alice, when you first came to us at Glyndyvrdwy Llyys and could not thread a needle, and the Argyllwyddes set you to matching pearls and stringing them?"

Tom, who had been listening, in a foggy way, gave a loud laugh then, saying, "The Argyllwyddes! What is that?"

"A lady I knew once, good and kind she was . . . and dead now. . . ." And Morgan turned away, her face still and grave, and picked up a mandol that lay upon a table. There was a little silence, for Morgan had that about her which commanded men's hearts; in her way, she was more royal than either of the Henrys. After a little, the prince came to her where she stood, fingering the music piece. "I cannot seem to get the hang of this," she said, "though I understand the lute well and some harp knowledge I have too—"

"It is the left hand that does the work," said the prince. "Look, I will show you—" And their two heads, fair and dark, bent above the mandol, while the hum of voices rose again in the hall.

It was late in the evening, many of the guests had taken their leave, and those few left were quiet or, like Tom, asleep; there came a loud knocking at the Chepeside door. "It is Oldcastle," cried the prince. "Let him in, before he spoils my new door-paint!"

I had a fine curiosity toward this knight, Sir John Oldcastle he was and the greatest Lollard leader in the realm, though he was the prince's good friend. Some said he had tutored Henry while he read briefly at Oxford Town, others that he was a mere drinking companion; for sure he had fought under the prince in the Welsh wars and was named a brave knight. A wily thinker he was named, too, having studied law and taught it, too. Many times he had been up for his Lollard beliefs, but no judge could outwit him, though all knew him guilty. There was a mort of heretic believers behind this man, too; some say his influence spread all over the land, even in the northern parts and Scotland. All men knew, too, that he operated a kind of escape route to Wales for all those who wished to avoid persecution or trial, though nothing could be proved against him.

This man must be brave knight, indeed, I thought, for he entered all alone, having come through the London streets without retainer or bodyguard, a thing none other would dare in these times. He was a tall man in his middle years, something broad of girth, too, with a bearing that was both genial and arrogant, like a homely god. His head was large and square, topped by a crown of close-curling hair, red as flame. There was high color in his cheeks, too, as round as apples, and his eyes burned blue from clear across the hall; he was known in the taverns as Painted Jack, for the English commons love nicknames. He, too, like the woman Alice, wore a plain wood cross; I thought it must be a badge of their faith.

He bowed to the Lady Morgan, saying that all men could see whose loins she had sprung from. "She is his image, Harry—you do not fear to keep your old enemy's stamped coin about you?"

"She is my talisman, Jack. Besides she loves me well." And the prince put his arm about Morgan, drawing her to him.

"They say that Owen lives still, mistress," said Oldcastle, his blue eyes keen as a sword. "And that he will come again. What say you?"

"I think not, sir," she answered, her own eyes not giving ground. "I have heard that he lives, and so I hope—but I think he will not fight more. My father is a man of peace—he was drawn into this conflict. . . ."

"So he says," Oldcastle remarked. "Owen I know from our youthful days—he was double-tongued even then—double-tongued as the Greek Apollo. . . ."

"I think you err, Sir Knight—my father's mind has many parts and not one only; he saw ever both sides of a question. It is his greatness, to my mind." She finished quietly.

He looked closely at her. "To most men," he said, "it is single-mindedness that is the virtue. . . ."

"What 'most men' think is never right, for in a mass men do not think but feel only, like animals—or it may be, like one great animal that runs and hides, or springs and kills. A mob is ever mindless, whether it be behind you in battle or facing you with spear and sword." A little flush had come up in her face, warming its beauty.

The prince spoke, quickly. "Ah—but if *one mind* rules—one leader at their head—there lies the greatness of man!"

"No, Harry," Morgan said, shaking her head, "men must not be bent to one will, like a herd of bulls led on to charge. Such a leader uses the baser part of people—for his own glory!"

The prince smiled; he loved her well. "But, sweetheart—even as a woman you must see," he said, with sweet reasonableness, "a battle-force must have a leader. . . ."

"I think," she said slowly, "there should in truth *be* no battle-force. . . ."

The prince laughed low, indulgently, bending toward her. "There speaks the soft woman's heart, knowing nothing of these things—"

"No, Harry, by my faith, she argues well!" cried Oldcastle. "Mistress, I read you well. It is that you have no patience with these men's wars and would see them gone from the earth. . . ."

A little smile played then about his lips, as he looked down at her. "What other game, then, Lady, would you give us in its place?"

"You have a keen wit, sir. It is true I think wars are a grisly game. . . . If I remember right," she said, her glance stabbing him, "the doctrines you hold by teach as I speak also. Do you not hold that all men are brothers and that there should be peace on earth and goodwill to men?"

The prince broke in. "You have the words wrong! It is 'Peace on earth—to men of goodwill'. . . ."

"That is the Latin—the other is translated from the Greek words—which came earlier," said Morgan. "The apostles wrote in Greek. Besides, it does not make sense in the Latin. God does not mince words or make conditions. His peace must be for all, or it is no peace."

"In truth, Harry, you have a very Minerva here. Did you not know?" Oldcastle looked sidelong at Henry; there was some irony in his eye.

"Why, sweetheart," said Henry, "I did not know you Lollard . . . see that you do not speak so in my father's presence. . . ."

"No, Harry, I am not Lollard," Morgan said, her brows drawn together as if she struggled with her thought, "I am not Lollard either—for I think in time they too will make wars to prove themselves right. . . ."

Oldcastle was silent then and seemed to look into space. He spoke at last, heavily. "It is the nature of man. . . ." There was an uneasy shifting of feet then and some clearing of throats among those that were left, for all could sense a web of tension.

"Bring ale!" the prince called, loud. "Or will it be malmsey, Jack? You must be dry after our dry talking. . . ."

Oldcastle roused himself. "Good brown ale!" he cried. "A pitcher to myself I'll have—a mighty thirst sits on me, it is true—good brown ale!"

"Will you have a pasty, sir? There is a fine hare pie," Morgan said.

He clapped his hands, laughing loud. "I will have—everything that is left!"

"Let us have music, too," said Henry. "Soft music—so as not to wake my brother." And he went to the musicians' gallery.

Morgan led the portly knight to the board, serving him with

her own hands from the food there. He picked up a leg of capon, tearing at it with his teeth. Through his chewing, he spoke. "Lady, I wish you all happiness, for I think you love our prince-ling well—as indeed, in some wise, I do myself. . . ." He swallowed, and took a long drink of ale, then spoke again. "But know him well, this prince—or he will cause you pain"—and he pointed the drumstick at Henry where he lounged at ease among the music stands—"he has much regard for you. And many of the sweeter things, like music, he loves, and fine-spoken words, but nothing in this life does that young man love—so much as war. . . ."

Chapter 4

That spring the Lady Catherine of Wales and Mortimer died in the Tower. She had been cured of the plague, if indeed she had ever had it, but she wasted after, coughing and spitting blood and growing ever weaker. Her little son Edmund followed her within two days, though he had been romping in the gardens for weeks. Ugly rumors were about concerning both deaths, as always happens in such cases; the smoke of that fire existed, of course, for the little heir of Mortimer was, in fact, closer blood to the throne than the Lancasters. It is a dark thought, and I, for one, did not credit it, though many did. The true Mortimer heir had been confined in the Tower for years, ever since Richard's fall, so it booted little, to my mind, to let him live, while killing the next claimant.

After, there were many plots against the royal family, for there was much sympathy for the Mortimers and even for the Lady of Wales. None came to any great threat though, for they were discovered in time. One only was a close call and might have proved successful. In the prince's Coldharbour mansion, in dead of night, while he lay sleeping, an assailant, who had been concealed behind the bed hangings, grappled silently with him, fingers closing about his throat. The prince, thrashing about in the bed, fighting for breath, woke the Lady Morgan beside him, and she, with great presence of mind, reached out to a table where stood a heavy candlestick and, miraculously in the dark, brought it down on the right head. It broke the fellow's skull, and he died instantly. On his person were found tracts of the New Learning, a wooden cross, and other evidence of Lollardy; it was assumed that he was a poor madman, though none knew his face. The prince made much of this incident, telling all who would listen of the lady's bravery. The king too showed much gratitude; in the way of old tales, he asked her to name her reward. It did not turn out as in the stories though, for she asked a full pardon for her father of Glendower and freedom for her brother Meredith, still in the Tower, and this he refused to grant, sending her instead a girdle embroidered in gold.

The Lady Morgan was much alone in these months, for the prince had been sent with his brothers into Scotland to put down a rebellion there. Such skirmishes were sporadic in that part of the realm and in Ireland, too, though never were they the concerted efforts which had occurred in Wales. The king was too ill to travel, much less command troops, so his sons assumed many of his duties, particularly Henry, who had much experience. The commons loved him, too, as I have said, for his victories and for the goodliness of his person, and demanded him for many public tasks. He sat in the king's council, presiding over it much of the time also. I saw the lady often then, for the prince begged me for her entertainment while he was away; almost every afternoon I sat with her, playing and singing, making up new songs. Some mastery of the mandol she learned then from me, though she had indifferent skill for music. She had a way with words though, this lady, and could think up fine rhymes. They were short verses and bold and not in the fashion, but, to my mind, they were possessed of much merit. Also, when we were alone, she would mime for me, though she rarely did this in company. She was able to take all manner of parts, old crones and gruff soldiers and could mimic the king and Joanna most cruelly. If I could have laughed, I would have then, with her, for they were merry sketches indeed, and for my sight alone. I thought it shame and told her so, that she was not born a boy, for she would have made her fortune in all the courts of Europe.

We sat one day in the small solar, she all in mourning white for her sister, and played together a duet, a song we had been practicing against the prince's return. Her woman Alice, who had been marketing with two pages, came in, her step quick. Her cheeks, too, were red as I had never seen them and her eyes bright. She sent the pages from her with the market baskets, to bring them to the cook, and flung herself to her knees before the lady where she sat. "Oh, mistress," she cried, "they live! They live! Our husbands live!" Then she raised her hands to her burning face and sobbed, the tears running down between her fingers.

This woman had been the wife of Walter Brut, the Lollard, who had been taken at the battle of Usk long ago; the lady's husband, too, one Rhisiart ab Owen, had been taken, he that was secretary to Owen. It was thought that all those prisoners had been put to death in the last reprisals of the war; but Alice spoke between her sobs, and shakily, of new word she had received. These Lollards, like all outlawed sects, have many secret ways of communicating; there is an underground web, insidious and spreading wide, that brings all news from one to the other so that scarcely is there any knowledge of one of their members that is not known to all. Much has been done to smoke out these lines of communication, but it is in vain; they are seldom caught either, for there are no informers among them.

She told a harrowing tale, indeed, of hardship and long years of captivity and, in the end, miraculous escape. The dungeons at Usk had been crammed full with Welsh prisoners; they had been overlooked all this time, though in other places all the prisoners had been executed without right of ransom. Sometime in the last year, though, an order had been given for their disposal, for the crown no longer gave any funds to that prison, and there was no way to keep the wretched creatures, even on bread and water. If they two went free, indeed, it was a very miracle, for one out of each three had been summarily butchered, the rest being released. They had been lined up and counted off; those who went free had to make their ways unaided through desolate and mostly hostile country to where they might receive succor.

The Lady Morgan listened with a face white and strained; no flush came to her cheeks, and when Alice's recital was finished, her mistress' eyes had a troubled look.

"And they live, both, and are well?" Morgan asked, low.

"So I believe," answered Alice. "Oh, mistress, it is a true miracle!"

"You believe . . . you will not tell me where you have learned this?"

"Oh, mistress—I *cannot!*" And the poor creature started weeping afresh.

"But it is sure?"

"Yes—it is sure. . . . They live. I even know where they are to be found." And her eyes slewed around to me, for these Lollards trust few men.

"You will tell me presently," said Morgan, putting aside her mandol and walking from us to the window, where she stared out into the warm May afternoon.

The woman Alice knelt still, her head bowed in prayer, her lips moving silently. She raised her head and spoke to the Lady Morgan. "Oh, mistress—is it not a very miracle?"

"For they two—yes—" said Morgan slowly. "But what of those other men cut down?"

"Aye, mistress—I will pray for their souls. . . ."

Morgan came over to the woman where she knelt, cupping her hand under Alice's chin and forcing her to look into her eyes. "Alice, who gave such an order? Who made that grisly lottery?"

Alice's eyes flicked away, as if she could not bear to look upon the lady. "Mistress, I am sorry," she whispered. "They say . . . it was the prince."

The Lady Morgan did not speak for a moment; I saw her knuckles go white among the folds of her gown, where she clutched it suddenly. "Yes," she said, turning away, "it has the Lancaster smell. . . ."

After a bit Alice said timidly, "I think, Lady, he meant to show mercy. . . ."

"They cannot deal out half-mercies," said Morgan, her face dark as I had not seen it. "They cannot—to get on the right side of their God. . . ."

"My Lady," I said, for it pained me to see her so, "my master of Lancaster would have pardoned none. . . ."

She looked at me. "Yes—perhaps," she said, her face clearing of its dark humors. "You cannot bring up a cub in a wild beast's den and expect it to turn into a lamb. Harry has known nothing but war since he was fourteen . . ." She sighed. "Yet does he think himself ever in the right. . . ." She looked at me with a sad little smile. "Withal, the king has been a kind master to his fool, Little Brother. . . ."

When Alice had withdrawn, she spoke to me of her love for the prince, how she had yearned for him all the years of the wars, never thinking to encounter him more. "And Rhisiart—that I was wedded to—never did we two love nor was I less than a maid when first I came here—for he went away to battle scarce an hour after we exchanged vows. I thought him captured at first; then we heard they were all dead in that battle . . . I do not wish him unalive, for we were good friends, but this news makes all unclear." Her brows were knitted together in thought, and her face wore a look of trouble. "I have vowed wifehood . . . and I know not where my duty lies now, for the prince is my only true lord. Yet do we stand at odds often and often, when we are private—striving each for our own convictions. And then, I can never be wife to Lancaster, were I free, for I am base-born. . . ." The lady spoke as though I were that wall in front of us—wanting no answer—and so I gave none; indeed there *was* none that I could see, for it was a pretty coil that she was in, between these two men. She went apart from me then, dismissing me, I think to weep; never did that lady show weakness in front of other folk.

It was the first hint that I had that all was not perfect love between Prince Henry and his leman, but not the last. Often and often, after that, I heard sharp notes in their two voices when they spoke and ill accord in their words. Perhaps, after that day, I was looking for it, or perhaps their disagreements grew. I do not know.

Often I heard the lady upbraid him, albeit gently, for his surly tempers toward his ailing father, deeming him unkind and intolerant; in this was she inconsistent, for she ever hated Lancaster and held him usurper and worse. Truly, all folk have their faults, even the best of women. In all other things I found her fair and just.

She tried also to make peace between the royal brothers, for she had a fondness for poor gay Tom, as did all females. There was too much rivalry of long years' standing between the brothers and too little of common tastes, so nothing was gained on that score; indeed, the prince seemed to take her partisanship right hardly and baited Tom the more.

As for Oldcastle, his great friend, the lady leaned toward Lollardy anyway, or so I privately thought; heavy arguments were afoot whenever this knight was present, for he could never hold his peace on points of doctrine, and the prince grew daily more intolerant of this sect. He did not sanction the persecutions and burnings though but held, like his uncle of Beaufort, that persuasion should be used of a gentler sort.

But it was on the question of war and battle that the lady fought the hardest; I think she hoped to convince her lover of peace's virtues, but war was bred in him from his earliest years and so seemed right goodly. He talked often, his eyes kindling, of the English claims in France, the lady contending that there were none such. "Who is it you are looking to become," she would cry scornfully, "Charlemagne—or that cruel boy of the ancients, Alexander, who laid waste half a world for the name of conqueror? Ever have I marked," she said, "how you must be victor always, even in a play-game! What is it burns in you? For in *you* it is—you think not of England's good, but of yourself only. . . ."

"I would have England greater than any," he answered.

"But it will not be so; you will beggar the realm." She spoke with quieter tongue then, and with sweet reasonableness. "Can you not see, Harry, how it will be? War is costly. My father of Glendower was wealthy beyond any Lancaster dream—yet is he stripped of all now and the sweet country of Wales beaten to its knees. . . ."

"God will be on my side. It will not happen so with me. . . ."

"Oh, Harry, your head is thick as English yew!" And scorn crept back into her voice, for she held her own powers of mind most high. "Each army holds that God is on its side, and fearful things are done in His Name. He cannot be on all sides. In truth, I think He is not on any—for what God would sanction slaughter and pillage?"

The prince's face would grow most dark, for he did not brook contradiction, but after, he would shrug it off and woo her with fair words. I think he persuaded himself that her thoughts were but a woman's piddling fears; this was not so. The lady had been reared more scholar than maid; she was a thinker of great subtlety and could quote all the old books besides.

It was not always so between them, of a certainty, for their love was very great; yet did these discords presage the end, for the end did come.

Chapter 5

The last I saw of the Lady Morgan was sometime shortly before Midsummer; I recall it because there was talk of some Midsummer celebration, and I was fetched to the prince's manor to have my brains picked. Oldcastle was present and Lewis Allen, with Tom Chaucer and Hoccleve and two young women of the town, low creatures but clean. A masque was planned with a classical theme, something of Theseus and his Amazon bride, which parts would be taken by Prince Henry and Morgan. Hoccleve was to write in a part for Oldcastle, some lines pertaining to rude merriment and revels, for it was thought he made a perfect Bacchus, or Dionysus, as the Greeks had it. They fell to talking of other Midsummer Nights, and the lady spoke of the lighting of the fires, a custom in the Welsh countryside, the prince remembering that they had done this, too, in Monmouth in the days when he was very small. As they talked, I saw it in my mind's eye, a brave sight.

After, I recall, there was singing and music, and much humorous chaffing, for the prince's purse was flat again and he had to borrow from Oldcastle to pay the musicians.

"Oh, Harry," cried Morgan, "and must I sew all these costumes? My fingers are all cramped from the making of those wall hangings for the solar!" She laughed though, as she chided, for the lady had much skill with the needle.

I snapped my fingers suddenly, remembering. "Is Duke Thomas coming?" I asked. "My master bade me tell him that the monies due him from his Irish expedition will be sent tonight . . . but late, close on midnight, for they are coming by barge. . . ."

"Tom was not invited," said the prince curtly. "Besides, the money will be going to his quarters surely and not here. Would that I could get my hands on it! For I am owed in the thousands —ten times more than Tom's share! Before God, does my father look to drive me mad? Tom has had payment three times these last six months, and I nothing for two years!"

The evening was spoiled for him, it was clear; he sat brooding at the window, looking out into the dark of the street; Morgan glanced at him once or twice but said nothing and went on with her talk, nodding as the poet Hoccleve described the verses he meant to use.

After a bit the prince took a tankard of ale from the board, draining it; he stood toying with the mug a while as if in thought. "Look you," he said, addressing young Tom Chaucer, "I know which way the retainers will come from the Tower Mint. They must land at the Chepe, then down Bread Street, then Cordwinders—it is the only way. There is a dark passageway that leads to the Savoy—they can only come through it one at a time. If we wait for them there, we could have the treasury purses out of their hands before they knew what hit them. . . ." A little smile played about his lips; all the company had stopped to listen. I saw Morgan's face, still and shocked.

"I'm with you, my Lord," cried young Chaucer; he was somewhat in his cups already and of a reckless temper besides. "It is a fine joke on Tom. . . ."

Oldcastle shook his head, smiling. "Not I, boy. It is my neck would be in a noose were I caught. I am too old and too serious for pranks. You would do better to comb the taverns for accomplices."

"By heaven, I will!" cried the prince. "There are doughty fellows looking to make a groat for breakfast or the next drink, and there is no great danger either. What say you, Hoccleve?"

"I will pass it up, my Lord. I am not in such great favor with your royal father as it stands, after that lampooning verse I wrote of the lady-queen. . . ."

"It is a way to get your debts paid," said the prince. "No? Ah, well, we cannot all be brave knaves. Come, Tom. . . ."

"Harry," cried Morgan, "you do not mean to *steal*—!"

"It is mine—the money—by rights. Tom has had much payment these last years and I none. I told you that. Would you have a beggar by you always that cannot buy you gowns or pay for your lute strings?"

"It is wrong nonetheless," said she stubbornly.

"Ah, do not preach at me like a praying sister. You are not so white as snow as that. . . ."

"With what do you impugn me? For my love or that I am prisoner and Welsh?"

"Oh, before God, sweetheart—let be. I meant nothing. . . ."
He took a step toward her, but she backed away from him, her face hostile.

He set down his tankard, making a ringing noise on the polished table. "I do not mean to give it up. There is no other way—I only take what is mine!"

"So said your father when he took Richard's throne!"
The prince, stung, drew back his arm in quick response and slapped her full in the face. It was a hard blow; she reeled and almost fell. Her cheek showed red, and a tiny trickle of blood ran down from her temple where his ring had torn the skin. She did not cry out, and none spoke; the silence held, for there was much shock in the moment.

The prince was instantly contrite, taking her in his arms and kissing her, begging her pardon. "Oh, sweetheart, I am sorry." He put his hand to her cheek. "Did I hurt you, my darling?"

"Of course it hurt. Do you think I am made of stone? How long ago was it *you* were hit across the face?" She drew back, raising her hand. "Shall I show you how it feels? Though, indeed, I have not so much strength—not having been bred to war. . . ."

He caught her hand. "Believe me, sweetheart, never have I hit anyone in the face before. . . ."

"I am the more honored, then, my Lord." But I saw the lady's face quiver slightly as if she suppressed a smile; she was ever quick to see the humorous side even when the jest was against her. "Oh, let it be, Harry—some would say I had much luck to be alive. . . ."

"Oh, my Morgan, will you forgive me?" He folded her in his arms again.

"Probably . . . for the blow." She stood away from him still, her eyes searching into his. "But not ever for the thought—for the deed you spoke of—for it demeans you. Harry, you must not do such a thing. It is true your father is unfair often and favors Tom; I grant it. But yet, two wrong things do not make a right deed. Promise me."

And in the end, he did promise, and he did not go abroad that night but sent all the company away, except for me, and his musicians, to play for them and sing.

They sat long at wine together that night, holding hands and listening to sweet music, though they spoke seldom, she gazing abstractedly into space while he fondled her fingers most tenderly. Close onto midnight there came a loud halloo at the doors, shut for the night, and when they were opened, there stood the king's treasury men, with heavy purses hung from their belts; the king had changed his mind and redirected the payments, letting Tom wait for once. The prince laughed loud, deeming it a great joke on himself that he had so fortunately escaped knavery. "You are my Lady Luck, sweet—but for you I had been a felon this night and doing penance for a twelvemonth. Never leave me, sweetheart. . . ." But she did.

When next he was sent on campaign, and it was soon, for the king had thought to sweeten the summons by sending the monies first, she found means to go from him. When he returned, his house was empty, and all the servants quaking with fear that they would be held in blame. I think they spoke true, for even under torture none broke but all swore they had no knowledge of her whereabouts.

The prince at first thought she had come to some harm; he accused his father and his stepmother, his brothers, too, for he was distracted by grief. Wild with it, he seized me from my master's house, thinking I was privy to the lady's secrets. He thought to have me tortured, too, but the king saved me, refusing to have his Little Brother put to the question. "For he can have no part in it, my poor fool. Get you another doxy! She has wearied of you, Harry. . . ."

Her woman, Alice, was fled, too; I thought it plain though I held my tongue, that the lady had made use of her woman's Lollard connections and the escape route those heretics operated for their own and had gone into Wales to her father and to join her lawful spouse. The prince sought Oldcastle, too, for he knew of this man's underground power, but he could not be found. Tom, that light-minded fellow, hinted, with a laugh, that they two had flown the coop together. "You cannot trust these Lollards, Harry—nor no man trust a woman." The prince, enraged, flew at his brother, shaking him as a terrier shakes a rat; the brothers had to be pulled apart, Tom swearing never to grace the prince's door again. Much ill was done by that sweet lady, if she had only known, with torturing and recriminations; the prince dismissed all his household, turning them out into the streets, charging them with laxity and worse.

There came to him within a week, a Welshman who had been lodged at the Vintry with Lewis Allen; he claimed some knowledge of the Lady Morgan. This man was called Davy Gam; it was a nickname only, for his given name was such a tongue twister no Englishman could say it. He had been loyal to Lancaster through all the Welsh wars, out of reverence for his beloved master of Nannau, who had been killed by Owen's hand. He promised to lead the prince's men to where Morgan was in Wales and also, he claimed, to the outlawed Owen Glendower. The prince gave him a small force of soldiers and free conduct over the border; he was away almost three months but came back empty-handed. "My Lord, I am sure she is there, and her scurvy father, too, but she is hidden well, and I could find no trace of her, and none would inform. The Welsh are loyal still, to their Glendower masters."

This ruffian, Davy Gam, was much by the prince after that; he knew all the lowest haunts, the prince accompanying him, often coming home in the smallest hours of the morning. Prince Henry brought home women, too, a new one each night, it was said; he was often drunk, sleeping the daylight hours through. My master was very wroth with him, summoning him to his bedside and letting him hear the rough side of his tongue. There was naught could shame Prince Henry though; mostly he shrugged all off, saying he filled his days and nights, too, as best he might. "After all," he said, "the war in Wales has been over for a twelvemonth, and council has not sat for weeks, nor have I any other duties. What would you? I must do something or run mad. . . ."

And so it went, tongues wagging in high places and among the commons, too. It was said often and often that the young prince was no better than another Richard; that his ailing father might have stayed forever in exile for all the good he and his seed would do the realm.

Chapter 6

My services were not needed much of late, for my master the king kept no court and the prince was much abroad, in the taverns and stews of the town, but one day I was summoned to Coldharbour to play my latest songs. I was much pleased, for I had been idle too long; like the prince himself, I knew only one thing, and without it I was lost and moping.

I had thought to see lights and hear music and laughter as I floated down the Thames, but the prince's house was as dark as his father's, with one beam only shining out over the water from the casements. I found the prince alone, with none but servants about him and a flagon of half-emptied wine at his hand. "Help yourself, Master Hercules," he said, waving at the table, which was piled with food in covered dishes. "There was to have been a fair company here tonight, but I had no heart for it, or stomach either . . . so all grows cold. Please eat, if you are hungry. . . ."

I answered that I had supped earlier; indeed, I had not much appetite when I was not working but lived, as it were, on my nerves and a little honeyed wine, for I have a sweet tooth.

"There is a song here," said the prince, reaching for his lute. "I have it in my mind, but it will not come right." And he strummed a while, breaking off after a bit and frowning. "You see how it goes—the tune? I made it some months ago but half-way only. I cannot get beyond this passage."

I listened, nodding. "It is a sweet air," I said and hummed the notes, fingering my own lute softly, till I had it clear. "My Lord, I think it is not in the melody—the fault—but in the tenoring only—thus. . . ." I played a chord or two, trying it over. "It is a passing sad tune—it is the minor key that will get it right. . . ." I had it now, for the ill measures were very short, and I played it through.

The prince caught the tune now, too, for he was very quick; we played together, he taking the melody, and at the end he looked at me with almost a smile, though his eyes had still a brooding look.

"There are sad words to it, too—for it is a lament." And he sang them softly. "When that the wind sets the golden leaves atremble . . . I cry in my heart—Oh, where are you, my bird of gold. . . ." He stopped then, throwing down the lute so that all the strings jangled in the air, a high, thin whining, sadder than the song. I saw the wine then in his face, blurring all its strong lines. He reached under his tunic and brought out a paper, folded small and much worn at the edges. "I have had a letter from her—the Lady Morgan. It was long months agetting here, but it is truly hers—I know her hand." He held it out to me, unfolding it; I saw that his hand trembled, from drink and from the force of his emotions, too. "Read it, sweet knave, for I know you had somewhat of love for that lady also. . . ."

Being small, I am afeared of those in drink, especially when they are powerful nobles, and I did not welcome my lord's confidence, thinking he might feel regret on the morrow; there was nothing for it though—I had to read that letter, though I quaked at what it might reveal, for I could not read the prince's face. I was not guilty of anything, of course, neither succoring the lady nor aiding her escape, but one never knew with the Lancasters which way they might jump; such uncertainty places guilt in innocent hearts.

I do not, of course, remember that letter word for word, and have not its copy, but much of it I do remember; it went like this:

"My dearest Love—for you are that and always will be, even when I am old—I would not have you believe that I went from you in anger. Arguments and blows mean nothing, though in time they might have hurt our love and its sweetness. I will not reveal how I found my way, or who it was aided me; I am safe though and by my father. Do not send for me, for I cannot come back—ever in this world. After the siege, when first I came to you, I thought myself a widow and you knew me a maid, for never had I bedded with Rhisiart ab Owen. It fell out though that I learned from my woman that my husband was yet alive; I was in anguish, for the knowledge nearly tore me in two. I

wanted to stay by you always—please believe that. It was many
weeks before I found my mind in this matter and knew that I
must follow it. I did not, even then, go to him for that it was my
woman's duty, for I am not bound by such things, being unortho-
dox in all matters, as you know.

After much thought, and pain, too, I made this decision, which
I will hold by while I live. I am bastard, a thing you know, and
all men also. Never has it harmed me, for my father was generous
and good; but I would not bring bastard children into the world,
though they be a king's. Twice would those children be defamed,
too, for their mother lived in adulterous wise, with her husband
still bound to her by holy vows. And so I have gone from you, my
only love.

However this letter comes into your hands, if it does in the end,
pardon, for my sake, the poor wretch who has it on his person, for
it will have passed through many hands before it reaches you,
and I would not have the innocent suffer.

Remember me, and our time together, as I will remember you.

> By her own hand, signed,
> Morgan ab Owen
> ap Griffith Fychan of Wales"

It was a letter of surpassing sweetness, and I blinked back the
tears which rose behind my eyelids, for I liked none to see me
moved; always I feared men's mockery. I could have let them
fall, for all the prince cared; when I looked, he was staring at
space—"looking at his own grave," I have heard it said. He
roused himself slowly and with sighing, holding out his hand. I
put the paper back into it, seeing its edges almost split at the
folds, and its heavy texture worn smooth; he had carried it long
beneath his tunic, for sure, and reread it many times over.

"Well—the lady loves me, it seems—for what it is
worth. . . ." He passed his hand over his face, as if to wash it
free of its grievous thoughts. He stood up, placing his hand,
heavy, on my shoulder for a moment. "Think you we shall ever
see her like again, Sir Hercules?"

I had no words but shook my head sadly, putting one hand

over my carven grin; it was my habit, sometime, to hide that part
of my face, out of consideration for other folk. He looked keenly
at me, a long moment. "You are a good fool," he said.

After a bit I asked him, "How did you come by it, my Lord—
the letter?"

"It was a poor woman who sells flowers in the square. The
servants caught her as she slipped it under the kitchen door. She
knows nothing or says not—will not tell, even, the name of that
one who gave it to her. . . ."

My heart gave a horrid leap. "You have put her to the question?"

"No, I have not—for Morgan's sake. Besides, the woman is of
the New Learning, a wooden cross concealed beneath her bodice; such do not break under torture. I have her tied up in the
stables, on bread and water."

"My Lord, I beg you—let her go! The lady enjoined you in
her letter—"

"You would not have the creature turned over to my uncle of
Arundel, then, to fry? And are you Lollard, too, then?"

"My Lord, I swear it, no! I have no need of such faiths. . . ."
A kind of scorn must have crept into my voice, for the prince
looked strangely at me.

"Yet will the Lord of All deal kindly with you, I doubt not,
poor Laughing Man . . . for that evil has been put upon you, an
innocent. . . ."

His pious words mocked me, though that was not his intent.
But I have courage of a sort, and I was weary, too, of fawning. I
risked my neck before this Lancaster sprout, though some would
say I had not overmuch to lose; I felt it all or nothing, and so I
spoke. "My Lord, what would you say if I told you I am not sure
there *is* a Lord of All, either Lollard or Holy Roman, or Avignon,
either, for that matter?"

The prince was silent for a little; then he answered, speaking
slow. "Morgan, for sure, would not gainsay you—she was ever of
a questioning spirit. And then, too, I would say you had good
reason—as all men do, sometimes. . . ." He straightened then
and seemed to throw off his liquorish and pensive mood. "But
each man must have a faith, I say—and live by it—and mine is
that one taught me long ago at my mother's knee—God rest her
sweet soul." He sketched a cross in the air and, turning, poured

out two glasses from the wine flagon. "Well, I will let the flower-woman go—and tell her two names to remember in her Lollard prayers—Morgan . . . and Hercules. . . ."

Chapter 7

My poor master worsened, though he had no strong attacks of his disease; he seemed to weaken from day to day, some days unable to leave his bed at all. He could take little or no part in affairs of state, and much fell to his young sons. Henry, in especial, being still greatly loved by the commons in spite of his roistering nights, was given many duties, chief among them being his appointment to the post of Captain of Calais. He was also warden of the Cinque Ports and Constable of Dover and, as I have mentioned, presided over the royal council in his father's absence. His Beaufort cousins had by now become the most powerful nobles in the realm; Henry was a cardinal, and Thomas Beaufort, the Duke of Exeter, had replaced Archbishop Arundel in the chancery. I have so little knowledge or understanding of politics, I cannot say how this last came about, but folk would have it that Arundel was ousted by the prince, with the help of the entire Beaufort faction, these nobles having many loyal followers among the younger nobility. Sentiment had run high always against Arundel, among all the more progressive minds of the kingdom, many deeming that he held too much power in his hands and wielded, too, more influence over the old king than was desirable. (I have fallen into the trap of so many others. The common folk wag their heads sadly and click their tongues, as they say, the old king, whereas their faces light as they name the young king, meaning that youthful victor of Wales and lover of low company, "The dear rapscallion, forever wenching and guzzling—wild he is, for all the world like our own Johnnie!") Strange it is to tell, that, for the people, young Harry can do no wrong, whereas for his kingly father, he can do naught else.

I must make mention further of these same Beauforts; they are dear to the prince and very close, perhaps because of their mother, the Lady Katharine, who raised him in his early years, showing him much loving gentleness. These Beauforts have a finger in most of the pies at court, including all the dealings with France. That country, because of its mad king, is torn between two parties, which struggle incessantly for power, the Burgundi-ans and the Armagnacs. The king favors the Armagnac faction, while the prince and his Beaufort uncles lean toward the Bur-gundians. There are fat pickings to be had from either alliance, for the Armagnacs control the rich vineyards of Bordeaux, whereas the Burgundians can offer the strengthening of the al-ready English Calais, plus much profitable commerce with the duchy of Flanders, where all the great weaving of cloth is done. (I have but small understanding of monies and business dealings; still it looks to me that, with the plentiful wool of England, the second alliance makes more sense.) Either French faction could offer an English king free entry into France though, which I sus-pect is the way the wind will be blowing when my master dies, for young Harry loves conquest even for its own sake. Being French myself and a cynic, too, I am sure neither father nor son realizes that the Armagnacs, under the Duke of Orléans, and the followers of Duke John of Burgundy are both playing their own foxy games, much alike. They are bribing the English—not to conquer France but to help them, one or the other, to power and overlordship. Ah, well, I shall not be asked—I am but a poor fool. Let them wind this coil as they will!

The prince, it would seem, had none such suspicions of Old-castle's guilt in the "escape" of Morgan as I had myself, for he sent that knight as his lieutenant into France; it was a position of much trust, for the whole expedition was done without his fa-ther's knowledge or sanction. It was the next September, the king having dragged on, too sick to rule, for almost a year, and the prince virtually making all decisions as the president of the coun-cil. The prince, that time, sent an expedition to the aid of Duke John of Burgundy. It was a piddling small force, some twelve hundred perhaps, but they turned the tide for Burgundy. They took Paris and routed the Armagnacs smartly. It was a pleasant victory for all the younger faction; the small force was rewarded handsomely by the duke, and there was much rejoicing and many high hopes for the future. Wine and mead flowed free in the Coldharbour house, and the music and revelry went on all night; I worked as hard as I had ever done, for all the prince's guests were of that expedition and were tired men, wanting the wild respite of laughter.

"To France . . . let's to France!" "Pick the lilies of France!"

"England forever!" they shouted. Thomas of Arundel, who had captained the expedition, sat beside the prince, they two sipping malmsey from the great festival cup, in quiet celebration. "My Lord," he said, "I cannot blame them—if you could have seen! How the French ran! My Lord—if so few Englishmen can do so much . . . what if we led an *army* into that land?" He lifted the cup. "To an English France!" he cried.

"Not so fast, Arundel," said the prince, laughing. "Don't count the chicken while it is still in the egg!" But he took the cup and drank, his eyes glittering above the rim.

That expedition, though successful, had its gloomy side, for the king was wroth with his son, that he had done this without royal sanction. He sent for the prince and railed at him, tossing under his coverlets. "You are deposed from power from this day!" he cried. "I cannot take my rest in peace, but you will have the kingdom all your way—can you not wait a little?" His choler, indeed, was such that it seemed, in a sort, to cure him, sending the furious blood raging to his heart and stimulating it; he rose from his bed the next day and was closer to a well man than he had been in many long months.

The brief reign of the prince and the Beaufort faction was at an end though, for the prince was summarily dismissed from council and banished from London itself for a sixmonth. Old Archbishop Arundel was recalled to the chancery, and the younger Beaufort ousted in his turn. The prince, with many of his household, rode in slow progress through the country, showing himself to the people. He was wined and dined at all the great nobles' houses and cheered by all the folk as he passed by. It was whispered then that there were plans afoot to place the young heir on the throne before his time, deposing the monarch father, but this was hearsay only. I think, from all reports, that such a coup would have worked, if dealt cunningly, for my master was sadly lacking in popularity. Truly, I think now, that the prince would not have done it, for though he seemed to hate his father well, still were they Lancasters both, and with full pride of race. And for sure, one could not blame young Harry for covetous thoughts, seeing an ailing king botching his inheritance; this must have been in his mind often.

At any rate, the way of Burgundy was abandoned for the way of Armagnac, in the last gasp of rule. The Armagnacs offered

Aquitaine in full sovereignty as bribe for English aid, and King Henry sent an expedition of three thousand under the command of Tom, his second son, and his favorite. They landed in Normandy and slaughtered and pillaged vast areas of the countryside; it was more like a pirate raid than a planned invasion, for Tom of Clarence had none of the prince's military genius. The whole thing ended in embarrassment for the English, and they were lucky to get home with almost whole skins, for the two warring factions of France made peace behind the English back, and no longer needed the Clarence expedition. Tom and his men were paid off but less than handsomely, and the prince, it is said, laughed loud and long in his castle of Monmouth where he waited out his banishment. The commons, angry, rose in council, near revolt, and refused to vote any more monies for the French adventure. They shouted, too, for the prince to be brought back, saying the kingdom was endangered without him. Though he refused to consent to it, this demand sent my master into another frenzy; he kicked his little spaniel across the chamber and pulled down all the hangings from his bed, tearing them in his hands and stomping on the pieces. After, he took to his bed again for a day, fasting.

Much has been said, and by myself also, of the prince's wild behavior and low habits; yet did his Lancaster brothers—Tom, John, and Humphrey, too—roister with as feckless a bearing as he, in all the filthy haunts of the town. They were an unruly family, for sure, having only a sick and choleric-tempered man to guide them and no woman's hand to restrain them after their first youth. Yet did no blame attach to these others in any mouths, but to the Prince Harry only, for that he was the heir. I remember me an occasion, indeed, where these three younger brothers were found rioting in the streets, brawling with some low fellows of the taverns, so that they were bloodied and in tatters and were arraigned before the king's bench to answer for it. Judge Gascoigne, the king's high justiciar, sentenced them to a night in prison and a stiff fine before their release. The prince paid this from his own pocket but got no praise for it from my master, or reimbursement either. But the king, indulgent, laughed at his sons' exploits, deeming them doughty fellows. It was a thing passing strange but always did he hold his eldest in much contempt.

It was long before these two were reconciled once more, and many grave charges were brought against the prince in the meantime. I do not remember, if I ever knew, who brought the charges, but my master was well-nigh gone into convulsions when he heard, judging them true. It was charged that Prince Harry had used the wages of his garrison at Calais for his own purposes, letting the soldiers go without pay and squandering their monies on women and wine. He replied in high anger, demanding a fair hearing before the council. At this time his enforced exile still stood, the king not having yet pardoned him. He entered London with a great company of armed followers, the people shouting huzzahs at him as he rode, all in chain mail, his face grim as it became in later years. He forced his way to his father's presence and knelt, throwing himself upon the monarch's mercy. I was not there, for council sat, and even the pet dog cannot go with his master to council, but it seems that both Lancasters wept, embraced, and forgave each other. The prince was exonerated fully from those foul charges by vote of council, and a sweet harmony reigned for a little. Here am I cynic again, but I cannot help remembering how the commons, and the younger nobles, too, held great love for the prince and wished him well always. In my doubting nature, there lurks still some feeling that the dark smoke of those charges had some fire under. But I will not swear to anything, of course.

True it was, though, that father and son were reconciled, if briefly. I remember me a day bright in October and warm as May when the prince came to his father's apartments, his face full of lightness, and carrying two fishing rods. "Come, Father, we'll fish together. It's a rare fine day."

The poor old man, hideous and bloated, struggled to smile through his hardened scabs. I am shocked to remember now that this "poor old man" was then forty-six! He said, gruff as a bear to hide his emotion, "There are no fish in the Thames."

"Well—eels, then," said the prince, still merry and hanging a light mantle over his father's armored shoulders. "Come, Father, it will do you good—no matter if there is naught to catch. . . ."

They bore the king down to the river's side in a great chair, for he could not ride. Upon our two horses, the prince and I spoke as we wended way through the narrow streets.

"Remember Morgan?" said the prince, his eyes bright with

tears unshed. "This is her saint's day. Ever she railed at me that I treated my father ill; this excursion is for her. Think you it will tax him too greatly?" He ended anxiously.

"Oh, I think not, my Lord; he is strong betimes, and the air is good also. . . ."

The sweating bearers set the king's chair down beside the water; the river flowed swift here, bearing upon it all the fallen leaves from the bankside trees, like a moving carpet of yellow and flame. The prince cast a line, putting it into his father's hands.

"Am I helpless then that I cannot cast for myself?" The king frowned upon his son. "Take you this line—I will go upstream. . . ." And he beckoned to his bearers that they should move his chair. After four casts his line reached the stream, dragging downriver with the current.

I played to them as they sat, half a day there on the bank; twice the king drew his line out, feeling a tug, but it was only leaves tangled on the hook. At last the prince pulled in his line, coming over where his father sat and throwing himself at his feet, stretching on the sparse yellow grass, his face upturned to catch the sun. Presently he spoke.

"You were right, Father. There are no fish here. It is not as it is in my Monmouth valley; I caught twelve salmon in an hour when last I cast there."

The king spoke heavily. "Monmouth . . . is there no other place! Is that name to be forever on your tongue?" His face was like a gargoyle's off a Paris roof when he scowled; the lines were graven deeper than humanity.

The prince looked at him, his mood all shattered. "Oh, Father," he said, very low, "it seems I cannot help but anger you, no matter how I try. . . ."

"Try!" The king exploded. "When have you tried to please me? Your acts of treachery behind my back—this fawning on the commons—the company you keep. . . ."

"I am no traitor, Father," the prince said quietly. "And the commons cheer me for my victories in Wales, where you yourself sent me when I was a boy. . . ." He sat a moment, silent and flushed about the neck. "As to my company—I must take my pleasure where I find it. . . ."

"Aye," said the king bitterly, "no marriage is good enough for you. When I am gone, my heir will sit issue-less upon the throne!"

"You have three other sons—I have never known you afore this to forget it—they can heir me." He finished on a curt note.

"Oh, aye—" the king railed. "You have not any bastards even—though Tom has two already."

"Never have I heard *that* was a mark of virtue—even in such am I wrong." The prince's lips curved in a sour-sweet smile.

"Wrong!" thundered the king. "You put me beside myself. . . ." He shot his son a sly look. "Is it that you follow Richard's way?"

I saw Prince Harry's fists clench beside him where he lay, and his eyes showed a flicker beneath his closed lids, but he spoke carelessly.

"No, Father," he said. "It is not that—I am careful, that is all. . . ." And he gave a great yawn and turned over onto his folded arms, pretending sleep.

The king sat on in a dark silence for a while, then beckoned to be taken home, not glancing at the prince where he lay.

I lingered behind, holding the bridle of my little mount, my master being borne ahead. The prince looked up, raising his head from his cradling arms. "You see, Master Hercules—how it is with us"—he sighed, a heavy, windy sound—"I cannot please him. . . ."

I looked at him, seeing the little lines already showing about his eyes and mouth, lines of sharp control and self-imposed rigor, belying his debauchings; a look of strain was on him, too; he was in his body now like a spring wound up. I said, with some little diffidence, "Will you not forgive him, my Lord? He is old before his time and riddled with disease and ugliness . . . a hard thing to bear when one has been a goodly knight afore. And he is eaten, too, with envy when that he sees your youth and vigor. Comely are you, also, and the people love you for it. He would be as you are again, and cannot. It is hard. . . ."

He shook his head. "That is not the whole story. Always my father loved me less than the others—you do not know. It does not breed love in return—that knowledge. . . ."

My heart was main heavy as I rode on, to catch up my master. I was bound up now with these Lancasters, father and son, and their discord hurt me to my very soul, for I found, to my surprise, that, in my inner parts, I loved them both well.

Chapter 8

At the end of the year—it was now 1412—I could see that my master would fish no more in any waters. In early December he fell into a faint which lasted many days; it was a deadness resembling the grave, yet did he breathe. His lady-wife and his four sons were summoned to watch at his bedside, for it was thought by all that the end was near. They sat beside him by turns, not leaving him alone.

I had nowhere to lay my head, for my master had kept me by him always in these last months; at night I had been accustomed to sleep on a pallet at the foot of the great bed. I had been forgotten though in this great matter of his dying, and no provision had been made for me; it was obvious, with my visage, I could not creep into a wide bed with some others of the court gentlemen, as was the custom in castles, nor was there a wench ever who would tolerate me. I had found a warm corner by the kitchen fireplace and would curl up there of nights, for the scullery folk were kind, in turn for a few songs. I did not mind, but news of my master did not come my way, and it grieved me.

About the fourth night, Prince Henry, having given up his vigil in turn to another of his brothers, wandered down to the kitchens in search of some ale and bread; perhaps he looked for some companionship, too, for that was a lonely household in those times. None were stirring in the huge kitchen either though, for it was somewhere in the small hours and not yet dawn. I watched from my dim corner as he tiptoed in, recognizing him from the gleam of his gold SS collar, the Lancaster insignia. I started up, unthinking, from where I crouched, and he drew back, the breath hissing in his throat, making a cross-sign before him as he stared into the shadows. When he saw, by the banked fire's light, who it was, he laughed, shakily. "By Our Lady, Sir Hercules, you frighted me . . . I have been too long with the semblance of death, and with my own shadowy thoughts. I took you for an imp, indeed!" He looked down at me, his face troubled. "Is there none else about?" he asked. "I had thought to find somewhat—wine maybe or a crust . . . I have had no supper. Why are you here? I don't understand—"

"My Lord," I said, "this is my bedchamber. . . ." and I gestured to my bedplace; the pastry cook had given me some straw from the hens' roost, and it lay matted on the floor.

"Oh—for sure," said the prince. "Poor Hercules—you slept by my father of nights . . . I had forgot. He will want to find you there, if so be it—by God's Grace—he should wake from his coma. I will find you some corner there in his chamber. . . ."

"My Lord," I said, "I would be grateful, for I am used to be by him. . . . He has not waked then?"

He looked most grave. "Nor will not—so the doctors think. We must pray."

I knew where all was kept there and fetched ale and a cold meat pie; we ate and drank in a kind of hush, I sharing the meal, not having eaten much for worry these last days. Always the prince made little of court niceties, not scorning to take his meat with the lowest; it was a thing the Lady Joanna complained of often, for she was ever mindful of her high place. I think it served him well in later years though, for his soldiers loved him for it, following him into hell itself.

The prince kept his word, too; when next he kept watch by the king he found me a little cubbyhole in the wall behind the royal bed, where my master sometimes went to soak his swollen feet out of sight of his courtiers. He had a brazier brought to me there, too, and coverings, for the nights were cold, and the place next to the outside wall. There was a *prie-Dieu* there, too, but I did not pray, for I had forgot how, if indeed I ever knew.

Though I knew him for what he was, I loved that ruined bully in the great bed and listened to his heavy breathing with tears behind my eyelids; indeed, all my fortunes were bound up with him, and I knew not what would become of me when he was gone. We are all selfish under; it is the nature of things that live.

When the other sons were there or the queen, I did not show myself, fearing they would drive me away, but at the prince's vigil I would creep out and sit beside him mournfully, watching my master. The royal face was yellow as if colored by saffron, but the ugly sores had near dried up; only a scant scattering of scars showed now, in his last days. There was a deeper scar going right around his forehead where the crown had pressed against it; he was a king who wore his badge of office always. He could not wear the crown as he lay in bed though, and it rested beside him on a padded stool; it looked a torturing thing indeed, seeing it thus, encrusted with jewels it was and surrounded at the top with spikes of gold.

Nicholas Colnet, the physician, came each morning early, during the prince's watch, to bathe the king's body and try to force a brew between his lips, but he did not rouse. It was a sad thing to see the withered limbs, with the skin all white and scaling upon them; they looked to be dead already.

The days and nights wore on, and it was near to the time of Christmas, though none spoke of it, the king's state driving away all sense of time. One night I sat as usual beside the prince, none other being by. There was a flagon of red wine on a table; Prince Harry rose to fetch it, being thirsty. As he did so, he brushed against the stool on which the great crown rested, nearly toppling it. He reached out and took it up in his hands to save it. "In Christ's sweet name, it is a heavy thing!" he cried, weighing it in his hands. "I cannot see how my poor sick father bore its weight so long." And saying so, he took the crown and fitted it to his own head. I saw a movement out of the corner of my eye, a movement in the bed. My master's eyes were open, staring at his son. He gave a sort of gusty growl in his throat, once, twice, and then, for a miracle, spoke.

His voice came rusty and the words blurred, but we understood them both. "Can you not wait, Harry? It is only a little now. . . ." And the sick man's lip curved in a ghost of a grin.

The prince set aside the crown and fell to his knees beside the king. "Father—I meant nothing . . . it was nothing. Forgive me, Father. You will have many years yet. . . ."

"That I will not, Harry—" he whispered in a thin rasp. "And there is much to forgive." He shifted a little, stirring the covers. "My mouth is dry—I would like a little broth."

I ran to fetch the doctor, carrying with me the look of horror that I saw on the prince's face as he knelt, fingering his beads.

It was a miracle, if I could believe in them, for the king recovered enough to keep the Christmas celebrations at Elpham Castle, where he had been used to go with his household all the years of his reign. He was paralyzed all down one side though and had to be carried everywhere. His speech, too, had a blurred sound, and a corner of his mouth twisted upward, for he could not control it. I played to him on the lute; he most loved songs of old battles and of the Crusades, for in his youth he had fought in Spain against the Moorish infidel. "A gypsy woman told me once in those Spanish parts," said he, when I fingered my lute softly by his side, "that I would end my days in Jerusalem. I do not see now how it can be, though those dark Egyptians are said to have the Sight. . . ." In a wise, though, her prophecy came true, for he weakened gradually in the New Year, and in March, he suffered another harsh stroke; the chamber to which they bore him, because it was nearest, had ever been called the Jerusalem Chamber, for the old Crusader hangings there were upon its walls. He breathed his last there, with none of the family beside him, for all were out ahunting in the first good weather. He spoke no word, though I sat beside him to the end.

After, candles were brought to stand at the head and foot of his bed, and I waited there with Colnet, the doctor, straightening out his cold limbs in seemly fashion and drawing the rich, furred robe over him. His face in death had a semblance of youth, as so often happens, the deep lines smoothed, and a look of peace upon it. The pits and scars of his old affliction looked like flaws in yellow marble, and one could look upon them without abhorrence. Will it be like that with you, Hercules, I thought, when they lay you away? Will the carven grin relax and the lips cover the wolfish teeth?

We heard the hunters' horns long before they came in sight, and I watched from the chamber window as the party rode into the courtyard, the serving folk crowding there to await them, falling upon their knees. The chapel bells had already begun, tolling the king's passing; as the prince dismounted, a loud cry went up from all the folk, "The king is dead . . . Long live the king!" One came running, I forget who, bearing the heavy crown upon its velvet cushion, to bring it before the prince. I shall never forget his face, flinching as from a blow, and the white look of it. It seemed to me that he looked upon the crown with loathing, but it was perhaps my sick fancy; I am ever, because I partake in so little life of the heart, placing in the inner parts of others thoughts that do not belong there.

Chapter 9

My master's embalmed body lay in state in Canterbury Cathedral until June that the populace might view it and the effigy that would adorn the final resting place be finished; I never saw him again after he was taken from the Jerusalem Chamber where he had died, for I owed allegiance now to my new master, he that had been Prince Harry, and he kept me by his side, as his father had once done.

I had thought at first to be forgot, in the dark days following the old king's death; I had monies saved, paid me for my services, and could have lived my days out in some abbey or other, where the good monks might tolerate the sight of my face in return for my gold, but it was not to be. I chanced to wander into the little private chapel at Elpham the night after the old king's body had been taken away; I had some thought of trying a prayer and burning a candle or two for my master's soul. Again I faced young Harry in the dark, where he prayed alone, and again we spoke, as in the dim kitchen that other time.

"Poor Hercules," he said, laying a hand gently on my head for a moment, "you are his only mourner. The queen feasts above-stairs with her four Breton sons and all her ladies, and my brothers are I know not where. . . ."

He spoke bitterly, and I thought to ease him. "My Lord," I said, "he still has you. . . ."

"I pray out of guilt only," he said, "for I could not love him. . . ." He went on, his words pouring from him as they would not to his equals. "Today I sought out a good priest of my youth, who was one time at Monmouth. He is a recluse now at Westminster. I begged him that he pray for my father's soul . . . and for the soul of Richard, whom he wronged. I would not see my father, black as he was, burn forever in hell. . . ."

I was stunned with horror and knew not what to say; I have said before this that I could find no truth in these Bible beliefs, for I believe our hell is here on earth, or so I have found it. "My

Lord," I stammered out, "is it—is it that you believe . . . such a thing?"

"I believe my father guilty of Richard's blood. It is a thing I have told no other. . . ." I saw he had not taken my meaning; the pious do not question hell. I had forgot.

I said timidly, "I have heard betimes—that Christ forgives all."

"I hope it may be so—I have vowed a new chantry for the abbey if the priests will intercede for him."

I had thought that Christ would do it on His own, but I am not versed in such things; perhaps it is a Lollard thought.

The young king led me by the wrist, out of the chapel and through the streets, some attendants coming out of the shadows to walk beside us to the river, where the barge waited. "Come with me to Coldharbour," said this Harry. "Will you be my man and serve me with sweet forgetfulness, Sir Fool, as you did my father?"

"Sire," I said, giving him my old master's title, "I could wish for no other life. . . ."

He thanked me courteously, smiling a little, but in the light of a suddenly flaring torch I saw that his face was wet with tears. He could not love his father, so he said, and yet did he weep for him!

In those next weeks, before his coronation, there were many black words against the new king, for that he turned his coat, so they said. He had always had those about him, gay and profligate, living by their wits and his bounty; I knew most by sight, for I had seen them while I tumbled or sang, but these did not deign to notice me, and so their names have no moment now. But many and many did the Lord Harry cast from him then, paying them handsomely withal. And several sobersides that would not drink or wench with him he kept, and others, too, that he hired from his father's household. The Lord Scrope and his followers he put from him, too. "For I would not be thought a sodomite king," he said to me in scorn and pity. So quickly then was his court changed—no idle gamesters, wine-stained; no wild girls with flowers in their hair.

The day set for the coronation was Palm Sunday, just three weeks after the death of his father. The workmen labored the nights through, building the tiers that would seat the folk that came to watch where the procession passed in the streets. At the abbey there was no quiet for the hammering and the crashing of great beams for the scaffolding; through all went the sound of the tolling bells, ringing the old king out.

King Harry ate nothing for two days before his crowning; on the morning of the hallowing he was drawn and spent-looking. His Uncle Beaufort chided him for this, saying, "You cannot get through the ceremony this way, Harry . . . you will be there in the abbey six hours and weighted down with the robes of state—you *must* eat!"

The king asked then for honey in the comb, a whimsical thing, for there was none to be had in March. His uncles looked at one another aghast, thinking him light in his head. "Aye—of course there is no comb-honey," he said, "but my stomach cannot tolerate meat—or wine either. . . ."

I had a bit of hoarded marchpane in my pouch, for sweets were my vice, and I fetched it, feeling foolish. It was a cunning thing, wrought in the shape of a sailing boat and colored prettily with Eastern dyes; it had cost a whole sixpence. He took it with a thin smile. "It is a small ship to take me to France, but I hold it an omen. Thank you, Sir Hercules."

And so the new king was crowned with nothing to sustain him but my bit of sweet; it took him through the long day.

A coronation is a rich and awesome sight here in England; since the first Edward they have taken their crownings seriously. The throne that is used is from that same Edward's time, thick-carved of oak and blackened with age; all else is rich as the trappings of Byzantium. Harry knelt for his anointing, barefoot and almost naked. Then he was robed in state, each furred and jeweled garment blessed. The robing took a long time, and the air in the abbey grew stifling and thick as a pall with the breath of hundreds. Several women fainted and had to be carried out, and sweat showed in beads on the king's face as he faced front to receive the weight of the crown.

Then the king was brought to St. Edward's throne, and the bishops and peers came forward to render homage and swear fealty. They swore on bended knee, their folded hands between the new king's palms. Each man, when he had done this, kissed the king's left cheek and touched the crown. The ceremony took a long time, for each oath was made separately, and the king so borne down with the weight of his crown and robes that he moved slowly.

The king's three brothers swore first, after the churchmen; then his uncle, Thomas Beaufort, Earl of Dorset, and his cousins, Aumerle and Cambridge. The next to swear was Edmund Mortimer; the king's first act had been to release this young man from the Tower, where he had been a prisoner since Richard's abdication. There was a rustle went around the great hall then, for this Mortimer was closer true heir than the king, by right of primogeniture, and his appearance, too, was like those Plantagenets, fair and golden, like to Richard himself; there must have been folk who minded that so looked all English kings, in times past, and bethought them, too, of his blood, more royal than Harry's own. He was tall and slender, shy from his lonely life, brought to a prison pallor by the years of his confinement. It was seen that he was afflicted with a stammer and spoke in halting wise, one time stopping altogether in the long words of the oath. There was a hush as of horror till he found the words and went on to the end, all breathing a sigh, relieved.

The king and court moved slowly through the streets then, the people cheering, and so to the palace for the coronation feast. I was at the lowest table, well below the salt, but even from there I could see that the new-made king did no more than touch the seventeen courses set before him with the tines of his fork, though he took, from time to time, a sip of wine. The banquet lasted five hours. My wits were addled from watching only, and in my light imp's suit my body ran with sweat, my head reeling. I could never have borne to sit in the high seat, under eight fur robes and a heavy crown all this long day. But then I am not a king, only a poor fool.

Chapter 10

My new master was less and less disposed to revelry as the first year of his reign wore on; there was much unrest and lawlessness in all the towns and warring factions within the court itself, and he had many and many sober duties. I was not called upon to mime or entertain but to play quietly sometimes of a night and by day write down my lord's own songs; often, after a long day in council or a hard ride, his face wore a look of weariness almost akin to his dead father's.

One of the first acts of the new king was to disinter the body of King Richard, which lay in an inglorious grave at King's Langley. He brought the royal bones, with great pomp and ceremony, to the beautiful tomb in Westminster Abbey which Richard himself had commissioned long ago. Over this grave are the golden effigies of Richard and his first queen, Anne; the doors were opened to the people, and for weeks, folk filed past, marveling and praising the pious and just action of King Harry. It was a gracious gesture of honor to the man his father had wronged, but my mind, ever cynical, read more in it, too. There were still folk who held that Richard was alive in Scotland; a mort of petty rebellions, indeed, had risen there in his name. King Harry, by this new ceremony of reburial, put down these hopes forever; Richard, now, was truly dead, and the whole realm was invited to mourn him. There would be no more Scottish rebellions; it was a political move of great shrewdness. This king, I have found, has more layers than an onion!

The deeds of his father weighed still on his conscience; again, in my cynic's mind, came the thought that this Harry feared those deeds might redound to his own disfavor; at any rate, he went to great lengths to expiate those sins. He undertook the reconstruction of the abbey at Westminster and lavished fine gifts, vestments, psalters, sacred vessels, and the like, upon its holy monks. He rebuilt Richard's royal manor at Sheen and raised a new Carthusian monastery near to it. A nunnery he founded near there, too, for Brigettines. I was present at its dedication;

238

there was some irony in it. The words went somewhat like this: "Henry, a true son of the God of Peace, who gave peace and taught peace and chose St. Bridget as a lover of peace." As a member of King Harry's household, I had been privy for some months now to his constant planning, in all his spare moments, for the invasion of France! But, of course, I am, as I said before, a right true cynic.

There were many more pious acts of great generosity (with the realm's monies)—a new-founded Brotherhood of St. Giles in London, a monastery in Anglesey, grants to Oxford and Cambridge, grants for life to his nurse, to old servants, to priests and hermits. He began to be regarded as a king of surpassing mercy and gentleness; some even named him saint!

His dealing with his first Parliament again illustrated his mood of appeasement; there was much cooperation on both sides. The commons made many brave demands, most of which were met with courtesy by the king; they asked that all Welsh and Irish be expelled to their own homes and that no commerce be permitted with these nationals. The commons cried, "England for the English!" and Harry bowed to them; those countries, part of England by custom and conquest, were now to be treated as subject races, a bitter policy. In return, Harry received ten thousand pounds annually for his own household upkeep, besides generous revenues to the new government's needs. So all went home satisfied . . . or nearly all.

One group which was not appeased was the Lollard sect, for Harry's coat had turned for them, indeed. I think the Lollards had expected an easing of the persecutions, for that their greatest leader, Oldcastle, was the king's own friend, and in his youthful past, Harry had consorted with many of their persuasion. Often had I listened as he argued doctrine with Oldcastle and others, too, in a mood of sweet reason and tolerance, albeit he could not agree. Now, though, was Harry become fiercely orthodox, satisfying even Arundel. After his coronation he had ordered a public burning of heretical books, the largest and most radical of which belonged to Oldcastle. Arundel and other orthodox churchmen were pushing constantly for the arrest of this man, and, in spite of many efforts on the king's part, it was accomplished at last. The king wept, but as he said to me privately (for I was becoming his confidant), his "hands were tied." Kings are powerful, as I see it, true—but they must play games also, like the rest of the world.

I was present at Oldcastle's trial; the king had got permission for his old friend to state his case. The man read a document of his own composing, very legal and impressive it was, for he had been a master of law; the churchly court, though, would have none of it, deeming it too general in thought and too wily in intent. They demanded answers to two crucial questions. Did the accused believe that in the sacrament of the mass the material bread remained after the consecration? Did the accused believe that confession to a priest was necessary in the sacrament of penance? Oldcastle replied that he had nothing to add to what he had already read out. The churchmen sternly read him aloud the official teaching of the church on these two questions, granted him several days to contemplate his answer, and warned him of the consequences of heretical belief.

Sir John was brought again before the court two days later; he had made up his mind, that brave man, and he answered as bold as the old warrior that he was. He said that if the church taught that no material bread remained after the consecration, the church was wrong and had corrupted the Scriptures. He said, also, that confession was not a necessity for salvation, but contrition was. They questioned him further; I can never forget him standing there, that ruddy, portly knight that men called Painted Jack. Calm he had and a pleasant bearing, but steel beneath. He was asked what honor he would pay to a crucifix. "I would wipe it," he said, "with a goodly cloth, milords, and keep it clean." "What reverence do you pay the Pope?" was the last question. "He is Antichrist," he answered quietly, thus sealing his doom. He was handed over to the secular arm, taken to the Tower, and condemned to die at the stake.

That night, late, the king sat alone, with none about but me, and he would have no music neither, for his mood was very low. He sat long, brooding into the fire; finally he slapped his thigh, rising. "He shall not die!" he cried. "For that I love him well— that great old fighter—and have known his worth. He shall go free if I strike off his chains myself! It is not weakness neither, only . . . but he is the stuff of martyrs, that man. A king cannot have martyrs about. . . ."

And the king called to him several fellows of his household, enjoining them to secrecy. "Go to that tavern in Nettle Row—the one they name The Fish . . . there is a silver-gilt fish-sign swings above it. . . ."

"Aye, my Lord, I know it," said one, a soldier, by the look of him.

"Ask for a man called Bardolf. . . ."

"I know him," said the same soldier. "A foul scrivener-fellow . . . one of those sort that spits on the cross as soon as look at it. Shall we bloody him up a little for you, sire?"

"No—no . . . I'll handle him myself. Just bring him to me. Go by the back ways. I want no witnesses."

When the man Bardolf came, hooded and cloaked as closely as a monk, he was closeted with the king for an hour, and I never saw his face but was sent to bed like an errant schoolboy, though before this, I had been privy to much. It crossed my mind that the king might be using this fellow as a procurer; he had had no women lately. It was not till days later that I put two and two together.

It may well be that my "two and two" made five—I cannot swear to it; but one night in October Oldcastle escaped from the Tower, though he was chained hand and foot. All men marveled, some mentioning the devil; others said it bespoke the great strength of the Lollards, that they could loose their leader from the strongest prison of London. I thought I knew better and think so still, though the king deplored the escape publicly and offered a reward for Oldcastle's recapturing.

The escape, though, was the signal, in a way, for open revolt, though the king could not have foreseen this. The Lollards saw, with the example of their leader's trial, that rational criticism and reform of the church had been counted as high treason, and they saw, too, that if Oldcastle were taken again and died, the priests would be able to destroy the whole sect.

By the end of the year, there were bills posted on all the many church doors of London, threatening that a hundred thousand Lollards were ready to strike a blow for freedom; propaganda went forth to all parts; messengers were sent all over England and into Wales, too, summoning all the sect to a rendezvous in London. The new king was called by them the Priests' Prince, and the Tool of Satan. The king, by Christmas time, knew that he would be soon faced with a full-scale rebellion. Some said that the Lollards planned to kill the king and place Oldcastle on the throne, dividing all the wealth of the vanquished church among themselves. I cannot credit this myself, for they were never a bloodthirsty lot; yet has much devastation been set in motion by the zeal of the religious, so it may be they would have been as all others, had they prevailed.

The king had his spies among these Lollard enemies, of course, and he learned the time and place of their rendezvous. It was to be at Fickett's Field, just outside Temple Bar, on the night of January 9.

The king, with his three brothers, his uncles, and most of those knights who had fought beside him in Wales, rode to the site of the rebels' meeting place and awaited them, ordering all the gates of the city to be closed and guarded and patrols to be posted all along the open fields.

From the midlands and the west country, from York and from Wales, the Lollard groups were making their way to London, unsuspecting. None of these groups had leaders, for their cry was that Christ would lead them. If He did, He played them false, for straight into the arms of the king's men they marched and were quickly disarmed, group by little group, and taken off to prison. What followed is grim and dreadful to tell.

Four gallows were set up in St. Giles' Fields, and as many as a hundred were executed there. Though they were urged to recant, none did. The field was called by the people Martyrs' Field, so that Harry's connivance in Oldcastle's escape, if such it was, happened in vain, for there were martyrs aplenty about the realm then.

I said this, in a commenting sort of way, just as though it were a random thought. I saw the king's face close in upon itself, as he sat thinking; I do not flatter myself that what I said influenced him, but it may have put a flea in his ear, as they say in country parts. By the end of January he had stopped the executions and was granting amnesty (to all who would pay a stiff fine). However much I helped, I gave thanks for it, that no more suffered.

The strange thing is, that, even for handsome reward, or for free pardon, none betrayed Oldcastle; he was not captured for many years.

Old Arundel died in February, but he had lived long enough to see the hated Lollards scattered, and the prince who once openly defied him now hailed as the "champion of Christ" and the "pillar of the faith."

Chapter 11

In the spring of the year, early April it was, and the yellow of the daffodil starring the pale new grass, I walked with my king in the Tower gardens. These had been once, as he had said, a prideful sight, in the days of Richard, but in the war-torn time of the Lancasters, the grounds had all fallen into sad neglect. "I must make all fine again," said King Harry, "if time permits. It was a gladsome place to sit once." There were no flower beds at all, and the grass was not kept cut, but a few stone statues and marble benches still stood, like relics of a happier morning, green with mossy lichen and discolored from the rain.

There came to him there Meredith ab Owen, brother of the lady Morgan, as summoned. The king had given orders that all the ladies of Owen's house that were still lodged, prisoners, in the Tower, should be made ready to go free, back to their Welsh homeland. "There are none so many, Your Highness, for some have died. There are the twins and their sons, and my wife, Elliw. . . ." I watched him as I spoke for signs of Morgan, but there were few. He was silver-gray now, not yellow, though he could not be much above the king's own years, and he was bent, halt of one leg, and one arm dangled lifelessly. His clothes, too, were shabby and of an old-fashioned cut, the red dragon of Wales almost faded now from his breast.

"Think you that your father still lives?" asked the king. "We have never seen sign of him. . . ."

"Sire," he said, slowly, "I do believe . . . he is hid somewhere in our hills, for there are many secret places there that he has knowledge of, and many of the wild hill chieftains would lay down their lives for him still—" A touch of pride crept into his voice then, a wistful-sounding note, too. "I doubt not that he has found shelter all these years." But a look came like a cloud over his thin features. "He has not many years, though, left . . . he is past his prime—and it would be not much more than a cave in a mountain that held him, for so they live still, in those parts. . . ."

"I would have you take him this pardon . . . full pardon from his king—" And King Harry reached into his tunic and brought out a scroll, hung with several of the royal seals.

Meredith looked up at him from where he still kept, on his knees; it was a sea-blue look and fey, reminding me at last of Morgan. "My Lord, there are some who would say that you do this thing to follow me with your men and spy out my father where he hides. How do I know it is not so?"

"It is the word of prince to prince," said the king grandly; he is ever given to fine words such as he learned in old books. "A squadron of my men will escort you to the border, for your safety —after, you will go on your way with the women."

"I will do it," said Meredith, bowing his head.

"It cannot take you longer than a month," said the king. "I will expect you back here at the Tower within that time. . . ." He stood for a moment, looking down at the Welshman's bent head, a strange look, almost of begging. "If so be it you see the Lady Morgan and none about . . ." He stopped as Meredith looked up, that same, fey, Morgan-look in his eyes. The king's face turned haughty, the soft look fleeing. "Tell the lady I am king here now in this land. Tell her that I command her presence here in court. . . ."

He waved Meredith to rise. The Welshman smiled. "It is two hard tasks you have set me, my king . . . the Welsh are a proud race. And I have been long a prisoner. How do you know I will come back at all?"

"As I have pledged my word not to follow—so will you pledge yours . . . prince to prince. . . ." The king was on his own fine noble ground again, the Welshman smiling still his lingering, graceful smile, almost as though he mocked.

But "I will do it," he said and bowed low.

It was closer to a fortnight than a month when Meredith came back from Wales, presenting himself to his jailers at the Tower. The king received him in those same gardens from which he had dispatched him. "What say you?" he asked.

The Welshman spoke heavily. "I am sorry, My Lord, he would not take the pardon. He said he had done no wrong and was no felon but a leader of his people only. He said he had led them to defeat—but not to disgrace. I am sorry . . . I told you he was proud."

The king stood for a moment, fingering the scroll, the seals still hanging from it. "And Morgan—what of Morgan?"

"She will not come," said Meredith. "She said a king could not command a married woman from her husband's side. . . ."

There was a long moment, while the king's face grew dark; I was reminded of his father and waited for the storm. It did not come though; the dark blood cleared, and he said mildly, "It seems the lady too is proud. How does she?"

"She is in good health, sire. She has two sons."

"Already?" spoke the king softly. "And there is none for Lancaster. . . ." After a bit he looked at Meredith. "And Owen . . . how was that proud man?"

"Oh, sire," cried Meredith, his control breaking, "he is sick. There is a heavy soreness in his chest, and he coughs blood— though he tried to hide it . . . I think I will never see him again in this world!"

The king reached out the scroll. "His pardon is yours—if you will take it. Get back to Wales and to your father. . . ." He paused and then went on. "The pardon was not to dishonor him —though he will not credit it. . . . I had thought to make all clear in the world's eyes, that is all. There is no man I honor more. . . ."

That night the king sent for a woman; it was the first time in many weeks. "Find one who is passing tall," he told his man, "and with yellow hair." He kept her for a night only; I saw her in the morning, going out by the side entrance, clutching a velvet purse. She was young, from the northern countries, big and pink-and-white; under the yellow hair her face oxen-dull, with a look of sullen greed.

King Harry's second Parliament sat soon after; among other things, it passed a statute which would have delighted old Arundel's heretic-hungry heart. It was prompted not by the commons but by the king's council directly, and ordered that all officers of the crown should "exert their entire pains and diligence to oust, cease, and destroy all manners of heresies and errors vulgarly called Lollardies." As I look back on it though, Lollardy was not stamped out, only damped down; those who bought their lives with steep fines did not cease their beliefs but kept them alive within their secret hearts. There was a book of sermons and tracts, painstakingly copied in the hundreds, called <i>The Lantern of Light,</i> and though it was death to own it or even to read it, it was known to enormous numbers of folk as a second Bible. I have read it (a thing which now I will admit) and it contains no word of treason, only simple faith that any lowly person may understand.

At that Parliament, too, it was revealed that the piracy of the French coast by the men of Cornwall and Devon was worrying all. For many years these folk had depended, strange as it sounds, on these French raids for their very livelihood; it was their trade. But the French also retaliated by raiding our shores, as is natural, to my mind, and so, in a sense, there was a petty war always with us in those coastal parts. The channel was never free for shipping and trade, and it was peril to cross it. Several times the commons referred in their speaking to the king's "adversary of France," and there were heated debates and much waving of arms and cheering, for all the world as if a full-scale war were awaging. Indeed, I saw that such could not be far away. I have read the writings of the famous French chronicler, him that is called Froissart, and remember one thing he wrote; true, it was concerning the old wars of the Black Prince, but watching the folk of England shouting in happy choler for battle, I think it is as true today. "The English," he wrote, "will never honor or love their king unless he be victorious and a lover of arms . . . their land is more fulfilled of riches . . . when they are at war than when they are at peace. They take delight and solace in battles and slaughter." It has a ring, that passage, for look you what happened to poor Richard, that peaceful king! And of course, King Harry, as a boy, had seen it all!

Another thing, though I am not excusing my king's march into the French lands, was that there were much unrest, much lawlessness in all the realm; unemployed soldiery plundered the countryside, raping and looting. None were safe, except behind the walls of the towns, the traveler taking his life in his two hands. Going to war against the hereditary French enemy might kill two birds with one stone; it is an unfortunate metaphor to use concerning war, but never mind, it is my own. The battle-hungry soldiery would be satisfied, and the channel freed of enemy craft, too, is my meaning. Also, if such a war were won, it would redound forever to Lancastrian glory. I cannot set myself up as historian, for all is too close, but sure it was to me that from all directions there came creeping the smell of war.

By the next Parliament, in November, all was out in the open. The commons and the council both advised the king to "negotiate . . . but not to shrink from the necessity of war." So fast had this temper of the times risen! As for King Harry, at night he pored over maps and played mock battles with an old set of toy knights. He studied his lineage, too, convincing himself that, by right of descent, he was the rightful King of France! This is hard to credit, for what claim there was was through Richard, whom the Lancasters had deposed. But men will convince themselves of anything, if they want it badly enough!

The Beauforts were back in power, and Uncle Thomas was sent to the court of France to offer terms. The king asked the crown of France, so it was not surprising that the peace terms were refused. I was present after Earl Thomas' return, when the king sat at meat with both uncles. He showed no rancor at the French replies; I think he did not expect compliance. "It is a start," he said, laughing. "Who spoke? The king or Isabeau?"

"It was the Duke of Berry," said Thomas. "For the poor king is in a fit again, and Isabeau plays her own game. She looks to have broken with Burgundy. . . ." They made some rude jokes then, for that queen is fair quarry, having played the whore with so many.

"I have heard she is shrewd though, Isabeau," said Harry.

"She is a lady will ever have her way," said his uncle, "and cares not how she comes by it."

Upon the great flat desk where the toy soldiers stood were scattered papers from France and several small portraits in frames of gold. The king picked one up idly. "Who is this?" he asked. "She looks like a stuffed owl. . . ."

"It is Anne of Burgundy," said Thomas. "You are offered her . . . with some few duchies. . . ."

"Not for all the wealth of Araby," said the king, carelessly tossing the picture down among the papers and taking up another. "They are not breeding them right nowadays, these noble damsels . . . Richard had a flower-face for queen. I remember her from my boyhood. . . ."

"She is dead, Hal. That is her sister you are holding."

The king looked down at the portrait; it was on ivory and prettily tinted, though I could not see the face. "She is not so pretty as was Isabelle . . . but some fairness she has." He studied it for a moment. "I know her name—Katharine—spelled with a *K* . . . someone knew her . . . I cannot see her hair, so tightly coiffed she is. . . ."

"I think it is a chestnut color," said Thomas, "for I saw the lady at court."

"And curly, or so I heard," said King Harry, "and needing no crimping irons—it is shame to cover it. . . ."

The Lord Thomas, seeing his interest, spoke again. "Hal, do not set your thoughts upon her, for they will not have you. It was told me plain."

"How is it, then, that you have her portrait?" demanded the king.

"She herself," said his uncle. "She gave it to me, looking scared."

"Offer for her," said the king. "She pleases me . . . You saw her there, Uncle. How does she look? Her nose seems something long. . . ."

"Hal, her father is a Valois," said Thomas, laughing. "Isabeau called him droop-nose . . . although I think she meant something else, in truth. The little Katharine's nose is as pretty as the rest of her, though . . . I spoke in jest." He looked grave then, Thomas. "But, Hal, I think they want to wait with her—they have held off these ten years, and she is the last of their daughters—their only pawn. . . ."

"Then have they waited too long!" said King Harry in some anger. "Soon she will be too old for a bride . . . offer for her. . . ."

The king kept the little portrait by him, in a coffer full of old trinkets, along with some unstrung pearls, a worn letter, and a lock of yellow hair.

Meanwhile, the Duke Thomas went on with his French negotiations. It is the measure of the turmoil and dissent among these French that they did not throw him out of the council room bodily, for Harry's demands were outrageous, to my mind. But perhaps their very boldness took the French off guard. King Harry claimed as his own the territories of Normandy, Anjou, Maine, and Touraine, besides many others, old spoils of the Black

Prince. He claimed, too, old forgotten monies due from the ransom of King John of France, dating from 1360; they were reckoned at one million and six hundred thousand French crowns! Also, he demanded the hand of Katharine of the portrait, with a dowry of two million crowns; she cannot have been flattered!

Amazingly, the French countered with an enlargement of the English duchy of Aquitaine, an enormous concession. They ignored the old ransom claim but offered a dowry of six hundred thousand. The haggling went on back and forth for nearly a year, the French finally offering eight hundred thousand, plus a costly trousseau and all the royal jewels.

"By God, no!" cried Harry, at the end. "We shall go in and take what we want! Enough of this bargaining . . . I am no merchant!" And so began the preparations for a full-scale war.

Chapter 12

During all the spring of that year, King Harry's emissaries were in the Low Countries to contract for ships that would transport his army across the channel, for in England there were only six royal ships large enough to do the job. Soldiers and sailors were levied at a fair wage promise; in all there were upwards of ten thousand, eager for the excitement and spoils of war. Such eagerness was not mine; I quaked in my new boots whenever I stopped to think on it, for I was going, too. I was listed among the fifteen minstrels, at the end of the muster rolls, after all the stablemen, physicians, lawyers, scribes, and cooks. I had a suit of chain mail, painted a fine red and boasting horns and a tail, so that I was known everywhere still as the most famous imp, even in war!

My master was grown more pious still; I think he sought to prove that God was on his side, for he made pilgrimage to all the famous shrines of England, sometimes spending all night on his knees, and taking horse in the morning to join his gathering forces. On a July Saturday we rode forth, all his household, to go with the king to Southampton, where camped his army, the greatest fighting force ever assembled in that realm, or so the chroniclers say.

It was a hot, wet day, the air fouled with fog, such as England is ever plagued with. The sweat ran down my body under my light mail, making sore places where the metal rubbed; I thought with pity of the knights in their heavy plate and the poor horses, mailed, too, and carrying their heavy loads. We came in sight of Southampton waters by noon; the fog had not lifted, and the masts of the ships at anchor there rose like ghost spires, half-seen in the gray air. There were fifteen hundred of them, a sight to lift your heart . . . or throw it down, depending upon your inner temper.

We lodged at Porchester Castle in Portsmouth Harbor, all us folk of the king's privy household. There was not sleeping room; we all bedded down in the courtyard—a good thing it was warm weather! Food there was, in plenty, though, oxen and sheep roasting whole in all the plains roundabout, requisitioned by the army. The smell from the cooking fires, pleasant at first, grew sickening after a while, so numerous they were; it was flesh, after all, that was cooking, and not so very different from a Lollard's!

I had nothing to do with my time, for King Harry was too busy for music or song-making, and I had no friends; I used to walk sometimes outside the castle walls, seeking escape from the crowds and the noise, though I could not get out of range of the charred meat smell. I would take along a leather wallet, filled with meat and bread, and sit on the green shoreside, watching the floating ships and the little moving figures, like ants, that were busy upon them. I made songs, too, trying them out on a little pipe. Once, two little girls crept close to listen; children of the people they were, filthy and ragged, and thin as weeds; it was their sheep, no doubt, that offended my nose, for soldiery ever lived off the land. I stopped playing and reached into my wallet, holding out my packet of food to them, but they ran away, frightened of my face; I had forgot again. I waited a while, but they never came back; when I returned to the castle, I left the food and a little bag of sugared comfits under a rock, for I fancied I heard a rustle in the bushes where they hid. It was small pickings, but I hope they found it; I did not see them again.

It was during these weeks of last-minute preparation that King Harry first learned of the conspiracy that was always after spoken of as the Southampton Plot; the lords involved were of the French expedition, strange to say, and pledged to the king's support! At the head of this conspiracy was Richard, the Earl of Cambridge, blood-kin to Harry; he had known him as a boy at Richard's court. Others involved were Sir Thomas Grey of Heton and Henry, Lord Le Scrope, of Masham, who had used, at one time, to be much about the king, before his crowning. I have often wondered if it was this lord's pique at being cast aside by the king which induced him to join with Cambridge, for he had never turned his mind before to things political. They sought to get Oldcastle and some of his Lollards, and the fugitive Owen Glendower and his Welsh; this all came out at the trial, though the plans had not got so far toward being carried out, and so those leaders were not suspect. The plan was to capture and kill the king, and place the Earl of Mortimer upon his rightful throne, proclaiming the House of Lancaster as wholly impostor. This was to take place on August 1, and all the plans were laid, the Lord Mortimer privy also to the plot. On the night of July 31, close on midnight, the Lord Mortimer came to Harry with the tale, throwing himself on the king's mercy.

The king did not lose his head, as some would have done, hearing of such a well-nigh completed plot; he, instead, summoned all his lords about him, as if to council, and revealed to them all that he had word of a conspiracy against him, asking what steps he should take. Among them, of course, were the guilty men. They were taken by surprise and knew the jig was up; they confessed all and were led off to prison. The king then had a commission of ten lords and two judges appointed, and a jury of Southampton citizens was hurriedly got together. The trial was held at Southampton Castle on August 2. So frighteningly fast did this king move, like a great cat apouncing!

The two, Grey and Cambridge, confessed all, but Scrope denied it at first. After, he pleaded mercy from Harry, begging that he forget not that they two had slept once in the same bed! This last public utterance did him in, for it implied an intimacy that would be sweet to gossips forever. King Harry fumed in his private chamber, cursing the wild nights of his youth, but a public denial would do naught but add to the bad look of the thing, so kept his silence. But poor silly Scrope suffered the full penalty of the law—hanging, drawing, and quartering—a hideous death. The other two plotters were merely beheaded. Bits of them were stuck up on walls throughout the kingdom, to rot and to warn.

All was ready for the embarkation; the ships were loaded, all, and had been for some days; each morning bedrolls and gear were got together for traveling and each night unrolled again. The wind was contrary and would not blow for France. No matter how hard the king prayed in the chapel or swore in his chamber, it blew soft in our faces from the sea. For four days it was contrary, and we were becalmed. I rode with the king on the fourth day to the shore to look at the ships where they rode the water like painted boats, their sides brightly daubed with the signs of chivalry and the arms of Lancaster, and the thin flags drooping at their mastheads. With us rode the Lord Mortimer, carrying a royal falcon upon his wrist. It was a gift from the king, and he thanked him shyly, for this young man was still like a youth, his stammer plaguing him.

"It is I must thank you, Edmund," said King Harry, "for that you revealed my enemies. . . ." He looked at Mortimer, his eyes keen. "Were you never tempted? There are those who say the kingdom is yours."

"I would not have a throne got by a trick," said the Mortimer, his stammer gone for a moment then.

The king still looked at him, his horse reined close, a little smile playing about his lips. "Yet did Lancaster gain it by just such. . . ."

The earl flushed, casting down his eyes. "You were a boy then, Cousin Harry . . . your father—" He looked up, suddenly. "One thing I would know from you, sire—how did Richard die?"

"I do not know," said the king. "A thing you will not believe. . . ."

"I do believe you," said Mortimer, after a moment. "I, too, will speak true. I would not conspire, but many and many a time—my whole life spent in prison—I wished you dead, and all made right."

The king spoke very low. "I carry no weapon, and there is none here but peaceful Hercules. Now is your chance."

Mortimer smiled, his face as guileless as a girl's. He shook his head.

"No, my Lord—it was a darkling prisoner's thought. I am not of that stuff either. Nothing pleases me so much now as my freedom—hawking and hunting, riding in the blue air—after so long. A crown would not sit so easy."

"It does not sit easy on any head, I think," said the king, shortly.

The Mortimer was flushed again about the neck, his fairness all bright. "Harry," he said, "I am not one to lead men, but my sword is yours. I have savored my free ways—but I yet will follow you to France. . . ." His words seemed to run down, and his old stammer choked him.

"No," said the king, "I have claimed enough from you, Cousin. Stay here and tend your estates." He stretched out his hand. "And—good hawking!"

Mortimer snatched off his bonnet, bending to kiss the king's hand. As he straightened in the saddle, his back to the seawall, his long fair locks, unbarbered, streamed out behind him.

"The wind blows fair, Cousin!" cried King Harry. "The wind blows fair for France!"

The first ship of the fleet was Henry's own flagship, where I rode, with all the privy household and some few lords. She was named the *Royal Trinity*, and none but me thought it blasphemous, for King Harry was worshiped now among his followers like a very warrior saint. She rode proudly ahead of the others, her masthead decked with Plantagenet arms and signs of the holy church, her waist red-painted and hung with silver antelopes and golden embroidered swans. But misfortune came out of nowhere; several of the bravely decked fleet caught afire and burned to cinders, the sailors perishing in the waves while all looked on helplessly. There were mutterings that it was a sign from heaven against the expedition, for there were some still who believed it was a foolhardy mission, but the king would not turn back, making light of all such prophecies.

Two days it took to reach Harfleur; I was sick the whole time, and many others, too, though the king paced the deck as healthy as a leopard. I had expected we would head for Calais, for it was our own English garrison, but the king chose the Harfleur way, to save time, for it was but a hundred miles from Paris, with a straight road cutting through by the river. No hostile sail showed while our ships beat down channel, though the walls of Harfleur had slit windows opening on to the sea. We came in sight of the city on the third day; it was an awesome sight, its walls rising sheer for miles above its deep moat, its three great gates closed, the drawbridges fastened up strongly. From the sea the town looked as if drawn upon a map, each turret, tower, and keep etched boldly against the sky. The earthworks fronted the whole, but we saw no soldiery, and no ships sailed out from the estuary. We made landfall in the shelter of the huge chalk cliffs, that rose above us like grim white clouds. We sent soldiers to spy out the way, but they saw no inhabitants; the place looked to be a thing of mists, silent as the grave.

No oppposition showing, all the men, horses, stores, and siege weapons were unloaded, and tents were erected in the lands before the city. It had been the king's plan to ring the city with trenches and ramparts, but before he could put it into effect, the garrison and citizenry of Harfleur flooded the flatlands to the north of the town, making an impassable marsh in those parts. It was a cunning stroke, for with it in the summer's heat came marsh fever, running bowels, disease, and death.

At first all seemed well; the men sang in their tents outside the walls and were merry as they set the siege machines to the walls, taking bets on how long before the city would fall. The king himself went among the soldiers at night, cheering them, bringing his minstrel folk among them to make music. I was a favorite again, as in the old days in the markets, doing my rudest antics and broadest jokes; I had thought I had forgot how, in my days at court. But all the rough fellows saluted me, stretching their lips wide with their fingers and aping all my movements.

By day, though all knew the people within were running short of food, we too were suffering. Our rations were running out, and there was not much to be got from the countryside that was undefended, except rotten apples and unripe grapes. One by one, the men fell ill, and a rotten-sweet stink lay over the whole camp; I know not what caused it, some named it the siege smell, though I think it came from stagnant water and from the dead rats that floated in it, thrown down by the people behind the walls. None of the water was good to drink either, and many grew sick and died. The Bishop of Norwich, the Earl of Suffolk, and the Earl of Arundel all died in the early days, and many followed.

After two and a half weeks, one out of every three sickened, and as many as two thousand died. The ones left were, for the most part, more dead than alive, and hundreds, too, were sent home. Our poor ships limped across the channel, filled with all those stricken souls. Thomas of Clarence, the king's own brother, that merry, feckless soul, headed the list, grievously ill. At least he was out of it, though he wept like a babe to miss the fighting. The other brother, Humphrey, did not take the sickness, nor did the king. Needless to say, for I am a puny sort, I was laid low for weeks. The king kept me by him, though, since I could not fight anyway, and I mended, in the end. I got my taste of war though, nonetheless; my first taste and, I hope, my last. But that is another story.

BOOK IV

The Goddam

(Told by John Page,
English knight-at-arms)

Chapter 1

The first time I heard that name they called us English, I saw red. I was first man up on the siege ladder outside Harfleur; before I was halfway up I saw her, a real witch she was, black hair and laughing, young. She was leaning over the top of the wall, between the spikes. "Goddam, go home!" she yelled, in her Frenchie way, and holding something up in her hand over her head. I saw her ready to throw and I ducked; it just missed me, a whole potful of boiling oil. Even so, a couple of drops hit my cheek, stinging like hellfire. She got hold of the top of the ladder then, and another slut came to help; they managed to push the whole siege tower over backwards. I was on top, so I just got a little shook up, but the fellow down under had a broken leg from it. I looked up at her, way above me now and mean-faced because she missed, and shook my fist. "You goddamned wild woman," I hollered, "wait till I get inside!" "Goddam, goddam, goddam," I heard from up there, "Goddam, go home!"

We got used to the name after a while, and it just went in one ear and out of the other; after all, it wasn't no worse than what we called them Frenchies, and a mild sort of oath, when you come to think of it. I used to wonder, though, what became of that black-haired girl; she stuck in my mind, some ways, till I saw her again.

That was one of the first days in the siege there; after, I got sick, like a lot of others, and just lay around shivering and puking, and dragging myself off into the bushes. I got over it, though some didn't and had to be sent home, back on the ship. They said the king's own brother was among them, but I never heard for sure. And some died, too. It was the dead rats those Frenchies threw in the water, poisoned it, like.

But, as I say, I got over it, and the siege got over, too, in the end, and they had to surrender. I got to say this for King Harry; he paid us for every day, even when we was sick, which was more than his father did. Sixpence a day I got, archer's pay; that was before I got to be a knight, though I had a horse and all. I was in the last battle of the Welsh wars, being just old enough to go; me and the king are about the same age, as I figure it, only I got me a wife now three years, and he just beginning to think about it. We got a whole squadron of those Welsh now, right here in France fighting on our side, them that used to be our enemies. Makes you think.

Still and all, it was the middle of September before Harfleur fell, and we landed there on August 2. When I look back on it, seems like we'd all have died there if it had gone on much longer. As it was, there weren't too many of us left. I can read, and I saw the muster rolls; the priest that kept them was the same one I confessed to every Sunday. There were six hundred knights and five thousand archers, our army almost cut in half. There was some said—the high nobles I mean—that we'd ought to go on back to England and get more men, but old Whoring Harry said no, we'd push on. That's what we called him in those days, not in a nasty way, mind, and not when there were ladies around, but just among ourselves, in a friendly way.

That other siege, at Harlech, in Wales, well, that went on so long you got sort of sorry for those that were left; they came out of that place looking like bags of bones, or worse, and some couldn't walk at all. But here it was different, they was no worse off inside than we was; a little hungry maybe, and I guess some of the women were scared. First off, Harry took all the rich folk prisoner and held them for ransoms, but he put them all together in a fine tent up in an airy place on a hill near his own quarters, which wasn't too bad, and more than they deserved; after all they had a chance to surrender in the beginning, without making trouble for everybody. The poor folk had to do what they were told, of course, so you can't blame them, and of course, they got the worst of it, too, like they always do. Harry lined them all up and gave them a fair choice though; he was always fair, Harry, even later, when his blood was up, as you might say. Anyway, he said those that wanted to swear allegiance to him and to England could stay in the town and nobody would bother them. Even so, though, there was quite a few that wouldn't swear; the priest said more than two thousand, and they got driven out, even the women and children. They were a devilish proud bunch, calling insults at us, and throwing stones, too, even the littlest. An archer near me fitted arrow to his bow, black-angry he was at their taunts, but Harry rode out from where he was and drew his sword and struck off the man's hand. "I've given no order to fire!" he cried, loud as a bell. The hand, with the arrow still held in it, fell right at my feet, with the blood spurting out a yard from the stump. He could be hard, King Harry, when he liked, but soldiers are supposed to obey orders—that's what makes an army.

Even so, King Harry gave all the women that got deported twelvepence each and permission to take all the possessions they could carry out of their homes; it wasn't much money but better than nothing, which is what most conquerors would have given. We heard later that farther up the French road those folk were met by their own army, and taken on to Rouen, so they didn't do too bad, considering.

Old Harry didn't allow any sacking of the city, or looting, so none of us soldiers had our pickings, and lots of men grumbled; he feasted us all like royalty though, letting the conduits in the streets run with wine and setting all the cooks and bakers to work. There was food there, behind the walls, see, only the rich were hoarding it, like always.

He wouldn't allow any raping either; this made all the folk that were left so grateful that they hailed him all over again, which I guess is what he wanted. It wasn't such a popular order with our own soldiers though, they having been a long time without women. There had been about three hundred whores came over with us across the channel and set up in a camp a little ways off, but they were right by the polluted water, on the north side, and most of them took sick and died; the ones that were left weren't worth the effort.

We didn't call him Whoring Harry for nothing; he had a nose for them. I don't know how he did it, so quick, but that first night he had that same whores' camp full up with a new batch— French girls from the harbor houses, and some of them pretty. That's where I saw the black-haired bitch again; she was one of those they rounded up.

Those girls, they all had names, I guess, but we couldn't pronounce them, so we mostly called them Marie; a whole camp full of Maries it was. Funny, how we called those whores by Our Saviour's mother's name, but it just caught on, like, and nobody gave it a thought. Just to tell them apart, though, we'd nickname them—like Mousey Mary or Mary Big-tit—according to the way they looked; the black-haired girl, she got a name first off, being one of the pretty ones. A high-nosed fellow picked her out, one of the dukes; he could talk the language, and he called her, after, Marie le Sauvage. He was full of scratches and had a finger bitten clean down to the bone. I had a mind to this same witch myself but resolved to let her cool off a while first.

The next day the high-noses, both French and English, parley-vooed all the time the sun was up, and the rest of us just slept it off, after we got the siege-stuff dismantled and stowed away; most of us had heads that felt like they'd been axed, from the free wine. By sundown, though, I was feeling better, and I rode over to the camp of the Maries, looking for that little black-haired wild woman; in my mind I already had my own name for her, Moll Savage.

Women's quarters are the same all over, whether they be high or low. I mind the great chamber over the dairy where my wife slept when she was still a maid; she had been tirewoman to the lady of the manor where I was a squire, in Wessex. She was born to scullery work, being an ostler's daughter only, but she had a knack for combing and braiding, crimping, too, and so got raised, as you might say; she still does the lady's hair on special occasions, taking our children with her to play with the manor babes. Margery is a good wife and not so ill-favored either, to my mind. Some folk hold that a pocked wench is ruined-like, but from a little distance you can hardly see the marks; besides, it kept her virgin, there in that manor, with all the lords about. Her eyelids are something thick, though, from the disease, and she looks always as though she wept. But for that she would be handsome, a sturdy armful; I love her well and have only had to beat her once, and that not hard.

I was talking about the woman places though. Margery used to sneak me up there to that chamber of an afternoon, her duties being light, and we'd cuddle a bit, with no one about. It had a woman smell, warm and fusty, and somewhat of paint and powder, too, though how those poor girls came to have those things I can't tell. Combs and tweezers lay about in a clutter, and little pots of stuff to use on their faces; headcloths, too, and stockings flung anyhow on the beds. Not like soldiers' tents or barracks, where everything is neat and spare, even the lowest. And it was

the same there, in the camp of the Maries, every tent like a war-
ren of packrats; I had to poke through three of them before I
found the girl I was looking for.

She was in the smallest tent, colored purple it was and hung
with silk, with even some fur rugs on the floor instead of straw;
they had put the prettiest girls there. Some of them were as beautiful as ladies, with hair dyed red or gold, and paint an inch
thick. Dressed up like queens they were, too; they must have
come out of the best house in town. My girl was sitting in a corner by herself, cross-legged on a red velvet cushion, filing her
nails. She looked up at me and grinned, like a street-boy getting
ready to pick your pocket; I saw her fingernails were a half-inch
long and filed to sharp points. " 'Allo, Goddam," she said, "wan'
another hot oil treatment?" Her English was as good as my own,
but funny-sounding. She recognized me; I didn't know whether
it was a good sign or not.

"How much?" I said.

"An English crown," she said coolly and went on filing.

I wanted to hit her in the face, after I worked it out; it was
more than a month's pay! "Nothing doing, Molly Savage," I
said, but sorry all the same.

She looked up at me, laying down her file. "Half? . . . I like
your face. . . ."

I was still figuring, when I heard a voice behind me. "I had a
mind to this one myself, soldier. . . ." I turned; it was the king's
own self! Dressed like one of us though, he was, in a plain leather
jerkin and bare head; only his belt gave him away, made of
linked gold lion's heads it was, and thick and heavy. Many a
time I'd seen it agleam by the night fires when he walked among
us. He wore it slung low around his hips; they were as slender as
any page's, though above he was bulkier, his shoulders wide, and
his throat in his open shirt thick and corded. "I saw her yesterday
on the wall . . . she glared at me like a black leopard—yellow
eyes she has, too, like a leopard, did you see? I asked them to
bring her here . . . but I'll toss you for her, what do you say?"
He flung a coin, catching it in closed fist. "Heads or tails?"

"Uh—heads, I guess. . . ." I was stupid-like and flustered, not
having spoke with him before, of course.

He slapped the coin down and looked. "I'm in luck. Tails it is
—and prophetic, I hope . . ." he finished, winking at me. He

reached down where she sat and took her hand, pulling her to her feet. "We'll go to my tent. . . ."

"And who do you think you are—the king?" She flamed at him, pulling her hand away.

"Yes," he answered, looking at her and laughing.

"He is," I hissed, "he is . . . for true. It's Harry of England. . . ." I watched, thinking to see her put a little low, but she shrugged and made a little face, like a child does sometimes, to show off.

"A king . . ." she said, drawling the words out. "For you it'll be three crowns—English!"

"Done, Yellow-Eyes," he said, reaching for her again.

She took his hand this time but turned and gave me a long look. "King—" she said then, "I would have done it for the goddam for half-a-crown. . . ."

I'll say this for King Harry; he laughed. Of course, he could afford to. She never came back to the camp of the Maries again.

The next morning the king called us all together to give thanks for our great victory. There was some thought it was hard-won and not so much of a much either, with no looting and so many dead or dying, but most of the men cheered loud enough to hear back home. And when we saw the king, we all fell on our knees; he was dressed like a pilgrim-sort, with a kind of gray-brown robe on, like a monk's, and his feet bare. He was carrying a cross, a big plain wooden thing like the painters have the Saviour carrying; it kind of took my breath away to see it. Archbishop Chichele, he that was a low-born Saxon but now high, he stood up in front of us, near the king, in his scarlet (they looked funny together, I can tell you) and blessed the king and the English and the siege-machines and the cannon, and the flag, and I don't know what all. He prayed, too, but the wind took his words away, most of them, and his voice wasn't as strong as most church voices. Anyway, the king went first, as I said, barefoot, behind the dolled-up bishop, and we all followed, a couple of miles at least, to the church of St. Martin's on the other edge of Harfleur, to hear mass there. We all were supposed to fall in line behind; when the king went past me, I saw, under his cowl, there was a long scratch down his cheek, from eyebrow to chin.

My knees were sore after, because we had to kneel on the cobblestones in the square—there wasn't room inside the church—

and the thing took a long time. Anyway, the king gave all us soldiers crosses made out of red cloth to wear on our backs, so as to
tell we was English, see, and the army of God besides. So it was
plain we were going to push on, no matter. I found another
Marie, a comfortable little thing, with round rosy cheeks and soft
hair; she sewed my cross on for me, clucking her tongue and
shaking her head all the time. Of course, you couldn't expect the
French to think we were the army of God. She was a nice little
armful, though, reminded me of Margery, though she couldn't
speak a word of English except swear words.

We were sitting around camp, polishing armor and that sort of
thing, and waiting for the order to march; I, for one, was hoping
it wouldn't come too soon. I wasn't really over my sickness and
every morning had loose bowels still. Well, old Harry called us
together before the week was out (I saw the scratch hadn't healed
yet, though it had a scab, but at least there weren't any new
ones) and had us listen to him. He was sending a formal challenge to the dauphin of France, which is what they call their
prince, like. Now that is something that heads of armies always
do, to make it look like they don't really want war. They say, you
come out and fight me, just the two of us, and whoever wins, that
country wins, see? Well, I was thinking, as he challenged that
dauphin, of how he was twenty-seven or so, Harry, and a fighting
man all his life, too—and that dauphin, he was only nineteen
and a sickly sort, even had fits sometimes, they say, like his father. Anyway, he wasn't known for any kind of swordsman, that's
sure; you'd hardly call it an even contest. Which is maybe why
he didn't even answer, though the king sent his finest herald to
proclaim the challenge. Some said he did answer, that he, the
dauphin I mean, sent back some tennis balls and said that they
should be the weapons. After, the scribes and poets made a big
thing of it, saying how angry Harry got, and how he vowed to
bombard France with harder shot than tennis balls and all that,
and how that was the real reason for war. But I was right there,
and I never saw no sign of such a thing; the king, in my opinion,
never expected an answer, and just went on preparing for the
next march; we were at war already anyhow, all of us drawing
pay and all, so how could that be the reason?

One of the terms of the Harfleur surrender was that some of
the French high-noses were granted parole to raise their ransom

monies; they were supposed to have their ransoms and surrender to King Harry on November 11 at Calais. Looking back on it, I think Harry fixed it this way so that his council would have to vote for him to push on to Calais, seeing how nobody wanted to give up all that gold. See, the king always wanted folk to think that everything he did was lawful and by council's wish; he was pretty shrewd, Harry. Even so, a good many of the lords spoke against going on to Calais; it was more than a hundred and fifty miles through hostile country, and the rivers were all swollen, so it was said, or turned to marshes. He won out though—he would anyway, being king, and we began to get ready to march. Maybe this is hindsight, too, but I don't see what else he could do but try for Calais; to come back limping across the channel with half an army and no booty—well, his name would stink!

The king's uncle of Dorset, Beaufort it was, stayed behind to defend Harfleur; about a thousand men were left there with him, all grumbling. It was done fair though; the soldiers were all chosen by lot, except those that were too sick to march. I had said good-bye to my doxy the night before, but when I looked behind, I saw the whole Maries' camp was on the move, too! Harry read his men well. I was in the rear guard under the Duke of York; while we waited, holding our mounts, for the first riders to go ahead, and the second force, the king's, I saw Molly Savage peeping out between the curtains of the royal litter. She was eating something; when she saw me, she laughed and tossed it to me. It was a sugared fig, and I caught it without thinking, cursing her after for my sticky hands. She thumbed her nose at me and shouted, "À bientôt, Goddam!" I'd picked up a little of the language by then; it meant something like she'd see me soon. I wondered; she had the king's own marks on her, all right. I hadn't missed the earbobs dangling and the gauzy head veil shot with gold.

We carried no guns or siege-stuff, for the king said it would just delay us, and each man had in his pouch rations for eight days only. It was cutting it a bit fine, but in those days I was young too, like King Harry, and thought nothing of it. It felt funny though, that first night we made camp; we had no tents, no pallets even, no braziers or cookpots. High and low, we just munched our cold rations, wrapped up in our cloaks, and lay down on the ground. Dark had come early upon us, for the day was a gray one and it was already October; we did not know where we were until morning. The king's brother, Duke Humphrey, studied a map as he sat his horse; he shivered a little in the chill dawn, chewing his hard biscuit. He was attached to our division, a dark stripling, much like his brother, but with a ferret's eyes, shiny and black. "I make it Montivilliers, just over the hill . . . 'tis the first town. . . ." We all looked where he pointed, curious. It was a tiny hamlet, with straw-thatched roofs, like any English town, and a little spire sticking up all alone, like a finger pointing to the sky.

We skirted the town, seeing no one astir; just as we were past, a pack of mongrel dogs ran out, yapping at the heels of the wagon train. One of the Maries threw them a bone, and they fell on it, snarling and fighting; I wondered where she had got it.

At Fécamp, on the coast, there was a few arrows came out at us from behind the wall, but they fell short; we saw no one, and none came out to defy us. The next town was a good-sized one, with a high wall, and spears bristling along the top, but otherwise no sign of life.

The word came to halt, but, being in the rear, I couldn't see what was happening. "You—soldier!" said Duke Humphrey, happening to catch my eye and snapping his fingers at me. "Scout ahead and see what's afoot!"

I wasn't his to command and began to look around for my own duke, but then I thought better of it, seeing he was the king's brother. I spurred ahead, hoping I wouldn't get caught between those two dukes, but the Duke of York nodded at me as I went past, so I knew it was all right.

Up ahead I could see the whole army milling about, some of the horses pawing the ground and snorting; nobody knew exactly what the order meant. There was a little knot of men this side of the drawbridge and two people standing right on it. It started to go up—the people inside had pulled something—and our men had to jump off quick. I saw then that one of them was the king, and even from where I was, I could hear him shout, angry-like, and he raised his arm. Somebody behind him sent a whole potful of Greek fire hurtling over the wall, and I saw them get ready with the catapults. Before anything else happened, though, there was a white flag showed over the top, meaning those inside wanted to talk, and a minute or so later, the big gate opened a crack, and a little fellow comes out. Bald-headed he was and fat as a capon, and even from a distance you could see he was scared stiff. King Harry shouted, cupping his hands, that all we wanted was some bread and wine, and then we would let them alone. He didn't trust their well water, see? The man said something but didn't come any closer, and I didn't hear; I guess King Harry didn't either, for he beckoned to him. He looked around then, Harry, at his army halted in back of him, and he raised up eight fingers, and shouted that he wanted eight thousand loaves. Another fellow came out the gate then, carrying that white flag, and the two of them came halfway down the drawbridge, and the king went forward, too, with the other duke—I think it was the one they called d'Umfraville, part French he was, see—so he could parley. I was pretty close now, and I could just make out what they said. The other man, the one with the white flag, he says they don't have as many as eight thousand loaves, not in the whole town, and Harry says, "Bake it!" He asks for two hundred kegs of wine, too, and I thought the fat one would have a fit; they both got excited and waved their arms a lot, but I couldn't make out their talk. Anyway, the king went stiff, sort of—you could see he was getting impatient—and he raised his arm again, and the catapult fellows began wheeling the machine up closer and stuffing the Greek fire in. So then the enemy fellows began nodding quick and counting on their fingers, too, and finally they went back inside. Everything must have turned out the way Harry wanted it, because he looked smoothed down when he came off the bridge, and gave the order to camp a little ways off. Well, that pleased everybody, I guess; we were all getting tired of marching on our cold stomachs, as it were.

Well, we sat there, waiting, doing little chores like mending leather and the like, and the smell of baking bread began to come over the wall; like heaven it was and made your mouth water.

The first batch came out in an hour or so, piled in three carts; I got a loaf early, being up front, still hot it was, and tasted better than cake. The wine came, too, but old Harry made us water it down from the stream; he wasn't taking any chances.

That was the town of Arques; we had bread and wine left over to take along with us, and we crossed the river—the Béthune—and went on. We still didn't see no sign of the French army. The next day we got more bread and some cheeses, too, at another walled town—Eu, it was, on the river Bresle; this time Harry didn't even fire, just threatened, like. We were beginning to think it was a breeze, this French march.

The next day showed us different; first thing was, somebody had felled huge trees and laid them across the road. There was no bypassing them, with stream on one side and marsh on the other; we had to drag them off, every one. After a whole day of this, we'd covered maybe a mile and were sweating from every pore. At first, the high-noses sat their mounts and watched us, giving orders, King Harry among them, but then he jumped down, the king, and set to, himself, impatient-like and thinking he could do it better. He could, too, I'll say that for him; he hadn't had the sickness, see, and most of the rest of us were still weak from it. It put some heart in us though, seeing him straining along with us and joking and singing bawdy songs. One of them was about her, the one I called Moll Savage. That name caught on and that's what they all called her now; everybody knew the song, except the king, I guess. But seeing him working alongside, the men got bold, and somebody struck it up. It had a catchy tune, too; it might have got started by one of the musicians, I don't know. It had hundreds of verses, but it began something like this.

> Oh, bow your heads to Molly Savage—
> And smile at her as she comes near . . .
> Bow your heads to Molly Savage—
> She's a wench that has the king's ear . . .
> To bite . . . to bite. . . .

And it went on like that, taking his arm, and leg, and so on, getting ruder and ruder, you can imagine.

The king listened, just working along; you couldn't tell what he was thinking. But after, it getting near to sundown, he announced we'd make camp. " 'Tis a lively air," he said thoughtfully, rubbing his chin. "I have a mind to have Hercules set it down fair for the lute, or maybe the mandol. . . ."

Chapter 2

The road was blocked by felled trees all the way to Blanche-Taque, where there was supposed to be a ford-place; it was slow going and took us two more days. We were five days out from Harfleur by then and still hadn't seen any French army people; we had stopped feeling like it would be a cinch, with the trees and all, and were beginning to feel uneasy, like mice that know the cat's around but not which way it will jump.

Blanche-Taque, though, was the place where the Black Prince crossed the river, and every Englishman has heard of it, how it brought him to victory finally at Crécy. I guess it was the greatest victory ever for us English; we were all brought up to remember that prince in our prayers. Our King Harry called a halt, offering up prayers, with Bishop Chichele on hand again to do the blessing. After, the king, in his loudest parade voice and with tears in his eyes, told the story of the archers covering their bows with their cloaks to keep them from the rain, and they themselves sodden with it, and how those longbowmen saved the day for England, and I don't know what all. Many of our archers sobbed out loud. Some of the Maries, those that were closest, wept, too, though they couldn't have understood; whores are always sentimental.

Word had been sent to the garrison at Calais that they should send out a force to cover our crossing, for the French were sure to be looking out for us there; at the first ford, though, we still saw no one, either English or French, and the whole river was staked to prevent the crossing of horses. There was a bridge a little ways up—King Harry had it on his map—but when we got to it, we saw it was all hacked to pieces, nothing left. Some few spars and beams stuck up from the water, like broken limbs. Column after column of men came to a halt, unbidden, their faces looking, all, as though someone had hit them. Many of the archers, who were on foot mostly, sat down as though they could not go farther. King Harry dismounted and went among them, speaking with cheer. "Up, lads," he said, "it cannot be far now—we will get across . . . there is another ford-place a little ways ahead . . . up, up!" And, for a miracle, they dragged themselves to their feet, though their faces were yellow as saffron from the sickness that was still with them and streaming, too, with fever sweat. I, too, was tired to my bones, though I sat a horse, for the bread was gone and our rations near an end, too; hungry men tire quickly and sick ones quicker. We were a sorry lot.

We came to two more fords, all staked, and another destroyed bridge; by now even the king wore a look of heaviness, and he called a rest-halt, men dropping in their tracks at the word.

Ahead of me were the Welsh battalion; from among them one rode out, shouting and pointing. "Look, you, sire," he cried in his lilting speech, "look you, yonder . . . it is the Calais men!"

He pointed across the river, and all turned to see, even those that had flopped down dead-like onto the grass sitting up or standing, hoping.

We saw horsemen on the opposite bank, both knights and common lances. It was hard to see them in the shadows of the setting sun, but they looked to be in full mail; they pulled up their mounts and stood staring across at us, stiff and silent. I knew before the king spoke.

"No," he said, "they're not the Calais men. . . . They are French."

His brother spoke beside him. "And in battle formation, too, by Jesus!"

I heard my own commander of York speak then, irritable like an old man; he was portly and the riding made his breath come short under his heavy armor. "What need have they to form battle-wise? The bridge is down anyway; we cannot cross."

"It is to warn us—the devils!" said King Harry, his face dark and his lips drawn in, shut-like.

"Well, brother," drawled the Lord Humphrey, impudent-like, "what do we do now?"

King Harry spoke sense. "Withdraw. Back into those spruce woods." And he pointed. "The Frenchmen can no more reach us than we can reach them—and my men are like to drop . . . all of us are near spent. A night's rest will clear our heads. Tomorrow we will think."

So back we went into the cover of the trees, away from the sight of the ruined bridge.

"We'll have fires tonight, lads," shouts Harry. "They know where we are anyway . . . and we'll be warm, at least."

"And maybe we'll find chestnuts to roast . . ." said Lord Humphrey. "We've precious little else . . ."

He spoke true, except that there were no chestnuts. We still had rations, cured strips of meat and biscuits, getting moldy now, but enough for a day or two; some of the men had hoarded their bread and munched it slowly around the fires, making it last. I was not among them, for I take each day as it comes—that is my nature; besides, bread is better when it is fresh.

After we had settled, some of the lords, those who had ridden the whole time, went scouting about to see what was there in that place. They found nothing but some green walnuts, not fit to eat, and two poor human relics. It was Lord Camoys and Talbot who brought back these men, bearing them up between them, for they could barely walk. They were of Calais, we could see, by the red cross sewn on their backs, though their mail had been stripped from them. Each, too, had had his sword arm struck off, and the bloody stumps were wrapped about with the remains of their padded jupons. One was a boy only, with down for beard; he could not have been more than seventeen. When the bandage was unwrapped, it was seen the arm was sore festered and smelled putrid; the boy was fevered and his eyes glassy. King Harry swore, softly, and dispatched him to where the physicians camped, to see what could be done to ease him. The other was a tough soldier, with old scars crisscrossing his face, and one eye gone. The other, though, was canny, and he spoke up sturdily, making nothing of his dreadful wound, save to curse that he could not use it to draw sword against the enemy.

They were the last, he said, of the three hundred men sent out from Calais a week ago to secure Blanche-Taque. The king spat, disgusted; he was at times as crude as any villein. He laughed then, shortly. "Was the captain of Calais addled in his wits—that he thought to hold this place with three hundred men?"

It was not a question meant to be answered, and the handless soldier nodded, grimly, his one eye unblinking. "They fell upon us about ten miles up, more than six thousand French, under the Marshal Boucicaut. . . ." He did not pronounce it so, but we knew who he meant, all right. He went on. "They buried the most of them there, I'll say that for them, and the rest they chased back, clear to the gates of Calais, they said, though maybe they boasted. The boy and me—they took our horses and swords and cut off our hands . . . the ax was dirty, too, the whoresons!" He was sweating from the fire and wiped his good hand across his face, leaving a smear of dust among the scars. "We been walking three days, trying to come up to you. The French knew you were here, like, you see, and pushed us in this direction. . . ." He looked on a sudden weary, passing his tongue over his cracked lips.

The king snapped his fingers. "Give him wine!"

We all looked around then, from one to the other. The Lord Talbot said, "Sire, there is not so much as a pint among us. . . ."

I pushed forward, bringing out my water flask. "Here is water, sire. . . ."

The man drank deeply, me watching as it disappeared, not knowing, see, where we'd get more. "There is wine in the pack-train," said King Harry, "where the pages ride, and the women . . . you shall have it presently. Naught much of food is there, though . . . but somewhat you shall have. . . ."

The Lord Talbot spoke then. He had been thinking over what the man had said. "Sire, we must back to Harfleur with all speed. We are ill-matched; not so many as six thousand even are we, and all sick and weary. . . ."

The wounded man shook his head. "No, my Lord . . . all the armies of France stand between you and Harfleur . . . the forces of Brabant, Berry, and Orléans, too . . . they set out from Rouen two days after you left Harfleur. They told us that, in all, the numbers were forty-five thousand. . . ." He looked frightened, as though he expected to be blamed for it. And indeed, for a moment, I thought King Harry would dash him to the ground with his mailed fist.

But the king's face cleared, and he laughed, saying, "Well, then, we are neatly trapped. . . ." He thought for a moment, rubbing his chin. "My lords and my men"—and he turned around so all who were near enough could listen—"the hunted hare has more hope of life than the snared one . . . we will go on!" Seeing all staring at him as if he raved, he dropped to one knee and, taking up a sharp twig, scratched markings in the trampled earth. "Look," he said, "here we are and here the river.

And beyond the river six thousand men of the French waiting. Here, at our backs, are forty-five thousand coming ever closer." He drew in the dust a semicircle. "The river bends. Thus. And the bend is toward us and in our favor, mark you? Even if all the bridges and fords be destroyed, we can track the river to its source and so win through. The forces of Boucicaut, over yonder, there"—and he nodded his head in the direction of the river's bank—"they cannot catch us, because they cannot short-cut the river's bend. . . ."

"You think they will follow us, then?" asked Lord Humphrey.

"My brother, I am sure of it—as sure as that I have a cramp in my leg from squatting here. . . ." And the king stood up then, all those who had heard laughing weakly. "The Frenchman's purpose is to stop us from crossing the river—at any point . . . most like there *is* no place left untouched by their axes . . . Boucicaut means to hold us on this side until the larger armies can come at us from the rear."

The Duke of York spoke then. "Cousin [I had forgot they were kin], to track the river to its source"—he stopped, shaking his head—"we do not know how far it is. . . ."

"Sixty miles," said the king firmly. "It cannot be more, even allowing for the bend."

"But—sixty miles!" said the duke, with a troubled face. "We have barely enough food to last out tomorrow. . . ."

"Then we must live off the land," said King Harry. "As Alexander did, and Caesar, too." He stepped onto a fallen great log, balancing himself, and addressing all those about. "Hear me, my lads! We will push on to Calais! We will follow the river. If we can cross, we will cross. If we cannot, we will go to the river's source and skirt it. We will take what food we can find on our way from village or farm. We will take naught else . . . no monies, no life, no women . . . no churches will be plundered— upon pain of death!" With his arm uplifted and his face stern as marble, he looked like some statue in a courtyard. I have marked before that he was good at speech-making and striking a pose; all the men cheered, but ragged-like, because they had dry throats. Our water had to last.

The king stepped down, easy as you please, putting his arm about the wounded soldier's good side. "Come, old comrade," he said, and meaning it. "We'll get you that wine, and I'll find a crust of bread . . . then we'll see to your arm. . . ." And they walked off to the king's own train.

We heard later that the arm of the Calais boy had mortified clear up past the elbow and had to be cut off at the shoulder to save it. The king's own physician did it, with the king holding the boy down and feeding him poppy juice and brandy from his own store, and sitting up with him half the night, too, till it was seen that he would live.

"I'll bring you back to Calais, boy," he said in the dawning, as he piled the litter with his own furred robe. "I'll bring us all to Calais. . . ." I heard him with my own ears, for my horse had strayed in the night and I found him near to the king's people.

My mind shook its head, in a sort, for I did not see how it could be done; yet when he spoke you believed him, King Harry.

Chapter 3

We made good speed the next day, the weather holding fine; it was the twelfth of October; I always like to keep count, from a boy. The French across the river made good speed, too; we could see the glint of their mail sometimes when the sun struck through the trees; and when we made camp we saw their fires, seeming very close.

We lay down, most of us, that night, on near-empty stomachs, many a man folding his pouch flat after; in the night, too, I heard some sob in their sleep, for all were restless from hunger, and one hard-hewn fellow next to me cried out for his mother.

In the morning of the next day we came to Pont-Remy; there had been two bridges there within a mile of each other, but both had been well hatcheted, and the river swirled noisily around the broken bits. The French formed again on the far bank, laughing and shouting at us; some of our archers took aim, but their arrows fell short—it only looked near.

We halted there, in that place, while some were sent to the homesteads roundabout to forage for food. The folk were friendly, or scared, more like, and gave what they had, but there was barely enough bread for a mouthful each and a few measures of dried peas and a dozen sacks of corn. Still, it was something, and we ate for the first time that day. They gave us sweet well water, too, almost as good as food it was, though some vomited it up straightaway. Those were the ones that were sickest, see?

Many of the men were beginning to look half-dead, some nobles among them; the young Earl of Suffolk, whose father had died already at Harfleur of the marsh fever, had taken the same sickness himself. The king liked him well, this boy-earl, for he had been a merry youth, with talent for music and singing; he and the Lord Talbot took turns bearing up the sick boy as we marched. We were slow this day, for men kept dropping out to relieve their loose bowels or to vomit. Beside me, one of the archers dropped like a stone, halting all of us about him. I bent over him, and he muttered feebly, his face gray, "Go on wi'out me, lad . . . I be a goner. . . ." His speech was the speech of Wessex, where I was born.

The king, ever restless, saw the halt and came back to where he lay fallen. He looked down at him; you could see he was thinking hard. "Where does he come from?" he asked suddenly. The man struggled to speak. I said, "My Lord—I think he is of Wessex. . . ." And the archer's head nodded, his eyes begging. King Harry knelt beside him. "I know the region," he said. "Good bowmen come from there . . . there must be others here from those parts."

I spoke up, and another, too, down the line. "My Lord," I said, feeling my way, "it might be two could carry him, if they clasped hands chair-fashion. . . ."

The king stood up. "Better it would be to make a litter. Cut two poles and sling a cloak between . . . Here—have mine." And he took off his cloak and handed it to me. It was a fine gesture, and we all gasped; of course he had many, but still. "We'll slow our pace for you," he said, "and for any who fall . . . I cannot afford to lose one even." His face was earnest, and he spoke firm-wise. "Listen," he said, raising his voice, "and pass on my words. I will bring you all to Calais. I have sworn it. I know that it is said that commanders abandon those who cannot keep up, but it will not be so with us. We are too few, and we are all brothers here. If the man beside you falls, prop him up; he will do likewise with you. And so will we come to Calais, with God's help." And he made the sign of the cross on his breast. Many did the same, though I knew there were Lollards among them.

One archer spoke up, hesitant, his face unbelieving. "Sire— you'll not leave any . . . no man?"

"Not while he breathes," said the king.

Some had gone past us while we fashioned the litter. I saw the old man from Calais, mounted, his arm in a proper bandage now, and looking as though nothing had happened to him. He looked at us, curious. "The king commanded it," I said, to his question.

He spat, shaking his head. " 'Tis a rare fine cock of a king we got, boys, for sure." And he laughed, admiring-like. "He'll bring us to Calais if he has to carry every one of us on his own shoulders!"

He rode along of us then, talking of the boy with the arm that

had festered. "Lopsided he is now, for sure, but the fever is gone."
His one eye glittered. "In the king's own litter he lies now, with a
black-haired wench to tend him. Soft. . . ." he said, drawling
out the word.

I spoke surprise at his own recovery. "You wear better than
the most of us with all our limbs. . . ."

He shook his head. "No," he said, "they pain me, especially
the hand that is gone. I feel it sore. 'Twill rain, for sure," he said,
looking up at the sky. He was a doughty fellow, and I liked him
well. We rode together all of that day, cracking jokes, cheering
one another. Even the poor sick fellow hammocked in the king's
cloak wore a happier face, yellow though it was. Some others fell
out and could not walk, but their companions, following that
example, made shift to carry them also. My new friend, his name
was Tom Franklin, for he had bought his own freedom, spoke, remembering the Welsh wars. "I served under Harry Percy—him
they called Hotspur. He was ever mindful of his men, and they
loved him well—but, if one fell, there he lay, for the crows to
pick. Glendower, no—all men were his brothers. I saw him once
put a wounded man on his own fine horse and walk along of him,
aholding of the bridle, and him near fifty then. . . ."

"You fought at Shrewsbury?" I asked, and he nodded. "On the
other side, I guess," I said, low.

"Hotspur switched over, and I was his man," he said. "I was in
front—we had just let fly the first volley. I saw the prince, that is
King Harry now—no more than a stripling he was, too—clap his
hand to his eye, like. And we all saw there was an arrow sticking
through his fingers. . . . They helped him off the field. But later I
saw him, all bandaged up, fighting on the walls, brave as a lion-
cub, he was. I thought after . . . it might have been my arrow."
He was silent a moment, riding along. " 'Course, we all thought
he'd lost an eye—turned out later he was lucky. I remember
though—I got this that same day." And he pointed to his own
empty socket. "I'd ha' been out of it and left for dead, maybe, if I
hadn't seen that there princeling fighting on with his bandages
. . . gave me heart, like. So when he was give the Calais command, his father still king, I joined up under him." And so we
rode on that day, exchanging stories and remembering old battles.

The rain which Tom Franklin's bones had foretold came that

night while we slept, pattering down on the dry leaves and on our huddled bodies.

We lay in puddles and, waking at dawn to the notes of the trumpet, heard it choke and gurgle through the music as the water clogged it. I caught Tom Franklin's eye as he sat up beside me, seeing a wintry kind of grin forming on his thin lips, and smiled myself; it was such a funny sound. All through the ranks of waking men went a titter, and we heard a loud voice—the king's. "Thump it on the back, Walter!" A roar went up then, all the men laughing like they were at a village fair-show; we were silly-like, see, from the wet and all. As the trumpet finished, the notes came clear and sweet through the sheets of rain, and we heard the king again. "Good work, Walter, that did it!" There came a ragged cheer then, and it got us to our feet, though we slipped in the mud and our numb fingers could hardly tend our sodden gear.

All day we marched in the rain, soaked to the skin, and the next day too; we felt like never had we been dry. My bowstring was sodden and useless; if we came up of a sudden with the French we were goners, for each man fared likewise. Someone said we were out of Normandy now, and in a part they called Picardy, but who could tell? You could hardly see three men ahead; the rain was like a gray curtain and the ground so wet we sank into it up to our ankles. Those of us who had horses had to get off, for our weight was sinking the poor animals in the mud. We staggered along blindly, leading our mounts, or carrying our next-door neighbor, for more and more of the men could not put one foot in front of the other. The high-noses too, were walking, my own commander of York floundering along like a big whale-fish. He was a sorry sight indeed, poor York, his jupon torn, and the padding coming out of it like feathers from a molting capon, his face covered with a grizzled growth. At one halt, I looked around and saw everybody the same, faces half-bearded and gray under, from being tired, and all our clothes ripped and shredded, and one color with the wet. The land around, too, was one color, the color of rain and misery.

The king kept riding back and forth among us, wearing no armor; his horse was a small gray mare, but even her light feet sank deep. King Harry, too, was unshaven, and there were white hairs in his beard; I figured it up in my mind, marveling—he was only twenty-seven! But he peered closely at all his men, going through the ranks as though he by himself could keep them going. "Cheer up, lads," he would say over the steady rain-sound. "Cheer up—Frenchy's no better off than we!"

It was true, too, of course. Tom Franklin, who had seen them, after all, said they must be in worse case, for they were heavily armed and their horses too, all in full mail. It was small comfort, though. We were wretched as men could be and hungry all the time. The countryside was sparse-populated, and we lived on the few slivers of bread and salt meat we could forage; it was not much, just enough to keep us alive. When next the king came among us, he shouted we should open our mouths and cup our hands, saving our waterflasks. "For it is God's good rain," he said, "sweeter than wine!" Wine! What a thought! I felt we would never taste wine or roast meat or lie in a bed again, but plod forever though this ceaseless wet.

On the fifteenth of October (I was still keeping count) the archer that was lying on the king's cloak died. Tom Franklin spotted him first; his one eye was ever sharper than any two others. "The lad's gone," he said. "There's no breath in him, and his face is almost black—look!" And he pointed. We halted, then, and found it was so. There was a shiver went down me, for this was our first to die, and I could not see how it would not be the beginning of many more deaths; in all our ranks there was not one who looked much more alive than this poor dead one.

We did not stop to bury him, for the French were still behind us, and the rain would have washed the earth away from over him anyway. The king kneeled though, not thinking of the mud, and some bishops said prayers for the man's soul. Then we marched on, leaving him there beside the way, already stiff but wrapped in the king's cloak for his journey into wherever we go. Almost I envied him; at least he could not feel the cold and the wet, and his stomach had stopped its rumbling and gnawing forever.

After this the rain let up a little and dwindled down to a steady drizzle. I noticed, though, that more and more of the men were looking sick, and staggered as they walked; some of them groaned aloud, holding their bellies. Our columns barely moved. The king came back through the lines, on foot now; even his light horse could not bear his weight. "What ails them? It does not look like the fever. . . ."

Tom Franklin, beside me, shook his head. "It's them apples, sire. . . ."

"There are no apples," said the king, looking puzzled. "The summer crop has gone, and there's been no frost either. . . ." He spoke like a real farmer; there was nothing he did not turn his hand to, our Harry.

Tom Franklin reached down and picked something off the ground. "There's orchards all along this road," he said. "Must've been a storm a while back. . . ."

I looked at his hand; he was holding a little green apple, no bigger than a marble. I knew then we had been stepping on them all day, in the mud; I had thought they were stones. The king took it. "It's hard as wood," he said. He raised his voice so the men around heard, they stopping now and staring at him. "You can't eat these—they'll poison your insides."

One of the archers muttered sullenly, "Well, they're something. . . ."

King Harry stuck the little unripe apple under my horse's nose. It snuffed loud and threw back its head, not taking it, though we had had no beast-fodder for two days.

"So," said the king, angry-like, "the horse has sense. . . ." He threw the apple away. "Be patient. We must be coming near to another village; we'll all have bread."

The archer who had spoken, the sullen one, said again, under his breath, "Aye—a mouthful each . . . enough to whet our hunger more."

Harry heard and answered, reasonably. "Yes . . . but all must share."

The man spat. "All!" And he laughed, a harsh sound more like a croak. "Not the high-noses . . . their bellies are full!"

The king lashed out at him, furious. "None has better fare than his neighbor! My own pouch is as flat as yours. Look around you! We are all thin as weeds. . . ." He saw the Duke of York, puffing, and leaning on his lance, his jowls gray under his matted beard. His lip twitched. "Even my cousin of York is losing his big pot," he said. "Soon he will be as other normal-sized men—" The Duke of York smiled good-naturedly, though he was a man of choler at times. He had a great fondness for this king-cousin, so much younger than himself.

At that, all the men relaxed, smiling behind their hands and shifting where they stood, like grinning schoolboys. One of them spoke then, timidly, asking the king, "Sire—is it far, think you, to the river's source—where we can cross?"

"It cannot be far, surely," said King Harry. "And if we find a bridge before—why, we'll cross before." He spoke with much coolness now, and confident.

His brother came near, the Lord Humphrey, and spoke up then, contrary. "Yes, brother," he said, "and we'll cross and climb up the other bank and right into the Frenchies' arms!" His eyes wore a more scornful look than usual, though always he was a sour pickle of a boy. "Remember," he said, "Boucicaut has the same number we have . . . six thousand men, about."

"Aye, I know that," said Harry thoughtfully, rubbing his chin; it was a habit he had. "But I have my archers, and they are each worth two of any others! So, you see," he said, and his smile was wide and sunny through the drizzle, "we outnumber them, for sure. . . ."

All about were smiling then, broadly, I among them, though I did not think my mouth strong enough to stretch to it, and some-one cheered, weakly. The Lord Talbot sloshed over to where the king stood; he had heard the whole thing. This was a lord who had been with King Harry since his first battle in the Welsh marches; he was growing old like an old sword, his face hard and weathered as iron. I thought he looked like one of those effigies you see on tombs, all bronze and stone. He clapped a heavy hand on the king's shoulder and said, "For sure, Hal—it takes a Lancaster to set six against six and figure he has the most!"

The men went on then, much heartened, though some still held their stomachs. And sure enough, before the hour was out, we saw the spires of a village poking through the mist. We had more than a mouthful, too, that day, for in those parts they bake for the week and it was baking day. The folk in the town had to do without, but none looked at us with resentment or hatred; I guess they knew the French, behind us, would take it anyway.

It was a good omen, though, for in the afternoon the rain lessened even more and was now just a thin mist blowing in our faces, and almost pleasant.

We came to no bridge that was standing that day either, though, and all the fords were staked, the water rushing past like a wild animal. At one ford the king waded out, up to his armpits, to try if it could be crossed, holding onto the stakes as he went. He disappeared suddenly and came up dripping. He shook his head then, spitting the water out. "No use," he said. "They cut away the ford here—there's no footing. . . ." Several men waded out to help him back to shore, and he stood on the bank dripping and wringing the water out of his clothes.

Tom Franklin spoke then, screwing up his good eye and looking disgustedly at the river. "Sire," he said, "what do they call this stream?"

"The Somme," said King Harry.

"Somme . . . Somme—" said the franklin, trying it out on his tongue. " 'Tis somme-thing, all right!"

The king laughed, walking beside him, with his arm laid friendly over Tom's shoulder, and asking him how his cut-off hand felt.

"Poorly, sire, poorly," said Tom. "It keeps acalling out to me from where it lies. Don't seem to know it's finished, like, or maybe wants burying. . . ."

Chapter 4

We stopped looking at that old river after a while; it was like an enemy. We just marched along of it in the rain, looking ahead, sick of seeing another bridge or causeway hacked to pieces or another ford-crossing bristling with pointed stakes. As I said, it rained mostly, but, when it stopped for a bit and the sun came out, our clothes steamed, smelling like sheep. And the ground never dried at all, the mud thick and sticky as glue. My left boot had a hole in it, and the mud came in, squelching in between my toes, a nasty feeling, on top of everything else.

I forgot what day it was we came to Boves Castle; we called it that because on the map it was right where the town of Boves was marked. We came first to a clearing in the woods and a few scattered homesteads, where children, mother-naked like all serf babes, watched us round-eyed from the doorways. Against the sky stood the castle, a squat hump with four towers, and smaller buildings clustered close to it. There was a wall around it, but outside the walls stood several big granaries and a vineyard with winepresses. The drawbridge was up, and there were red flags all along the walls, which didn't look too good, being that they mean defiance. The big house standard hung above the first turret, but it was wet and hung limp, hard to make out.

The king called for the herald; they can tell any chivalry of Europe at a glance, of course. He came to the king's side, running; Hugh Stafford was his name. He looked a scarecrow, like all of us; the bright colors of his livery were all faded and running into each other, and mud caked his hose clear up to the thigh. He shaded his eyes with his hands and squinted. There was a kind of fog over everything, though it wasn't raining at the moment. He looked a long time, the king snapping his fingers impatiently. "Whose standard, Hugh?"

"Let's see—bar azure . . . fetterlock . . ." muttered Stafford. "It is Vaudémont—the Count of Vaudémont. . . ."

"Never heard of him," says King Harry. "Is he fief to France?"

"Not France, sire," said Stafford. "Burgundy. He holds from Burgundy."

The king gave a whoop then, looking happy. "Then is he our man!" He called d'Umfraville to him. "You go, d'Umfraville," he said. "Your French is the best. Take a herald and a trumpeter—whoever looks best. Say it is Harry of England and that I have treaty with his master of Burgundy. Say my soldiers are starving and I want bread. If he will not give, tell him I will burn his outbuildings and tenant farms."

Well, we all sprawled on the wet leaves there, thinking of the good bread we'd get, and wine, too, maybe. All our mouths were dry; we never had enough water. Being that this castle was friend to us, we thought we'd get more here than anywhere, see?

It was a long while before d'Umfraville came back, but at least we had a rest; most of us fell asleep—we were so weakened—waking groggily when we heard the trumpeter returning.

Well, you could see right away that d'Umfraville had bad news. He kept running his tongue over his lips, and fidgeting with his bonnet like an old woman. "Out with it, man!" cried the king, speaking for all of us.

"My Lord," said d'Umfraville, "the count in there says you may have thought you had treaty with Burgundy. But Burgundy has repudiated the pact and has ridden to join the armies of France." He had a look on his face like a dog expecting a kick.

"Christ's nails!" cried the king, stabbing his lance into the ground. "The goddamned whoreson fence-straddler!" Talking of Burgundy, of course, he was. The count here had to follow; it wasn't his fault. But it meant we'd get nothing without using force. Also it meant a whole big piece of the French army was not for us, but against us. Most of us, though, hardly took it in, being so dull-like, but it was a hard knock for us English.

"What about the bread?" said the king, calming down a little. "Did Vaudémont give any?"

"He did," said d'Umfraville, "once he heard we were going to fire his village . . . two basketsful."

"Two basketsful!" said the king.

"Sire, he swore it was all he had . . . by every saint he could think of, he swore. He said they grind tomorrow, and there is no meal yet. He swore . . . Shall I go back and parley again?" But you could see he had no heart for it.

"No," said the king, looking tired, too, for him. "It's probably true. . . . Have them divide out the few crumbs as best they can. We will have to press on. . . ."

The Duke of York spoke then, purple in the face. "By God, Harry—burn his barns anyway, the damned turncoat!"

The Lord Humphrey started shouting, too. "At least have a look at those granaries, to see if he is lying . . . we've got time enough for that!"

"All right," said the king, "take a few men, those that feel up to it. . . ." And he lay down, right on the ground like the rest of us, and closed his eyes. He could go to sleep just like winking, when he had a mind to it, Harry, and wake up just as quick.

I went with the Lord Humphrey, me and some others; I felt better after sitting a while. We looked in all the granaries, but they were as empty as though they'd been swept out. We couldn't find the wine vats either, no trace of them. When we told the king, he said he guessed they'd been moved inside the walls. He was wrong there, though.

After we were some ways down the road, starting up our march again, we heard a lot of noise and shouting behind us. I was in the first ranks now, see? The king had changed us all around, being that he was fond of his cousin York and liked to have him by to talk to.

The king turned his horse, calling upon some of us to go with him, and rode back down the lines to see what was up. I was with him, being curious myself, and having a horse and all. When we came up where the noise was, we saw a big press of soldiers kind of grunting and pushing one another, and all around were coming others to join them. The king jumped down from his horse. "Jesus," he said, "they've found the wine casks! They'll be drunk as goats in five minutes!" And he went in among them, pushing them out of the way. They moved aside but kept on with what they were doing, passing flasks from hand to hand and drinking, dipping into the big vats that had been hidden by the roadway. The king began to shout, but they paid him no mind; they were like sleepwalkers, or maybe drunk already—it was hard to tell. Never before nor since did I see King Harry not obeyed. He came out from them, grinning and shaking his head, but you could see he was angry, deep down.

"They've had no food . . . they'll make themselves sick." He looked up at the Lord Humphrey, who rode with us, and turned back to the reeling mob.

"Save your breath, Harry," said Humphrey with a little sneer. "It'll take more than the king's Majesty to pry them away!"

The smell of the wine lay on the heavy air; you could get drunk from it almost, sharp and sweet at the same time it was. To those men with their empty bellies and tired bones, it had a greater strength than the king's own self; if they hanged for it, they would have it.

King Harry sat his horse again among us, watching as one by one the men who had drunk their fill staggered out from the others, their lips slack and shining, their eyes witless. By the time darkness fell, half of the archers were dead to everything, sleeping it off, and the rest useless as babies. They fell where any stone tripped them and lay like the dead, without even a cloak between them and the puddles. The king and his nobles and all us sober ones were helpless to prevent it, there being so many of them.

I saw King Harry looking down at one where he lay in his russet jerkin, almost the color of the leaves and a part of them. The king held a lantern high, shining it on the man. He was snoring in grunts like a scared pig—it would have been funny any other time; his bow and his drinking bottle were hugged to his chest, and every time he breathed, wine from the open bottle ran out, spilling over his shirt. The king put out his foot, nudging him roughly, but he did not move or feel it. Not an eyelid flickered.

"God grant that the Frenchies do not catch up with us this night!" said the king, and signed himself. " 'Twould be our end, for sure!"

The king himself did not sleep, keeping every watch, in turn with those of us who were fit. When morning light came, and we saw the archers, one by one, stir and get up from their puddles and heaps of wet leaves and creep away, shamefaced, to wash their faces in the river, the king laughed. "Well, they'll have thick heads, but they'll draw bow again, praise to God." And he ordered prayers of thanksgiving for this deliverance, funny as it sounded. He was a great one for praying, Harry.

We marched again that day, the king having no pity on drunks or on himself either. The archers trudged along, the wine stains mixed up with all the rest of the crusted dirt; the air all around them was stinking with the fumes of stale wine. I looked, but I couldn't tell who the drunken ones had been, we were all in such a sad way. Almost every archer was barefoot, hose hanging at the knee in tatters and sleeves torn away; their arms would, at any rate, be free to draw bow. I looked down at myself and found I was not much better, though I had ridden a lot and still had shreds of boot and hose. By now all were well bearded, a fashion not seen in England in my time; we looked like the images of the apostles on the frescoes at Westminster, gaunt-cheeked and hollow-eyed. I had been taken to Westminster when I was a boy to see them when they were new-painted; I smiled now, to myself, wishing myself back there again, and all to do over. But then, thinking it over, I remembered something I read, by a holy monk it was, that if we had a chance, we'd all just do the same thing again. And I thought to myself it was true; what else was there for me but soldiering? I was bred for it by the world I lived in and world that was within me, too, like my king.

Chapter 5

The next day was the worst, almost, as I remember. It rained without stop, and hard; our clothes stuck to our bodies and rubbed us raw at every step. There was not a crust in the camp but all along the road were hedges with ripening nuts, and the archers and high-noses alike grabbed at them as they marched past; they were those little round nuts with hard shells that break your teeth, and even in my hunger I did not care for them. My fingers were too numb to pick them anyway.

We marched and marched, I leading my horse like all of us who were lucky enough to own one, to save it from breaking a leg or worse. More and more of the men dropped from exhaustion and had to be carried, but the king would leave none but the dead. He brooded over us like an old hen, King Harry, on that march; none will believe it, for when have kings cared? But it gave the sick men heart, like, to know he would not leave them to die alone by the wayside, as was always their lot before. That was one of the reasons why Harry was loved by his men, those that did not feel his wrath.

On the next day, I think it was, we came to the town of Nesle.

It was a fine, fair hamlet, set in among little rolling hills; it looked for all the world like a monk's picture of Our Saviour's city, Bethlehem, pretty and clean, with the little chimney fires smoking up to the sky. It wasn't raining either, for a wonder, and the sun came out just then, like it was smiling; it made you feel good just to look at it—Nesle. A bunch of village folk came out part of the way to meet us, too, all rosy and smiling, well-dressed. There was no overlord there, all were free tradesmen and farmers; you could see it was a prosperous place, in a small way. They offered us all the bread they had, and King Harry said we'd buy it! Which was unheard of, but he was so pleased at the way they behaved.

He made another one of his speeches before we got into the town proper, reminding everybody that these were inviolates, and *his* people, and there was to be no looting or pillage or rape or anything else, on pain of death; he sounded real serious, too. When we marched through the town, people stood alongside of the road, and in their doorways, cheering us, and running out to put something in our hands, tears running down their faces over their smiles. They called us Goddams, too, but you could see they didn't mean it bad; the king said they hated the French royalty and nobles because they were always being bled by taxes or just plain robbery, their harvests grabbed without even a thank you. One old dame handed me a rush basket full of eggs, and some of the men got chickens.

I saw my Marie, the one that had sewed on my cross for me, run out from where she was walking with the others and straight into a farm-wife's arms. I saw the woman's face, too, shamed-looking but glad to have her back, a mother's look, if you know what I mean. I guess the girl had run away, seeking another life and thought better of it when she saw her home again. Well, you have to have the temperament for whoring or it's no good.

We went on through the town and camped a little ways beyond, waiting for our bread. They must have baked that morning, and, sure, nobody in the town kept any back; three bakings while we were there, too, and plenty for all, loaves as long as your arm and crusty brown, delicious. The king paid five sous a loaf; they acted like it was a good price and brought us other things too, honey in the comb and baskets and baskets of red apples. It was a real feast, and we stuffed ourselves and had some left over. I'll remember that all my life, I guess, us sitting there, all raggedy and filthy, and fires going, with chickens over them, and the sweet taste of the good bread and licking the honey off our lips and the sun shining all the time.

We hated to leave there, I can tell you, and took our time packing the food that was left; I didn't have any trouble, having my horse and all, but some of the men had loaves hanging from their belt, all around, and strings of sausages like necklaces. Well, just as we were about to get on, a priest and two nuns came out from the town and walked right up to the Duke of York, and the priest grabbed hold of his bridle; it took a lot of nerve, I tell you. Most soldiers don't have much respect for such folk, thinking they got an easy life and no work, see? It held us up for a minute or two; I couldn't hear what they were saying. The king looked back and called out to York, asking what was the matter and why the delay, and the duke kind of beckoned to him, looking grim. The king came riding back, and York says, "These people say one of our soldiers stole something from their church."

"One of *my* soldiers!" says Harry, like he can't believe it; it was almost funny, when you think what soldiers are.

"They say it was one thing only," said York. "A pyx . . . they'll take its value in silver and let it go."

"Well—pay then, Harry, and let's be off," says Lord Humphrey, riding back too.

The king didn't answer but got down from his horse; his face had that look it gets sometimes, all shut-in, like.

Another high-nose, I think it was Talbot says, then, "Oh, sire —time is precious. We've overstayed here already. The French must have gained on us."

"Anyway, Harry," says Humphrey, "what can we do? We can't find the man—it could be any one of six thousand!"

"We'll find him, Brother," says King Harry, grim as anything. Then he shouted for d'Umfraville. That lord came running; he had been taking a quick shave, and one half his face was still stubbled, the other half bare as a baby's behind, and the water running down his chin. He looked comical, but of course no one laughed.

"Yours was the battalion camped closest to the town," the king says. "Did any of your men go back?"

"Well," says the lord, thinking, "they all went into the bushes —I never saw which way. . . ."

"Bring them here," says the king. "All of them."

"By Our Lady," says Humphrey, "are you going to search them? There's no time, Harry—the French may catch up with us. . . ."

"I'll search the pouch of every whoreson in this whoreson army if I have to!" says Harry, shouting it out so that everybody around could hear, and his face getting red.

So he stood the men up in long lines, all those of d'Umfraville's detachment, and that lord and John Bromley, the king's standard-bearer, along with a couple of squires, went through them, opening up their pouches and turning out their pockets. They even looked in the archers' quivers and under their clothes. You could have heard a mouse squeak, it was so still.

Most of the men stood very quiet, all of them scared and

guilty-looking though some hadn't even heard what they were looking for. But I saw one man down the second line kind of inch his hand toward his pouch in a funny way, and the Lord d'Umfraville saw it just about the same time and grabbed him quick. Something bright rolled out of his pouch and onto the ground right in front of where the king stood. King Harry picked it up and wiped the mud off it on the front of his jupon, holding it up.

It was a little cup, like, but a holy thing for the sacrament, and lots of the men crossed themselves, seeing it. It was a hard thing to believe that a man would risk his soul to steal it; it wasn't even gold, though the outside was gilded. Maybe the man was Lollard though; such would not think it sacrilege. I looked to see if I knew him, curious; I saw he was the one who had spat at the king's feet and accused the high-noses of eating better than the rest of us. He looked now gray-faced and cringing, crouched between the two that guarded him.

The king gave the pyx to the priest, speaking in French and handing him a purse, too. Then he knelt down and the priest signed him, so I guess the church forgave the sin. Even after the holy folk went away, carrying their precious vessel, King Harry stayed on his knees, his head bowed; we could see his lips moving but heard nothing; it was an uncomfortable feeling.

When he stood up, finally, the Lord d'Umfraville asked him what penalty the thief should have; it was his archer, see?

"He hangs," said the king. And again it was as still as if no one breathed. The king looked at his nobles, seeing them all with the same shocked faces. "He knew this," said Harry, looking at the thieving archer. "They all have known it. I told them before ever we marched and again at Blanche-Taque, and once again when we entered this town . . . there would be no pillage of holy places on pain of death. . . ."

The Duke of York shifted his heavy bulk, uneasy, and said slowly, "Harry, it may be you will need every man you have. . . ."

"Not that one," says the king. "We're better off without him." He turned to d'Umfraville. "He's your man," he said. "Make an end—but quick."

So four of d'Umfraville's archers strung him up to a big beech tree, while the rest of us watched. It wasn't a pretty end, but what could he expect? Even the Maries didn't weep for him.

I heard the Lord Humphrey say, looking up at the swinging body, "Well, there's three more hours wasted."

But York answered him roundly. "No, Humphrey, it was a right thing. I thought, among the wine casks of Boves, that Harry had lost his hold . . . but he has it back now. They will follow him now. . . ."

When our lines were formed again for marching, the king made another speech. "Get this through your heads," he said, "English oak as they may be." A lot of us smiled at that, feeling relieved, see, that he could joke. "Get this through your heads. Don't think because we have only a few men, that he who does wrong will not suffer. I will have no sacrilege committed, nor pillage, nor rapings . . . such men are not fit to march in God's army. . . ." He always called us that, see; I think he believed it himself. "The man who does these things will hang, if I have only a dozen men left, and the French a hundred thousand strong!"

Chapter 6

It was another two days before we came to the bend in the river that the king had promised. I was in the next battalion after Harry's now and saw an archer sent up a tall tree to reconnoiter, and the king in a taller one, seeing for himself. Down they scrambled, all smiles, the archer's bare foot grimy and calloused, scratched from the bark. The king threw his arms about the fellow and did a little dance, like. "It bends! It bends!" he shouted.

"Aye, my Lord," said the archer in a thick northern speech. "It bends for sure. A canny bend."

"We'll fox them now!" said the king, directing the march into the woods and away from the river, for a shortcut, see? It was harder going though, for there was no path and every foot of the way had to be cut through the trees and brush growth, brambles slapping into our faces and tearing at the few rags we still had hanging about us. We could not any longer see the glint of the French mail on the far bank though, for we were soon out of sight of the river, and it seemed to lighten us a little, as though they were not there at all, our enemy.

Our bread at last gave out; it had been so hard all that last day that we had to soak it in water to get it down. And so we went, not marching but crawling-like, for two days more, our stomachs fair empty, all. I felt dizzy and said as much to Tom Franklin, beside me. His face had no weariness showing, but a wooden look; he said, yes, that was the effect of hunger after a while, making the head light. I felt as though I floated beside my body, and all the men around me had the same dazed look; it was like walking in a nightmare.

At noon of the third day we came to a cleared place, with a few poor homesteads clustered together. The people, almost as ragged as we, stared at us in fear. It was not until d'Umfraville brought gold pieces to show them that they would speak. They said we were coming again to the river; it was now only a mile away. They sold us what grain and breadstuffs they had, just enough for a mouthful each, and said that there were two fords ahead, one at Béthencourt and one at Voyennes. They did not know whether they were still fordable or not; there had been, they said, some scouts of the French, wearing the livery of de Ramburés, seen in the district four days back, boasting that the English king's men were a rabble of scarecrows, unable to cross anyway. So, the king figured, maybe they had left the fords alone, seeing they were so confident about our weakness. So the king flips a coin and says we'll make for Béthencourt ford.

It was the longest mile I ever knew; all the way to the river was bog and marsh, sucking at our feet till we were pulled in clear to our knees. And when at last we came to it, the river flowed almost as broad as an ocean, it seemed, and powerful currents swirled in it. There was a causeway, or the remains of it, for it had been hacked to pieces like all the rest. Those who saw it first did not even bother to call out to the others but accepted it as a doom; some of the men would not even look but stared at their feet, covered in mud as though they wore leggings.

The king, when he saw how it was with us, called a halt, saying we would rest all that day and go on to the next ford in the morning. "This is the place they called Voyennes, anyway," he shouted. "This is not the place I flipped coin for . . . Béthencourt will be our luck!"

After we lay at rest a while, the king set all us archers to cutting willow staves four foot long and sharpening them at one end; good thick old willow trees grew there by the stream. He said they would come in handy for crossing maybe, but showed us all a battle stratagem he had planned. We stared as in a daze, for we had almost lost sight of the fact that we were there to fight the French; the river seemed our only enemy. But we listened, storing it in our heads that were empty of all else.

We fell into sleep early, scarce waiting for the light to die, not hearing the howling of the wolves in the distance, but only the frogs croaking in the near marsh, like a lullaby.

At dawn we set out again, in a gray rain, as usual. At Béthencourt the ford was destroyed, too, but the king waded in, looking at it, rubbing his chin in his thinking way. In a bit, he turned and spoke. "They did a poor job here," he said. "With a little straw and bits of wood, we could rebuild it sure."

All the high-noses looked doubtful, and the Lord of York said, "It would take a long time, Harry—the French may come upon us as we work . . . at any rate, Boucicaut's forces are yonder, on the bank. They'll catch us as we cross over."

"No," said the king, "that they are not! They had to stay with the river, remember? We went the short way, with the bend . . . we have outdistanced them."

"Not more than twenty-four hours," said Humphrey. "It'll be that long before we cross. . . ."

"We'll have to take that chance," said King Harry. "This river is taking all the heart out of us . . . we must cross here!"

He spoke right, I thought to myself, for the men looked already like creatures of hell, without hope.

I spoke up, though before I had not dared address my king; now all was equal, seeming, or I cared not. "My Lord," I said, "on the edge of the bog I saw two old barns, as we passed by. They looked to be stuffed with bales of hay, or straw, maybe. . . ."

He snapped his fingers. "Sharp eyes you have, man . . . what is your name?"

"John Page, sir."

"We have spoke before, John Page . . . you are he that would be bedded for a fraction of my fee, is it not so? Back in Harfleur?"

I could not read his face; it told me nothing. But I had to answer, and light-headedness made me bold. "It *was* so," I said, smiling a little. "Or so she said—I had not a chance to find out. . . ."

He laughed then, clapping me on the back, hard. "Well said, John Page! You may yet get your chance . . . if we come out of this! Although I think the wench would think neither of us good bargains today!" We stood there looking at each other, he covered with mud and slime to the armpits, his velvets matted and black, and I with my leather tunic stiff as iron and my shirt in tatters, my hose torn completely away. He must have seen amazement on my face, for he said, with a whoop of laughter, "Have you seen yourself in a polished shield lately?" And indeed I had been gawking at him, for he was a sight, his beard covering his face and the helm cut grown out to meet it at neck and temple; he looked like one of the beast-men that used to roam in our hills, or so they say. I knew myself the same, rubbing my hand over my face, and laughed, too.

Tom Franklin and I with some others stripped the barns of their straw, and others cut brushwood from the scrubby growth or hacked off branches from the trees. It was cruel hard work, for all had to be dragged through marsh to the water's edge. We were so weak by then it took three to carry what one could have formerly done alone. We had to take turns working in the river, at the ford; the water was freezing after ten minutes, and we came out numb, our teeth chattering and our hands swollen and blue like drowned things. Some of the men whimpered like dogs as they worked, making little sounds in their throats. I'll say one thing, though. The high-noses worked alongside of us, grunting and groaning; even the chaplains kilted up their robes and waded in, and the Maries dragged branches and brush through the mud. We were all one, see, about that river. We'd cross it or die.

We worked from eight in the morning till dark fell, and us with it, but we got it built, the ford. It was makeshift, of course, and wouldn't take much weight, but it was there.

We slept right there by the side of the river, just as we were, waiting for first light. We daren't build fires, see, for fear the French'd see them and hurry up to us; anyway, there wasn't anything to cook, and maybe the chill kept us from dropping off to sleep forever.

I woke early, feeling rain on my face, and voices around me cursing, weakly. I heard Lord Humphrey say, fretful, like a child, "Oh, sweet Jesus, will this rain never stop!"

"It falls on the French, too, remember?" said King Harry. "And we English should be used to it . . . Cheer up, all—think how we've brought our own weather with us for a plague. . . ." He was never at a loss for the right word, and watched as all the men crossed on the precarious causeway, speeding us on. "Keep on," he would say or, "Look out next you—help that archer, he's falling. . . ."

Many of the men hung back, fear in their faces, as they looked at the waters raging past the narrow ford. "I'll go last," said the king. "What say you, John Page? Will you keep me company? They will see then that I mean to get them all across."

We stood together, the king and I, at the brink of the water, close enough that only one at a time could pass through, and to keep down panic. To the huddled archers waiting their turn the king said, loud and strong, "All of you will get across—go calmly . . . The calmer you go, the quicker it will be done."

The king had sent most of his knights ahead, men and horses breasting the water and swimming, too, in places. He thought to protect the rest of us, see, in case Boucicaut and his army were waiting for us on the other bank.

All day it went on, unending, a long, snakelike chain of men, stumbling step by step through the river, going between the king's self and me. If a man hung back, we pushed him on; if he was too fast, we slowed him down. It was like sailors playing out a rope, as I had seen them do when we were on shipboard. The sun rose high and marched across the sky until the slanting shadows fell and it was almost dusk; still they came, the line of men, one by one. "I had thought us a few only, John Page," said the king. "But, by God, it is a multitude, for sure!"

I pointed to the water, where bits of brushwood and straw were floating past. "Sire," I said, "it is working loose. It will not hold much longer—go now. . . ."

He shook his head. "No, I can swim," he said. "Most of the men cannot. . . ."

"I, too," I said. "I stay also."

"Good man," he said, his teeth flashing white in his grime and whiskers.

He stopped the line then, to let the sick ones get across before the ford gave, and the women, too, for all that they were doxies only, and French, as well. When they were across—and it was a slow business—the six hundred or so archers that were left had to race both the gathering darkness and the disintegrating ford.

It was almost done, but more and more brush and straw was swirling downriver; you could see the causeway was about gone. At last, there were only about twenty men left; the king stared at their leader. "Davy Gam!" he cried. "Get across, man!" I saw they were the Welshmen, their leader a little squat, dark bantam of a fellow.

"We can all swim," he said, "so we waited." And he stepped boldly out onto the sunken causeway, careless of his feet as a hill goat.

The king stopped the next man, looking into his eyes in the near-darkness. "Is it true," he asked. "Can you swim?"

The Welshman's lip twitched. "I do not know, sire," he answered, "for I have not yet tried . . . but Davy will have it that we can. . . ." He disappeared into the dark ford-place, and each followed, up, all, to his armpits, holding his bow high above his head to save it.

I turned and looked; the bank all up and down was deserted, the bog gleamed wetly through the marsh grass. No man was left but us. The king said to me, "Go, now, John Page. I will follow."

I mounted and dug heels into my poor famished horse's side, for he balked at the dark water. "Giddap," I said softly in his ear. He whinnied but stepped out. In a second he was up to his belly, and the next step he swam. I heard the king's mount come into the water behind me, and the king whistling low. Ahead of me I could just see a dark dot on the water; the last of the Welshmen had lost footing, or the bridgeway had gone entirely. I called to him, reaching out my lance; he grabbed it, hanging on. The king's horse came abreast of us as we floundered there, and the king reached down, grabbing the man from the other side and drawing him up out of the water to lie across the saddle.

When we reached the other bank, the king let the man down from his horse, where he sprawled, gasping, among his Welsh fellows.

"You could *not* swim then?" the king called to him where he lay. The man sat up. "My Lord," he said, "I never tried. I lost my bow and went looking for it in the water . . . I had no time for swimming sport. . . ." He laughed, and the king with him.

"And did you find it?" said the king.

"Aye, sire . . . but the string is a little wet!"

Chapter 7

That night all things were good to us, the feeble fires we kindled on the shore, the singing of the Welshmen who had once been our enemies, the thin gruel the cooks concocted from the last of our barley, even the walnuts that hurt our teeth; we had crossed the Somme at last. Heedless of the French somewhere behind us, we made more noise than if we were at a banquet, cracking jokes and laughing loud, singing bawdy songs.

In the morning, too, we all came to line up eagerly, knowing that now our marching would take us toward Calais. Sour Humphrey, even, made light talk. "Not far now, are we? Oh, Harry—never in this world will I eat another walnut!"

"There is fine sturgeon in the waters about Calais," said one high-nose.

"And fat capons in every pot," said another.

The Lord Talbot's weathered face cracked in a smile, dirt crusted deep in its lines. "We've got past the king's army, and Boucicaut's, both," he said, and chuckled deep in his throat.

" 'Tis the Lancaster luck," said Lord Humphrey, looking smug.

All that day and the next morning we pressed on through a gentle drizzle, but cheerful we were, every man. Never have I known soldiers so cheerful, as though a load had been lifted from us. Beside me, Tom Franklin lifted his head, listening. "I thought I heard a trumpet. . . ."

"Walter blowing the rain out of it again, I guess," I said, and we both smiled. We rode now in front, behind the Lords d'Umfraville and York, the king riding in the rear, talking to Lord Talbot.

Suddenly York reined in his horse, bringing us all to a halt. "Christ save us," I heard him say. I looked ahead and saw a group of horsemen riding toward us out of the bushes by the side of the road. I could not see their colors at first for the mist of the rain, but then I saw; something turned over in my chest. On their blazon were the three silver lilies of France!

"Heralds!" I heard d'Umfraville say. "Oh, God, they've found us!"

There were three heralds and two trumpeters, dressed as though for court. The leader wore rich herald's gear, silk, embroidered with the arms of France and fringed deep to the knees; under, his legs were encased in chain mail like a knight's. He recognized my duke by his chivalry, as heralds can, and spoke to him, calling him "Your Grace of York." He spoke with courtesy and in good English, asking to be brought to the king. York turned to me, his ruddy color paled now, and whispered, "Go—warn the king—tell him of this. I would not have him shamed before these French, in his muddy rags . . . Tell him to put on his crown at least, it is in the pack of the first sumpter mule."

I rode backwards beside the lines, all the men looking at me as though my wits had left. I found the king and gave him my message, not telling him to put on his crown, of course. There was not time anyway, for the French herald was close behind me, riding with d'Umfraville. The king watched them come, his face unchanged and seeming calm, but beside his jaw a muscle twitched. I saw, all around, the men-at-arms and archers gawking at the peacock-herald as though he had dropped from heaven.

"Herald, here is the king," said d'Umfraville. I saw a look of disbelief on the Frenchman's face, for I have already said how our Harry looked.

The king smiled, a little grimly. "It is I, Harry of England and France," he said, as though he were on a throne; what a cock he was, Harry!

"Who sends you, herald?" he said, still as calm as calm.

The herald started speaking in French, fast as anything, but Harry holds up his hand. "Say it in English," he said, "and loud. I want all my men to hear it."

So the herald says a long speech and flowery, like the Frenchies always talk, although he does it in English. The gist of it was that the dauphin sent him (though afterward it came out that he couldn't have, because he was too sick, see? People said that the Duke of Berry acted for the dauphin and his father, the king, who was always sick anyway) and that he, meaning the dauphin or the king, or whoever, had stood a lot from his cousin of England (which they weren't); he'd stood for his trampling up his land, and besieging his city of Harfleur, and challenging him to single combat and all, but he wasn't going to take anymore. He was demanding reckoning, and the only way he wanted it was to get it by battle. And he sends his gage of battle. And then the herald threw down an embroidered glove at the king's feet. And then he says what was the king's answer?

And then the king, still just as calm behind his whiskers and dirt, says he'll answer him when he sees him. And he asks, when will that be?

And the herald says his master won't say where or when, but he'll bring him to battle somewhere between here and Calais. And then that herald turns to all us soldiers and speaks even louder, and says, "My master says to the soldiers of England, you must by now see how foolish your king has been, and what fools you will all look to the whole of Europe, if you are alive at all. So," he says, pausing to look around, "knowing all this, do you still follow your fool of a king?"

Nobody spoke. They just stood still, looking. Tom Franklin, who had somehow got up next to the king, gave a great hawk in his throat, gathering spit, and just as cool and calm as the king, he spits it right at the feet of the herald. Then he says, "We'll follow."

Everybody broke loose with a cheer then, and yelling, "We'll follow! We'll follow!" They were jumping up and down and waving their arms. That herald's face was a sight to see; I guess he thought we looked like madmen, our eyes glaring through our grimy faces and all raggedy. One man, I saw, was all but naked; he only had a strip of cloth wrapped around his middle. But we meant it, see?

And the king was grinning from ear to ear, pleased at the way his men were taking it. "So," he says to the herald, "is that all?"

"My master would know if you seek terms?" The king shook his head.

The herald went on. "Then he wants to know by what road you march to Calais."

"By the straightest." There was a ripple of laughter at this through all the ranks behind us, and then the king said, "Tell your master that if I can avoid him I will—if not, so be it. We are in God's hands." He looked around him at the fields, all yellowing and sodden. "Tell him also my archers still have it in them to dye the tawny fields of France a bloody red."

Another cheer went up. Looking back on it, I think we were all crazed that day, our gnawing bellies taking our wits away; to look at us, you would think we could not even hold a bow, much less draw one.

After that the king relaxed, like. He asked the herald his name and how he learned the language so well. The man replied that he had been prisoner long ago to Harry Percy.

"Hotspur?" said the king, all lit up.

"Yes," said the herald. "I was captured at the battle of Boulogne." I looked close at him, and then I saw he was old enough, his face seamed and his hair showing gray under his bonnet. The battle of Boulogne was before Wales even. "He was a great soldier, Percy," says the man.

"God rest him," says the king, bowing his head. "He was my teacher in war," he says.

"Then shall we see battle indeed," says the herald, bowing low from his saddle.

The king looked pleased, and they smiled at each other like friends; that is the silliness of chivalry—it is like a game.

"Tell me this," says the king. "Did you have knowledge of where we were this day?"

"I should not say it," says the herald, "but we have hunted you for a long time, days have we been in the saddle. We did not know even that you had crossed the Somme. It was quite a blow to discover it."

"You have earned your herald's fee," says King Harry. "I cannot give you a horse, though that is the custom; they are all famished and worn out." He rubbed his chin, like always, studying. "What was your ransom to Hotspur?"

"Two hundred English crowns," said the man.

"You shall have it back," said the king, sending a squire for a purse.

The herald thanked him, taking it, and he rode away with his followers.

When he had gone, the king's brother came near and said, "Did you mean what you said, Harry? Will we take the straightest road to Calais?"

"Why not?" says the king. "It is the shortest."

And so we marched again, straight for Calais.

The next day we came to a large town, all walled, and with

guns atop the walls. The road was a little ways off and we all of us tried to march quietly, foolish as it sounds. It was no good though; they got wind of us and some crossbowmen rode out and started shooting at us. There must have been two hundred, at least, and we were too tightly packed in the lines to shoot back. Old Talbot showed an angry face and asked the king if he could not take some of his men and go after them, but Harry said no. He said, "Look at those guns. They're harrying us to draw us near enough to use them . . . that would be the end. We'll soon be past."

Once we were clear of the town they let us alone; I guess that was all the men they had. But still, quite a few got wounded. And now we had another smell to add to all those we already had— the smell of blood. Some of the horses began to rear and snort; it makes them crazy, see?

That was the town of Péronne. And then we came to a smaller town, Frévent, and, below it, another river, smaller than the Somme but swollen with the rains. It had a vicious look, with dark whirlpools and a rushing current. God, I thought, we got to cross this, too.

The king beckons to me, knowing I could swim, see, and on account of I had stood with him crossing the Somme, and we waded in first. It came up to our chests, no further, but it was mighty hard work to keep your footing in that current. We paced it off to the other side, making sure there was a clear crossing, and holding hands. Even so, we slipped twice, the current almost sweeping us downstream. The king decided we'd make two chains of strong swimmers and pass the whole train between them.

It worked, though it took many weary hours, and twice the chain snapped. Four men were drowned on that crossing, wounded who were dragged under and had not the strength to fight the waters.

The king gave us only a half hour's rest after the crossing, fearing that the French would catch us all weakened, so we marched on. At twilight the king, riding ahead, gave the order to halt. He jumped down from his horse and knelt, not praying, but examining the ground. Some of the other high-noses joined him, and we could hear their voices, excited, like. When we got there, we saw the ground, all mangled, the grass churned up for miles, as far as the eye could see. Here and there, you could make out a hoof-print clear. Our hearts sank. Only a vast army could have made such a mess. Only the French army. So that we knew they had somehow got ahead of us. We made camp that night, our bows and lances on our chests, at the ready, no man daring to wrap himself from the cold. Most of us didn't have anything to wrap up in anyway.

The next day we kept on, but feeling that the next bend in the road we'd come upon that army. Every hour that passed was like a miracle, for we saw yet no more signs. We came to a village called Blangy, where the people sold us bread and dried meat; we got enough for each man's stomach to quiet down a little. A little ways past the village was a bridge over yet another river, called the Ternoise. We could see it far away; it rose in a high arch. But there were figures with axes on it, and we heard the sound of splintering wood. "Oh, sweet Christ," said the king, "they're pulling it down. My men can't ford another river—" He beckoned to d'Umfraville. "You, go ahead of us—take your men. Secure that bridge, no matter what."

So they spurred ahead, Talbot going too, with all his knights. By the time the main body of us got there, the road was clear, and the knights were lolling against the bridge, waiting.

"How many men did you lose?" called the king.

"Not a one, sire." It was a thing to make you hope again, seeing the French would turn tail so easy.

The king turned in his saddle, shouting so everybody, almost, could hear. "That's the last river, lads," he said. "Ahead lies Calais!"

We marched hard then, as though we could see Calais in front of us and were in a hurry to get to it; all afternoon we marched. When it neared to dusk, the king told me to spur ahead and tell d'Umfraville to find a place to camp. That lord's men were in front, see?

So I pushed on, up a little hill. The d'Umfraville men were halting on the top of the rise, staring down into the valley before them. The archers were sagging against the longbows and pointed stakes they were carrying, and one man had sat right down on the ground, his head in his hands. I hurried then, to see what it was they saw.

The Calais road ran down into a broad valley, and across that

valley was spread the huge army of France. It was still day, and
the thin rays of the sun picked out the shining armor, blinding
bright, the lances and shields polished to a dazzle, the wicked
gleam of axes. While I watched, more came out from the trees
that skirted the valley miles away. It was a multitude, staggering
the mind that tried to count it, and more and more pouring into
it. "Like locusts they are," said a lilting voice. It was the Welshman, Davy Gam. "A swarm of locusts, blackening the
land. . . ."

The king spoke, behind us. "You speak true, Davy . . . gilded
locusts. . . ."

Below, the French knights, those near enough, looked up,
laughing and pointing. I saw us then as they must, a small horde
of ghostly scarecrows, scrawny and haggard, scarce able to stand.
Indeed, as they came up the hill and saw the sight below, many
of the archers dropped to the ground, heads and hands sagging.

King Henry shouted to the trumpeters, "Marshal the host," he
cried. "Sound for the battle array!" A groan went up from all the
men who could hear. The trumpets sounded, but the men did not
rise from the ground.

I heard the Lord Humphrey say, "Oh, Harry, give over—what
use is it?" His voice was thin and sullen. "The French will walk
in and butcher us like oxen!"

The king grabbed his standard from his bearer and set spurs to
his horse. He rode among the host, crying, "Up, lads, up! Hunger
has not stopped you—nor rivers—nor wounds. . . . You have
done well—look how far we have come! Don't be afraid to look
at these peacock whoresons!"

One by one the archers got to their feet, looking ashamed.
They formed ragged lines about the standard, but like sleepwalkers they were, and slow.

The king sat his horse, pity crawling in his face. He rubbed his
chin.

"Sound for parley," he said. "They cannot fight tonight."

I knew how he must feel, so hot for war as he ever was. And to
parley now, when the French are finally at hand!

He spoke low to York, Talbot, and some other lords, too low
for me to hear. But I heard the Duke of Talbot say, almost in a
cry, "Sire, no! They will never accept such terms!"

The king nodded. "I doubt not. But it may give my men one night of rest. And they must have it—or we are lost. . . ."

Sir Hugh Stafford, the chief herald, rode up, saluting. His faded livery was spattered with mud, his horse drooped; in fact, he looked much as all the rest of us looked. The king squinted at his bearded face. "We'll trim your beard to a point, Hugh. . . . 'Twill set a new fashion, and among us we mayhap can fit you out. Who has leggings?"

And so the nobles stripped themselves of whatever was whole of their gear, and Sir Hugh, when he rode out with his under-heralds, looked almost, but not quite, presentable.

Chapter 8

When Hugh Stafford rode back from the French camp, we did not look at his face but stared instead at the horse he led, his herald's fee. It was a fine black stallion, bridled in painted leather and polished to the gloss of mail. It was no better than we had had ourselves when we started out, but none could remember back that far; it looked a wonder among our poor sick nags. "You are the richest man in this army, Stafford," called the king, walking around the horse and clucking his tongue. "We have not even a lump of sugar . . . think you it will charge for England?"

It seemed he did not care to ask what passed in the French camp, but presently he said, heavily, "Who treated with you, Stafford?"

"D'Albret," he said, "the High Constable of France. He did the talking mostly—a shrewd man, and goodly. The horse is his gift. There were others too—Orléans, Berry, and Bourbon. The dauphin is not there."

"That figures," said the king, laughing. He had little respect for this royal lord, who was known for a fool, and puny, too. "Well, what passed? How did they take my terms?"

"Oh, sire," said Stafford. "They refused to listen. They said, begging your pardon, that it was not for the King of England to make terms, but to hear theirs."

"Thus did I figure also," said the king. "Say on."

"They bid you renounce the Plantagenet claim to the throne of France."

"And?" said the king.

"You must likewise renounce the hand of the Lady Katharine . . ."

"I had not known I had it," said the king, laughing.

Hugh Stafford had a funny look and did not speak.

"There is more, Hugh—say it!" said King Harry.

"They demand the person of the king and of every man who marches with him, all horses, all baggage, all weapons, all the king's jewels . . . all are to be yielded as right of conquest."

"And what will they do with my soldiers?" asked the king. "Will they treat them well?"

"Oh, sire," said Stafford, "they are wolves. The Duke of Bourbon said they will strike off the hand of every third archer as a warning. They spoke of selling the fingers in the streets of Rouen. . . ."

There was a kind of windy, sobbing sigh went up in all the ranks, and the king's face went all shut about the mouth, his eyes narrowed, too. After a moment he said, "D'Albret is a man of honor and courtesy . . . does he go along with this thing?"

"Sire," said Stafford, "he spoke against it, but he was oversaid. . . ."

The king thought a moment, rubbing his chin, while all stood silent and afraid. Then he spoke slowly. "Well, my lords," he said, "I think these terms were not meant for us to take. I think they mean to force us to battle by these words."

"Afore God, Harry, take the terms!" cried Humphrey. "They are five times our strength!"

"And not half-starved neither, and worn out," said York, looking glum.

"How many men have they, Hugh, think you, in truth? Forty-five thousand?" asked the king.

"It is hard to say. They are spread all out into the woods, unseen . . . Not less than thirty-five thousand, for sure, at least."

The king walked up to the brow of the hill and stood watching the scene below. In the stillness we heard high laughter rising from the French ranks, and much noise where the baggage lines stood, a sea of wagons. We could see many nobles and men moving about, too, in clustering groups.

"What is it they are doing, Hugh?" said the king, shading his eyes. "Over there by the carts?"

The herald, Staffofd, would not meet his eyes. "Oh, they are playing the fool. . . ."

"What, Stafford?" demanded King Harry.

"They are painting a peasant's cart," said Stafford.

"In God's name, why?" exclaimed Talbot.

"They are going to drag the king through the streets in it," said Stafford reluctantly. "This they told me. Through Rouen first, and then Paris . . . with a halter around his neck, like a mule. Then he must make submission to the king and the dauphin on his knees. This they said."

All the high-noses muttered at this, as they had not at the archers' fate. "For the saints' sake, Harry," cried Humphrey, throwing his helmet onto the ground. "We'll fight!"

And all around the word went up. "We'll fight! Let's fight!" Even the men drew anger from this and shouted too. They loved their Harry, see?

The king looked at them, his eyes moving over the scarecrow ranks.

"We'll give them what they want, lads," he says. "We'll fight." A cheer went up; of course, it was what he wanted too, and they knew it.

The king said to Stafford, "Go back. Tell them their terms are too harsh for us. Tell them we will give them battle."

Stafford was soon returned from the parley. As we watched them riding back, we saw a lot of movement from the French lines, though it was hard to see what went on for sure; the rain was making a kind of veil over the valley. Davy Gam went partway down the road, daring a stray French arrow. He ran up, saying, "They break ranks, sire, 'tis for sure! They will not risk their filthy necks today!"

"I pray you are right, Davy . . . that is what I hoped for." We all watched; slowly the French pulled up their stakes, moving their camp back into the woods. "Why do they do that, I wonder?" asked the king, of no one. "We must follow; they maybe mean to encircle us from behind."

And so we were set to follow, staggering gray-faced through the rainy mist, with the darkness coming fast. Almost we went too far, our first lines almost stumbling into the French; Harry had to order retreat, sending his commands in whispers through the lines. We turned tail and groped our way back. When the king gave the order to halt, we flung ourselves down upon the ground, not caring, though it was plain the French camp was not far away; we could see their fires, and in those gleamings a blazoned shield upright among the tents and a liveried servant scurrying with wine or food. We could smell their roasting meats and hear their laughter. They were not quiet, having no fear, and hammered away at armor or struck shoes for their horses.

They were like a living army camped next to a dead one; us being the dead, see, for all the sound we made.

Tom Franklin and I had found a farmhouse, abandoned; it was one room only and had plaster-daubed walls and dirt floors, but we brought the king there—it was some shelter for him and his nobles. The high-noses flung themselves down, but King Harry said he had to set the watches, and so he began going around the camp. We had some fires going, seeing that the French knew where we were anyway; it was a comfort, I'll tell you, and took some of the stiffness out, too.

I sat me down with Tom Franklin and the Welshmen; those folk were always cheerier than the rest of us, and good for a song, too. My father, rest his soul, used to call them Singers and spit when he said it; the old people always hated the Welsh, saying they'd ill-wish you soon as look at you, but I liked these well.

Anyway, we were lying around, just looking at the fire and thinking, maybe somebody'd say a word or two or hum a tune, but mostly quiet we were; all at once, on the edge of the light we see a gleam. It was that belt King Harry wore, with the lion's heads in gold; it was the only way he was dressed different to the rest of us. Well, we started scrambling to our feet, but he signs us to stay the way we were and sits down himself, cross-legged, and holding out his hands to the flames. I noticed he had a big ring, with the royal arms; it was slipped down to his knuckle—that's how thin he'd got, see? One of the Welsh was singing, kind of a sad tune, like; only we didn't know the Welsh of it—it just sounded that way; King Harry chimed in at the end and sang along—he knew the language. When it was done, he started another that nobody knew, though they hummed it after they'd got the hang of it. After, he clapped Davy Gam on the shoulder and said, kind of serious, and shaking his head, "Oh, Davy—would you had found her!" So it was about a girl, I guess. Well, Davy shook his head, too, and they just sat a while.

Then Davy said, "Some say he died . . . Owen. Up in the hills somewhere. So they say."

The king crossed himself then and fell onto his knees; you could see he was praying. And then he said, "That's heavy news for me this night. . . . He was a great man, Davy." And then the rest of the Welsh began to mumble, and I heard the name Glendower, so I knew who it was they meant. That whoreson nearly won England, and here was our king mourning for him!

"Well . . . he killed my master that I loved . . ." Davy said, but not speaking hard, just sad, like. And the king sang another song, with the name Morgan in it, so that was the girl. A funny name like all the Welsh names, out of old stories they are, all. And Davy looks over at him and says, "You'd best forget about that lady, King . . . proud she is, like all the Sycharth folk. . . ." And the king didn't say anything, just got a soft look on his face like he never had usually; she must have been some wench!

After a while, one of the Welshmen spoke, a big man, kind-faced, that they called Broch. " 'Tis a vast lot of scurvies there, Your Grace," he said, jerking his thumb toward where the French made camp. "How much greater than we ourselves does Your Grace reckon them?"

"Well," said Harry, "let's say you must strike down four men before you can fight on equal terms with the fifth."

Broch shook his head. "Then are we dead men already. . . ."

"Not so," said the king. "Heroes have been overmatched before. . . ."

"Sire," said another soldier, a young lad, his beard no more than a down upon his cheeks. "Sire, some of the men say you and your nobles will pay your ransoms while our throats are cut. . . ." He spoke timidly and with fear.

"No," said Harry, shaking his head, "no man will pay ransom. We fight without quarter tomorrow. No prisoners taken, none given. . . ."

"Do you speak true, sire?" The boy's face was alight under its sickly pallor.

"I swear it," said the king.

"Well," said Tom Franklin, holding up his one hand, "we'll claw some of them down in their blood, anyway. . . ."

"Good lad!" said King Harry. "Can you lift a mace in that hand?"

"As sure as you're born, King!" said Tom.

"You shall have my brother's then," said the king. "He left it behind when the sickness took him home."

"My second blow shall be for him," said Tom, "and for Lancaster. . . ."

"Come, then," said King Harry. "It is with my gear on the farmhouse floor. . . ."

Davy Gam uncorked his water bottle, holding it out. "Will you not drink, sire . . . there is wine . . . the last. . . ."

"Is there enough for all?" said the king, taking it.

"If none guzzle," said Davy. And so it passed around, the king drinking as easefully as they say he was used to do in the London stews, and wiping his hand after on his sleeve, like any apprentice.

"God with you, friends," said Harry, as he rose. "Shoot straight tomorrow!"

His words were brave and put great heart in us, but when I stood my watch, looking around each sleeping cluster, a fancy struck me, ugly and sad, but I could not shake it off.

The bodies of our men lay sprawled anyhow, uncovered, some clutching bow to breast, some curled upon their sides like children. I thought, oh, God, what pity to wake them, with all their dying still to do!

Chapter 9

At daybreak I woke, as did we all, to the thin trumpeting; very still and far away it sounded in the hush. The rain had stopped, for a wonder, though the ground was as soggy as bread-sops. All around me the archers were sitting up, groggy and blinking at the light, looking scared as rabbits. The horses were tethered behind the shack where the high-noses had slept; when I went to fetch mine, I saw them through the broken door, armoring, looking as dazed as the rest of us. Over their torn and filthy shirts their squires were hanging fresh link mail, and over that the plate, polished like glass, transforming them to the images of true knights. I had no time to polish my own mail, flinging it on anyhow. At least I had it to hide my tatters and protect my skin a little, which was more than most had.

I saw the king all armored too, a marvelous sight. He had the royal arms on his jupon, the gold lilies of France on blue, quartered with the gold leopards of England on crimson. It was as brave as brave. He wore also the Lancaster SS collar, silver; no one knows what it signifies, but it's been in his family since the time of the Black Prince. In his belt he had his huge sword. He was shaven, too, and looked most royally handsome, though the shaven part was white against the weathered skin. Most of the other high-noses had been shaved, too; Humphrey had cut himself, and I heard him cursing. "I should have left this for the French to do," he said. "It's their work . . . God help me."

They urged King Harry to change arms with one of them, that he might escape hurt in the battle, being taken for another. This was the custom, and his father had done it at Shrewsbury, arming five knights in his image, but our Harry would have none of it. He joked it all aside though, taking no great credit, saying, "I'm all dressed up now. Would you have me strip it all off again?"

His uncle York begged him, saying, "We need your brains, Harry, to direct the battle. Even the Black Prince watched from a windmill on the hill at Crécy. . . ."

"There is no windmill here," said Harry. "Besides," says he, "we need all the men we have. We can spare none but the wounded, the priests, and the women—" He clapped his hand to his head. "By God," he said, laughing. "I had not remembered the women. For a full week I have not given them a thought. It is a true miracle!" They all laughed then, saying things I could not hear—obscenities, no doubt, as men will at such times, to ease their minds. I heard the king give orders for the baggage and noncombatants to be sent up the hill to safety.

I had not gone far though, for my horse was slow to leave its pasture-field, when Harry caught me up. "John Page," he said, "my bowels gripe me . . . always before a battle. Where do the men . . . ?"

I pointed. "The Welshmen dug a pit," I said. "Davy Gam hopes to lead some of the French into it before the day is out. . . ."

The king laughed loud. "A fine thought! If only the dauphin were here! Him I would like to set in it."

We walked together for a bit, the king thoughtful. "Do you know London town, John Page?" said King Harry.

"Oh—aye, sire . . . I spent all my leaves there, being stationed at the border only. . . ."

"You fought in Wales then?"

"The last year," I said. "I was at Harlech."

The king walked on, his head bent; I could not read his face. Presently he said, "Harlech . . . ah, yes, Harlech . . . eight months of siege—and I in love with a damsel behind the walls. . . ."

I did not know what to say, but he was silent still. And so I said, "We got the most of them out. . . ."

"Oh—aye," he said. "She survived, and we were together for a while." He sighed. "I know not why my mind turns on her now . . . I loved her well. . . ."

We went in silence; the air was soft as May—it would be hot work today on the battlefield. As we watched, the sun broke bright from over a low cloud. The king said, "It must be the hour of prime . . . in London they'll be setting open the gates. How often have I cursed the first cart on the cobblestones! But now—now I pray to hear it once again. . . ."

With the light we saw that the French were very close, not

more than two bow-shots away. Our army was on the crest of a little hill, and tangled woods were thick on either side; beyond stretched wheatfields, flat and yellow in the early sun. They said we were near to the town of Maisoncelles.

The trumpet sounded for prayer. You could see it was not a welcome sound to any of us; neither was the tearing of cloth, as the surgeons made strips out of old shirts and smallcloths, stacking them in piles for bandages. They had been at it since early light.

We knelt, all, in the wheatfields of Maisoncelles, the king and nobles in full armor, to be shriven. The banners were unfurled above our heads and stirred faintly in the breeze. The host was offered on the king's shield, to bless it, see? And all the chaplains moved among us, giving holy bread; it was the first taste of bread some had had for days. And I could not help thinking that also it might be the last.

After, the king began to marshal us for battle, but before he got full into the business, the same French herald rode over again. Harry's face looked dark and angry, because all these delays were nothing more than torment for the men. "Go back," he says. "Tell d'Albret there'll be no more treating. . . ."

And the herald says there's another two thousand French joining them, and doesn't the king want to yield? But Harry shakes his head and says an archer's not much good to himself without his right hand, nor a king with a halter around his neck either, so we'd just as soon get it over, whatever, and don't come again, that's his answer. God will take care of his own, he says; it was brave words, but Harry's face looked a little pinched in the morning light.

When he'd gone, Harry talked to us all. "We take no prisoners!" To the high-noses he said, "Look you—remember, no ransoms! Any man who offers his glove to somebody in battle is giving a severed hand of an archer in it, too. I don't think any noble of England would be that gross." Then he dismounted and gave the order for all of us to do it, too, and sent the horses back with the ones who couldn't fight. Some of the high-noses looked pretty grim, then, because that meant nobody could ride off when things got tough, see?

I saw the Duke of York stumble, and he cursed, saying, "That damned shoe! The sole is just about gone. . . ."

The king looked almost merry, for a wonder, and he said, "Pray to the shoemaker saints. This is their day, remember? The feast of St. Crispin and St. Crispinian. . . . They'll be celebrating in London."

"I wish we were there!" says Lord Humphrey, bitter-like.

"We're better here," says Harry. "Men will envy us this celebration—in after years. . . ." He seemed to have changed, like a whole new spirit was in him. "Give me my crown," he says. "I want the whoresons to know who they're fighting!" He put it on his head, not a crown really, but a helmet with a crown sort of embossed on it; right in the center was a big ruby. I didn't like to think of it, but it looked just like a great gobbet of blood.

But he was almost gay, the king, and he said, "Cheer up, lads . . . think of all the men in England who wish they could be here with us. . . ."

"I wish they could be, too," says Humphrey. "About ten thousand of them."

"Oh, be quiet, Hump—" says the king. "I wouldn't have a single man more! Why, just think," he says, "how thin our glory would be spread . . . This way we'll have it all to ourselves!"

I couldn't help looking down to where the French were forming battlewise. Their lines were forty deep, at least, knights alone, and God knows how many archers behind, with great guns on either side. Everybody else was looking, too, and looking sick. The king saw and said, "Don't look at the show-off Frenchies! Look to yourselves! Remember we are the finest archers and knights in the world. So we are few, what of it? If we die, we will be mourned the greater—and if we live and come to victory"—and here he signed himself, and most of the rest of us did, too—"why, we don't need any more than just ourselves." Somebody started a small cheer then, and we all took it up. "Cheers, too," said the king, "for our shoemaker saints—" And there was more cheering then. And then King Harry said, and loud, "I name you my bulwark, my wall, my yew fence of England—and who can stand against you? Hold fast, my lads—and, with God's help, we shall prevail!"

Then there was so much cheering that you'd never think our parched throats could make such a noise; over in the French ranks they started mocking us, but by now we didn't care and just thumbed our noses at them.

The king set us in battle order then, the men of Camoys and d'Umfraville on the left, us of York and some others on the right, and the king in the middle. He set his archers in wedges all in between and told them to set their pointed stakes in the ground with the points facing out on a slant.

It didn't take long, seeing we were so few, but then the French never made a move, and we just stood there, waiting. It must have been hours; the sun was way up in the sky, and still the French didn't come.

"Oh, God," said Lord Humphrey, "I wish they would come and get it over!" He took off his gauntlets; his hands were sweating, and he wiped them on his jupon.

The knights shifted from foot to foot in their heavy armor. The archers, behind their pointed stakes, checked their bows and arrows, smoothing the feathers at the tips and trying the points with their fingers. One of them turned suddenly and shook his fist at the enemy. "Come on, you bastards!"

Why should they, I thought. All they have to do is wait, and we'll drop from weariness and hunger.

I saw the king, looking over to the French lines, all unmoving, and he rubbing his chin. He snapped his fingers suddenly. "My Lords," he said, "I'm going to order an attack."

The high-nose Talbot shook his head, being an old soldier. "Sire," he said, "we've got the advantage of high ground here now—for what little it counts. I don't think—"

The king interrupted him. "I *must*," he said. "We'll all go crazy else. Tell the archers to pull up their stakes and move to the attack. Tell them to go slowly though and be ready to halt when I signal." And so it happened, one by one the archers drawing stakes from the earth, their bowstrings ready. Down in the valley the French were even stiller, curious they were, see?

All the knights kissed their swords, that is the custom, and King Harry signed himself with his mailed hand. "Forward, banners," he said. And then he turned and shouted, "For England and St. Crispin!" His voice was like a bell, and seemed to hang in the air after.

Slowly the banners streamed downward toward the French lines, through the wheat, over the plowed earth, the slender line of our army with them. The French still did not move; it looked as though we would hit against them and break. Then I saw a shiver in the air, a glittering movement; it was the French lances, all being lowered at once. Then came their loud trumpeting, and the first battle cry, I think it was "St. Denis," but I don't rightly remember, for all at once came others, and the French lines started to move. Immediately the king, ours I mean, turned around and flung up his hand. The archers halted instantly, ramming their stakes into the ground in front of them, points out, as he had ordered.

The French knights, on horseback, streamed forward; they were so close together that their spurs locked, and they came so fast they couldn't stop and were onto the stakes, their horses pierced through and the riders thrown.

"Kneel!" cried the king, and the archers knelt on one knee. "Stretch!" And our bowstrings went back to our ears. The king flung up his hand, and at once you could hear the high, thin singing of the arrows as they sped to the French lines. We drew again, right away, and another volley of arrows went, us kneeling behind a whole mess of fallen French knights, floundering in their heavy armor. They couldn't get up, see, without help, and so, after another volley, we just waded into them and clubbed them where they lay. You couldn't see what you were doing even; it was like sticking pigs, sort of, with the screaming and all. After a while, we were standing on layers of dead bodies, slipping in the blood, and fighting from on top of a mound of them. The French we'd fired on weren't hit, see, on account of their armor, but their horses were, so they were on foot, like us, and floundering in the mud up to their knees. We had the advantage, even though we slipped, too, because we *could* get up, being half naked and light, like. I noticed that, instead of killing the fallen French, some of the men were taking prisoners, even though the king said not to. Most of our poor soldiers couldn't resist the thought of ransom; it was like untold wealth was lying there at their feet, so they didn't want to destroy it. The only thing is—the thought went through my head—they were disarmed, those knights on the ground, but supposing they picked up a weapon off some dead one! They were fully armored, and they could have turned on us easy. So it was better to do what the king said. But the archers went on taking prisoners; some of them had a dozen apiece and weren't fighting anymore, just herding them up and collecting their gloves.

They were collecting the knights' weapons, too, and stacking them neatly, like grisly housewives, there in the muddy field running with blood. I ran among them shouting, but they paid me as much heed as if I had been speaking Chinese. The French were rallying for another charge; we had hardly made a dent in them. And someone pointed up the hill where the wagons were, with the sick and the priests and all. There was much confusion and distance, but it could be seen that the French were there, too. There was fierce fighting on the other side, where Camoys commanded, while all about the king's forces lay piles of French dead. He looked up, his sword in his hand, dripping. "What ails them, John?" he shouted. "Do they play games, then?" Talking of the soldiers on my side, see.

"Sire," I shouted back as loud as I could, "they've taken prisoners. They're taking ransom pledges. . . ."

"Sweet Christ!" he cried. "And the French near ready to come upon us from all sides. . . . Do they mean to ward off French fire with promised gold?" He struggled toward us over the slippery piles of dead and dying. "I gave orders . . . no prisoners . . . kill them!" The men, stayed in their game, stared at him as if he spoke from another world, their eyes fevered. The captives began babbling in French most piteously, and begging, with their hands outstretched.

York stumbled near, saying, "Sire, they are unarmed. It is against the laws of chivalry!"

"We are above the law now—or below it," the king said, his face hard as flint. "Shall we all die for these? Or for English greed?" he cried, looking at the archers holding their prisoners. "Do it quickly now—or I call my guard!" The men looked their resentment; I knew it was not pity they felt, but the good ransom money snatched out of their hands. None moved to obey him, and he clapped his hands, hard. I know not how they heard him above the din, but his own bodyguard came running from center field, going among the prisoners and chopping right and left with ax and mace. I saw York's face, crumpled-looking, and indeed it was horrible to hear their screaming.

The king saw York, too, and said, "Well, Cousin, do not look then . . . it is soon finished . . . to battle!" he cried. "Form your lines and hold!"

I guess it was no worse than anything else in war, and it made sense, of course, but it was butchery, for sure; my stomach turns still, thinking of it. Unarmed men. He did worse later, Harry, but we were all harder by then.

I have forgot what came next. I know there was a fresh charge from the French, and we were too busy to think more; my sword arm ached as though it would fall off, and still they came. We fought on mounds of bodies, as I said. We could not keep to our formation either, but all was confusion; it was hard to tell friend from foe, so covered with mud were we all.

I saw, somewhere to my left, the Lord Humphrey fall, his leg pouring blood from between the gaps in his armor. The king bestrode him, sword in his right hand and ax in left, laying about him on all sides like a demon. They had spotted him, the French, though his jupon was mud-crusted and showed no colors; they saw the ruby in his helm, see? One by one they went for him, he fighting fierce and keeping them off by a miracle. At the last there was just one knight, hacking away at him, and the king looking as though he slowed. I saw the ax flash above his head and shouted; he ducked, and it hit him a glancing blow, knocking off his headpiece. He reeled, but did not fall; I came to life then, and ran over, getting my sword into the French knight's throat, the only place where the armor gaped. He fell, and I finished him off, and turned to the king. "Help me get Humphrey off the field," he said, gasping-like, for he was stunned and the breath was knocked out of him. We dragged Lord Humphrey to the sidelines; he was alive still.

There, on the sidelines, too, was the young Duke of Suffolk, he who had near died before from the fever-sickness. Dead he was now, for sure, his chest caved in, and all the mail over it twisted and mangled; a gun ball must have got him. Next to him lay my own commander of York. There was not a mark on him, and his face looked as though he slept. The king's physician, Nicholas Colnet, knelt beside him. "Sire," he said, "there is no wound. . . . I think his heart failed him. It happens sometimes when too much weight is carried." He shook his head. "Many and many a time I warned him—he *must* lose flesh—"

"Let be, Colnet," said the king wryly. "He cannot heed your warnings now. What of Humphrey?"

"It is an ugly flesh wound, nothing more. We have only to keep it clean."

Back we went to the battle, the king setting d'Umfraville in his cousin's command. Three times the French attacked, floundering through the mire, stiff in their steel, but all fresh; they had plenty, see? But three times they withdrew, leaving hundreds wallowing in the mud and in their blood, till we finished them off, those we could get to. I felt it less a miracle that I had not been run through by a French sword than that I could still stand and still swing ax. The sweat poured off us like rainwater; we peered through it blindly, trying to see who was who.

Another attack; the French came, trampling on their own dead and dying, but they fought fiercely. Against their fresh armor we English showed blackened and bloodied, caked in slime to our eyebrows. I saw the man who had had nothing but a loincloth; he was full naked now and laying about him with a great mallet. He looked like one of those wild berserkers they used to have in the north countries; his member was shrunken and pale, looking as if it wanted to hide.

Some of the French, cut off from their own lines, began to seek quarter, holding out their gloves. I saw one surrender ten times before he found an Englishman who would take his glove; we were all afraid of our Harry, see? But always, at the mention of ransom money, there'll be one that'll set all aside. So there were a few prisoners, after all.

They called that attack back, too, though there were a lot of the French still on the field. D'Umfraville stood watching a moment, pushing his visor back and taking deep breaths. "God," he said, "it cannot be—" He broke off, afraid to say what he was thinking.

Harry heard and said, "For sure they'll come again, friend. Hold fast!"

D'Umfraville's voice came shakily. "I know not if I can. I'm near to bursting in the chest—and cannot lift my arm."

"Your strength will come back," said the king, though he himself tottered as he spoke.

There came a kind of lull that happens in battles sometimes, hard to describe; the din seemed far away, and all around us the fighting seemed to die down. I guess maybe the French were taking counsel; we could see them a ways off, lining up and milling about. We all stood there panting, leaning on swords or maces.

Davy Gam ran in among us, shouting, "The priests and boys—
they've killed them—killed the priests!"

Up on the hill the baggage train was a bloody shambles; all
was plundered—the civic crown, the privy seals, the jewels, the
purses. There was a smoldering heap where clothes had been
burned, a senseless thing, and time-wasting, too. The pages had
all had their throats cut and lay naked, stripped of their gear,
with their legs all twisted under them, like boy-dolls thrown
away. The monks and priests were dead, too, their skulls split or
worse, and bloody gashes where their crucifixes had been torn
from their throats. There was no sign of the women; they had either been taken or gone willingly. They were French, after all.

The wounded had all been slaughtered and stripped naked,
like the pages; I saw the armless youth the king had been at such
pains to save was among them, a sick irony.

The king's litter still stood, though the hangings had been
wrenched away. Inside it was Moll Savage, a dripping dagger in
her hand; with the other she was mopping the forehead of the little fool, the merry imp Hercules. He looked to be conscious; I
could see his doublet rise and fall with his breath.

A little ways off were two men, one a knight or squire in
French armor; he had been stabbed in the throat and was barely
alive, blood and mucus spewing still from his wound and mouth
alike. The other was a rough fellow, a peasant from these parts.
He was full dead, his brains bashed in, the mace that did the
work beside him on the trampled earth.

The king leaned over the little man, shaking him gently. "Hercules—Little Brother . . . do you yet breathe?" The fool looked
up and nodded; his mouth smiled always—it was his trademark
—but his eyes, too, had a little light that danced now. I had not
seen before that they were beautiful.

"He saved my life when this *cochon* came at me," said Moll,
jerking her head toward the dead peasant. "And so I stung his at-
tacker, yonder squire, with his own weapon . . . to make all
square . . . I think he is not bad cut, our Hercules, for the dagger
came out easily. . . ." She bent over the fool, lifting a wadded
cloth from his side. "Yes, it has stopped bleeding." She looked up
at the king, her yellow eyes crinkling. "He has a mighty arm—
the little Hercules. . . ." And sure his blow had left little of that
poor villein's head.

"Good girl," said the king. "Tend him well, my little Hercules. He is my good friend. I'll send Colnet when he can be spared. . . ." And he bent and kissed her on the cheek. "*Au revoir*, my brave Michele. . . ." So that was her name, though I liked "Molly" better.

We could hear the French battle cries, so could do nothing more there, though I finished off the stabbed Frenchie, just in case.

As we came on to the field, we saw the jewel-like colors of the plumes in the French helms, a whole new line. Out through the trees came the banners of Brabant, fresh and unmuddied by battle, the mounted knights gleaming like holy angels, or devils, maybe. Our men struggled to form lines and meet them, the king shouting, "Your stakes, lad—your stakes!" They rammed them in, and again the horses ran upon them, goring themselves and falling, the French knights unhorsed and floundering till we clubbed them down. All was confusion by now; our brains were reeling, and still they came, and still they fell, and still our maces rose up and then down to the slaughter. I was using both hands for mine; I had not enough strength left in my right arm alone. My limbs were so weary—it was as if I wore heavy iron chains upon them—and my running sweat ran into my open mouth and choked me. The French came on like a sea, engulfing us; but one by one they fell, their wounded horses, riderless, neighing in pain and terror, and the painted reins flying loose.

I saw Brabant fall, hacked from his horse, and the Lord de Rambures, also. They were brave Frenchies, riding like madmen upon us. The Duke of Orléans yielded, and Bourbon, too. The Duke of Berry fled the battle, riding off into the woods; I saw it with my own eyes—the coward.

We all felt our strength was fair done. Many of us fought with open wounds, blood running down to mingle with the sweat. No matter how many we hacked down, there were more still, as though they rose up, the enemy, from the earth. I heard more than one of our soldiers sob from tiredness as he laid about him with his ax, my own voice, too, rough and grating in my ears. The king croaked at us like a sick crow; his voice had failed him. "Keep on, lads," he gasped, rustily. "A little more and it is done."

So we kept on, our arms rising and falling, but slower and

slower each time, and our legs like water. There came again, gradually, that lull, that strange ebbing of sound. Suddenly I heard the king sigh, as if in amazement; he was not near either, but I heard. I looked over and saw him, dropped upon one knee, pushing his visor up and staring. I looked where he looked. There was the dark, still woods, with the straight white Calais road between, but where the thousand glittering French had stood was nothing but riderless horses, tents, and the flung dead. There was no sound but neighing, no Frenchmen but these mangled heaps. As one by one we lifted our heads to look, there came a little hollow cheering from the archers; it died away from its own weariness. We all looked at one another, weaving on our weak legs, like ghost-things.

From the little knot of royal French that had yielded, Orléans came out, kneeling to King Harry. "All is yielded to you, sire," he said in careful English. "The field is yours."

"My Lord," said Harry, "it cannot be. There are thousands of your countrymen left . . . when they re-form. . . ."

"My Lord," said Orelans, "it is so. We are all scattered. You hold the field. We place ourselves into your knightly chivalry. . . ." And he bowed his head.

The king still argued; it would have been funny at another time to hear them argue thus, like each was too polite to claim victory. But in truth it was a hard thing to believe. We all took off our helms, and blinked at one another like owls. We'd been squinting behind the visors all day, see; it was like coming out of the half-dark. What a sight we were that day! Yet had we won.

The king asked for the lists of our dead. "My archers––" he said to Talbot.

"Aye," said old Talbot, blood streaking his face from a gash on his forehead, "it may be a lot have died. Still. . . ."

From over the slimed and bloody field men came lurching, one here, one there, looking like they'd just come up from hell. Hugh Stafford, the herald, plowed through the mud to bring the lists of those slain. The king took it, his hand shaking. As he read he steadied, looking up in wonderment at Stafford.

"Sire," said Stafford, seeing his face, "it is complete. Except for your cousin of York, and Suffolk, only one other noble died. Thirty men-at-arms, seven squires. I think not more, in all, than two hundred."

The king looked around. "Then all these dead. . . ."

"They are all French," said Stafford. "I think we have killed more than twice our whole number."

"Oh, sweet Jesus, Harry," whispered Humphrey, from where he sat propped up among the wounded, "you have done a miracle."

The king crossed himself. "My Lords," he said, and his voice was husky; almost he sobbed. "My Lords, surely it was the hand of God. . . ."

None spoke for a moment then. The king raised his head. "What field shall we tell them back home . . . what field were these battle-deeds done on?"

D'Umfraville said it was Maisoncelles, but the king did not like that name. "It makes me think," he said, "of last night and the hardship and the rain . . . it smells of our despair. . . ." He pointed to a turret showing above the trees and spoke to Orléans in French. I guessed he asked him the name because Orléans said, "Agincourt."

"Agincourt . . ." said the king, trying it out on his tongue. "It has a good sound. I like it." He turned to all us archers, where we dragged our wounded off the field. "Agincourt. That's the name you'll tell your grandchildren. This was the battle of Agincourt."

Chapter 10

I was knighted in that battle; you could have knocked me over with a feather. Some of the men—after things simmered down and it looked like the French were really gone for good and we'd truly won—foraged around the French tents and brought back hams and cheeses and fowls and all kinds of foodstuffs, such as we'd never seen. We being so starving, some just gobbled and threw it right up again, wasting it. But Tom Franklin and me, we thought we'd make a fire, see, and set a pot to it with a chicken and let it boil up for soup; we figured that'd be an easy thing for our sick empty stomachs. I fetched some great torches, still burning, from one of the royal tents and started a fire with them; they were soaked in resin, see, and the smell was sweet and clean, clearing the air. I think I'll remember it always, that smell, and it coming on to evening and all.

Well, I was kneeling down, piling on brush for kindling, and even some of the Frenchy tent poles; they weren't using them again, that was sure. Well, I felt a tap, like, on my shoulder, a smart one, and heard a voice, the king's. "Arise, Sir Knight!" Just like in an old story. "For courage and fidelity beyond the line of duty . . . for battle valor . . . for my life that you saved," he says. "I make thee knight . . . so rise, Sir John Page of Wessex!" I had forgot all about that French high-nose I'd killed, the one that had knocked off the king's helm. But he hadn't; that was Harry for you. "There's another one, too," he says, "if I can get to him in time. . . ." And he beckons to me. "Come," he says. So I follow, sort of dazed-like, not taking it in yet.

He went over where the wounded was, still carrying his sword that he'd knighted me with. There, on the ground, his legs all blown away, but alive still, was the poor little devil of a Welshman, Davy Gam. He must have been suffering sore, but he looked up and smiled, and the king touched him with his sword and said the words. Well, he couldn't rise, of course, and the king said, "You'll rise up new in heaven, Davy, lad," and Davy's face was like he was there already. It couldn't have been long neither, poor sod, though his bright eyes followed us as we left.

"One more," said the king. And he went to his litter and knighted the little fool, the mountebank. "For that you saved this lady," said Harry, meaning the whore Moll. It's funny, she had the kind of skin that doesn't flush, being smooth and olive, but when he called her lady I saw a kind of color creep up her neck; she kept her eyes wide, too, because there was tears in them, see, and she too proud to let them fall. She was some wench. And the little man was mending, too, for he stood to receive his accolade, tottering and holding his sore side.

The king, though, still didn't quite believe his victory and made us keep to the field; he feared the French would come back. All the high-noses were still in armor, though they lolled about on the ground, and all us men were just as we were, too, so tired we could hardly eat, even though we had the food at last. We just lay and waited, while the shadows got longer and longer, and darkness was creeping all around us. The Lord d'Umfraville said, finally, "My Lord, I think they are not coming back."

And Harry said, just as quiet, "No, I think truly the day be ours. . . ." Then he bade the trumpeters sound the retreat. I think it was the sweetest sound I ever heard, not thinking ever to hear it again. All the men gathered, ragged-like, about the king, and he spoke, not like he usually did, in a parade way, but kind of halting; you could see he meant every word. "I would give my thanks to you for this day's work," he said. "Believe me, no king was ever served better. I would like to say more . . . but the words won't come . . . Thank you, thank you, lads. . . ."

And so we came to Calais rich men, or almost. There were French horses, enough to go around, and much armor that we could not carry, and it rotted there on the field. Clothes we had, too, and weapons, and food; it was a paradise-change for us starvelings. And then, too, I had my knight's pay from then on, a big raise.

They watched us from the Calais walls as we marched in; we were not ragged anymore, but still a funny crew, I can tell you, with all our looted French clothes and armor. It must have been hard to make out who we were. But then all of a sudden someone must have spotted the king's arms, for a great cheering came, and all the bells of all the churches starting pealing, and the people came running out to meet us, crying and laughing at once. The bells never stopped for a week.

At home, too, the people were like crazy folk, cheering themselves hoarse. When our ships came into the Cinque Ports, men waded out chest-high and carried the king into shore on their shoulders. And in London wine ran from the conduits and great splendid ceremonies went on. We all paraded behind the king through the streets, the cheering almost making us deaf. What a sight Harry was; his face was all bruised from the Frenchman's blow. It had been black and blue and now was yellow and purple, like a painted thing. The people loved him anyhow, calling him the Bonny Warrior and the Handsomest Prince of Christendom. I never saw such crowds, even after, when there were great victories and more gained; they were packed so close that even if one man fainted, he'd still stand up.

It was a great victory, for sure, Agincourt; there was never another battle like it, I think not in any time, let alone ours. But when I think back on it, I see it this way; maybe God had a hand in it—I wouldn't know—but for sure the Frenchies did. What I mean is, they made their own defeat; we were just there, the few of us. Oh, we fought well, and more than well, I'm not saying that, but the French didn't have no main leader, see? And they didn't know who to follow; they were all mixed up and divided. And they were so old-fashioned! Why, they didn't even have longbows, just old-time crossbows, that you have to wind up before every shot; it takes a lot of time. And their armor was like two hundred years ago; we weighed one suit—the Duke of Brabant's, I think it was. It weighed more than ninety pounds! So you can see they could hardly walk in it, let alone get up if they fell. Well, to my mind, all these things had a hand in bringing us to victory that day, not just God, or even Harry. Though some that weren't there would say I spoke treason, almost.

But as I say, there was no battle like it. I followed our Harry clear through the fall of Rouen, when I got my leg blown off and got retired. With full pay—Harry was good to his own. But all those battles—Caen and Bayeux and Falaise, Rouen, too—they were just siege-warfare. Not worth writing about or remembering even, though there were some grisly things happened. Those sieges, though—they made Harry a conqueror and won all Normandy for him.

He changed, though, Harry. Got hard, like. He was always full of care for his own soldiers, thinking about them all the time, and easy with them and all; most of the time he was fair and just with his enemies, too. Even the French said that when they wrote about him, though his punishments were cruel sometimes; he once hanged some of the defenders from the wall of their town, those that wouldn't give in, leaving them there to rot forever. And there was that soldier he crucified. Margery, my wife, that is, said nobody would do such a thing and I must have been fevered or dreaming, but it was true. This soldier took a potshot at him, see, when he was going into the tent of another high-nose to parley. It was at a town called Louviers; well-fortified it was and held out three weeks. But when it fell, Harry had all the gunners put to death, and this one he put on a cross, I swear it. So he was beginning to show a side of himself that hadn't been there before. Even so, he was one of the best; war makes brutes out of all men in time. Though maybe it sounds a funny thing for me to say, me being all my life a soldier. But I ought to know; the things I've seen. And done.

Tom Franklin got retired right after Agincourt, with a good pension; he settled down right near where I myself live, in Wessex. I used to visit with him between campaigns, and now, two old cripples, we have a good time remembering and reordering all the battles.

As for Moll Savage, that I had a hankering for, the king kept her by him for two years, maybe more. And when he got shut of her finally, he married her off to that good little man, Hercules, his fool. They kept a kind of inn, right in London-town, famous it was, because of the fool's mumming and singing and, of course, because of her whoring, too.

I myself wouldn't want a whore for a wife, but mummers are a different sort, everybody knows. I wouldn't have my face carved up to make people laugh neither, though lots of those mountebank folk have done it since his time. He didn't live long, Hercules; that wound he took at Agincourt must have been near some vital place. Often he swooned, they say, holding onto his side and losing his breath, and finally he dropped down dead while he was mumming, right on the stage. He was much mourned, and the king buried him in Westminster, near his own father, the king before him, though the fool's grave was unmarked.

She set herself up then in a fine house, with the king's own arms over the door; I saw them myself, finally. She was still good-looking, not like a leopard-thing anymore, but a queen maybe—fine clothes and jewels, and fattened up some. She was a good whore too, like I'd thought all those years, made a man feel good. Nothing fancy—she had Ay-rab girls for that—but just a fine bit of fun.

Funny thing, I think the king himself, Harry, loved those two girls—Moll, and the Welsh one before—more than his pretty little Frenchy princess. That Katharine, I saw her at her crowning; butter wouldn't melt in her mouth.

A man with one leg—nothing to do but sit in the sun and whittle maybe or tell stories to your grandchildren—you get soft. I keep forgetting all the blood and the filth and the boredom and the hunger. And I remember Agincourt and the king and glory. There'll never be a battle like Agincourt, and never was before. I said that. There'll never be a king like Harry neither.

BOOK V

The Prize

(Told by Katharine of Valois,
later Queen of England)

Chapter 1

I hate my mother, Isabeau. My hand trembles as I write it, for I think sometimes that she is everywhere about; certainly her spies are. I never think of her as my mother really; she is always the queen. I think my sisters hated her, too; certainly Marie did. And once, when I was very small, and peeping from behind a screen, I saw Michele hit Isabeau back, after she had been whipped; of course, she was a big girl then and should not have been whipped at all. It was before she was married, and had something to do with that; she didn't want to marry Burgundy's son. Who would? He looks like a toad. She did marry him though. Everybody always does what Isabeau wants, in the end. Marie didn't want to go into a convent, but she did. Isabeau said that it was so that she could pray all her days for the health of our papa.

Poor Papa, he is so sweet, when the fits are not on him; but they are now, almost all the time. I remember, long ago, he was often well. We had parties sometimes, and once, on my saint's day, I was given a pearl ring and some little cakes. Isabeau had taken the boys, the dauphins, to Melun, which was good, or they would have gobbled up all the cakes. I did not much like them either, though they were my brothers; they had hung about Isabeau's skirts since they were babies, fawning on her like little courtiers, kissing her hand, and making fancy speeches. Of course, all men, young and old, acted like that about Isabeau; it was only the women who felt differently.

For Isabeau was very beautiful; even now, getting fat, she is still one of the most beautiful women in France. Her skin is like thick new cream, without blemish or color; of course, she is painted, but still, one can tell. And her eyes are large and brilliant, almost black. It has been said that we princesses all take after her, but that is policy only, to flatter and to quiet ugly rumors; we do not. We are merely pretty, and none of us is tall. When Isabeau came here first, to the Castle St. Pol, right after she married Papa, they had to make all the doors higher! Papa told me himself. It was partly the headdresses she wore, a foot high, but mostly it was Isabeau herself, tall, as a queen should be.

We all have thick, curling hair like Papa's (though most of his has fallen out by now), and Michele and Marie have the de Valois nose, with a little hump, though mine is flat.

Once, when I was very small, I heard two servants talking—rough girls they were, such as were always about us in those days. One said, pointing at me, that for sure the Mad One never sired her, look at her button-nose! And the other answered, yes, it is Orléans to the life! I was very ignorant then and thought they meant I was not Isabeau's either, but the Duchess Valentine's, and I was happy in that thought, for that lady, Orléans' wife, was gentle and good; I used to dream that one day she would claim me.

I stopped that dream early; it was not long before I discovered that Uncle Louis of Orléans was my mother's lover. He was not the only one I saw in Isabeau's chamber; in those days I had a little bed there, as was the custom. Even by moonlight, I could see that none of them wore even their smallclothes. I used to lie awake with my fingers in my ears, so I would not hear them, and hold my breath, so they would not hear me. And, in the morning, I would feel shame, as though I had done Isabeau's deeds.

I am, of course, no longer ignorant; when I grew older, I understood all the gossip. None lowered their voices either; I was as nothing in the castle, for all I am a princess. Not only was Isabeau the scandal of this court, which Père Le Grand called the most vicious in the world; she could not go abroad except in a covered litter, for the people pelted her with filth and shouted insults. Once, when I was five, we were taken—Marie and I—to a wedding at Senlis. We were both much elated, for we had new dresses. Not new, really, of course, but I had Marie's court gown cut down and refurbished with new lace, and Marie had a beautiful velvet made over from Michele's betrothal robe. We rode with Isabeau, splendid in cloth of gold; there was a special litter, new, with a roof, and prettily painted doors, like a little house. All the way to Senlis there were thuddings in our ears, as the stones and clods of earth hit the doors; the shouting, too, was terrible. Isabeau never spoke at all, except to tell us to sit up straight. She acted as though nothing were wrong, or perhaps she was used to it. But, for us, so little, it was a frightening ride.

The wedding, too, was frightening; one of the brides wept and the other fainted. It was a double ceremony; my sister Isabella, she who had once been Queen of England, poor Richard's queen, was wed to Charles that was my Uncle Orléans' son; it was she who wept. She entered the church with a cloth held to her eyes, and in the pauses one could hear her sob. I never knew why she wept, though I wondered often, in after years. Was she sad to set aside her queenship and become a mere duchess? Or was she crying that she was marrying a boy of twelve? When, three years later, she died in childbirth, I thought that perhaps she had the Sight, like those ladies of Wales, and, at her wedding, had seen her own end. I never knew this sister; she had gone early to England, before I was born. I never saw her after either, for she left Paris for her own duchy, and there she died.

The other bride was marrying my brother Jean, then the dauphin. She was dressed very beautifully, her clothes stiff with gems, and a crown on her head, though she was just my age; her name was Jacqueline, and she was from the duchy of Hainault. They said her robes were too heavy and that she collapsed under their weight. Her mother said the words for her as she lay on the floor, for they would not interrupt the solemn rites, and a squire carried her out from the church after. As they passed us, I saw that she had lost one of her silver shoes, her small foot dangled limp, stockinged in red.

All my early years were marked by sadness, fear, or disaster; one would think I would have hardened to it, but I did not. We girls were hungry often—the servants kept all for themselves, there being no one to order them; Papa was mostly ill and Isabeau uncaring.

In the night sometimes we would wake, the three of us in our little bedchamber, cowering at the sounds that came from Papa's room, when they had to chain him; screams of rage and piteous sobbing all at once. We lay awake all night then and starved all day, for none tended us, and our door was locked; we beat upon it with our shoes and shouted till we were hoarse, but no one ever came until Papa was right again.

He was not always so, of course, Papa. Sometimes he would lie for days in the deepest melancholy; we would tiptoe in and look at him, but he never knew us. Sometimes he would talk a lot, like an old nurse babbling; at those times he said he was a man named George and not a king at all, and he thought we, his daughters, were harlots.

"Poor children," he would say, sadly. "So they have taken you and sold you into slavery . . . poor little girls. . . ." And he would shake his head and mumble, weeping.

Michele answered him once, being the oldest of us. "Sire," she said, timidly, "you are Charles of Valois, the king—and our father. . . ."

"Oh, no," he said, with a cunning look, "I am George . . . they have taken Charles away. His wife . . . and his daughters, too . . . away . . . they are harlots . . . harlots are they all now. . . ."

Once, when we gazed upon him, and he lying all filthy and his beard grown out and uncombed, his eyes empty, he came suddenly to his wits and was himself, our papa. "My poor little girls," he said, tears in his eyes, "what have they done to you? All ragged you are, like peasants, and your faces dirty. . . ."

"We are hungry, too, Papa," I said, made bold by his concern.

All weeping then, he cried for his servants; none came but a slops-wench, looking scared. When he demanded food for us, she said that there was none in the palace. He was horrified and angry; he stomped out of his chamber, us following, right down to the kitchens; our footsteps echoed in the empty corridors. He fed us from the spit there in the kitchen fireplace, burning his fingers on the hot roasting meat; I remember too the taste of it, salted by his tears.

All was good then for a long while, maybe a month; the servants tended us and Isabeau, even, was kind, buying lengths of cloth for our dresses and ordering new shoes. It did not last though, and all wore out, the clothes and shoes, but we were never quite so hungry again.

There is a story told of Papa's madness, how it came upon him. He had gone to the southern parts of his domain to tour and show himself, as kings must do; Isabeau, in her fourth pregnancy, could not go. She had lost two children through miscarrying and still had not got an heir, but a girl only. Our father had been away for several months; on his return, his brother, the Duke of Orléans, rode out from Paris to meet him.

Before they met, however, a wild man, all unkempt and hairy, came out of the woods at Le Mans, grabbing the bridle of the king's horse, and speaking impassioned words, low. The king, hearing him, flew into a rage and galloped to meet his brother, drawing his sword. It took eight men to subdue him, and the Duke Louis was slashed across the arm. Four others, too, were wounded, and they brought the king, bound, and out of his wits, into Paris.

After, none remembered clearly what the wild man had said; neither was he ever seen again. It has long been a mystery, but I think that I have solved it. I think the wild man told my father of Isabeau's taking Orléans for lover; I think his madness was caused by that, for he had loved Isabeau greatly. But, ever after, when his raving fits were on him, it was Isabeau he longed to rend in two, Isabeau at whom he raged. Once, indeed, he beat and kicked her cruelly, being taken with his madness suddenly; she miscarried then, too.

After my youngest brother, Charles, was born, Isabeau found herself pregnant for the twelfth time. She would not go in to the king anymore, saying she feared for her life, and there were enough heirs now anyway. She found a young girl of the petty nobility, who looked like Isabeau herself, somewhat, and sent her into the king's chambers, thinking to delude him. None knows what happened there, for sure he did not take her for Isabeau but loved her dearly. She is by him still, living in his rooms and caring for him tenderly, even when he is sickest. She resembles Isabeau no more than the dove does the hawk; they are both birds.

This is Oudine, and I ask Christ's blessing on her every day, for my poor papa's sake.

She is very clever, Oudine, as well as pretty and sweet. Some would not say so since she has no more Latin than most women, but she is clever in other ways. She can paint beautifully with colored inks on parchment; I think, if she were trained by a master, she would not be worse than the court painters; but who would train a woman? Many charming things she has made—a lovely likeness of my little dog, Melusine, is one. I have put it into an oval frame and wear it sometimes at my girdle, as one might hang a purse. She makes pictures for my papa, too, to amuse him, and herself, also; often he is sunk into a state of half-sleep, and she has none else to talk to, and little to while away her days, for she lives always in his rooms. There is a game she has invented, indeed, several. She has made pictures of court people on squares of parchment—the king, the queen, the dauphin, the princess, and many duchesses and dukes; on the other side she has numbers, all different, or sometimes heraldry. They are brightly colored and boldly, so one can tell them at a glance. One keeps the pictured side up, you see, and bets on what is under, in all manner of ways, according to the game. Of course, no one has monies, so we usually play with the same sous over and over. But it is a fine way to pass the time, especially for a sick man; one game we call court, and another, simply, cards, for the squares are small, like our menu cards.

Oudine is wonderful with Papa; she can calm him even when he raves, and none else will venture near. She cleans him, too, when he fouls himself, which he does sometimes, like a babe, and feeds him gruel from a spoon, too. For the sickness makes him childish often. When Papa is well, though, I read to him sometimes, for I have learned how and she has not. Papa used to read a great deal, but his eyes are weak now. I read romances mostly, like the story of Melusine, that I named my dog after, because Oudine and I love these stories well. Sometimes, though, Papa will ask for the works of the ancients, when he is fully intelligent, and I can do that, too. Not many girls can. I, too, am grateful for Oudine; with my sisters gone, and Owaine, too, I have little else to fill my days. But I am ahead of my story.

I was telling of my early years and the fearful things that happened. I remember the night that Uncle Orléans was killed; it was terrible. He had come to visit Isabeau; she had just been delivered of a stillborn babe. I do not remember whether it was a boy or girl—I get mixed up—she has had several. This one, though, was his, and he came to condole with her; she was still abed, for she had been very ill. We girls were asked to supper, mainly so that we might wait on them; she did not like servants about when she entertained that lord.

They supped off silver dishes from a serving table drawn up to the great bed, he sitting on its edge; we got what was left. After, when we had cleared all away, she sent us to her dressing room and drew the curtains of the bed about them both. So perhaps she had one last night of love, though it was a sin, for she had not yet been churched. But sin did not worry Isabeau. I suppose she felt she might as well be hanged for a sheep as for a lamb, a saying of the country-folk.

When he had left, she called us in; she had bled all over the sheets, a fearful sight. Michele was afraid and wanted to call the doctor or midwife, at least, but Isabeau would not, though she groaned most piteously. We had to hide the bloody sheets and clean her up; while we were about it, a distasteful task, a knock came at the door.

It was a little page of Orléans' train; he had run all the way. He carried something wrapped in a cloak; when he showed it to Isabeau, she fainted. We had to look then, too. It was the hand of Orléans, dripping blood from the wrist. We could see his signet ring and the long fingers with their polished nails. And then there was more blood to clean up, and Isabeau to see to. It was a dreadful night.

The page was almost unable to tell; he had near lost his voice from fear. But finally we made out his words. Orléans had come with but a few retainers; though the world knew about those lovers, still he pretended, and it was his downfall. They were set upon by a great body of assailants, who struck the duke down from his horse, spilling his brains out all over the cobblestones. The little page, quick-witted, hid under a stone bench; it was near the fountain square of the Rue Barbette. He saw it all; the men who struck the duke down were all masked—the leader wore a red hood pulled down over his face. They axed the body again and again; it was in many pieces.

We brought unwatered wine, giving some to the page, and forcing the rest between Isabeau's lips. When she recovered, she gasped out hoarsely, "You must take it back! Take the hand back! It must not be found here. . . ."

The little page fainted at these words, being sore afraid; it was clear he could not go. So we three girls crept out in the darkness, Michele carrying the bloody hand in a napkin.

One cresset lighted the fountain, and he lay beside it, that handsome duke, what was left of him. There was no head at all, just a sort of mash puddling the stones, and parts of him were scattered all about. Another body lay across him—his squire, headless, but wearing the Orléans livery. Michele dumped the hand beside the body, spilling it out of the cloth. After, she pushed the napkin at me, whispering, "Take it . . . I think I'm going to vomit—" We none of us vomited though. And we got back home, through the dark streets, past the shuttered houses and inns. I do not remember how. I was just six years old.

It was two years after that night that my oldest sister, Isabella, died. In the same year, Michele married the toad Burgundy, and Marie was given to the Poor Clares.

I was almost alone; I did not count Isabeau or the dauphins either. They were a sorry lot, except for little Charles. As I say, I was alone, except for Papa, in his times of health, and Oudine. And Owaine, my friend.

Chapter 2

If it had not been for Owaine, I would not even have learned to read, for there was none to teach me. In the years after Orléans' murder, my father seemed to come fully to his wits again. Even when Isabeau took another lover, he did not rave or run mad but merely sewed the man up in a sack and sank him, with stones, in the Seine; the words "Let the king's justice take its course" were written on the sack. So, you see, he was sensible. If killing is sensible at all, which I doubt. What I mean is, he acted as the world expected. He awoke, one might say.

Everyone knew who did the murder of Uncle Orléans; it was Duke John of Burgundy, he who is nicknamed "The Fearless." And indeed he showed no fear but boldly admitted the deed, saying further that it was justified, for Orléans had been a tyrant! These two factions, Burgundy and Orléans, have torn our country in two for years, laying waste with their wars. The people starve because of them, the cities ground down and the countryside trampled and plundered, and still they fight. The Orléans party is called Armagnac, from holdings in the south. But Burgundy is strong—so strong that he forced the family of Orléans, his wife and sons, to legally absolve him from all guilt. He married his son to a king's daughter, too (thank God it was Michele and not I), for Isabeau plays canny politics. And now she is his paramour, too.

I can never understand this—he is as ugly as his son, old, too, and thick as a barrel. He has no accomplishments except butchery and no learning at all. Orléans, like all our Valois House, was gallant and fair, though corrupt under. But Isabeau and Burgundy are a fine pair of vultures and deserve each other.

After my sisters were gone, our part of the house was so empty and sad; I spent much time in Papa's chambers, just moping about. Oudine tried to teach me fine needlework, but I am all thumbs at such things. One day Papa saw me turning the pages of one of his books; it was a missal with beautiful pictures, picked out in gold, a gift from his Uncle Jean of Berry. There was one picture, an imp sticking his pitchfork into a lady; the expression of his features was so cunningly wrought, a mixture of mischief and ferocity, I burst into laughter. Papa took the book from me, saying, "But child, it is not funny . . . that is a saint he tortures!"

I pouted, for he seldom reproved me. "Well," I said. "I did not know, Papa . . . I cannot read."

This so astonished and saddened him that he began looking about for a master to tutor me. He had been sick so long, and out of things, as one might say, that he did not know how to go about finding one. He turned to that same uncle of the missal, the Duke of Berry, begging him to help us.

I had not met this old man, though he was my great-uncle, for I almost never went anywhere; I loved him on sight—he had such a merry face. Bald as an egg he was, as my father would be soon, and of a very great age, though he did not look it; Papa said he was upwards of seventy!

When he saw me, there in Papa's chambers, he pinched my cheek and gave a deep chuckle in his throat, though I had not done anything funny. Except to curtsey low, as Oudine had taught me; I thought perhaps I had done it clumsily. I found later, though, that this uncle had a habit of chuckling like that; I have seen him do it whenever he first glimpsed a treasure he coveted, such as a fine-wrought manuscript or gem or one of those yellow teeth belonging to a curious great animal from Africa, for he is the greatest collector of such things in the world. So perhaps, after all, I had pleased him.

Indeed, it seemed so, for Papa said, "Well, Jeannot, what do you think of my smallest girl-child?"

He chuckled again and said, "She is a very cat, dainty and sleek . . . Her hair is like little copper wires, twisted." I did not like this very much, for my hair is a curse to comb. I must have been standing in a slant of sun, also, for it is brown only, the red showing only in brightness.

"Yes," said the duke, "she is a right dainty small wench . . . you must fatten her up, though, Charlot." There they stood, those two nobles, calling each other by mountebanks' names! As though they played a masque! I learned, after, that all his intimates called the duke "Jeannot"; he was an easy sort of man. No one other, though, have I heard nickname my father. He is the king, of course, so only an uncle would dare.

"I would fatten her *mind*," said Papa, tapping his forehead. "She cannot read! All my children they have neglected while I have been abed. . . ."

"It is no great failing," said the duke. "Most damsels cannot read. . . ."

"She is a Valois," said Papa, drawing himself up. It was sweet, but sad, and almost funny, Papa showing kingly pride, for he was in his nightshirt still, with dirty ankles, and his poor face all hanging like a hound's.

But they settled for a Latin master; he was one Morris Stove of Wales, and an Oxford scholar. He had been at the Duke of Berry's court in the train of the Welshman, Owen Tudor. This Owen had been ambassador during our French alliance with Wales; now that that war was over, or nearly, and his cause was hopeless, he acted as agent or buyer for the duke, traveling to all parts to seek out curios; that duke would pledge his own head for a costly treasure that he coveted!

And that is how I came to know Owaine; that is not his name, really; he is another Owen Tudor, like his father. I called him Owaine because of its French sound, and also for that it was like Gawaine of the Arthur tales, of which I am most fond. Owaine's father had brought him here to France when he was only two, because all the rest of his family had been killed in the Welsh rebellion; that was in 1404, so Owaine is a year, almost, younger than I am. One would never have known it though; I have always been undersized, and he was big for his age, even then, and very learned, having been tutored by this Master Stove for all his years.

Master Stove is a little dark man, much bent, with a nose that is longer than the Valois'. He has no teeth either; they were all knocked out by an English lance in some battle. It is funny to think of Master Stove as a soldier; one would picture him as tied always to his books.

The alphabet was easy, and Latin, too, but our French tongue, written, is not ordered and is difficult to recognize; English is worse, and Flemish, too. Everybody spells just as they please in these languages, and each piece is a new puzzle. Master Stove, though, says, being a princess, I must learn something of them all, and Italian, too, seeing that I may be placed anywhere in marriage. I had much trouble with the English, and the duke said perhaps Owaine could help, seeing that he knew it well and was a child, too. And so we met and have become good friends.

In those days, it was most pleasant, for each morning we studied with Master Stove, and Owaine never crowed over me either, for all he was so far ahead. Owaine knows Welsh, too, though he does not remember his country; these people have much pride of race, not like us French, who are all divided.

Besides my lessons, many pleasant things happened then, because of Owaine, and my great-uncle, Jeannot, Duke of Berry. Owaine lived in the duke's household; he was a boy-squire only, but you could see he was a great favorite of Uncle Jeannot, for he trusted him with the care of his pet bears. This duke, as I have said, was a collector—of everything that is under the sun! All of his curios were fascinating to us, of course, but the animals especially. His house in Paris that was called Hôtel de Nesle, was the largest in the city, larger even than any of the royal residences. It was very close to our St. Pol house, but I had never been there until these lesson-years; I had never been anywhere.

It was a beautiful house, Nesle, with huge grounds about it and many outbuildings, just like a small city. Inside, there were special rooms for all his possessions; one room had jewels only, under glass, rare stones, and most costly, from all over the world! There were paintings kept in all the galleries, and books, both scrolls and missals; tapestries, too, of a wondrous magnificence. I cannot begin to describe them; it would take a scholar, indeed. Furnishings from the Orient, Cathay, even, and thick glowing carpets upon the floors. The windows were all glazed, too, with colored panes set in patterns; more beautiful than a cathedral it was there with the light coming through all rainbow-like, a joy to enter, truly, even for a child.

But a child could go wild with happiness in his garden places, with the flowers and animals and birds; a paradise, truly. Owaine's father was not the only one who bought treasures for the duke; he had many traveling agents, and every week new curios came in, packed in straw or transported in gilded cages, depending upon their nature, of course.

There was a profusion of flowers; some that came from hot countries had to be grown in glass houses! There was one, from Africa, I think, a huge blossom, that they said could eat a man; we used to creep by it very carefully. Owaine said that once my brother Louis had fed it a frog; it disappeared without a trace! A cruel thing, but all my brothers were cruel boys, except for little Charles, who is merely weak.

There were marvelous birds, too, colored like gems, in cages in a house to themselves, with seven maids to care for them and clean their cages. I did not much like them though; most of these rare birds had ugly voices and rapacious beaks, and frightened me. I preferred the homely larks and linnets; there were hundreds of these little birds in one great cage, making sweet music like a heavenly choir. One gaudy bird, though, we could not get enough of; he was so comical. He could talk, this bird, though it is a hard thing to credit. Latin couplets he would recite, wonderful to hear. Most of the time, though, when we stood before his cage, he would swear at us in the vulgar tongue, scandalously, like a shrewish wife; he had been brought there by a sailor from Marseilles, and all sailors swear dreadfully.

The part I liked most, though, was the Palace of the Beasts. It was built just like a manor house, with many rooms, all richly furnished and filled with all the animals of the world. There was a room of cats, not little ones only, but big creatures, caged— panthers, lions, and leopards, beautiful and strange. They were most terrifying when they roared or opened their great jaws to eat; whole sides of beef they would consume at once, raw and bloody. Outside, in the grounds, were many deer and, in an enclosure, odd beasts from other parts, a small striped horse, and a spotted, long-necked creature with beautiful eyes. Camels from the desert, too; I did not like these—they were very bad-tempered and tried to bite. One mammoth animal, though, loved me and would eat from my hand. It was called an elephant; big as a small cottage it was, with a sort of tail in front as well as behind, and wicked horns, though it was always gentle; I fed it little nuts that grew there in its place. I still remember the soft lips so delicate on my palm, like a caress.

Inside was a special apartment for the monkeys, great and small, a delight to enter; these beasts are most like humans, comical to watch as they play. The duke had them all dressed, like servants, in his own livery, and they could sit at table and eat with spoons, like very Christians!

All manner of dogs he had, too, in kennels all apart. That was how I got my Melusine; we watched her being born, one of a litter of seven brachets. The duke was always generous; he saw my delight and told me to choose a pet for myself. It was not hard; I took the smallest, a bitch-puppy, with soft brown eyes.

All these creatures are tended with great care, mostly by natives of their own countries, who understand them well. There are blackamoors, and little slant-eyed people, and Turks in baggy trousers; I was afraid of them at first—they are so foreign —but they are good and have no harm in them, though they cannot speak French at all.

Owaine, of course, as I have said, loved the bears most. I think the duke did, too, for all his personal things have bear symbols embroidered on them, and his dishes, too, have many carvings, all representing bears. Owaine will stand and let the bears hug him, a fearful sight, though they never hurt him at all. He has trained them, too, to dance, for it is a thing Owaine does well; even then, when he was a child only, he knew all the latest steps from court.

He taught me, also, to dance; at first I was as clumsy as the bears, never having done it, but later I became more graceful. It is still one of my most favorite pastimes, and I have been highly praised for my skill.

Owaine, like his father, is tall, with slender limbs and long, straight, yellow hair. His eyes are bright blue, deep-set in their sockets under fair brows, and his mouth is most fair, curving and soft, with large, square teeth, very white. I notice teeth very strongly, for so many nobles have rotten ones, and the servant-people often lose theirs early. My brothers all have crooked teeth, which spoil their looks, and Isabeau's are a dark color from a black sweetmeat that she fancies, though Papa's teeth are strong still and sharp enough to bite to the bone, when he is in a fit; Oudine has marks still, on her arm, which Papa cries over, for he did not mean it, of course.

Owaine, also, was kind and merry; he did not tease or pinch, like other boys, though of course I knew my brothers only. Besides taking lessons with me, Owaine was much with me all the day; none ordered us, Papa and the duke were lenient, and Isabeau was not often about. We had the run of the two houses, St. Pol and Nesle, too; I seldom went hungry either, for Owaine would bring me good things from the duke's table—that whole household lived like emperors.

Owaine had many accomplishments; he knew falconry, and some jousting and hunting, being reared by that great old duke. I knew nothing, really, till he taught me; I could not ride a horse even, though most girls are bred to it early. It is hard to credit how ignorant I was.

I grew to love Owaine well, more than Papa even; I could not help it. We would hold hands and kiss; our caresses were innocent and sweet. After, when we grew older, we were constrained, and there was much pain; even in my ignorance I knew I must not lose my maidenhead, for I was a princess of France and must remain virgin or demean my house.

When my woman's times came upon me, and I bled each month and was melancholy before, I would weep into my pillow that I could not marry Owaine; at such times I thought my heart would break. Though, in his own country of Wales, he was of the finest heritage, descended from kings on both sides, yet was Wales discredited; here, he and his father, too, were nothing, not even knights! And I must marry nobly, at least; I was reconciled to it; I prayed only that it would not be an old man or ugly.

Chapter 3

I had not been much at court, only on occasions of high state, and I do not recall much of them, only a great bustle and ceremony, with loud voices announcing people. The first time I really can remember well was the visit of the English embassy. Wales had been put down, that we had been allied with, and there was an uneasy peace between England and our own land. I say peace, but it was never so; always there had been raids and counter-raids, each side pillaging the other's shores, across the Narrow Sea. This embassy was sent from the new king, he they called still the Tavern Prince, Harry of Monmouth, his father having died only months before. I must have been near thirteen. Even then, I did not have a new dress to wear, only my old green velvet, rubbed in spots, and short to show my ankles, for I had grown.

It was a morning late in May, the air still fresh and a little cool. I had been to the duke's bear-pits with Owaine, for there had been no lessons that day, Master Stove being abed with a cold in the nose. We had stopped in the gardens—like Eden they were, the ground all white with pear blossom. He had flung himself onto the earth among them, and I sat, making a wreath of the fallen flowers for his head, and laughing; we were very free and careless together, that boy and I, for much love went between us, as I have said. And there Isabeau came upon us, she who never sought me from one year to another.

She had some lords and ladies of Burgundy with her, though the ugly duke himself was not present. They stopped, all, when they saw us, laughing lewdly, for they were a scandalous sort, the women's bodices cut low to show their rouged nipples, after Isabeau's own fashion, and the men dabbling their fingers in those same bodices in the sight of all.

Isabeau scowled when she saw me, pulling me roughly to my feet. "Has he had you then, doxy?" she hissed, shaking me by the shoulders. "Who is the sprat?"

"It is Owen Tudor, of the duke's household," I said. Owaine

scrambled up and fell upon one knee, most courtly he was, yet she scowled still.

"Has he had you, girl? Answer!"

"No, madame," I answered, my face all red with shame before them all. "He is just twelve years. . . ."

"He is big for that," she said. "Stand up, sirrah!" He stood then, near as tall as that tall woman.

She eyed him, a strange look, and, loosing me, stepped close, her hand going up under his tunic, between his legs. For a moment only she stayed thus, then stepped back, laughing harshly. "Pah!" she said. "Nothing there . . . the little one speaks true." Her whole train laughed loud then, clapping their hands as at a mummer's jest.

"Come you, then, Katharine," she said, and whisked me away.

I was taken to her solar and plumped down under a broad window, a head-veil over my hair, to have my picture painted. It took all the morning; after, she gave it into my hands, the paint all wet still and coming off in my fingers. "Give it to the Lord Thomas of Dorset, when you are presented. Say it is for the king."

It was a poor thing, that portrait, all pink and white and simpering. The painter had given me a fur hood, too, with lappets of ermine; between them my face was a rabbit's. I exchanged it for one Oudine had made, a simple likeness, before I went into court.

He looked at me startled, that Lord of England, hearing me called daughter of Valois; for sure I did not look it, in my skimpy old gown, with my head barely covered and no jewels except my little pearl ring. I gave him the little picture, as I was bid, whispering, "For the king," and he took it with grave courtesy; he was a goodly knight, though I heard later he was one of the bastard Beauforts, son to Gaunt by a lady of the commons. So, it *can* be done, I told myself, thinking of Owaine. Princes do marry commoners, sometimes. And why not a princess, too? For I dreamed always in those days of Owaine and a miracle that I knew in my heart would never happen.

I did not take my lessons with Owaine anymore; Isabeau had forbidden it, shrieking at poor Papa for a dotard and a fool. In spite of all that has passed, he is still much in her power, when she wishes it; it is easy to see that he loved her greatly, once.

So I must slip out, unseen, to meet Owaine; it was not difficult, for none kept watch on me. We met behind the bear-pits or in a grazing field between our two houses. All that summer we met and through the fall of the year; if he was still a boy, yet was I a woman already and weak with sick desire. We kissed and caressed all our short moments together, pressed close together all along our bodies' lengths. I would have given all; I cared nothing for our Valois House that would not even buy me a decent dress to cover me or a woman to tire my hair. But he would not, Owaine. He was right noble, or perhaps he was too young. And now, maybe, I will never see him again.

For that same Thomas of Dorset came again from England, asking for my hand in marriage with his king! It was Oudine's picture that caught him, the king; I should never have exchanged them. For sure the court painter's simpering idiot-face would have captured no one's fancy! Because the little Oudine painting is fresh-looking and alive, though she has made the nose and chin too long.

Isabeau is all for the match, though Papa is none so sure, deeming the whole Lancaster line impostors. It is difficult to understand Isabeau's politics; but Burgundy has all along had treaty with this king, even when he was a prince only, so perhaps that is it. The king has asked a huge dowry with me, a million crowns! It is ironic, when you think of it, I, who have never in my life held even a half-crown in my hand! He has asked all of Normandy, Anjou, and Aquitaine, too, an outrageous demand, so it may perhaps all come to nothing. There has been parleying back and forth between our two countries all this year. And now it looks, even, as though we may go to war!

All the duchies are arming, calling up their vassal lords, and mustering their foot soldiers. Even the Duke of Berry will play the warrior, though he is seventy-five if he is a day. He has withdrawn to his own duchy holdings and has closed up his Paris house, taking all his people with him, except for those who take care of his animals and flowers.

I hoped against hope that Owaine would not have to go, seeing that he has been bear-keeper here, and overyoung for warfare, also; he is gone, though, and his father, too, and now they are training for battle in the country dukedom of Berry. Of course, Owaine will be a squire only and not bear arms, but he will be in the thick of it anyway, wherever the duke goes. I did not even say good-bye to him; I had not the chance. I keep remembering, though, what he had told me of the deadly English longbow that was copied from the Welsh; it is as tall as a man, and the arrow can pierce iron at forty feet. I pray every day that he will not be hit by one.

It is coming on to summer again, and the heat is terrible. Poor Papa is ill again; he is always worse in sultry weather. He is not raving, though, but lies all day upon his bed and often does not know anyone, even myself, or Oudine. When he comes out of his trance, he does nothing but weep; it is sad to see.

Isabeau keeps from his sight, for which I thank Our Lady; it is a fact that she sends him mad, or more so. She is living openly now with Burgundy; sometimes they are here at St. Pol and sometimes at the Louvre Palace. It is strange; with Orléans, that gallant creature, she was always at least discreet, though everyone knew or guessed, but with this ugly monster now, she flaunts her love, if one can call it that. I think it is a power liaison only, theirs; they are both getting old for cuddling.

She makes all decisions of state now, Isabeau, with Burgundy, Papa being ill—here at home, and with England, too. If there is anything to sign, they send me in with the paper to Papa's bedside; thus they make use of me. If he is well enough, he signs, for he loves me, and is beyond thinking. If he is sunk in a coma, Louis can sign, for he is dauphin now.

I call all my brothers dauphins, as one would say, princes. But the true dauphin, the heir, is, of course, the oldest; this is Louis. He was never pleasant, Louis, but now, at seventeen, he is grown into a young man most horrid. Not that he is ugly, truly, though he has pimples; it is his *inside* that is not lovable.

I was not raised with my brothers, so do not know them well. Jean, that I saw married to the little girl that fainted, is mostly away in his bride's duchy, but I remember him as arrogant and spoiled. He is nearest my age, barely a year older; Charles, who is rather sweet, is almost two years younger than I am and lives now in Anjou, where he will someday rule (if we do not lose it to England).

The Dauphin Louis, though, is kept here now, where Isabeau and Burgundy can make a tool of him, when they must. He lives wildly, drinking all night and sleeping all day, though it is bad for him; his health has never been good. (He has fits sometimes, they say—not like Papa, but foaming at the mouth and rolling on the floor.) So I do not see him too often, thank Jesus. When he has nothing else to do he taunts me with my only suitor, the King of England, naming him wastrel and tavern-crawler. A case, clearly, of the pot calling the kettle black, but I did not deign to answer.

"He will come to you a worn-out sack," he said, picking at a pimple on his chin. "He has had a different woman every night since he was fourteen, sometimes two. How many does that make? He is twenty-seven now—you have a head for sums, they say, add it up. . . ." And then he laughed, a nasty sound. "Mayhap, the morn after he beds with you, he will forget and leave a purse under the pillow. . . ."

"They say, also," I said, angry but not showing it, "that he is the champion of all that he turns his hand to, jousting, swordplay, tennis—for tennis, he is a wonder. . . ." This last was pure spite; I had seen Louis in the yard, knocking balls across a net. He could scarce hit them, though each was sent easy to him, seeking to flatter; of course, he was always allowed to win, though his serves fell nowhere near the mark, and he could not return at all. I know something of the game; I have watched often lately, having nothing else to do.

This stung him; there was a little flash in his dull eyes. "Aye—" he said. "I will send him a gift of tennis balls and bid him stay home and play with them."

"Take care," I said, "that he does not round them with iron and send them back to you—out of a gun!"

I had no wish, God knows, to marry that king, or any, but what Louis said was silly; all the world knows King Harry for a warrior all his years. Look what happened in Wales! Besides, I would defend the devil himself against my brother the dauphin.

Besides, if the truth were told, though I loved only Owaine, I took some pleasure in the thought that King Harry held to me through all the long parleying, even though he did haggle over the dowry. I, who had been as nothing all my years!

Anyhow, I was not plagued with Louis longer. He too took up arms, going to Rouen where troops were mustered under his own lily banner. Before he went I saw him, all mailed, and with his hair clipped around his ears in a helm cut, a revolting sight.

The castle buzzed, and folk ran round aimlessly like headless hens, the people howling at night outside our windows from fear. The news had come that Harry of England had landed at Harfleur, with a huge fleet of ships and ten thousand men; he was now outside the walls of that city, with his siege-machines drawn up and his army encamped.

Chapter 4

Harfleur has fallen; the English held it under siege for more than three weeks, and none of us French came to its succor. There is so much discord among our armies it is a wonder they can agree who is the enemy! But all the bells of the churches here toll day in and day out, a mournful sound, and the people wail in the streets, heaping ashes on their heads.

And now he will march to Calais, King Harry. Calais is a strong port; it has been English for years. If he reaches it, the English forces will be practically upon our doorstep, here in Paris, for it is not far away, a bare hundred miles. Only the common folk have fear, though, for the castle people, all, brag that we will stop his march and put him to rout. They say the English army is decimated by the marsh fever, many having been sent back home; they say that King Harry marches with but half his men, and those full sick.

So all our forces march to cut him off, and Owaine with them; I tremble for him and pray each night to Our Lady. Everything here at St. Pol is at a standstill; I thought myself idle before, but now there is nothing to fill my days. Papa is still sick; he knows nothing and does not even hear the folk outside our windows, shouting and throwing stones. They burn Isabeau and Burgundy in effigy, for they blame them for this war. And we hear that the Duke of Berry's house and grounds have been attacked, some of the gardens near destroyed, for there are not enough defenders. The common folk hate all our nobles, on account of taxes and other things, although they have always loved poor Papa.

Louis came once again to the palace here, I guess to take counsel from Isabeau and Burgundy; he is completely under their thumbs, one can see, although he is supposed to act for Papa. I saw him before he went back to Rouen; he taunted me, saying that he would bring my English bridegroom to me within the week, in a peasant's cart, with a rope around his neck! He said the English are all starved and half-dead, near naked; they have been on the march for weeks now, through hostile country and in the rain.

"But the rain falls on the French armies, too," I said.

"Pah," he said, snapping his fingers, "*that* for their chances. When they catch sight of us they will turn tail and run, without a fight. We are fifty thousand strong!"

But it did not turn out that way. I can hardly write what happened, it is so dreadful. This city, that mourned before, is like a city of the damned now. There is not one family that does not have its dead. And it is the same all over France. The tolling bells never stop; we are so used to the sound by now, I think we would go deaf if it ceased, from the strange silence.

The armies, French and English, joined battle in a wheatfield near Maisoncelles. Our forces were routed, all, and the French dead cannot be counted, though the English lost almost none. No one understands what happened; it is a miracle in reverse. The poor folk cry that God is English!

The French who died, nobles and common soldiers alike, were piled on that field in heaps higher than a man's head. After, widows and their fatherless children journeyed to that battlefield to find their dead and give them Christian burial, while the English king marched on, undeterred, to his holding at Calais. Many of the dead men were so mangled they could not be identified, even by their own, who loved them. Many thousands lay on the open ground, corpses stripped naked by our own peasants or by the English. One good thing that toad son of Burgundy did, he that is my sister Michele's husband; he gave a great plot of land there, that he owned, for a common grave; those unknown dead were tipped into it and shoveled over, 5,800 by count. Of course, none of Burgundy's kin were there at all, in that battle; he lets others do his work, that lord, for all he is named Fearless! Nor was my brother Louis in the fight; he sat safe in Rouen through all the slaughter.

Isabeau wears black, but it is rich velvet, and the color makes her look thinner; one can see no sign of grief upon her face. Indeed, it is alight with excitement; she and Burgundy sit all day with their secretaries, drawing up new treaties, arguing thus and so. Those two will always be on the winning side, somehow, you may be sure. They will send new terms now to the King of Eng-

land, he having gone back to his own land across the channel. I
do not know what will be; of course, he has more to bargain with
now, that king, after his great victory. They say he has named it
the battle of Agincourt, after a petty castle that stood there, in
those parts.

Papa has recovered, somewhat, it being November and cool.
After he came to his senses, hearing about the terrible defeat, he
scratched long runnels down his face with his nails and tore out
part of his hair, too—which he cannot afford, he has so little left.
He goes in sackcloth, like the begging friars, and Oudine says
there is a chain drawn tight about his waist, under, but of course
I have not seen it. He is a good man, Papa, when his wits are
about him, with a heart as big as all our poor land.

Owaine has come back, unhurt! He was there, in that battle,
but only for a little, at the end. The old duke, arriving late with
his forces and seeing the dreadful slaughter, fled the field. He has
been called coward by Burgundy, who was not even there; Isabeau, too, is putting all the blame on his shoulders. As if he could
have turned the tide, that old man, when all the flower of French
chivalry had fallen already. Most men of seventy-five would
never have gone in the first place—a thing they forget.

I have seen Owaine, for Isabeau keeps no watch on me now,
being busy with her scheming. He has described the field there at
Agincourt, most horrible to hear. Corpses cut in half and headless men, piles upon piles of dead, with living men trapped
under; and the English, fighting naked, covered in mud for clothing, looking, he said, like black devils out of hell. He saw the
king, also, he said, or at least he thinks so; the warrior bore the
Lancaster arms. A giant he said, all bearded black, and fighting
fiercely, laying a space about him with mace and ax; a king to
fight in such wise, like a barbarian! He sounds a brute; I hope he
will forget about me.

Owaine and I are back where we started, when we can con-
trive to be alone. Separation and war have put an edge upon our
loving; we make wild moments of joy and pain, though I am virgin still, thank Jesus.

For Owaine has a noble heart, like Galahad or Gawain; and
besides, Papa has talked to us. Papa likes Owaine, though he
does not approve of my name for him; he says he should be
called Owen ab Owen ap Tudor, his right as a Welshman. Papa

much admires this race; he knew the great Glendower in his youth. Indeed, he names Owaine like to him, tall and golden fair as he is. Only Papa says, smiling a little, that he is Glendower-with-water, meaning, like watered wine. Of course, he did not say it in front of Owaine, but to me only. I made a little face, and he shook his head, Papa, saying Glendower's like would never come again, not in a hundred years. "But your playmate is a good lad," he said, sighing. "Would I could give him to you, Katharine, for husband. But love matches do not happen in this world," he said, sadly. "Not for princesses." And so I wept sometimes, a little, into my pillow at night.

Just after Christmas, this year of Agincourt, 1415, the Dauphin Louis, my brother, died. He fell into a fit with all his revelers about him; it was at dawn, in his own apartments. There was much wine there, and he lay in a pool of it, his limbs jerking wildly and foam coming from his lips, while all the low women shrieked in terror. He lay as one dead, but breathing still, all through Christ's mass, until the feast of Epiphany, when the life went out of him. He was only nineteen, Louis.

Much money was spent on his funeral and many candles burned. The inside of Notre Dame Cathedral blazed with light, like noonday; they melted down the candlewax after, and it weighed 2,150 pounds! He was not much mourned, though. Only Papa, Oudine, and I, from our household, followed his coffin, with that good old man, the Duke of Berry. Little Charles was brought up from Anjou, though he had a fearful cold and coughed all through the services. Brother Jean, though he was dauphin now, was not present, nor Isabeau. They gave it out that she was too prostrate with grief.

We had to follow the coffin through the streets, nearly a mile, and it was snowing hard; none of the common people lined up to watch us pass, for all that they love a show. Poor Louis was too much despised.

I did penance every day for the bad thoughts I had of him; it went on through Lent, before I was absolved. I cringe inside when I think of my acts of contrition if Isabeau dies; I shall have to walk barefoot clear to Jerusalem!

For I hate her more than ever now.

The winter wore on, and spring came, and summer—1416. The good old Duke Jeannot fell ill and, in June, himself lay dying. This whole year has been marked by death, as though God cursed it; all those thousands at Agincourt, many of them my kinsmen, and then Louis, and now my friend, and Owaine's master. I went there every day, to ask of him, though they would not let me into his sickroom.

One day, though, Isabeau appeared in Papa's chambers, saying we must all go to the Hôtel Nesle, for the duke's will was to be read. She pulled me roughly by the arm, as was her custom always, scolding me for that I did not look overclean. As if it was my fault that I wore always the same dress! Or nearly—I had two.

It was a solemn sight, there in his great room. The duke's two daughters were there, though his wife was not. She was near fifty years younger, his second wife she was and a wanton who did not love him; or so it has been said. Many of his house servants were there, gathered in the background and weeping loud; I caught a glimpse of Owaine among them. The duke's confessor was there, dressed in his robes of holy office, and bearing the host on a red silk cushion; physicians, too, wearing the hoods of their order. At the sick man's feet his pet bear nuzzled among the coverlets, seeking his feet to lick them.

Isabeau sailed in, like a great ship, all in black still, pushing her way to sit upon the side of his bed. His eyes had been closed, but he opened them, feeling her weight beside him; his face was gray, but he looked then almost merry. He tut-tutted, shaking his head and wagging his finger at her as if she had been an erring child; perhaps, to him, she was. He was so old, and wise, too.

He waved her away and called me to him, taking my hand. He spoke so low I could scarce hear his words and had to bend my head right down.

"Look you," he said, patting his belly, "how flat I have grown. . . . Just a year ago they had to cut a window in my armor so that I could fit in." He held my hand for a moment, then let it go, seeming to sleep. Isabeau dragged me away then, twitching at my head-veil as though I did not wear it in seeming wise.

When the will was read, I was amazed to find that he had left me a casket of jewels and a chaplet of emeralds for my hair; it was a sweet thing and made me feel most loved, though Isabeau took them all away when we got home, saying I was too young

and would have them when I was wed. She herself got nothing,
nor Papa either, except a pair of little gold cups.

After the reading of the will, we all were shooed out; in the
crowd Owaine managed to come near and slip a square of parchment into my hand. I tucked it quickly into my hanging sleeve,
under the lining, but I felt eyes and, looking, saw Isabeau's upon
me, a dark swift glance.

In my father's chambers she turned on me, railing. "Where
have you hidden it, doxy? Out!" And she poked about in my
sleeve, tearing the cloth and ripping the parchment in two. Her
face grew dark red as she looked at Owaine's words; I never
knew what the letter said, some love speech, maybe, or a bid to
an assignation, but it sent her wild.

She turned on me, beating me about the face; when I put my
arms up to protect it, she grabbed one of them and twisted it till
it cracked. The pain was agonizing, but my fear was worse; she
was so big, my mother Isabeau. "The truth now, wench!" she
cried, forcing me to my knees by that twisted arm. "The truth!
You are a used-up purse. . . . He has had you these many times!
My God," she wailed, "Harry will never have her now! Our
sweet France is lost . . . lost! All for a doxy that must wallow in
dung with a pricked-up Welsh beggar!" I cannot, in truth, even
write the words she used, filth of the gutters, and she a queen.

"I have not, madame—I have done nothing . . ." I cried
aloud at her, but she did not listen, and went on beating me and
kicking me with her sharp pointed heels where I lay. I saw poor
Papa's mazed face, mild as a sheep. He came between us, trying
to raise me up; she hit him, too, full in the face, and spat. I was
not angry before, but now I was, seeing him used so, that poor
sick man. I turned my head where she held me in her hand, biting it, sinking my teeth into the soft flesh till I met the hard bone.
She howled then in rage and pain, and loosed me. I saw, with an
ugly satisfaction, the bright blood well up from the white hand,
just above her rings.

I stumbled up, gaining my feet, and cried, my wits all gone
from me, "I have done nothing . . . nothing! Do you take me for
a whore—like you? Whore, whore, whore!" I screamed. I had
not ever said such a word before.

She stood still then, her head high, her arms down at her sides,
the blood running off the fingertips of her hand.

She spoke, laughing harshly in her throat. "No—you are not like me. You are all Valois. . . ." She laughed again, an empty sound. "Sometimes I think none of the twelve I had were mine . . . got as they were on poor shuddering flesh by a madman . . . I was beautiful—and they gave me to a madman. . . ." God help me, though I hated her, almost I pitied her then. She walked away, out of the room; a little trail of blood dotted the floor where she had gone.

Papa held me in his arms after, weeping, and mumbling endearments. I wept, too, for everything, for all my life that had been. And for Owaine. They sent him away, the duke's people, to escape Isabeau's wrath, into one of the far duchies, and it was many years before I saw him again.

Chapter 5

Four years have passed, and I am growing old, and still unwed. All Normandy has fallen to King Harry, and still Burgundy and Isabeau parley; as though it were a game, the ruin of France. The English king still holds to me, though he has not lowered the sum of my dowry; of course, he has most of his other demands, by conquest. Perhaps he wants Papa's crown! Though he has not said so. I do not know whether to be glad or sad at his constancy; he has never met me, so it is no compliment, unless to Oudine's painting skill.

The last of our great northern cities has fallen—Rouen. It was under siege for a year, almost. The poor people! They say as many as thirty thousand perished, one way or another. Paris will be next, God save us, if Isabeau does not play her politics better. Already the people starve, for no produce reaches them from the country; from my windows I can see the little children, thin as wolves, fighting the pigs for offal. And last winter the wolves themselves came inside the walls to seek for food. There were wolf hunts every night, though often the wolves won.

The price of food is sky-high; a loaf costs fifty sous, and the carcass of a cat a hundred. Even in the palace there is a scarcity. Often, as a child, I went hungry when there was plenty; now that I am grown, I steal from the larder, I have become most cunning. It is steal or die.

It is not for myself alone that I steal. Papa and Oudine would starve if it were not for me—Charles, too. He is dauphin now, for Jean died, some say poisoned by his wife. (That is ridiculous, for they never lived together, and he was sickly anyway.) At any rate, Charles is here now, living in the castle. I am thankful, for he is someone to talk to, though he is younger. He is like me, Charles, a hungry reader of romances; we both go about with eyes all red at the rims and swollen. What else can we do but read? We are not allowed to leave the castle; indeed, it is dangerous, for the people would tear us to bits—they are frenzied with famine.

Strange to tell, Isabeau bears herself differently toward me now—ever since that day long ago when I called her whore and bit her (she has a crescent mark still on her hand; paint will not cover it). It is as though by my viciousness, I earned a measure of her respect. She even, now and then, tells me the news of the war or asks me, in a manner most sickeningly roguish, if I will have English Harry to my bed. As though I had a voice in it!

She has given me some clothes, too, old ones of her own that she used to toss to her serving ladies. They are big enough, both lengthwise and around, that three such as I might fit into them. But Oudine is clever and has made them over; I still do not look a royal princess, but the effect is not bad, and at least I am decent and clean, though none of her colors become me, being gaudy and strong. She plucked my eyebrows for me, too, Isabeau, one day when she was idle, awaiting Burgundy; it changes me greatly, making my eyes look larger. For she has arched them, two thin lines, curving high, as if penned by a quill. A barbette, even, she has given me, which I longed for. She invented these headdresses, Isabeau; all the ladies of Europe have copied them, they say, especially the older dames. It is a most becoming fashion, framing the face and hiding the hair (a blessing for me, with my thick tangle!). Isabeau wears hers pulled very taut; when she removes it, the flesh of her chin falls slack, a double fold, making her suddenly ugly and old.

I have been so lonely these four years, moping about, reading, playing at cards or chess, and painting my face over and over again, different ways (I stole these, too, the paint-pots, from Isabeau; she never missed them), a prisoner in these walls of St. Pol. But now suddenly all has changed! We are to meet with King Harry! I, too, for he wants to have a look at me. I am dreadfully nervous; Isabeau says the outcome may save us all. I, to save France by my beauty! And I am none so beautiful as that, as she has told me time and again.

But, all at once, I am being treated like a princess! Bathing in milk (when the children are practically eating each other in the streets), wearing cucumber pastes on my face all night, and being measured for a gown of my own. The cloth cost three thousand crowns! Our Lady have mercy! I am sure I shall stumble or stammer; Isabeau says I must say nothing and smile only, for my teeth are good. They are making special shoes for me, too, with soles six inches thick, so that I will look queenly. That frightens me even more; I am sure now that I will trip on something, not being used to walking in such.

The meeting will be at Meulan, which is still neutral. It was set for May 15, but Papa got nervous, too, I guess, and had a relapse, trembling in his bed, and sweating with fear. So they have changed it to May 30, hoping he will be better. I am glad, for my shoes have come and I practice walking in them every day. They have got me an escort, too. A young count of the House of St. Pol. (This is hard to explain; the castle we live in is called that, but long ago his family gave it to the Valois people, though they retain the title—his family, I mean.) He is as horrid as my brothers were, but in a different way. He is small and dainty and minces when he walks; his eyebrows are plucked thinner than my own, and his hair, dusted with gold, lies in lovelocks on his shoulders, though his face has little lines showing, under the powder. His voice, though, is like a boy's, high and fluting; I hope they will not let *him* speak either! Isabeau has given it out to the English that this St. Pol is an old playmate, for whom I have much love. I do not even know his Christian name! But she hopes to whet King Harry's appetite with jealousy.

We went by barge to Pontoise, a town on the river Seine; I had never set foot on a boat before and was afraid, among all my other fears, that I would be sick. I was not though; the trip was like gliding on a cloud. I would have been filled with delight, had it not been for my trembling nerves and the fact that Papa, at the last moment, had to be left behind. He had seemed well again until the day, but when Oudine in the morning came to dress him for the journey, he could not stand at all, his legs giving way beneath him.

At Pontoise, we took up residence in the royal palace there, a poor place, dating from two centuries ago or more, without chimneys, hangings, or carpets on the floor. It was as cold as the tomb, though outside the sun shone in full splendor. The King of England was then at a place called Mantes, which had handed over its keys to him without a struggle. Meulan was halfway between the two, almost to the measured mile.

To my surprise, I was not taken to Meulan on the date of the meeting; I had thought I was important, for once! But no, Burgundy and Isabeau went alone, leaving me with that fancy youth, St. Pol. They did not come back all day, and at nightfall, Burgundy strode in alone, black as a thundercloud. I say strode; his legs were too short for that, but he thumped them down hard on the stone floors, his iron heels ringing. One could see he was angry as a stoat!

"She has been bid to supper," he said, and that is all, and he left us, going apart, no doubt, to sulk. She did not return, Isabeau, till past midnight; I heard the noise of her litter-bearers' feet on the flags and ran out into the hall, for I had not slept. She came in, walking with a bounce, like a girl, for all her bulk; her face had that look it used to have long ago when she had been with a new man, a sort of glow on it. Had she got to my king before me, then? Probably. All the world knew him for a lover of whores; how could he resist her?

All the next day I was put through my paces like a show horse, wearing my platformed shoes, going up and down stairs, curtseying three ways. My hair was washed and brushed and rubbed with silk, my teeth scrubbed until the gums bled; I was not allowed to dress at all but had to lie in a bath of almond milk and musk, hours at a time. That night I was given drugged wine to make me sleep, so that I would be morning-fresh.

At dawn they woke me, for I was at last going to meet the king. Isabeau herself painted my face, she is a master. My hair they coiffed under a new barbette, very tall, of a silk the color of smoky violets, that almost matched my eyes. My gown came last, for they had to sew me into it—at the back closing, it fitted so tight; I reddened with shame when I looked down, for it showed every line of my body, I might as well have gone naked! It was of a soft silk from the Orient, sheer almost to see through, and no shift under; when I walked, it went between my legs, outlining them like a page's hose. There was a long train behind, trailing; I prayed no one would step on it. The whole was embroidered in tiny gold fleur-de-lys, our Valois arms; the silk was white and shimmering along its folds, my skin showing faintly rosy through. The bodice was cut very low; if I breathed too hard, all would be lost. Or won, perhaps, according to how one saw it.

Around my neck they hung a pendant jewel, an amethyst from among the gems left me by Duke Jeannot. It was as big as a thrush's egg, and fell, cool, between my breasts, half hidden. Isabeau pulled it out, shortening the chain, and stepping back to look between narrowed eyes.

"No," she said, twitching it long again and dropping it down into my bodice. "It is more enticing so. . . ." She gave a last jerk at my sleeves, pulling them down to hide my hands, for they are too small and the nails are bitten to the quick. "Now!" she said. "We are ready."

On the way to the litter, there was a great shield hanging in the passage; it was polished, and I could see my reflection. No one had thought to show me a mirror. I near swooned; it was not myself I saw but a marvelous fairy out of one of my own romances, not skinny and small, but pleasing tall, and curving sweetly, with a face all peaches and snow! I walked with a better grace, knowing myself a beauty this day and not my own poor self. Though they threw a large veil over all as we rode, hiding me from the folk that lined the roads, as though I were one of the Duke of Berry's treasures!

The meeting place was all laid out, a pavilion, raised off the ground, the tent-roof worked in the arms of France and England, a gay sight to see. It was halfway between our two tents, French and English. We waited in the tents until the trumpets blew, I sweating sore in my finery under the canvas. When they sounded, it was like a call to the lists. Cheering broke out as we went forward, Isabeau in front on Burgundy's arm, and I following, with that same youth of St. Pol; his perfume near knocked me over. I caught a glimpse from behind Isabeau's shoulder of a figure all in blue and green, coming from out the English tent; it was the king!

I cannot remember how many walked with us; it might have been hundreds. I know we were two full processions, that we walked slowly, and that we stopped, each side, in the center space before the pavilion. The king bowed to Burgundy and gave Isabeau the kiss of courtesy, but I saw his eyes slew around to me where I stood, draped in my veil.

And then he stood before me; I had been told to keep my eyes down in maidenly wise, but I heard him give a funny sound, low, a little sort of cluck, exasperated. Then he stepped forward, throwing off my veil; I felt the wind of it as it whipped past my face and raised my eyes. Then I could not have spoke if I had been bid to; the breath caught in my throat, and I near swooned. For he was beautiful, Harry, and none had told me.

We stood thus, staring, a long second, till I dropped my eyes. Then I heard him sigh a little, a shaky sound, almost, and he said, "Welcome, little Katharine," and taking my face between his hands he kissed me full on the lips; it was not the kiss of courtesy, and I heard a great guffaw go up from his lines, and some soldier called out, "Go it, Harry!" In English it was, but I understood. He took my hand then to lead me inside the pavilion; in the heat I could smell his smell, so different from St. Pol, a warm smell of horse and leather and, sweet and sharp, mint. His hand, too, was dry and warm, with a firm clasp.

There were four chairs inside, all gay decked in ribbons, with cushioned seats; one stood a step lower—mine. He led me to it and seated me; his own was on the dais above, next to Isabeau, but he did not sit, standing still before me. No one else could sit either; it was not proper, in his presence; I saw Isabeau standing above us, and Burgundy, both cross as crows. He looked around, too, Harry, exclaiming quick, "Sorry—please be seated, all . . . Look—I will sit!" And so saying, he pulled the cushion from off his chair and flung himself upon it at my feet! He sat cross-legged, like a Turk; it reminded me of Charles, at home, when I read to him, and he sitting before Papa. I smiled and King Harry smiled back.

He never left his post at my feet that whole parley-time, though the talk went on for hours. He did not seem even to listen, staring at me all the while, though every now and then he would turn and throw out a word or two, swift, in English, state language which I could not follow. Once he took my hand, playing with it, and twisting my little pearl ring; one time, also, he reached under my long gown, encircling my ankle with his fingers. "*Jolie* . . ." he murmured. His French was terrible. And later, looking into my eyes, he said, "Ah . . . *tu es belle*, Katharine!" His accent was so comical that I laughed aloud; he laughed, too, as if he knew my thoughts.

I had been bid to silence, but I spoke, for his attentions made me bold. In my best English, and slowly, I said, my eyes lowered, "It is most kind of you to say so, sire."

He clapped his hands delightedly then and, rising quickly for a moment, kissed me on the cheek. He plucked then at the edge of my barbette, where it lay on my forehead and whispered, "Is your hair curly, little Katharine, under that ugly tower?" And I had been so proud of my new headdress! I blushed all up from the neck of my gown, for all eyes were upon us, and none spoke, watching. There was a teasing look on him, though it was not cruel at all, but tender, almost. "Tell me, little Katharine . . . does it curl?"

How had he heard that, I wondered. I nodded; then, for the look, so intimate, in his eye, I reached out to pull him closer, though it was not seemly. "I hate my hair," I whispered, in French.

He laughed again, and pointed to his own head, all cropped like a warrior; on him, though, it was becoming, his head having a goodly shape. "I have some curl, too, Katharine . . . we will make curly-topped babes between us. . . ." Oh, then I reddened dark, for all the company heard and a laughing murmur went up.

I cast my eyes down then, in earnest; I was in much confusion. He sank again to his cushion at my feet, still holding onto my hand; I prayed it did not sweat. The talk went on; it was terms they talked, of Falaise and Touraine and Maine. Monies, too, I heard mentioned; when our spokesman of the French side let fall, slyly, a bid to lower my dowry, I felt him stiffen a little. The final offer was eight hundred thousand crowns, down from his demand of a million. "Done," he said, loud, without taking his eyes from me. "Done . . . I will take it. . . ."

There was much clapping at this, from our side, but, of course, being greedy, they could not leave well enough alone but asked for six hundred thousand crowns to be deducted from my dead sister Isabelle's dowry that was never returned with her after Richard's death. He frowned then, Harry, shaking his head; it changed him greatly, drawing his lips in and making him grim as a bishop. "No," he said, heavily, "no." And then, with a wave of his hand, most lordly, "We will talk of this another day. . . ."

He rose again, bending over me, his face all soft again. His eyes went to my bosom. "Will you show me the jewel you wear, fair Katharine," he asked. "I have been longing to see it all this hour. . . ." I reached down and pulled the pendant from under my gown. "It is most rare," I said. "I got it from the good Duke of Berry when he died."

"Amethyst," he said, holding it in his hand. "It matches your eyes." He held the stone for a little in his hand, leaning ever closer, then he whispered, "May I put it back, little Katharine?" And he slipped the jewel back into my bodice. The touch of his fingers made me tremble and go weak. I do not know how I stood up, even, or walked beside him to our tent.

Back at the castle at Pontoise, they stripped me of my finery, Isabeau ripping the stitches of my gown as though it were a beggar's shift. My cheeks were flushed, I could feel the heat of them, and little bubbles of laughter kept rising in my throat, remembering the king.

"Take off that look, cat-face!" Isabeau commanded. "The cream is not yours yet. . . ."

"I think, though," I said, for I could not forbear, "that I pleased him well. . . ."

"Pah," she said, slamming the lid of a chest, "he uses all women so. . . ."

I smiled inside, for I knew her angry. He had not looked once in her direction, Harry. She that no man had ever withstood. Her day was done, Isabeau.

Chapter 6

I was back where I started, in a way; back in my made-over gowns and kept under lock and key in the castle at Pontoise while negotiations went forward. I say forward, but it seems they did not, just dragged out in endless haggling for more than a week. At night, Burgundy and Isabeau would quarrel, their voices rising in those echoing walls. The St. Pol boy and I knew nothing, though he was able to hear more, being in the men's quarters; he said the snag had something to do with my brother Charles. That could not be, of course; Charles is a boy still, caring nothing for politics. But, since he is dauphin, it must be that some faction is using him, trying to put down Burgundy. Anyway, we went back to Paris with naught accomplished. Except that now I had seen King Harry I no longer dreamed of Owaine. Perhaps I am fickle. But, at least, with Harry, there is a chance, however small. And one must be practical. Besides, it would be nice to be a queen and away from Isabeau.

No sooner had we gone back to Paris than the English stormed Pontoise. So it seems we are still at war. There is no town in Normandy that is not English now. Indeed, the Duke of Clarence, Harry's brother, rode with a great force right up to the gates of Paris; the people were in a wild state, the bells ringing alarums all the day. He did nothing, though, just rode up and down before the closed gates in formation, showing off. Perhaps it was to strike fear that it was done. It worked, too—as if folk were not terrified before. And now, if possible, there is even more famine here, with supplies from Pontoise, our last stronghold, cut off.

All through the hot summer the officers of Paris sent petitions to Papa, begging him to capitulate before the city be ruined. It was pitiful to see poor Papa, wrinkling his brow, trying to understand. As I have said, he is always sickest in summer.

I never knew what went on that summer; little Charles, the dauphin, was not in the castle but had been sent somewhere south. At least that is what Oudine said; certain it is that he was used, somehow, by the Armagnacs, Burgundy's enemies. As will be seen when I have told how all fell out.

For, on September 10, on the bridge at Montereau, the Duke of Burgundy's skull was cleft in two! No one will ever know what happened exactly. I have even heard it said that Charles did the crime! That boy could not even lift the ax! Besides, he would not step on an ant, even. But he was there and saw it all, though it happened so quickly. He was taken, like a hostage, I guess, by a large group of the Armagnac faction, to meet with the duke and his Burgundians to discuss a truce (between they two, not the English). White flags were carried by both sides, but weapons, too, he said. Charles was very much afraid, for he knew the men that held him would stop at nothing. And they did not. One stepped forward, as the duke knelt in formal homage before his dauphin, and raised a battle-ax, bringing it down on his head and killing him instantly. Charles said that man was called Tanneguy du Chastel and had been his jailer all that summer. He was their pawn, Charles, you see; they needed him to get close to Burgundy. Of course, I did not mourn Burgundy, and the deed paved the way to peace, for a while, with England. But it was, just the same, a barbaric vengeance.

They said that King Harry, when the news was brought to him, cried out in joy, "Now none can keep me from Katharine!"

It seemed a cruel thing to say, even about horrible Burgundy, but I could not help feeling pleased, when I heard. The duke's son, Philip, the one that was married to my sister Michele, swore vengeance on his father's killers and then and there donned black clothes which he wore for years; never did I see him out of mourning. He and Isabeau got together quick as a flash (this time I think it really *was* only political) and offered to hear King Harry's terms. The strange thing is, that before, Burgundy's enemies had been called Armagnacs; after the murder at the bridge, they were called Dauphinists. A very unfair thing, for poor little Charles was nothing but their tool, and captive, even. Certainly he did not deserve the bad name he had for so long, in all France, and in England, too.

One might think that events would march fast now, but they did not, at least for me. Nothing more was said about my marriage, and all that fall and winter (it was 1420) there was still much fighting; only now the Burgundians fought alongside the

English. The Dauphinists, as I have said they were beginning to be called, harried all the free towns of middle France and occupied the entire south.

I was still marking time, as usual, but in a different place. At least in these last months I had traveled a little. Isabeau pulled us all up by the roots, Papa, Oudine, and me, and we removed to our castle at Troyes. It is smaller than the St. Pol but much more attractive, for it is almost in the country. Troyes is a market town, and all the land surrounding pretty and neat, with little farms laid out behind fences, and cows and sheep grazing on the slopes. I had never even been to the country before, can you imagine? I had not known the sky was so vast and so blue or that the land stretched, unbroken, for so many, many miles. No one will credit my ignorance, but I had known almost nothing except the narrow streets of Paris.

We spent the whole of that winter and spring in Troyes. The castle was walled, with a moat and drawbridge, very old-fashioned and charming. There was a little tower even, where you could see far out over rolling hills and watch the ribbon of road unwinding back to Paris. Oudine and I spent many hours there, though Papa could no longer climb. For weeks, in the cold months, a blanket of snow lay over all, a wondrous thing to behold; in the sun the whole landscape would sparkle like diamonds. Within the walls, too, were gardens, in disrepair but charming nonetheless; in early spring moss covered the wall and went right up the old tree trunks. Creepers, too, hung down from the branches, thin as cobwebs they were, making a veil, almost, about the trees. Oudine said they were bad for the trees' growth, and would strangle them in time, but I thought them very pretty. Certain little flowers came up, too, in the first spring days, even peeping out from the snow; it was enchanting. Indeed, I was almost happy there at Troyes, but not quite. I was sad about Papa, who grew worse every day, though he no longer raved or had fits. He no longer listened when I read to him but mumbled throughout; also, he could not concentrate on the cards when we played. So I grieved for him. And then, too, I was nervous about Isabeau's spies, who watched me constantly.

Isabeau had brought a huge household with her, ladies and chambermaids, spies all, though I had still not one to sew for me or tire my hair. I thought at first that she feared I might poison her, but Oudine said that was not it; she said that Isabeau was making sure that I was virgin still and would remain so. Sure it was that I could speak with no boy or man, though there were many squires and pages about. Isabeau, if I so much as smiled at a pretty page, would rail and rant at me, and sometimes pinch me; my arms were covered with little marks, black and blue. If she had not been so much bigger and with so many to do her bidding, I would have hit her back. For I no longer feared her; I knew now that I was truly her last weapon.

For she favored the English match; without it she would have no power—the Dauphinists wanted to topple her.

It is all she has left, Isabeau, her power and her politics. She has changed greatly since Burgundy's murder. She has no bedmate to replace him; perhaps she is past it at last. She is still vain, painting her face with great care and dressing sumptuously. But her dresses, all, have had gussets let into them, for she grows ever fatter. She spends much time closeted with her counselors and various people of state.

Papa will not address her even, though he no longer grows violent at her approach. That is how I learned about the treaty that was a-making with the English. I had to read the terms to Papa, you see, for he would listen to no other.

The toad Philip of Burgundy joined us here at Troyes in March. The Dauphinists almost caught him on the way; he got his helmet all battered by a slingshot as he rode by a castle that they held. He says the lands between here and Paris are all rife with danger; there are Dauphinist troops roaming in bands, and deserters, too, from the English and his own armies. Just after he came the dispatches arrived from King Harry. Those were the ones I read to Papa, for he had to agree, and sign; he is still king, though Isabeau does all the scheming.

The first thing in the treaty made my head swim, I can tell you. I almost choked on the words as I read them. King Harry offered for my hand, but this time he did not ask a dowry, but said instead that I would be given a dowry by the English government, an amount of forty thousand crowns a year! Because, he said, "she has pleased me greatly"—which brought me much joy and pride. The treaty went on that Isabeau and Papa would remain queen and king for the rest of Papa's life, but on his death the crown of France was to belong to Harry and his heirs forever.

He was to be regent, straightaway, on account of Papa's illness; the Dauphin Charles was to be disinherited and fought to the death; I gasped at this, but no one else made a sound. All Harry's conquests, including Normandy, would be subject to the French crown when Harry became king, and he promised also to rule his new kingdom according to French laws and customs, retaining a French Parliament, and keeping all the privileges of the universities and churches as they were. At the end, Papa, who had listened intently, said nothing and just signed it. I do not know, truly, if he understood.

So all was settled, or nearly, and I was so excited that I could not sleep at night; Isabeau, too, roamed the corridors after all were abed. I would hear her heels clicking on the flags and see the faint light of her candle through the crack where my door joined. She spent many hours with her dressmakers, too, and left off eating sweets, in order to lose flesh. Who was getting married, I wondered.

For it was not till my sister Michele arrived that I was measured for clothes, even though they said that King Harry was coming in May. She, too, had changed, my sister. Where Isabeau had grown fat, Michele had grown thin as a weed. Her face was narrow and sharp; with her nose that broke in the Valois bump and her brilliant-colored clothes, she was almost like the Duke of Berry's speaking bird that I had seen back in Paris. She was kind, though, supervising the making of my dresses and the embroidering of my shifts and bedgowns. Rolls and rolls of beautiful cloth she gave me, too, demanding payment from Isabeau, raising her voice to match Isabeau's own.

"Harry will take her without expense to her parents—he has said so!" cried Isabeau. "I will pay for her wedding gown, that is all!"

"You cannot expect him to buy her smallclothes—before they are bedded even," shouted Michele. "Would you have her go to him with rags under?"

"It is what the King of England is used to," said Isabeau with a lewd smirk.

Michele gave her a crafty look. "Harlots do not all go in tatters. . . . There was at least one I knew who wore a crown," said Michele, nastily.

"There is another—still at it . . . a duchess," said the mother to the daughter, with a quiet venom. And that is how I learned that Michele had taken a lover; though it was plain to see if one had eyes. It was a gentleman of her train, a petty noble, not even a knight; when he sat beside her, she could not keep her hands off him.

"And he is not the first," she confided to me later. "How not?" she asked, shrugging her shoulders. "I cannot bear Burgundy— or ever could. . . ."

It was sad, though, to see her going Isabeau's way, and frightening, too. I wondered if such was inherited; Isabella, my oldest sister, I had not known, and besides she died young, and Marie, alas, was safely hidden in her convent, but what of me? Did Isabeau's blood run wild in my veins, too? I remembered how I had felt at Owaine's touch; was that a weakness or did all girls feel so? I had none to ask, for I knew none. I was not even a girl, really, myself, anymore. I was almost twenty!

Chapter 7

"So you see—he is used to paying!" It was Isabeau, railing at Michele. I could hear their voices as I walked along the corridor behind the waiting woman who had been sent to fetch me. They quarreled night and day, those two, a wearying sound.

Isabeau met me at her chamber door, grabbing my hand and jerking me forward. "Come, Katharine . . . all must be done in a day, don't dawdle!" She held a roll of shimmering stuff which she began swiftly to hang about my shoulders. "It will look well," she said, narrowing her eyes, "with a pinker powder. . . . Your Lancaster swain bids you wear his colors . . . he has sent it ahead, a fortune it must have cost . . . from the Flemish weavers. And he follows close behind. Men! They think we can wave a wand and make a gown. The women will have to work at this all night! Stand still, wench—stop fidgeting!"

And now Michele, too, was hovering about me, undoing my hair from its knot; I had worked on it all morning, and now all was to do over! "We must have ringlets, so!" said Michele, winding a hank of hair around her finger.

"Oh, no!" I wailed. "It is too curly already!"

"He likes it so, Harry," said Michele. "Where is the letter, madame? It is writ to Katharine."

Isabeau pulled it from her bosom—can you imagine! My letter! It was all crumpled now, with the royal seal of England broken and dangling.

"Why did you open it," I cried, "if it was mine?"

"I am your mother, Miss Cat-face, had you forgot?" She thrust the letter at me, and I read it, standing there in the middle of the room with at least six pairs of hands poking at me from all sides, for the women had begun to drape the material for sewing.

The letter was in a fair Latin, writ in a beautiful hand—his own, for the signature matched.

"Wear this for me, my Katharine," it said. "It is the latest cloth from Flanders, changeable, as you see; in some light it is blue, then along a fold it shows green, a subtlety for Lancaster.

Green is the color of love, and blue for constancy. I would have you not wear the hennin either, but let your hair show waving and long." I smiled at this; the hennin has not been worn in my time—it went out twenty-five years ago. But perhaps, in England, they are backward. The letter was most goodly and sweet, with many endearments and love words. And signed, "Your Impatient Bridegroom," which made me blush like a flame.

I looked at the shining cloth then; it was most exquisite, stiff almost to stand alone, with a fine rustle when it was handled. All day I stood to be fitted and to have my hair dressed; I had to sleep that night with my head in a sort of wicker cage, to keep the style.

I looked, the next morning, all attired, most beautiful again. Truly, fine clothes can work magic! "May I not wear the emerald chaplet that was left me by Duke Jeannot?" I asked. "It is mine, madame, and I have never yet worn it . . . besides, it would look well with the green of my gown."

Michele turned the chaplet around and around in her hands. "I have never seen such a fashion . . . Like a monk's cap, but all jewels. . . ." She fitted it on my head, pulling loose curls out all around. "It is unusual," she said, "but most charming, I think. . . ."

"But I cannot see it at all," I cried, looking into the mirror. "You have put it too far back. . . ."

"It is the only way," said Michele firmly.

"And you do not have to see it anyway, Miss Cat," said Isabeau. "Would you sit at state with a mirror in your hand?" There was much noise below, in the courtyard. "Come—let us go down," said Isabeau. "I hear trumpets. . . . He is coming!"

Papa was in hall before us, sitting on his throne; Oudine had brought him down, but Isabeau would not let her stay. When she was sent back upstairs, Papa began to weep, and none could stop his tears. "Look, Papa," I said, "look at my new gown that the king has sent me. . . ." But he just gazed at me blankly, his face all mazed and wet.

"God's nails!" cried Isabeau. "The fit is on him again . . . get him upstairs!"

But it was too late, for Philip of Burgundy had come into hall, and they were already crying his name. King Harry followed close on his heels. There was just time to seat ourselves and hope for the best.

Harry strode in, clanking; he was all in armor—a strange sight—but passing fine. For over all the shining mail, he wore a jupon rich with gold embroideries and jewels, and from his bascinet there floated a long green scarf; on it was worked in gold thread, "Katharine". He went first to Papa and knelt before him, waiting for the kiss of courtesy. Papa did not even look at him but stared ahead. I heard a gasp behind me—Isabeau.

We were all watching Harry; none knew how to mend the situation. For a long moment he waited; when Papa still said nothing, he took Papa's hand and raised it to his lips. "It is your son-in-law," he said gravely. "The King of England. . . ."

"Ah," said Papa, peering at him. "You are most welcome . . . I am George. . . ."

Harry spoke then, with a calm face, unchanging. "It is a good name," he said, "an English name . . . most courteous of you, sire. . . ."

Papa gave him a cunning look then. "It is not really my name, you know."

"I know," said Harry, "you are the King of France, and my father."

"Then will I kiss you," said poor Papa, doing so, on both cheeks. He waved his hand, then, Papa, toward us. "And now please greet the ladies."

King Harry came last to me, cupping my chin and kissing me. "I thought you fair before, my Katharine . . . you are twice so today. And my colors become you well—does the cloth please you?"

"Oh, yes, sire. . . ." I whispered; I have been so little in company that my voice has a way of dwindling. "It is my favorite dress. . . ." I smiled to myself, hearing what I said; I had only two!

"Why do you smile, little Katharine?" He held my hand still.

I was confused then and said, glancing around, "I will tell you —some other place. . . ."

"Are there gardens here? Let you show them to me, Katharine. . . ." He turned to a bench where some nobles sat, Philip of Burgundy and some English. "Tom can speak for me . . . it is all set down anyway. Come, Katharine." And he raised me to my feet. Someone near the yard door opened it; I heard a skittering sound on the flags, my dog Melusine. Isabeau would be furious.

We all watched, and some ladies tittered, as the little dog trotted through the courtiers, a frayed rope dangling from her neck. She was making straight for Harry! He stooped down and picked her up; she licked his chin.

"Sire!" came from Isabeau, quickly. "Do not handle her . . . she has fleas!"

"Madame," he said, bowing, "who among us does not?" There was a loud laugh from the bench; it must have been brother Tom. Papa clapped his hands like a child; he had been attending after all.

"It is a sweet little dog—who owns it?" asked Harry, stroking its ears.

"I, sire," I answered, "her name is Melusine."

"Melusine! It was the name of my first hunting bird . . . and you love the legend, too?"

"Oh, yes, sire," I said, "she is my favorite fairy, Melusine . . . after Morgan le Fay."

"Morgan—you know our Welsh tales, too? Well-read, my bride is. . . ."

"Only romances," I said, feeling modest, "and some Latin songs."

He drew me to the door and through into the sunshine, leaving the whole court looking silly. I heard Isabeau's voice rise impatiently. Harry looked at me, smiling small. "She will do all, Isabeau. . . ."

We walked through the gardens, I seeing them for the first time as shabby. He had put Melusine down, and she ran through the bushes, wetting on several, so happy not to be tied up. For a moment we went silently; then King Harry said, "I would not force you to this match, Katharine . . . if it does not please you. . . ." His face was dark and set in that hard way I had seen him once before; I could not read it. Dismay flooded me. Did he want then to back out of the bargain? Isabeau would flay me!

We had been speaking English; I could not find the words. I burst out, in French, "Oh, sire—please . . . I—no one has asked me, but—if one did—I would say yes!"

He wheeled suddenly, his eyes all lighted. "Truly, Katharine? Truly? Even if I were not king?"

"Truly . . . even if you were not," I said, he catching me close to him against his armored chest. "But," I murmured into his shoulder, "but it will be nice to be a queen. . . ."

He laughed then, a joyful sound, and I laughed, too. I thought him wonderful, but I was not used to voicing my thoughts, even in French. He held me away from him then, looking down a little into my eyes. "Oh, Katharine . . . I had been afraid you would be tall above me, like your mother . . . but even with my middling height, I top you right well."

I laughed for sure, then, and said, "Oh, sire, you do not know!" I lifted my gown at the hem and pointed to my platformed shoes. "Look! Look what they have made me wear!" I kicked one off and stood, smiling up at him, on the stockinged foot; I did not reach his chin.

"Oh, Katharine"—and he lifted me into his arms—"I have done this before, now and then, but it was hard work, and I was younger then. You are light as a kitten." He buried his face in my neck, kissing and kissing. I nearly swooned, there in his arms, the heat from the sun upon us, almost noon it was, and the heat within me, too.

"Shall I tumble you in that grass over there?" he said, smiling. "The tree above with its creepers will be our bower. . . ."

"Oh, no, sire, it is too close to the palace . . . and my dress! The grass will stain it!"

"It will be lost, the stain, in the green." But he put me down, smiling still; I smoothed my gown, he watching me.

"Your favorite dress," he said, musing. "Why did you smile then? You promised to tell. . . ."

It seemed a lame joke now, even to me, but I told him. "But then—what do you wear—on ordinary days?" He looked puzzled.

"Isabeau's castoffs," I said, watching for him to smile, and smiling too.

"Very thrifty," he said. "One can serve to make three. . . ."

I laughed, too. But then I said, "It is not much fun—being thrifty."

"I know," he said. "You are marrying me for the forty thousand crowns. That is why I offered it—I knew I would not get you else. . . ."

He kissed me then, very hard and long, upon the mouth. When he drew his head away, I saw his eyes, looking past me, over my head. "Quick, put on your shoe—here is Isabeau!"

And, true, there she was, moving grandly down the paved walk, her face flashing annoyance above the barbette at her chin; she had been too hasty to wait for a page, and her hugely long train was all bunched up under one arm, showing her purple-clad legs, still long and slim, to above the knee in front. "How many dresses will that one make?" whispered Harry in my ear. "At least six, I warrant!"

I giggled and saw Isabeau frown. "All is waiting on your signature now, Harry . . . you will have the girl the rest of your days—can you not wait?"

"A thousand pardons, madame." And he bowed very low. "I had forgot the time—she has some of her mother's fascinations. . . ."

And Isabeau simpered like a maiden! She carried a large fan made of feathers, against the heat; she tapped him lightly with it then, on the wrist, saying only, "Flatterer. . . ." But she brushed against him as she turned, as if by accident; old habits do not change. I felt shame before Harry, but his eyes glinted at me and he pressed my hand, his lips indented at the corners.

Inside the hall, King Harry left my side and went on both knees before Papa. "Sire, Father," he said, in French, "your daughter has consented to be my wife . . . for which I much rejoice."

Poor Papa looked bewildered for a moment, at the sight of this fair nobleman kneeling there; one could see he was trying hard to puzzle it out. There was a long moment while the court held its breath; at last a light seemed to go on in Papa's face, and he said, "Ah, yes—but be good to her, Richard, she is only seven. . . ."

"No, sire," said Harry, with quiet reasonableness, "I am Harry of England, and this daughter is Katharine, a lady grown to full beauty."

"Katharine. . . ." Papa passed his hands across his eyes. "I have been sick, sir—sometimes I forget." He spoke with great dignity. "Yes, I see you clear now. You are not Richard . . . you are He That Must Conquer All. Ah, well," and he sighed. "What must be must be—we must be conquered."

Harry spoke. "No, sire—it is *she* who has conquered me. . . ."

I broke from behind Isabeau then and ran to Papa, stumbling in my unwieldy shoes, but I did not care. "Oh, Papa," I cried, my head in his lap, "I am your Katharine . . . wish me happiness, Papa. . . ."

He laid his hand on my head. "Little Katharine. . . ." Then he raised his face to Harry. "Keep her well—my little one—she is a good girl. . . ." He looked around him then; I saw he wandered. "And now I must go to my bed. I am not well. . . ."

Harry lifted the poor King of France to his feet. "Let me escort you, Father . . . if one will show me the way. . . ." And he led him from the hall, his arm about Papa's shoulders, king leaning on king.

The Treaty of Troyes was signed that day, and I betrothed. The wedding was set for twelve days hence, a barely decent interval, some said.

Chapter 8

I am in love with my own husband! Michele says it is positively indecent, and Isabeau hints darkly that I am riding for a fall; she says a night will come when he will not show up in my bed, so used is he to many women. So far, though, it has not happened, even though he has fought or besieged cities each day; each night he has been with me, sometimes riding miles to the rear where he left me.

Because, in spite of the treaty, there is war still; I understand little of it, save that the Dauphinist forces swarm all about and must be put down. Poor little Charles! I suspect he is in a dungeon somewhere; how glad I am I was not born a boy! A thing I never thought to delight in until now.

City after city has fallen to us; I say us, for Harry takes me everywhere, and Isabeau follows, too—worse luck! I had thought to be rid of her. Harry says, though, that she has a mind for policy that is finer than many a man's; he consults often with her. I would not mind, except that still she paws him; I cannot bear for any other woman to touch his hand even.

The garrison at Sens fell, after a week, and Montereau (where the Duke of Burgundy was murdered) held out for a fortnight. At Melun it took much longer; so long, in fact, that Harry had a little house built there, outside the walls but out of range of the guns, just for me and my ladies. For I have ladies now to wait on me, I who was once so unnoticed! They are mostly English, for I asked that none of Isabeau's come near; only Michele and one other are French. Most of the ladies cannot speak French, so I have much opportunity to perfect my English before we go home (I call England "home" because it is Harry's).

One night, in that little house near Melun, I thought that what Isabeau had predicted had come to pass; I was still pacing the floor of our bedchamber, wringing my hands and sobbing low, even after the clock had struck midnight. I did not let any of my women in, giving it out that I had a raging toothache; I did not want to feel shame before them, and my Harry absent from me. I thought that surely I would die. There was a flagon of wine, a pale one I liked, from Champagne; I kept taking swallows from it, not even bothering to pour it into a glass—I was distraught. It was near empty when I heard horses' hooves below. I ran down, all as I was, in my bedgown and robe, mazed with tears, and still clutching the bottle's neck. There was a thin slime of frost on the ground, cold and sliding under my slippers. I saw Harry, in the light of one torch, drooping in the saddle; another was with him, I cared not who. He had to help Harry from the saddle, and I saw him near to falling. There was blood running down his face from under his helm, and more seeping through a cloth wound round his hand. I flew into his arms, sobbing loud. He looked down at me with a little smile. "Katharine, you are shivering! Get you inside!"

I turned on the man with him, who was holding him up, and said fiercely, "Go—go away! He is mine—I will help him. . . ." I got a glimpse of the man's face, shocked. It was the Lord Camoys, a kind and gentle lord.

I got Harry upstairs, he panting a little but walking easily. When I had washed the blood away, I saw his face was gray with exhaustion, the wound a scratch only, at his forehead; the bleeding had stopped. There was a deep cut though, in the palm of his hand, a grisly sight, like a mouth grinning.

He told me, his breath laboring, what had happened. They had been mining beneath the walls of the town, trying to make an entrance; the defenders, too, had mined, outward, and the tunnels had met. There, in the gloom underground, my Harry had closed with a knight of the town, one Sire de Barbazon, the commander of the garrison. They two had fought for more than four hours, with swords only, neither winning at the end, though both drew blood. Finally, no longer able to continue, they had made truce between them, according to the laws of chivalry. "And now he is my brother-at-arms, that lord," said Harry, "and, if he is captured, he cannot be killed. . . ."

"Oh, Harry," I cried, sobbing anew. "And I thought you had been with another woman!"

He laughed and drew me onto his knee. "Oh, Kitten"—that was his name for me now—"oh, Kitten—would you rather, then, that I had died?"

"Oh, no, Harry! Well—yes, maybe—oh, I do not know. . . ."

I still held the flagon, though I had not noticed. He saw it and said, wrinkling up his nose, "Kitten—are you drunk? That is an empty bottle, and you smell like a wine-vat!"

I was, of course, though I did not recognize it, never having been so before; I saw two of everything, and the room reeled. He put me to bed, piling coverlets on me with his good hand, for I was shaking with cold and the drink, and sat beside me while the doctor dressed his wounds. That Lord of Camoys had fetched the doctor, though I had bid him be gone; I was most thankful, and begged his pardon in the morning.

Harry did not love me that night, for we were both past it, in our different ways. But it was the only time; always we joyed greatly in each other, my Harry and I.

It was not till November 18 that the town of Melun surrendered; by then many of Harry's army had fallen ill and some had died even. They call it siege-sickness; thank God, Harry did not take it! The poor people inside, they said, died like flies, mostly from hunger. I cannot see why they did not surrender before that happened. But then I do not understand much of this whole war. Harry believes that he will unify France; I do not see how it can be done, this country of ours has been so long in strife.

The terms of the surrender were very harsh, but just; even those who do not love Harry name him the most fair and honest ruler that ever lived. I cannot help feeling sorry for the wives of those that we hanged, though. How dreadful if it were the other way around! The bodies were still hanging from the gibbets as we rode by on our way to Paris; I hid my eyes and would not look.

All the citizens of Paris lined the streets as we went by, throwing flowers in our path; I could not imagine where they had got them, for it was December. Michele said they must have broken into the Duke of Berry's hothouses; they are not guarded properly anymore now that he is dead. I said, looking sidelong at him, not to tell Harry, or he will hang the thieves. I meant it for a joke, but he did not laugh, only said it would be impossible to find the culprits, after the deed.

I was so proud of Papa; all the way to Paris he was not sick at all, and rode straight and tall, smiling and waving at his subjects. Harry and I did not go back to the old St. Pol, though he lodged Papa and Isabeau there; we went to the Louvre Palace instead.

It is magnificent; I had not known our family possessed anything so fine.

We kept Christmas there; you cannot imagine how many gifts I got! Not just from Harry either; his brothers all made presents to me, jewels and plate and gold ribbons for my hair. I have so many dresses now I could not wear them all in a year! We feasted, too, all the day; I ate so much that I made myself sick. Harry says that is foolish—he does not know, of course, how scantily I have fed all my life. After, though, I restrained myself; I do not want to get fat, after all. I could not see all go to waste, though; Harry let me give what was left to the poor. He had not thought of it himself, but then he had not seen, as I had, the little starving children of our city fighting the rats for garbage.

And at night we danced! Harry can do that well, also, learning all the latest steps quickly. He can do everything better than anyone else. He can play on the lute and the mandol, and write songs, too. He has many minstrels, who are with him always, wherever he goes, for he loves music above all things. He insists that he cannot sing, but when we have drawn the bed curtains, he sings to me, and it is very sweet. Oh, how I love him!

After Christmas, Harry got letters from England, from the Parliament there, begging him to come home; he has been away from his kingdom for over three years! Besides, he said, of course they want to see me; I hope I will not disappoint them. Perhaps Harry will let me wear my tall shoes when I am crowned; I am so little for a queen. He is going to crown me in the place where he himself was crowned; it will be the first time ever that a queen has had a coronation in England, all by herself. I am brought so high that I must pinch myself now and then to see if I am not dreaming. Just think, Isabeau used to pinch me; now she must bow the knee!

Of course I wanted to go home with Harry, but it was dreadfully hard to leave poor Papa; I may never see him again, for he is growing weaker by the day. It is not just his wits now, for they come and go, as always; he cannot leave his bed—he has a dropsy and his poor legs are all swollen. He did not know me either when I said farewell; I wept and wept, but he did not seem to see. I am rich now, for Harry has given me part of my year's dowry; I gave Oudine two thousand crowns to help take care of Papa, for I do not trust Isabeau.

We went first to Rouen, for Harry had business there, treating with Burgundy, and setting all in order under his captains. I did not see him at all by day, he was so busy. Michele, though, was with me, and my ladies. One of them was the girl I had seen married to a brother of mine; she was Jacqueline of Hainault that had fainted at her wedding. I like her well—she is pretty and has a lively wit; imagine, she is the first person of my very own age I have ever known! I call her Jacquette. I wish she could come also to England, but the toad Burgundy will not let her. After her first husband, my brother, died, she was married to his nephew, the Duke of Brabant, so now she is Burgundy's subject.

She does not like this husband, for he will not come to her bed, though she is so pretty. Her first husband did not either, but that was because he died so young. So Jacquette is still virgin, though twice married. I am so sorry for her.

I did not ask her why Brabant did not bed with her, but she told me, when no one was about. He is a catamite, she whispered. I did not know what that was; she said he loved men. I was aghast! After, though, when I had thought it over, I think I could understand. If I were a man, I would still think Harry more beautiful than any woman. I do not think women are beautiful at all, compared to men, except when we are all dressed up, of course. We have a funny shape, like a pear, and are too soft to touch; when I touch Jacquette's arm my fingers sink in, though her flesh is young. And it is the same with my own; it makes me shudder to touch myself. Though Harry says not, laughing.

Jacquette much admires my Harry, as who would not? I have told her if she so much as smiles at him I will scratch her eyes out, jesting of course, but meaning it, too, in a way. She says that everyone knows he has eyes only for me—it is like a romance in a book. Which is sweet of her. I asked Harry if he thought her fair. "Like a Saxon," he replied, making a face. So I guess he does not like her kind of beauty—hair like flax and round blue eyes; I am glad.

We parted with tears, Jacquette and I, though we have been friends so short a time. She has promised that she will somehow get away—escape, she calls it—from under Burgundy's thumb, and has made me promise that we will receive her in England. I hope Harry will do it for me; she has been unfairly used, Jacquette.

We left for Calais at the end of January. It is Harry's own town, of course, and all English, or nearly; the folk all came almost halfway to meet us. They brought presents for me, too, cloth which they make there, and golden buckles, and a huge key to the city!

I liked Calais; it is a fine city, with no poor people or sad sights. It has belonged to the English for years, and there have been no sieges or battles there, so food is plentiful and the folk look happy, a welcome change. We had to wait for several days because the wind was not favorable, but I did not mind; we spent all our time together, Harry and I, dancing and listening to sweet music; it was like a holiday.

I had been afraid I would be very seasick; the boat was so little and tossed about like a cork, even in harbor. When we got onto it, I felt my gorge rise at the motion, before we had pulled up anchor. And when we began to move under sail, I said I must go to my cabin and lie down; I did not want to vomit in the sight of all. My ladies had all gone below immediately; they had made the trip before, being English. Harry, though, said to stick it out on deck, as long as the weather was good, and keep on my feet, too. He walked me around and around the deck, all bundled up we were to the eyes, for it was bitter cold. He was right, though, as I should have known; he himself is never seasick. I did not exactly *like* the crossing, but I was not sick once. My ladies were all green as new grass throughout. My Harry is always right.

We arrived at Dover on February 1; it is so beautiful, that port, seen from the sea. Great chalk cliffs rise high behind, white and dazzling, and the little city nestles at their feet. I was amazed to find that some men had waded out to us where the ship lay at anchor, bearing gilded chairs; they meant to carry us to shore! They were all richly dressed, too, these men; Harry said they were barons of the Cinque Ports, and that they had done that once before, after Agincourt. Only then, they had carried him on their shoulders. He whispered to me, "My English know their Harry . . . I would have the head from any shoulder that touched your little bottom, Kitten. . . ." So I was glad they had brought chairs. I would not like to be the cause of any cruelties; though I exulted to hear him speak so, my Harry.

Chapter 9

We went first, in England, to the shrine of Thomas Becket at Canterbury. I have not said how pious my Harry is; every night (even that first night, our wedding night, when I lay in the great bed trembling in my ignorance) he will say his prayers; sometimes it takes an hour, and he on his knees all the time. I was ashamed; I scant mine, especially when it is cold, and sometimes have forgot them even. He does not mind; he says it is a private thing, prayer, and I have most probably not sinned very much anyway. That is not true; look how I have hated Isabeau! And my brothers, most of them. And Burgundy.

Once, when I had waited for more than an hour for him to come to me, I asked him why he had taken so long (I guess impatience is a sin of mine, too). He said it was the anniversary of the death of a friend, Sir John Oldcastle. I was curious, and he told me the man had been burned for heresy and treason! I could not see how such a one could have been my Harry's friend, and I said so. He rebuked me, but gently, saying he was a good man, much misled, and that he prayed for his soul. He prays often, too, for the sins of his father; I did not ask what sins, for everyone knows he murdered good Richard, and many more besides.

We stayed so long in Canterbury that we did not reach London till late in the month. It was a wondrous sight, London, all decorated for us, and the people cheering. I cannot describe it, truly. At the city gates were giants, fearsomely real, which bowed to us as we went through; beside them, lions rolled their eyes. Harry explained how it was done, by a machinery cunningly hidden inside. There was a row of castles with armed warriors, and gleaming thrones with angels chanting. (After the song they rose on their wings into the air!) Truly the English are clever. Also real folk welcomed us, dressed as martyrs and confessors and apostles, singing loud and sweet. The streets ran with wine, and the people, full of it, shouted till they grew hoarse. They called me Fair Kate, a nickname most charming.

We lodged that night in the Tower of London, all decked with evergreens and bright with many candles; I do not like the place though—it is gloomy and has a musty smell, in spite of all that was done. Harry told me that he was hostage there, Richard's hostage, when he was a boy. We climbed the stairs to the Lion Tower, but there was only one very old one left, and when he yawned, I saw he had no teeth. "I have been too long away," Harry said. "There have always been lions here. . . ."

"Let me buy you some, Harry," I said. "I am rich now—and I have given you nothing. . . ." But he said no, he wanted no gift but myself.

On the next day, a Sunday, I was crowned Queen of England. It happened in Westminster Abbey, and the ordeal was terrible; it took all morning and the robes weighed many pounds, to say nothing of the crown itself.

The banquet after, though, I will never forget. It was Lent, and the menu was all fish; I never knew there lived so many kinds in the sea! I was too excited to eat, with all eyes on me, though I had to pretend. Harry was not with me, for it was against protocol; I missed him sorely, there in the midst of all those English. They were good to me though, all those noble people; many spoke French in my honor. On my right sat a most august two, the Bishop of Canterbury and the Bishop of Winchester. But on my left was the King of Scotland, a captive, but an honored one. He was very bonny, as they say in his own country, with goodly fairish brown hair and bright blue eyes. He had a ready wit, too, and made me laugh often; I was thankful for him that day.

There were huge pastry subtleties, three, all of Saint Catherine, in my honor; there was the saint with a lion, reading Scripture, and the saint with a serpent, and also with a whale! King James, the Scot, whispered in my ear that the lion was cross-eyed; I choked on my wine, and it went up my nose, burning it, and making my eyes water. It was a good thing, for just then I saw Owaine; I was able to cover my face with a napkin, and so hide my consternation. He had brought in the last subtlety; I did not even see what it was. Just after, I recovered myself, and said to Jamie, as all called that king, "I did not thank that gentleman just now—on account of your foolery. Do you know him, that I may send . . . ?"

"To be sure," said Jamie. "He is in my own train. A Welshman, Owen ap Tudor. I will carry your regrets to him, madame. I shall tell him the Queen of England has choking fits when she drinks wine. He will muse upon it all the way to Scotland, and mayhap carry the tale. He goes tomorrow to my court; perhaps they will find my ransom—I do not know."

And so I had seen that old love again; he meant nothing anymore; why did I feel so glad he would be gone from the kingdom? Glad, of course, also, that he was alive still, for it had been long since I had heard any news of him.

I much loved London; it was such a bright and busy place, with all kinds of people rubbing shoulders, and not many fights. In Paris, even when there was no famine, swords flashed at the slightest pretext; of course, here there are not so many factions, and the folk are as one. Harry says it is not so in the university towns though; he says the students there are constantly bashing the townsfolk's pates, and vice versa. Harry has told me something of his own student days, when the Oxford masters taught in the taverns, because they preached dissension. He has told me of the London inns, too, where he used to spend his nights when he was a prince only. I have not seen any of them on the inside, for he says only low women go there. He took me, though, to a mummer-show in the courtyard of the biggest and newest; it was called The Panther and the Smile. The Lancaster arms hung above its door, which was odd, but I had not time to ask about it, for the show had started.

It was in my honor, a play of the life of Saint Catherine. That part was taken by a beautiful black-haired damsel, very graceful and quick. It was all in dumb show, with music playing; it was wondrous to see how much these people could express, without uttering a word! The most marvelous agonies and sadnesses, as well as antics to make one laugh.

There was an imp that tortured Saint Catherine; there were a whole train of them, but one did not notice the others, they were just dressed-up children. The leading imp was small, but a man, one could tell, and incredibly agile, able to bend and twist his little red-clad body all manner of ways, dancing, leaping, and turning somersaults in the air. All the while, though his eyes frowned or winked, according to his actions, his lips remained grinning, as if they had been carved that way. Suddenly I realized that they *were* carved! Then I remembered some little dwarfs of the Duke of Berry, that had been thus mutilated, with slit noses or eyelids; it was to make them comical to look at, but I never found them so. To me they were but sad, and I avoided looking. This little fellow, though, was so wonderful that all applauded his every move, and I with them.

It was a frightening piece, ending with the death of Catherine on the flaming wheel; I covered my eyes—it was too horrible—so I never saw how it was done. They had stripped her naked before though, and all the men watching whistled. After the wheel part, when I uncovered my eyes, I saw her, all robed in white, with a crown and wings, being borne right up to heaven; even though I watched carefully, I could not tell how that was done either, though Harry said wires and pulleys. It was a fine show, for sure. When all was over, Harry gave me two purses, that I might present to those mummers, and called them to us. The little man, in spite of his ugly smile, had a fine speaking voice and much courtesy, and his look was kind; the damsel I did not like, close to. She had eyes like Isabeau's.

The little man was called Sir Hercules, and everyone has heard of him, all over the world; he is famous. The girl's name— Moll Savage—teased at my brain all the day. I woke suddenly in the night, remembering, and shook Harry awake. "Harry," I cried, "is she the girl you had by you in your tent—that Moll Savage?"

He was startled, being half asleep, and said, "Yes . . . but not for a long time now. . . ."

I pummeled him with my fists, sobbing. He caught them in his hands, almost laughing. "Why, Kitten—would you have me white as snow? I am nearly thirty-five . . . and no monk either. . . ." I quieted a little then, and he asked me how I knew. "Michele has told me, and St. Pol, and Isabeau, too! And so it is true, then!" And I fell to sobbing loud all over again.

He sat up in bed. "Katharine," he said firmly, "she has been here in England these two years. She is married now to Hercules, that was my fool; they bought that inn there with their savings."

"She has put your arms over the door!" I burst out.

"Katharine . . . I granted the arms to Hercules . . . to help his custom, for he has served me well."

"And has *she* served you well—that whore-eyes?" I was disgraceful, but I could not help it.

He smiled down at me. "Yes, Katharine . . . when I was at war and lonely. Have sense, Katharine, a man needs a woman." "They say *you* need many. How many have you had?" He laughed then, Harry; I could have scratched his eyes out, and I lifted my hands, all curving, to do it, but he caught them again. "I have had a hundred women in my time, little Katharine. . . ." He looked down at me, and his face changed, the smile going from it, and said simply, "But none have I loved . . . save you. And, for a little time, one other, long ago. . . ."

"Who was she?" I asked quickly.

"She was Welsh," he said, and was silent a moment, his face going all shut again, so that I feared to speak either. "She ran away from me. . . ." Then he caught me to him, holding me very close, so that I could scarcely draw breath. "*You* will not run away from me, my Katharine . . .?"

"Never . . . never . . ." I whispered. "Never will I leave you."

Chapter 10

Poor Tom is dead, Harry's brother; and I never knew him! Except to know that he was careless and gay; handsome, too, though not as handsome as my Harry. He was kind to me, making me presents and compliments, too, when we celebrated Christmas together in Paris. But I hardly noticed him, being so taken up with Harry. I mourn him greatly, though, as do we all, for besides being sad, his death is a very great disaster for our English side. You see, I feel myself English already!

After my coronation, we made a royal tour; Harry wanted to show me all of his country. We went first by horse-litter, for the weather was still damp and cold; when we came to a town or village, the curtains were thrown back, and we had to wave to all the people. Sometimes my arm felt as though it would fall off, at night—it was so stiff and sore. And my face, too, ached from much smiling. It is a small hardship though, in return for being queen; surely I had never thought to be so happy! The people love Harry, cheering wildly and making us rich gifts; me they cheer also and sometimes compose songs and poems in my honor.

Each night we stayed in a different castle; Harry has many of his own, but often his nobles made us welcome. Some of them are wealthier than we are; it is strange. But they were all kind, and many of them offered one or more of their daughters for ladies-in-waiting to me. I have more ladies now than I could ever need; I who had none at all!

It was at Baynard Castle, near the town of Beverley, that we got the hard news from France. Harry had timed our visit here for Easter week, there being a very old shrine here, dating from the times of the earliest Christians; he much loves all such holy places. Though we had attended the mass for Christ risen, and vespers, too, on Sunday, still Harry went back next day; he wanted to pray for his soldiers, he said, and give thanks, too, for all his great victories. "But, sweetheart—" he said. "Stay here in the castle gardens and wait for me. There is no need for you to grow chilblains, on the cold stones." And indeed I did not want to spend the day inside, even in a holy place; it was April, and England at its loveliest. The hills all around were covered with the yellow flowers of the broom, which I have not seen in France. It was like a golden carpet as far as one could see; cherry trees were in bloom also, and birds sang in them. Three of my ladies were with me; I remember, because their names made me smile. They were Joanna Troutbeck, Joanna Mugwort, and Joanna Berthold; they were all young, like me, having been born about the time Harry's father had married Joanna of Navarre, hence their names, all alike, in that queen's honor. I liked them well, especially Troutbeck and Mugwort, whose comical names matched their plain faces. The other was most comely, but round as a partridge, so I felt I had nothing to fear from her either, as far as Harry was concerned. We were all working at a great tapestry; the English are most adept at this—artists even. I was learning fairly, though I still stuck myself often with the needle. A little page played to us softly on the lute, as sweet music, almost, as the birdsong. It was the fairest day!

Troutbeck looked up, her plump fingers still flying in and out. "I hear hooves on the drawbridge. Can it be His Majesty back so soon?"

"No," I said, "he could not . . ." but I rose, anyway, my yarn silks tumbling to the ground, where Melusine began sniffing them as delicately as a cat. "Heel!" I said to her absently, as Harry had taught me; she paid me no mind, gnawing at the silk ball. A tall man came hurrying around the yew hedge, Lord Thomas of Dorset, Harry's uncle. I ran to him, seeing his face white with shock. He took my hands.

"Lady," he said, "Katharine . . ." He wrung my hands hard. "There is dread news . . . I know not how to say it. Where is Harry?"

I told him. "Is it far?" he asked.

"Not far," I said. "I will come with you . . . just down the road and around the first bend. . . ."

"Will you ride before me on the saddle . . . there is haste. . . ." On the way he told me the sad tale. After we sailed for England, the Dauphinist forces crossed the Seine. Tom, left in command, took a small band and met with them at Baugé, where the river forks. They were overmatched, for the French army was huge, and they were utterly routed, and Tom lay dead.

I was shaking like a blown leaf as he mounted me before him. There was another horseman there, young and exhausted-looking, his hose caked an ugly brown with mud. He had ridden all night and day from the coast. Thomas Dorset named him dead Tom's squire.

The little church's door stood open to the bright day; within all was thick gloom, except for one large candle in front of the altar image. In its spill of light we could just make out Harry, lying flat before it, his arms stretched out in imitation of the cross. Lord Thomas hung back. "I would not disturb him at his devotions. . . ."

I would not either, but someone must; I went in. Stooping, I touched him gently on the shoulder. He turned a face all wet and smeary with running tears.

"Oh, Harry—I am sorry. There is bad news. . . . Will you come outside?"

"Katharine. . . ." He looked mazed, but got to his feet, staring hard at me in the poor light. "What is it? Is it Calais? Is it my soldiers?"

I nodded, dumbly, and drew him to the lord his uncle.

"Tom is dead." Dorset's voice was thick, and I saw him swallow hard. "Here is his body-squire, come to bring you the word. . . ."

The young man began, in a halting manner, for he was shy in Harry's presence, and much worn, too, with traveling. "We heard the French were at the Baugé fork . . . Your Grace's brother was encamped at La Lande Chasles. We were only a small force, for the Lord Salisbury had not yet come with his men, the main army. When your lord brother heard of the French advance, he insisted to ride upon them as we were, though the Lord D'Umfraville pleaded to wait." The messenger seemed to choke then, going on after a little pause. "Your lord brother called that lord coward. . . ."

"Oh, Jesus," said Harry, putting his hand to his head. "And so he must go. I might have known . . . he was ever jealous of Agincourt and himself not there to share. . . ." He looked straight at the squire then. "How much outnumbered were they then—our men?"

"Oh, sire—three times, at least . . . and they had crossbowmen and pikemen . . . it was lost before it was even begun. But they fought like fiends, sire, your lord brother, and the other lord. They drove straight into the middle of the French, laying about them strong with lance and sword. It was the Sire de Lacey took my master in the end—through the chest with his lance-point. The other, D'Umfraville, died trying to unseat de Lacey."

"And my soldiers?" said Harry, in a small voice.

"About half got away," said the squire. "The Lord Salisbury came up with his reinforcements and rallied them. The French gave chase, but it was dark and we slipped away."

"Thank God for Salisbury," said Harry. "The French will say now, though, that our English bowmen are not invincible . . . that they still can run from a battle . . . and that their captains can die. . . ."

That night, as we lay in bed, I knew Harry restless and tossing. His flesh burned to the touch, and in his sleep he sighed, twice. I could not sleep either, beside him, and I rose and went to sit by the window, looking out at the moon. Presently he came to me there, moving silently on his bare feet, so that I started when he touched me.

"It is cool, Katharine . . . come back to bed. I must have waked you—I am sorry, sweetheart. I had a nightmare. . . ." He drew the coverlet over us and lay down, his face upturned to the moonlight. "Oh, Katharine." He sighed. "I did not agree well with Tom while he lived . . . all our lives we were at odds, for we were much unlike . . . but now he is dead I remember how gay he was, and how simple and good. Brave, too. Rash and a fool, but a brave one. I hope he knew I loved him, under."

"For sure he did, Harry . . . for sure."

He spoke again. "They told me that Tom's bastard, that is called Jack of Clarence, went in among the French lines, with but one other, to find his father's body. He brought it back for burial. That boy . . . he is scarce turned fifteen." He was silent for a little, then he spoke again. "I envy him his son, though he is base-born . . . I would . . . Can we not have a son—soon now, little Katharine?"

I did not speak right away, for I felt shy of this, but presently I spoke. "My Lord—I had not thought to tell you before it is certain . . . but it is more than ten days now that I have been late with my bleeding . . . I think—it may be. . . ."

"Oh, Katharine," he cried softly. "It must be! That is a long time! Oh, Katharine, tomorrow I will send for Colnet. . . ."

"There is, mayhap, a midwife in these parts . . ." I said.

"Oh, no—not for you, sweetheart—not for my son. A doctor must be with you! I would not lose you as I lost my mother!"

"Oh, Harry," I said, chiding, "it is a different case. Your mother had a babe every year—it weakened her. . . ."

Just the same, we had a doctor. We had Colnet, he that Harry thinks the greatest of all. I was right; I was with child, for which we both rejoiced greatly.

I moaned greatly, too, for I was queasy-sick to my stomach every waking morn and long into the day. My three Joannas nodded and smiled, wise, saying that was as it should be. I would not suffer any of my prettier ladies about me then, when I looked so horrid, blotched and swollen of face, and green as grass. I have grown very vain, I fear, with Harry and his spoiling love.

Harry hated to see me suffer so, and asked Master Colnet why it must be thus, when a woman carries her child within her. "I know not . . . It affects the balance, I think. It will not always be this way. Someday someone will discover a remedy . . . but it is not yet. In a month it will pass. . . ." A month! Mary help me, I cannot stand it.

I chew the leaves of mint and take small water-sips all day; by twilight, sometimes, it passes, and I feel as always, and wild-hungry. The ladies say I must eat for two, but Master Colnet says not. He says that fat bodies have no ease in labor, and I must curb my appetite, but it is hard. Soon it will be all I have of pleasure, eating. For Harry must go back to Normandy or lose all he has gained.

I wept bitterly, but it did not help; he says he is needed there. "Oh, Harry," I cried, "what if it goes for you like Tom? I could not bear it. . . ."

"I never had more than a scratch or bruise in France," he said. "It will be the same now . . . No fears, my sweetheart! I do not fear for you either, for I am leaving Colnet here . . . he will be by you always . . . and mayhap I'll be back before it is born. If I am not . . . Katharine, if it is a girl, I would have you call it Katharine, another Katharine . . . there cannot be too many!"

"It will be a boy," I said, laughing a little now for pleasure. "A boy, another Harry!"

"I would you would have the babe at Monmouth," said Harry, taking me by the shoulders. "I was born there . . . and besides there is an augury . . . Monmouth is a good place. . . . I will come to you there, if I can."

I counted again on my fingers; I did it every day. "He will be born on Christ's birthday, Harry, or a little before . . . you can be back by then—if you try. . . ."

He smiled down at me; I know he thought me then a silly girl, or a woman whimsical and womb-ridden, but I did not care—I loved him.

He reached under my coif, pulling out a curl and winding it around his finger, smiling tenderly all the while.

"If you do not come, Harry," I said, "I will think you have taken another woman. Oh, swear you will not! Swear!"

"I swear," he said, pulling me to him. But, upon my shoulder, I saw his fingers, crossed.

BOOK VI

The Conqueror

(Told by Henry V of England,
also Regent of France)

Chapter 1

As ever when I took ship for France, we lay becalmed in harbor, the sea like glass, our banners drooping in the June heat. Three days we waited there in Southampton, twiddling our thumbs and pacing the decks. At such times I cannot listen to sweet music even, being restless beyond bearing; I had no mind for women either, my thoughts being all with Katharine and the babe she carried. Letters came to me there from her, which sent my plans all awry; I gave thanks then for the wind which would not blow—it gave me time to think. With great joy she told me, Katharine, that that troublesome dame, Jacqueline of Hainault, had fled her husband and was in England, beside my Katharine, throwing herself on our good mercies. I would as soon pack her off back to her own duchy, for there is sure to be trouble with Burgundy because of her; she is his subject, and married, moreover, to his cousin. It will be a coil to unwind, for sure. But I could not deny Katharine her company; my poor little kitten has never in her life had a friend, and she is most fond of this Dame Jake. I felt some joy, indeed, that Katharine will have a companion throughout while she carries the child, for I fear it will be many months before I can come back to her. That lady has no monies neither and must be provided for out of the exchequer, though her Hainault duchy is one of the richest of Europe; of course, she can lay her hands on nothing, with Burgundy guarding it like a broody hen, in his right as liege lord.

I have written to Katharine to give Dame Jake nothing of her own; my kitten's monies burn a hole in her purse always, she is unused to handling even a sou. Instead we will see to the lady's needs out of Queen Joanna's estates; she cannot use any herself, Joanna, having been convicted of witchcraft and confined to one manor only. I have had qualms about this witching thing of Joanna, having been absent, but brother John insisted that it is true as rain. He never liked our stepmother; for sure none of us did, and certainly she dabbled in sorcery with her Breton ladies from the first. Ah, well, it is another coil which I must unwind; I will see to it when I have time . . . later.

Meanwhile, there was Burgundy to placate. Katharine had put me in a pretty spot; women will ever do this if you suffer them to it. But I loved her well, my little fool of a kitten, and besides, she had conceived. In my darker moments, I had fears of my powers, for, with all my women, none had borne bastard to me.

I had planned to set sail for Harfleur; the Dauphinists were rife in those parts, even attacking the abbey at Bec, though Salisbury, that good soldier, had put them to rout. So I prepared instead to land at Calais, for Burgundy was encamped near there, and I must think how to best woo him from his sulks at the Hainault affront. I would deny any complicity in Dame Jake's escape, of course, and lay it all to Katharine's blame; Philip of Burgundy despised women, anyway, except to debauch them. I made note to take along a few of the lowest kind.

When the wind freshened, at last, and we made sail, passing the Dover cliffs, I saw them mantled in green, as emeralds, a bonny sight; my heart gave a leap, and a voice inside me said, "Never . . . never again, Harry, will you see this sight. . . ." A foolish fancy, sure, for I would be coming back within the year, but I could not dispel it—a melancholy sat on me, a strange thing. A stranger thing still, that sea journey; I was sick from the pitch of the ship, though our crossing was not rough. It was the first time I had ever felt this disease of the waves; I had counted myself immune to it.

I softened up Burgundy; it was not difficult, with the women, though for myself I could not stomach any of them, after Katharine. I had to pretend to a dead drunkenness, but he swallowed all, and promised to hold Picardy for me, while I rode forth to tempt the dauphin to battle.

For close on two months I rode through Normandy with a small force of horsemen and foot-soldiers but none would give battle; the Dauphinists ran from us as though we wore armor of magic, melting into the trees and forests at our coming. I decided to march straight to the Loire with all my new army, fresh longbowmen from the marches. We took Dreux by the first part of August, and Beaugency, too. It was miserable work, though, for the heat was almost intolerable, lying on the land like a stifling blanket.

Many of my soldiers fell ill, with fever and running bowels, and we lost some few. I, too, lay tossing for three days in wretchedness on my pallet; I had not been so sick since I was a boy. The countryside was dry and stripped of supplies; we had little to eat and the water was foul.

I decided to make for the east, up the banks of the Loire. We went slowly, all weakened as we were. At Orleans, my captains urged me to attack, but I said we were not strong enough, though we raided close to the walls and got pickings enough to last us for a while. I wanted no more famine-ridden men; the miracle of Agincourt does not happen twice.

On a hill, high above the Loire, rises the castle of Rougemont; it resembles nothing so much as a Roman fortress, grim and gray and pitted and scarred with age. It was thought to be impregnable, and bands of raiding Dauphinists were holed up there, from whence they ravaged the countryside, robbing and murdering their own peasantry. It was a nest of thieves I longed to smoke out, for the evidence of their savagery leaped out at us as we marched toward it. In cottage-yards beside the road whole families lay dead and dying, the women, raped many times and staked out to four posts to perish, naked; headless babes; and ancients impaled horribly on blackened spikes. Our scouts, sent ahead, came back to us, staggering, their hands struck off and tied around their necks, babbling in pain and fear. I threw all my siege-engines at that place, though it was small and not worth the trouble, for I cannot bear senseless cruelty. I burned the castle and hanged or drowned all those who refuged there, except one man. My captains brought him to me, all ragged and unkempt he was, but wearing a robe of rough hair next his skin, and a cross about his neck. His tonsure was all grown out, and his hair hung matted about his face; a long beard, yellow-gray, reached to his waist. His eyes stared from this thicket like a madman's. Men named him a holy hermit, though, saying he was called Jean de Gand; I asked him what he did in such a lair of beasts. He answered that he was their confessor. I was glad to hear it, for I would have no man go unshriven to his death, though he be the vilest.

This hermit Jean, though, railed at me for upwards of an hour, his wild eyes starting from his head, and foam upon his lips. They say that in ancient days there were many such in Israel, holy prophets, and that the great kings listened, Saul, and David, too. So I forbore and let him rail; one cannot be sure what forms holiness will take.

He knew much of me, this hermit-monk; pointing to my forehead, he said that God had marked me for the good, sparing me in that first battle of Shrewsbury. "A star he has given you, Almighty God, upon your temple, O King of the English. . . . He does not lightly give these signs of grace! A holy war you waged then, as Prince of Wales, against the heretics—"

I interrupted him, saying that I fought at my father's bidding then, being a boy only, and against none but Welsh rebels, for the good of the realm. "I make no war against heretics unless they be of treasonous intent," I said, I thought with reason. "A man's soul is his own . . . I cannot, in conscience deny it. . . ."

He shouted then, to wake the dead. My trusty old Lord Erpingham stuck his head into my tent, alarm sitting on his seamed face; I waved him away, shaking my head and smiling. I could see, though, out of my eye's corner, that he did not leave his post outside but left the tent flap swinging a little that he might hear what passed. He is a good old man, Erpingham, gone white in the service of Lancaster; I have several such about me, for which I thank Jesus every day.

That hermit said, warning, that I must get me out of France, and go fight the infidel, and heresy. He said the Almighty had suffered me so long to ravage France, but no longer would he give me leave to pillage that fair land. I would be cut down, he said, in my prime, like the Assyrian in his glory. I answered that I hoped to unify this land of France, which has known nothing but civil war for many long years, that I wanted no crown here, and no lands other than English heritage to leave my heirs.

"Your son will wear a double crown—for France and England," said he, "but you, Henry, will die within the year!"

I said no more, but let him run down, like a wound-up clock, and furnished him after with food and wine; they must have half-starved him there in that garrison, for he ate like a wolf, with no more manners. I never saw him again; he left my tent and the camp, too, unmolested, after he had eaten his fill.

The next day, though, I was moved to send out searchers for this man, remembering his eyes, fixed upon me. I was seized on a sudden with violent pains all down one side of my body and my breath came short; I could not leave my bed. The Lord Erpingham said for sure the "holy" man had used witchcraft against me, for I had been recovered fully until he marked me with his staring eye. The sweating-sickness, too, came back upon me, and I could not hold my food; we were held up there in those parts for almost a week, and I lying helpless as a babe. We did not find hide or hair of the hermit, though we searched the woods all about.

The morning of the sixth day I sat up to sup a little broth, still weak as though my limbs had gone to water; there was a soft scratching at my tent flap, and I called, "Enter!" It was my new body-squire, Lewis, that had been poor Tom's, he that had ridden to bring me the sad news. His boy's face was all white and scared-looking, the freckles standing out upon it. In his hand he held, but away from him as though he feared it, something like a foot-long stick. I looked closer; it was a manikin, made of twigs, cloth-covered, with a twisted brass wire for crown. Piercing its side was a small knife, such as we use for nail paring. I reached out my hand for it. "Oh, sire, do not touch it . . . it is evil! I found it just now under your body-armor. . . ." The lad was so frightened that he stammered. I tut-tutted, but called for Thomas Elmham, my chaplain. He exorcised it with Latin words and a cross, and, after, took it apart, scattering all the pieces and covering the whole with earth and bracken.

I saw, for a moment, in my mind, Morgan's faraway face, laughing, but crossed myself just the same, in case. She would never credit such witching powers, naming them child's play and old-fashioned barbarism. But evil forces may take many forms; I have seen it myself. And, after, my strength came fully back, and we marched that day.

I had not thought of Morgan in a long, long time; it was passing strange. That night, after we made camp, I wept a little, on my pallet and alone, for my sweet lost youth; I was still weak from my illness, though I had not known.

Chapter 2

Try as I might, I could not bring the Dauphin to open battle; town after town fell to us as we marched, with no resistance. Indeed, the people seemed to welcome us, doing all our spy work for us; the peasantry and the burghers, too, of France hold much hatred for their self-styled leaders. It is small wonder, for they have suffered much and for many long years. One faction, and then another, have bled them dry with taxes, laying famine on all the land; there is scarce a town that does not have its starving children, homeless as rats, swarming on the dunghills.

I feared for my men's morale; there was no enemy to be seen, except disease and privation, and soldiers must practice their trade. I decided to swing due north, along the river, and bring them to Meaux.

Much has been told me of this stronghold; in Paris, almost a year ago, the bailey and the council, too, begged me to root out this Dauphinist nest; from Meaux the marauders ride forth to burn and pillage all about, even to the outskirts of Paris, for it is a bare forty miles away. I have been told hair-raising tales, too, of the Meaux commanders, especially one they call the Bastard of Vaurus; that man is hated and feared beyond any in the realm. Even as we marched, we heard his name; the folk make the sign against the evil eye, cursing, and calling him Antichrist. Such beasts are often brave; it would be a good fight.

I went forward with my scouts when we came in sight of this town, leaving my army encamped at Lagny, a few miles behind. It would be no easy task to besiege it, I could see from the first. For one thing, the river Marne splits the town in two; I would have to divide my forces. Meaux is an old Roman town; one can see the roads and canals, straight as a knife-cut, that none has learned the art of since. There are some few suburbs; I would take those first for bases, and from them beleaguer the two towns. For there were two—the town proper and, connected by a canal, another, that they call the Market. This would be most difficult to take, the Market, for it stood, by virtue of that canal, upon an island.

That night, back at Lagny, I did not sleep at all but studied this knotty problem. Old Erpingham I had with me, and Salisbury, that fine soldier; we worried that problem until dawn. I hit upon it, finally, with the aid of those old toy soldiers that I keep by me always. Poor Tom used to laugh at me that I would not leave them behind, calling me a play-baby; great pity it is that he had not some of his own. For it is plain to see, when they are laid out in formation, just where one is and where the problem lies; I cannot work without them.

I decided to make a bridge of boats, which could be moved to any point on the river as needed, and would connect my split forces. At dawn I lost no time but sent my rear foot-soldiers to forage miles around; that night they brought back upwards of three hundred small vessels. It would slow us on our way, but it was the only answer. Even in our slowness we took them by surprise, capturing the suburbs without the loss of a man. And so the siege began.

I had few commanders with me; indeed, as I have said, my forces were small, no more than three thousand, and less as time wore on. I had hoped by our few numbers to gain open battle, but the Agincourt glory hung about us like a charmed cloud, in spite of poor Tom's foolish defeat at Baugé. I dreaded this siege, knowing it would be long and wearisome; I could not blame deserters even, though we hanged all we found, as examples. There is no high glory in siege, it is all sickness and death, famine and boredom—on both sides. But we were in for it, no mistake.

I put the good Duke of Exeter, with his men-at-arms, to the north wall not far from the abbey of St. Faro. The Earl of March lay on the eastward side, while to the west were a force of picked knights, under Erpingham.

Warwick took the stickiest post (we had had to draw lots for it) south of the place called the Market; it was across the Marne, and separated from the main army. The bridge of boats would help, but God help him if it was broken! I prayed for him every night. I myself kept fluid, as it were, sometimes fighting here, sometimes there.

We had brought good country-folk from the rear, with their

produce to sell, and set them up in market-stalls all around the camps. There were some harlots too, but not nearly enough; the men had to line up for hours sometimes. But it was the best I could do; the pick of the country girls will always run away to the city.

I had quarters for a while in the castle of Rutel, a mile from the siege works, but it was too far, and besides, the lady there gave me no peace, her husband being away under Burgundy. The abbey of St. Faro was closer, and the monkish life suited me, my little Katharine's image being under my eyelids always. I wrote often to her, as the time wore on, there being plenty of ink and parchment there in that abbey. Sometimes, though, the letters would pile up hugely, till we could find an envoy; she must have got a dozen at once, like reading a whole romance. I pictured her poring over them by the light of one candle (why one, I do not know—we can afford more—but that was my fancy), her brow knitted, her other hand resting where our child lies. Poor little kitten—she must be as broad as she is tall by now, tiny creature that she is! For it was November already.

It was my custom, and has been since first I tasted battle in the Welsh hills, to walk abroad at night among my soldiers, greeting the watch, exchanging a word or a sup of wine and crust of bread. You get to learn much this way; men's tongues are looser under the cover of dark, and they are not so mindful of their low station either. They will talk, sometimes, as man to man, forgetting that I am king; it is a thing I pleasure much. I had forgot, though, that these troops were raw, mustered from backward places. Some of them did not know me by sight, or without my helmet; I was taken for a herald, maybe, my speech being courtlier than most. I heard much in those first weeks—much that helped me, and some that was worrisome.

Often a man would say, picking his teeth by a dying fire, that 'twas too bad to take out this morsel from between the teeth—it was half the day's portion. Then I knew that there was privation and reordered my food-bailiffs, to see that all was done fairly. Or another might complain that the wine that night was thin and sour; I made sure no one among my cellarers made profit in this way. After, I had all the measures tasted before they were issued.

One night, an especially dark one, I remember, I heard music and voices raised in song, soft on the crisping air, for it was growing cool. I went to where the song went up, listening hard to catch the words. I cannot remember all, but the refrain went something like this—"How many weeks will the walls hold out?" and the answer, "Threescore and ten!" Then on and on, till, "How many years will the wars go on?" "Threescore and ten!" There were all manner of variations, ending with, "How many winters has a man till the grave?" And that answer, of course, the same. A most wry and cunning air. There was another, too, all the troops sang. "Peace in the grave . . . only in the grave. . . ." It worried me some little, hearing these. And mutterings, too, I heard, that the English had said, "Yes, Harry," to the conquest of Normandy, but the whole of France was a hard nut to swallow. I took counsel with some of my nobles, and we decided to offer terms to the garrison, announcing this to the whole army; I called a special troop meeting, asking for a show of hands. There was no need to count; we offered the terms.

Their answer was to point to a great elm that grew there, inside the walls; each prisoner that they took they hanged there, from the topmost limb, in the sight of all, some of those poor wretches only lightly noosed and taking a long time to die. I pressed to the siege again; we were in too deep now, and there were no more mutterings. A just peace I will sanction but not insults and the name of England a stink forever!

This elm indeed was a dreadful sight; when the English prisoners gave out, they took Frenchmen captured from Burgundy, or their own peasants, too poor to pay ransom, that had been held there in the dungeons. One was a young woman, stripped naked and hung in chains, her head just touching the dead swinging feet of her hanged husband; it was seen that she was pregnant. We put a siege ladder to the wall to get her down, and three were killed upon the ladder as they strove to rescue her. When one finally brought her down, she was dead some hours, stiff and cold, her eyes picked out by the crows. I swore vengeance on the Bastard for this, for all named him the hangman. I think, indeed, if we had taken Vaurus then, he would have been torn apart in seconds; there were other wives a-bearing then back in England, besides my Katharine.

The siege went poorly though; the garrison was strong. We broke the walls with mangonel and engine, but they mended them; we choked their ditches with earth, and they cleared them; we dug mines beneath the walls and heard the sound of their picks and shovels countermining. We got every man that ventured forth, but their guns did damage in our ranks, too; they must have had as many as we did. The noise from them went on sometimes for hours at a time, deafening us. It was getting on for winter, too; one could see it would be a hard one.

December was wet in those parts, and the river flooded its banks, cutting off our armies from each other and from the supply lines; we were compelled to evacuate our siege lines and make new ones farther away. It was a weary fortnight wasted. Our strength was wasting, too. Every other man had a cold in the nose or a cough that would not leave. I shook with a kind of ague myself from working knee-deep in icy water; it seemed that four braziers going at once could not warm me. My fears for Katharine struck cold at my heart, too; I knew her near her time.

I took to my bed, finally. The good monks of the abbey tended me well, and I was soon on my feet again. Good old Erpingham sought to make light of it, saying that husbands often ailed when their wives carried. He knew me baffled and angry at my weakness.

I could not help it; I had not been ill for nigh on thirty years. And now, on a sudden, I had been laid low twice in a bare four months!

Chapter 3

I have a son! He was born on the sixth day of the month, St. Nicholas' Day, and tonight is the eve of Christ's mass; they have brought the news fast! Uncle Thomas came to my tent, his broad face all beaming like the sun; he had been with the watch and saw the messenger ride up. That rider had an arrow through his sleeve and his horse so blown it died within the hour; I have given him a purse of gold nobles and a knighthood because, with all the dangers that beset him on the Paris road, he had kept my letter safe, next to his skin.

Imagine, Katharine has written! Most women, the big strong ones, too, could not hold pen on the day of their bearing. She will bear many more, God willing! She feels wondrous fine, and the babe thrives; he is a big boy, she wrote, and has a head of yellow curls like a carven cherub in a church nave. And from the letter one curl fell out, soft as goosedown and pale as gold; she had clipped it from his head, my sweet Katharine. I wept at the sight. Another Harry for England!

I stayed all day on my knees in the abbey; when the bells sounded for vespers, I got up from the stone floor, stiff as old wood. I smiled to myself, thinking of Katharine, her beads slipping through her fingers as though greased, in such a hurry was she always to hop into bed where it was warm. When I crept in later, it was snug as a nesting dove's, smelling sweet of Katharine. And my little Kitten is all flame, too, tiny as she is. I have only loved two virgin maids; my other beloved, Morgan, came to my bed as proud and grave as a young warrior. Like a battle or a tourney it was, swift and clean, and we two both victors, in the end. But Katharine has all a woman's wiles, by instinct; she took to love like a duck to water. She might have done it for a living.

One thing troubles me; she has signed, "Katharine, Queen, on this sixth day of December, by her own hand, at the castle of Windsor." I made great point of bidding her to have the babe at Monmouth! She may perhaps have forgot; women in her state often lose many of their faculties. And then she is still a stranger in my land; Windsor is the place she knows best, and it is well heated, too. Still, it does trouble me, because of the augury. I mentioned such to Uncle Thomas, but he pooh-poohed it, calling it Welsh foolishness. True, it dates from my days in Wales, so long ago now, and the woman was mad, too, and hostile as well. It is strange how well I remember her, an old, old seeress that lived in the Ladies' Tower at Dinas Brân. Cataracts filmed her two eyes, but still she knew me for the prince that I was. It was the fashion, when we were garrisoned there, and all in idleness, to seek this lady out, for she was believed to have the Sight. Morgan, who was there once, would never tell me her fortune, and most did not take the lady seriously, but her words to me stuck in my mind. They were in Old Welsh, so I may have mistook them, but, as I remember, they went like this. "Harry born at Monmouth shall small time reign and gain much, but Harry born at Windsor shall rule long, but lose all." I shall offer benefice to the Welsh abbeys, just in case, those that are still standing in that land.

The messenger said that the bells of Paris were tolling when he rode through, for joy at this birth. Calais must be a festival, and London a fair! I would I might be anywhere but here, besieging these stubborn walls! There is little I can do to celebrate, though I will have a mass sung, of course, and we will keep Christmas in our tents with a right good spirit.

Katharine writes also that she has asked, at my bidding, my brother John and my uncle Henry Beaufort to be godfathers; she begs to have that Dame Jake of Hainault for the other! Ah, well, she is his mother, and my dearest love; I must put up with some of her notions, though men will snicker, I am sure. The Lady Jacqueline is thought a fool and headstrong. I have had criticism from all sides on her score already, some hinting that I show her favor in return for favors received! Such gossipings once outraged me, but I am accustomed to them now. The higher the image, the lower men will bring it, if they may.

Though Katharine had been successfully delivered and is well, I suffered still; I said as much to old Erpingham, who had blamed my weakness on husbandly sympathy. "It is not that," I said, "but I am growing old. . . ." He laughed at that, for he has twice my years. But truly, I ached in my joints like an ancient; at night I could not sleep for the gnawing soreness in my side, and on the siege ladders I had been twice assailed by a chest pain as sharp as a lance-blow. It was perhaps the weather, which was worse than our English clime, growing daily more severe; ice and snow stood in our ditches, and a clammy chill like the tomb hung in the abbey walls. I wondered how my poor soldiers fared in their flimsy tents; many of them had been sick and never fully recovered.

The Duke of Burgundy arrived in January with a large retinue and accompanied by several other high Frenchmen. One among them made my heart stop; I thought he was my bishop great-uncle of Arundel come back from the grave. This man was a churchman, too, the Bishop of Beauvais, one Pierre Cauchon; he was just such another heretic-hunter, I was told, and they two wore, both, the same hangman's smile.

I had summoned the duke to conference, hoping to treat of terms to offer the dauphin; this war has gone on too long. I think I might have persuaded him, but for that bishop and for Isabeau, who are hot for complete conquest. Isabeau came, too, though by litter all the way; she has grown too fat to ride, or even walk, and is carried everywhere. It takes six men to bear her state chair, and still they stagger under the weight. Her mind, though, is still sharp as a new-honed blade and as devious as a water-snake. One must keep all wits about when she is in council or lose all. In that mountain of flesh, too, there lives still the siren-nymph; she looks out of the black eyes, sunk like raisins in white dough, and tingles in the touch of the dimpled fingers. For Isabeau, still, cannot leave off her pawing, though I am her son-in-law! The poor mad king they brought along for show; he looked more than ever like a begging friar, and did not know me.

Nothing was gained from those conferences; Burgundy urged me to order an all-out assault upon the Meaux walls, a thing not feasible, with many of my engines still in the making. I said we would be ready by April. Burgundy insisted he could do it alone, and Isabeau seconded him. I replied that he was welcome to try, and he departed to muster all his forces. So I was left with my huge and hungry mother-in-law.

For a week till Burgundy's return, I must sup each night with Isabeau, though I was weary to the bone from the siege-day. I could eat little, partly because each bite increased the small gnawing inside, and in part because I grudged her the food, taken, as it were, from my soldiers. She devoured me with her eyes while her teeth tore at the leg of a fat capon; between courses she caressed my arm, with an absent air. She will gain nothing, for I am too weak for dallying, even with the fairest. Ten years ago might have told a different tale.

What she cannot have, though, Isabeau, she will destroy, or try to. I had marked she showed but little interest in her newest grandson, or her daughter either; they were ever on my lips then, as they were in my heart. She made little answer, except to voice the hope that the child did not take after his grandsire; I thought it rude and said so. "Besides," I said, "my father was no leper—" She cut in, smiling, saying that she had meant his *French* grandfather. I had a vision of poor King Charles, as slobbered as a babe the last time I saw him at table. I pushed the thought away and spoke then of Katharine. She threw me a keen look, full of malice. "You love the little cat-face well, it seems, Harry . . . I would have you thank me, sirrah, for I had much ado to bring her to your bed a maid. I beat her once for it—and would have had the Welshman's head. But they sent him away. . . ."

I took the bait, of course, though I kicked myself for it later. "What Welshman?" I said.

"Why . . . that Owen Tudor, emissary from the other Owen, your enemy," she answered, smooth as milk.

"Why," I began, "that man must be upwards of fifty. I cannot credit such a tale. . . ." For I knew of that Tudor; he had fought at Shrewsbury with Glendower.

"Not him," she said airily, "it was his son—a youth all golden fair and tall as a poplar. Cuddling in corners they were and meeting in the arbors . . . even using the poor king's chambers, and he all mazed and unnoticing . . . I wondered, truly . . . was she maid?"

"She was, madame," I answered shortly. I changed the subject and feigned indifference, but the poison lodged in my mind and my thoughts were all awhirl. There was an Owen Tudor on my English household rolls in the train of Scottish Jamie, my prisoner. I had seen the name when I sealed the order for payroll, for I assumed all the Scots king's expenses until his ransom was paid. Katharine's debaucher, if Isabeau spoke true, and in my pay now in England! Perhaps in Windsor Castle, who could tell?

I twisted on my bed that night, my agues all forgotten. Back and forth in my mind the thing went, pro and con, giving me no rest. By dawn I had decided there was nothing in it but Isabeau's venom, for never had a breath of scandal besmirched my Katharine. Besides, was she not a princess of the blood, daughter of a noble line? And then I thought . . . daughter of a madman and a whore! I was sick with jealousy; in all my years I had not been plagued so, except, long ago, at the thought of my Morgan in her young husband's arms.

I could not rest but resolved to spy it out. I called Walter Hungerford to me; he was a captain now and knight, but he was the grandson of my own grandfather's steward and had been *my* steward in my youth. This Hungerford had never been my intimate, for I felt him something dour of temperament, but he was a man to trust. I did not tell him all but made up a story to do with Wales and treason, asking him to find out where this Tudor was, and his business, too. I gave him letters for Katharine, too, and enjoined him to look at my son and see how he was cared for. And then I sent him off to England, bidding him make haste.

I slept little those two weeks while Walter Hungerford was gone, though by day I was much occupied. Burgundy returned, with a goodly force, and, on his own, made sortie at the walls of Meaux. It was complete disaster, as I had known it would be, and he was put to rout. I took no pleasure in it, though he thought I did, as men will who have been proven foolish. He railed at me, calling me coward that I did not join with him; I answered only that Meaux would fall as I had planned it, after April. He left in some high temper, though he did not break treaty with me; he needs me as much as I need him, as I well knew.

When Hungerford came back, I could have shouted for joy. He told me Katharine had taken ship for France two days before he landed in England. She had left the babe in the hands of his doctors and nurses, and he was well. Of that other mission, when I asked, Hungerford said the Tudor was in Scotland, on his master's business, raising ransom monies; he had been at it a year. I told myself, indeed, it would be many a year yet, if I knew my Scots. So that bogey was laid to rest and my heart all lightened. I asked Walter how the little Harry looked and how much he weighed.

"He is a good weight," he said. "But he is a solemn little soul, your son . . . I could not make him laugh, though I tried all manner of ways. . . ." I smiled to myself. Walter, with his glum face, all down at the mouth, and his gruff voice, tickling at a babe! For sure it was a wonder the little Harry did not cry; he must have a valiant soul.

I longed for Katharine but feared for her. I sent word ahead to Rouen, for she was bound for that place, that she must stay there till this siege was lifted; the roads were unsafe. I packed off Isabeau and the poor king though, sending them to the Bois de Vincennes, under a large escort. I was heartily glad to be rid of that lady and her viper tongue.

Chapter 4

By February I had word that Katharine was safely in Rouen; her letters were blithe and cheering, full of love. My fears about the young Tudor were quieted, knowing him far away; moreover, through discreet questioning, I had found that Katharine had shared his Latin master long ago—she had not seen him since Agincourt. It does not do to harbor jealous qualms about the past. Some few words of childish affection and a kiss or two, what is that? For sure she came to me a most pure virgin—unless, indeed, she had all the arts of a Circe. I do not credit Isabeau; however, I have struck that Tudor name off my payrolls. Let him find his fortune elsewhere!

My ill humors had left me, all, and we pursued the siege with much vigor; our great engines were almost ready. So it was exceeding strange to find that my physician, Colnet, came to me, journeying long over the endangered terrain. I frowned upon him, saying he had not been summoned, and I wished him by my little son. I can never intimidate that man though; he has known me too long and too well. Patients are all one to him, kings or no. He sat me down, tapping my chest and listening, kneading my belly. There was pain, but I denied it, he saying wryly I must be filled up with poppy juice, if indeed I felt nothing. He prescribed for me, saying I must take nothing but watered wine, broth, and gruel; I did not bother to tell him it was all I could stomach and had been so for weeks now.

"You have lost flesh, too," he said. "You must rest . . . leave this siege to your allies and your captains."

"I cannot," I answered. "This is my war . . . my soldiers will follow none else."

"Is it so important, war," he asked, "beside your life? You are not thirty-five . . . do you want to end up like your father?"

I was much startled and spoke up, saying, "I have none of his symptoms. My skin is whole, and I have no swellings. . . ."

"Symptoms do not matter," he said. "It is all one. The same

end is in sight—if you do not mend your ways. You are sorely
ill."

"That I am not!" I cried, roundly. "I have not felt better all
this winter!"

He looked at me hard then, a canny, keen look. "Then do you
lie to me—and to yourself."

I said nothing, and after a moment he went on. "Well, I will
give you some potions—for sleep and for the pain. If you will not
heed me otherwise, I can do no more. . . ." He began to put
back his instruments into his doctor's trunk. "At least let me stay
by you. . . ."

"That I will do," I said, clapping him on the shoulder. "If my
son. . . ."

"Your son is in good hands," he said. "He has five doctors and
seven nurses. Besides, *he* is in health!"

"Well, then," I said, putting on a cheerful face, "stay, certainly. You are my good friend . . . we will have a chess game in
the evening. . . ."

"Plead me no games," he said. "You will get between sheets of
an evening, with my potion inside you . . . and see you let others
climb the siege-ladders by day!"

I thanked him courteously, but of course I could not heed him;
my men follow only me—it is my duty to put heart in them.

Our mine beneath the walls of Meaux was almost finished; our
spies, too, told us that most of the townsfolk were of a mind to
admit us. The garrison, knowing this, too, began moving their
defenses to that part, islanded, that they called the Market. We
feared greatly that they would fire the town itself and butcher the
folk there; it was an occupied town, and the people had no love
for their invaders. In the hasty move, one part of the wall was left
unguarded; a towns-person, prosperously clad but not armed,
climbed to the rampart top and shouted to us in right fair English. "Attack!" he cried. "The defenses are gone—attack! Scale
the walls!" Someone drew up a siege-ladder and the man descended, running to me and falling on his knees. "For the love of
God, Monsieur King, be bold! There is none to stay you . . .
they have fled to the Market! Take the town . . . the Market
will fall next. All are with you—our savior!"

He was a burly fellow and strong, only a little haggard from
privation. "You speak our tongue well," I said.

"The good monks taught us, sire . . . there are others of us, too. We have waited for this day . . . they will welcome you, Monsieur King. . . ." I raised the man up, thanking him; it was good to hear. My cause was just. I repeated his words loud, so all my soldiers roundabout might hear, and take good heart. Cheers broke out, and we scaled the walls with a will. I was first man over; when I reached the top I had to stop for breath, my chest feeling as though a band had tightened around it. But no matter; we were in.

There was but little resistance—a few fighting men that had not got across to the Market yet. We dispatched them without much trouble. We saw no other folk; they had taken refuge in the churches. The habit of fear sits long upon the oppressed. I had it cried through the streets that I came not to tyrannize but to set free; none should come to harm. They poured out of the hiding places then, women catching me by the hand to kiss it and lifting babes in their arms that I might bless them. "I am no bishop, ladies," I said, laughing. "Go about your housework—we shall soon have you free."

Their good churchmen and monks came then, all, to bless me; many of them wept. I fell upon my knees, giving the sign that all should do so. "For we are the army of God," I said. I always believed this, but for sure it was true that day; these folk had been most sorely used. The tales they told, going back for years, made the hair rise on my scalp. I resolved their brutal rulers would pay dearly, especially he of Vaurus that they called Bastard.

Spring was at hand; there were other places that needed our English forces; the Dauphinists had come out of their winter lairs to ravage the villages all about Paris and along the Seine. Besides, I had not seen Katharine for near ten months, and my son was not yet known to me. I pressed the assault on the Market with all the vigor at my command, falling into bed at night with every bone gone to water within me. I did not need Colnet's sleep potions or even wine; I could not stay awake.

The Market was exceeding strong; we had to throw all our artillery at it at once. Sometimes the town rocked with our guns, and the folk went about with wisps of sheep's wool stuffed in their ears to deaden the noise. At the end of the long bridge that stretched from the town to that fortress I placed many engines; the stones from them bombarded incessantly.

I had been working for some time on one great invention, a huge structure of wood, raised on wheels; when it was set into place beside the bridge, it near spanned the river. From there, we captured all the mills built on and under the bridge, and cut off the supply of grain. We seized another island, too, near the Market, mounting a great force of artillery; soon we began to see great damage done. We began a second mine; the end was near.

At Easter I called a truce, shouting it from all the ramparts; we did not fight for three days, praying all that while.

The walls were, by then, broached in several places; I sent fair terms to the defenders, but they refused most insolently. Upon their one well-defended wall they set an ass, a poor bony creature, covered with mange and filth. They beat it with cudgels; it brayed long and loud. They shouted to my soldiers, "Come, rescue your king—he calls you!" I looked around; most faces wore a grim look, but on some few I saw a sniveling smirk. My soldiers! I have seldom been so angry, and stood still.

"By God, Harry—I would have their heads!" cried Uncle Thomas.

I nodded grimly, watching. "I shall."

Wars had not been fought so, in my youth, to demean a warrior before his followers.

They did worse; at nightfall, when we rested, from our camps we heard a trumpeter upon the walls, playing airs I recognized well. Snickers rose all around; every bawdy song ever heard in English taverns, including the one my men had made for Moll Savage, before Agincourt. But, listening closer, I heard enemy voices, behind the ramparts, singing the words, loud. They had substituted for "Moll Savage" the name "Katie Cat-face." I said nothing but closed my tent flap; my heart, too, I closed to mercy for those men that night. They died the death, after.

We gave them all we had; they could not hold out, and on May 10, the Market surrendered. I tempered justice with mercy, as I have always done. Only the fiercest ruffians suffered. Those who had reviled my Kate, and that same Bastard of Vaurus, at whose death all the townsfolk cheered. We hung him on that same elm upon which so many had agonized at his hand. As far as I know, he hangs there still.

Chapter 5

The Bois de Vincennes, as it is called, for its thick forestlands, is one of the most beautiful holdings in France. It is the hereditary castle of the Valois house and, like all their manors, has fallen into sad disrepair. Still, coming in sight of it, the breath catches in the throat; one might almost be entering the pages of an old romance, so hung with magic is that place.

I rode to meet my Katharine, for she was there, waiting for me. My heart went far ahead; I could not make haste, for I had been ill again, after that hard siege. Colnet rode with me and commanded a rest-stop every hour, making me lie flat upon my back. He would have had me go by litter, but I would not; I could not so shame myself before my soldiers. So it was not till the end of May that we arrived.

It was late afternoon; in the slanting sun the castle seemed to float above the tangled growth, its fairy spires and turrets like a mist half-seen. Katharine rode to meet me, down the narrow road that winds between the old forests. Her white palfrey was all caparisoned in green and blue for Lancaster, a long veil floated from her head, flashing gold; the colors dazzled in the dappling shadow. I spurred my horse to meet her, riding ahead, though I caught a glimpse of Colnet's face, set grim, as I passed by.

She had not changed, my Katharine, blooming still; I saw a startled look in her eyes, a fleeting thing, soon gone. I clasped her in my arms, lifting her from the saddle and placing her before me on my mount; even her thistle weight strained my arms though —I was weaker than I knew. We rode on, up to the castle, silent and folded together, her head against my heart.

Isabeau and King Charles kept court there at Vincennes, if one might call it that. The place was shabby beyond belief and looked as though it were inhabited by ghosts. A thick tangle of thorny brush covered part of the great doorway; its branches, all twisted and gnarled, were as thick as a man's arm, and sharp brambles caught at our clothes as we passed through. Inside, cobwebs hung from the rafters, like some macabre decoration, and the rugs and hangings had moth holes peppering them. The gilt paint peeled from the walls in long strips and lay flaked upon the floor. Even the chairs of state, the very thrones, were rickety with age, the velvet cushions worn and torn and the stuffing coming out.

They had given my Katharine a little turret room, bare of all furnishings save a cot and clothespress, with an arrow-slit window high upon the wall. I say "they," but it was of course Isabeau; the poor king knew nothing, not even who he was. I stormed up to my mother-in-law, whose chambers were the only swept ones in that place; she said there were no rooms opened and that mold and mildew covered all. "And I am poor," she said. "I have no train of serving people as once I owned." She had brought upwards of fifty—I took tally later! These French, though, do not serve as our English do; they lounge about all day, dressed finely, and keep much scraping ceremony, but turn their hands to nothing, and the lesser servants are either surly or untrained. I set my people to work, turning out chambers for me and my queen, and for my nobles, too. They aired the rooms, tearing down the rotting tapestries and throwing out the moldy mattresses. "We will sleep on army bedrolls, my love," I said to Katharine. "Our lice are soldier-trained and do not bite. . . ." And so it was, in truth; but at least we had clean floors and a fire, and the windows opened to the stars.

We could not care, my sweet love and I; it had been so long a parting. After, my Katharine tugged at my hair in play and whispered, "You crossed your fingers when you swore to no women. . . ."

"Did I?" I murmured. "I have forgot . . . but truly, sweet, there have been none. And I swear again . . . Look—they are all straight as sticks—" And I held up my two hands to the moonlight so that she could count them.

She kissed each one and wept a little, happily. "Oh, Harry—it has been so long . . . and you have not even seen our son! He is over six months old now. . . . When do we go home, Harry?"

I answered, "Soon." But this time I did cross my fingers, for I knew it could not be. There was still so much to do, in this, my other kingdom.

We stayed there only four days in that lovely, shabby palace, for I received summon after summon from my citizens of Paris; I

owed them much for all their courtesy, the Parisians, and, besides, I had business there which would not wait. I could not bear
to leave it as it was though, for I resolved to spend all my leisure
there; it was to me as Monmouth in my own country, a place of
much charm, that spoke to me. Katharine said the old Duke of
Berry had been born there, and its faded splendor dated from
those years. She has told me much of this great old gentleman; I
much regret that our paths never crossed. I left there, at Vincennes, some worthies of my household, with monies and good in-
struction to refurbish that manor for my use.

We proceeded to Paris, Colnet staying me again at every turn;
the journey took nearly a week! Katharine asked me of this, and
I told her I had caught a distemper in the winter's siege; it is as
good a word as any for what ails me. "But you do not want for
strength," she murmured in my ear, smiling small and sly, so that
I caught her meaning.

"You are a doxy," I whispered back. "For shame. . . ."

Her face fell a little then, and she said, "So Isabeau, too, has
called me—long ago." We were both sober for a while, I thinking
of that Tudor boy but not speaking; I did not know her thoughts.

The bells of all the churches rang for us as we entered, and
people thronged the streets in the thousands; I reeled in the saddle from the din and the crush, and it took all my will to smile
and salute. It was slow going, and the heat bore down, relentless.
I was in full armor, for my citizens expected it, to do them honor;
I did not think I could make it to our lodging at the Louvre, but
that I must surely topple. "Sweetheart," I said, low, to Katharine. "Here is Notre Dame . . . all cavernous and cool. Will you
come in with me and pray a little—out of this press?" She nodded, and I gave the sign to halt; we stayed there on our knees for
almost an hour. My poor retinue chafed, I knew, at this delay,
sweating and jostled, but I could do no other; I was sick and
dizzy until the spell passed.

When we came out again into the light, Katharine looked at
me, her face all in alarm. "What ails you, Harry? You are yellow
and trembling. . . ."

"It is the heat, darling—I never could abide the heat. . . ."

"Papa, too," she said, "poor Papa always ailed in the Paris
heat." It was an unlucky comparison; I pushed away the
thought.

We were happy there, as always we were, Katharine and I, when we could be together. And the Louvre is a charming palace, modern and comfortable, freshened by its many new windows and bright with a thousand candles by night. Besides, we had sent Isabeau and the king to St. Pol, and we were all alone, or it seemed so, without them; in truth my brothers were with us, and many of my train, but it made no matter. These sentimental English ever look upon Katharine and me as though we had drifted among them from out the pages of a love ballad.

It was Whitsun next day, and there was a great feast in our quarters, planned for weeks. All manner of food and drink, but I could only toy with either. I could not dance at all, though Katharine took great pleasure in it; I made her dance with my brothers and my friends, and sat in the corner, watching, like an old dame with the dropsy. She moved among the dancers like a little bright kingfisher, her long hair like a russet ribbon as she whirled to the music. For our love nights, neither, had I the strength I longed for, though she pretended well, my little Kitten, and I blessed her for it.

I could not take the rest that Colnet urged; there were councils to attend, and entertainments, too, rehearsed for months.

There was a most cunning Mystery play, put on by some of the Paris citizens; they were not professionals and forgot some of the words, but still they did passing well. It was the life of St. George, and the saint was got up to look like myself, with my own surcoat and armor copied, and the face, too, painted to resemble mine. The princess was Katharine, hopefully, though I thought the maiden too coarse-featured and too big in the bosom for the part. The dragon was the most comical; he wore the face of the young Dauphin Charles and howled most piteously when the saint dispatched him. Katharine, though, did not like that part and cried big tears. "He is no dragon, my little brother!" she said. "They are cruel folk to use him so!" He had changed much, the dauphin, since she last knew him, or so I had been told; profligate and extravagant, vindictive too, he had grown to be, by the tales. But she would never believe it of him. "He is a good boy, Charles," she always said, "and much maligned."

Much policy went forward there in that short time; the garrison of Gamaché surrendered without a fight, making treaty, and the garrison of Compiègne, too, offered. This last, though, would

surrender to none but me, so we must travel again. To please
Colnet, I let him look me over again; he said my liver was near
normal and my color good, all of which surprised me, for he is a
worrisome sort. I did, in truth, feel stronger, though it was perhaps his words that made me hopeful. I had more than a fortnight, though, to get to Compiègne; the date of the surrender
had been set for the eighteenth of the month.

Chapter 6

Event after event followed close in some few days; it is exceeding hard to sort them out. Smallpox came to Paris suddenly, and many took it; the household at St. Pol had two deaths among the kitchen folk. We removed to Senlis, another Valois holding; the air was cooler there, and the illness had not struck either in that place.

No sooner had we come there, though, than a message came that a plot had been discovered in Paris, a Dauphinist plot. I must travel back to hear the trial and see justice done. The traitors were all common folk that did not rate the headsman's ax; I had no stomach for more gallows' sights and had them drowned. The woman among them I would have pardoned, but she hung herself in her cell. They found her hanging by her own belt the morning of her husband's execution; there was some gallantry there, poor soul. She died unshriven and in mortal sin; I had ten candles lit for her and paid a priest to say mass. I hope it helped a little, wherever she is.

I went back to Senlis for no more than a day; it was all the time I had before going on to Compiègne for the promised surrender. Katharine begged to go with me, all tears she was; she was getting as bad as Colnet, fussing over me and feeling my forehead for fever. Truth to tell, she gave me some respite, for I had traveled too much in those last few days. We went by litter, for she pled it was too hot for her, riding horseback in the sun; I could never have done it otherwise and keep face.

We journeyed back to Senlis by litter also, the heat still holding. After, I felt almost as I had of old, stronger and with a better appetite, though Katharine said my face had still a yellow tinge; I did not tell her that my urine was bright gold.

The Dauphin Charles had sent to me, indicating that he was ready to talk of peace terms; before Katharine had time to say "What did I tell you?" his armies had moved, in full strength, against the town of Cosne. This was a Burgundian town; it had been lightly garrisoned, and Duke Philip feared it would fall. His messengers came while I walked in the gardens with Katharine, one coming to me there.

When I came into hall, I could hear them talking with my uncle of Dorset. ". . . Their case is hard, my Lord. They cannot hold out more than a week. My master begs the king will come to his aid, for he has not force large enough to save the town of himself. . . ."

Uncle Thomas spoke. "We can send some thousand men . . . I will lead them."

The messenger spoke then, saying, "Your pardon, my Lord— my master the duke wishes that the king himself will come. He needs his siege-skill. . . ."

"The king is not in his full health," said Uncle Thomas, heavily.

I stood in the doorway, Katharine on my arm. I heard the messenger say, again, "My Lord, Duke Philip bids the king remember the treaty that is between them. He says he has aided the Lord Harry—now let the Lord Harry aid him."

I spoke from where I stood. "I will come," I said.

Katharine turned, flinging her arms about my neck. "Oh, Harry—no! You are sick!" She flew at the startled messenger. "Tell your toad master he is a coward! My Harry is too sick to go. . . . Let him fight his own battles! Let his garrison fall! Let them all die! I care not. . . ." And she burst into floods of tears, sobbing and shuddering.

I went to her, taking her in my arms. "Let be, Katharine, sweetheart. I *must* go. . . . I have given my word, as he has given his." She sobbed softly against my shirt, I could feel her tears, wet against it. I turned to the envoy. "Tell your master I will come."

I worked late into the evening to prepare for the journey. When I came into our chamber, I saw Katharine sat before the window. There was a moon, and it shone full upon her; her rippling hair was purple in its light. She wore her bedgown, but she had not slept. I chided her a little, saying, "You will make dark circles under your eyes, my sweet. Come to bed."

We clung together that night as if it were for the last time. The thought shivered through me, what if it is? The last time. I shrugged it off, that thought; it was a sick fancy, born of much weariness.

She felt it too, I knew, or something of it she felt. For she said, after, "It will be only a little siege, will it not, Harry? You will come back soon?"

"Yes," I said, "very soon." And I laid my head on her breast. Her heart was beating fast, very fast, as if it hurried.

"Oh, Harry," she said, on a sigh, "we have been married two years—and for one whole year we have been apart . . . and your son—you have not even seen him. . . ."

"I know," I said.

"Can we go home soon, Harry—soon?" She tugged at my hair to look into my eyes; her own were only dark pools in the moonlight. I could not read them. "Can we go by autumn . . . by Christmas, anyway?"

"By Christmas," I said, "if God wills it. . . ."

She sat up then, pushing me away. "What kind of thing is that to say? If God wills it! *You* will it! You can go if you want to . . . you are the king. . . ."

"He is a higher one," I answered, but lightly.

She laughed a little. "Oh, Harry—I had forgot how pious you are . . . pious as a very monk. . . ."

"You know I am not a monk," I answered, pulling her down.

"I know," she said. "You are all mixed up inside . . . no wonder you are sick sometimes—it is all those humors moiling around and tearing at one another. . . ."

"Leave off your talking, girl, and kiss me. . . ." After the kiss, though, I fell asleep, like a very log of wood. Poor Kitten!

She came down into the courtyard with me at dawn, to see me off; she was in her bedgown still, with a mantle slung over, my soldiers having gone on before to scout and beat the bushes for spies. Her hair was tumbled anyhow, and her eyes had blue smudges under them like swipes from a sooty finger. She shivered a little, though it was not cool; she had slept less hours than I had even. "I am sorry about last night," I said. "I was like a drugged creature. . . ."

"Oh, Harry—I care nothing for that . . . we have a whole lifetime of nights!" She fussed a little with my jupon, straightening it at the shoulders and pulling the belt low upon it. "Only—hurry back! It cannot take long . . . just start the thing and let Burgundy finish. It is his siege, after all."

"I will come back as soon as I can—"

"Harry!" she cried, little spots of color coming up in her

cheeks, and her eyes brightening. "Harry—let me come with you! I was with you before . . . and that was a very important siege. Let me come!"

"No, sweetheart," I said, "I cannot. There is nowhere for you to stay—and besides, it is not fair . . . I do not let my soldiers have their women by them." I held her to me for a moment. "Look, darling—cover yourself. Here comes Uncle Thomas and my squire. . . ."

My body-squire, Lewis, ran up, pulling off his cap as he saw Katharine. His fair, freckled skin was all red above his tunic collar, seeing her in her pretty disarray. He gave me a shoulder up to mount by, for I was in full mail. Katharine ran over to take my horse by his bridle. "Harry," she said, her little face all anxious, "are you feeling sick again? You have never needed mounting before. . . ."

"I am tired, sweetheart—that is all. And this steel of mine is heavy in the heat. . . ."

She stood watching until we passed from sight around the road's bend. I saw her as we made the turn, her robe dark blue against the pale blue sky, her hair catching red gleams from the dawn's pink streakings. The sun was almost showing over the hill; it would be a fine, fair day.

Chapter 7

It was a hard ride, all day in the sun; there had been no rain in those parts of late, and the roads were sunbaked, the horses' hooves striking hard upon them, each step a jolt. We dared not unarm either, for the Dauphinist forces were all roundabout, though we saw none that day. By nightfall we reached Corbeil.

It is another pretty castle of the French, looking in the twilight like one I had had in my boyhood, made of marchpane. I remembered, as in another world, the taste of it; in these days my gorge rises at food, or the thought of it even. We lodged inside, in stuffy little chambers, without windows, or nearly, my nobles and I; my men were in tents within the walls.

That night I could not sleep, though all my bones ached from weariness; I thought to walk in the gardens in the cool, and wander, too, among the tents. I have always liked the rough cheer of my soldiers, the homely jest about the campfire, and the voices raised in song. There were no fires, of course, for it was too hot, even with the sun down. But I saw a little knot of men, squatting in a corner, playing at dice. I went over to them, meaning to sit beside them on the ground and share a little of their ease. As I bent forward, though, a dizziness came upon me, and blackness, . though the moon was full. I fell; I must have swooned or struck my head, for I remember nothing till I woke again in my bed.

Colnet was beside me, and Uncle Thomas, and my squire, Lewis, looking scared; he was only a lad. Colnet was mixing something in a mortar; it smelled vile, but he shoved it under my nose, saying I must drink. I threw it up twice, but the third time it stayed down, and I felt the pain in my side leave me, slowly, and finally I slept.

I thought to go on in the morning, but I could not move; my bones were heavy, like the great bones of a monster, too heavy for a man. Heavy, and as nothing, too, like water; a feeling most strange, though there was no pain.

It was decided that Warwick would lead the men to Cosne, and I would join them there. The next day, though, and the next,

I could not. Colnet clucked at me on and on, saying I must go back to Senlis or to Paris, where I could be nursed in safety. I had little will to argue; there was no strength in me for anything. At least, I thought, I will see Katharine. At least I will have my Katharine. And so we set out.

They had rigged up a barge for me, that they poled downriver. I lay upon it on cushions, too weak to sit up. The barge was slow and the way smooth, but my side was gnawing at me again, giving me no peace, and Colnet's potions had no effect.

Great trees hung over the river, all brown with the heat; the very paint of the barge-side showed as blistered and cracked, and the sweat ran off the toiling sailors in little rivulets. My own sweat sickened me, for it turned the bedding and the cushions yellow, and it smelled sour. I could not pass water or void myself either, and there was pain in all my vitals from it.

The river narrowed as we neared Charenton, where we would land. I saw the people lining up along the river, as though it were a street, and a great crowd waited at the landing place. The trees were hung with bright ribbons, blue and green, my colors, and flowers, too, were heaped in beauteous masses to welcome me. I saw that the ribbons had some words writ upon them, a message of cheer for me and my men, though I was too far away to read them.

Bois de Vincennes was about a mile away from that landing; I would rest there for a little—I liked that castle well. They had brought a litter down to the water's edge, to carry me. I looked about me, borne on the arms of Dorset and my squire; the people stared at me, it seemed with love and awe. I could not bear to be carried so, among them, and called for my horse.

"Oh, Harry," said my uncle of Dorset, "you cannot sit a horse! I watched you lying upon the cushions . . . you could scarce bear your pain. Do not deny it—put down your pride for once, sweet Harry."

But I would not. I waved them all away, mounting myself, though, truth to tell, I know not how I did it; the pain was shocking, bringing weak tears behind my eyelids that I blinked away. We went forward; the hanging ribbons fluttered in my face, one catching, too, in my helmet. I smiled and nodded to the people as they hurrahed, trying to sit straight. We made it through the crowd there and onto the open road, but that was all. I could go no farther; I was like a man of wood and fell forward in a swoon again. I came to my senses on the grass; they lifted me upon the litter then, and I was past protesting. At least the people had not seen my weakness. But all about me were faces of concern, and pity, too. I caught my uncle's hand. "Oh, Thomas, Uncle—you were right . . . I could not. . . ."

They brought me to the room where I had been with my Katharine, but now it was furnished in goodly fashion, with a great bed hung with velvet. They had brought two skilled physicians from Paris; I could hear Colnet arguing with them, softly. He is ever against bloodletting, though most doctors use the leech so freely that they are called by that name.

I have lost track of time somewhat, as one does when ill; I think it was the fifth day that I lay there. The Lord Warwick came to me, all as he was, in spurs, and his armor yellow with the road's dust. I struggled to sit up, Colnet putting many pillows beneath my shoulders. "How did it go, the siege?" I asked.

"Sire, it is over—two days ago. I left half our men there with the Burgundians."

"You did not need me, then," I said, in feeble jest.

"Oh, sire—they ran away . . . there was nothing to do. . . ." I saw his face then, wearing a look of shock. "But you, Harry, are you not better? We thought it was the heat only. . . ." It was a measure of his concern that he spoke me thus, by name; he was a lord most prone to protocol and custom, an old-fashioned man.

"Oh, I am much better," I said, trying to speak heartily; my voice sounded like a croak in my ears. We spoke a little more then, I thanking him for his work at Cosne, and bidding him bathe and rest. I slept, then, for a while.

When I woke, I heard low voices in the chamber, talking, Colnet, and my uncle. ". . . He has lived hard, taking no rest. He has drunk the tainted waters, too, at Meaux. There is some infection which I cannot recognize. . . ." It was the voice of Colnet, rasped with worry. I heard my uncle say, too, "He had the sickness, too, like all of us, the marsh fever and the running bowels . . . perhaps it has not left him. . . ."

"No," said Colnet, "it is some other thing—some internal trouble. His liver is swollen to twice normal . . . and gives him much pain."

"Will he mend?" asked my uncle. "Will he mend, do you

think? I should not say this, for he is the king—but always—I
have no son . . . he has seemed—" His voice broke, and in the
silence and the dark I knew that he wept.

All my old comrades came to me there—Erpingham and Hungerford, Thomas Camoys. "Shall I send for your lady, sire?"
asked Hungerford once.

"No," I said, "we are too near enemy lines here . . . I would
not endanger her. I will go to her soon. . . ." But I saw in his
eyes that he doubted.

My days bled into one another; I could not tell them apart. I
know that it was near the end of August that my brother John
came to me, having taken ship from England. I stared at him, astonished, and chided him, too. "I left you, John, as custos in the
realm. . . . Why are you here?" I thought I had spoken stern
and passing strong, but he bent close to hear my words; I must
have whispered.

"Oh, Harry," he said. "Humphrey is there . . . and there is no
great difficulty there—beside this sickness of yours. . . ." He
told me that there were masses said daily for me in the churches
there, and the people prayed openly, too, in the streets. "And
many of the taverns are closed, too," he said, "out of respect for
you. . . ."

"Oh, no," I protested, trying to make a jest, "not the taverns
. . . they were ever my second home. . . ." But he did not smile;
perhaps he did not even hear. I could not tell if my words were
loud or soft. I remember wondering, though, if he thought I was
close to death: I was fevered and only felt surprise.

It was while John was there that my coronation ring fell off
from my finger; I had raised my hand from the bed, and then let
it drop, out of weakness. We heard it fall, skittering into a corner
somewhere. I remember all going down upon their knees to hunt
it; it seemed there were dozens of people in that room. At length
my squire, Lewis, brought it to me; it had rolled under the bed.
There were long streaks left by tears on his face; I saw them,
though his features were all blurred, as most things were, then, to
my vision. They bound the ring to my finger with red thread, for
I had grown very thin, and it would not stay on. I was surprised
again and tried to look down at my body where I lay. It seemed
to me, swimmingly, that there was nothing there, under the
sheet.

434

I called for Colnet to come to me. "Nick," I said, "you have
fought long and hard, but I think no one can win this battle. . . .
How long, think you, do I have left?"

He did not speak at first; I saw his throat working. Then he
said, "Sire—God willing—you will have many years yet. . . ."

I looked at him hard, or tried to, through the mist in my eyes.
"Do not lie to me, Nick. . . ."

He fell upon his knees, and bent his head. "Oh, sire," he said,
low, "I think there is not more than two hours left to you. . . ."

"So little . . . ?" It was hard to believe; I was still young. Yet
could I feel the strength go out of me with every moment that
passed.

There was work to be done then, and in a hurry. My will must
be signed and depositions added; I must not leave a tottering
kingdom to my little son. I named John regent in England, and
Burgundy regent of Normandy. The care of little Harry I gave to
my brothers, and to Hungerford, for he was a sober-sided soul
and honest. "Take care of my little Katharine," I whispered to
John. "She will grieve sore . . . and it is too late now to send for
her. . . ."

I called for someone to bring my confessor, but they said he
was already there; I could not find him, for my sight failed. "Inside my hauberk," I whispered to my squire, "there is a little
packet . . . I would have it by me. . . ."

He brought it. I took it in my hands but could not open it; my
fingers would not work. Someone did it for me—John, I think. I
looked again upon the little picture I first had of Katharine, so
sweet, so young. I tried to open the old letter from Morgan, but it
had been folded small so long, it fell into pieces. I could not read
the writing either and thought it was my eyes. "Read it," I said
to John. "Oh, Harry—I cannot . . . there is nothing here, the
ink has all faded. . . ."

It was not so long ago as that, not fifteen years. But perhaps
she had used some made-up ink, squeezed from a berry, that
would not last; Wales was so poor, as we had made it, my father
and I.

That lock of hair, my little son's, fell out, too. I held all these
things a moment, and said, "I would have them by me, when I
am laid to rest. . . ." There was another something, too, a ribbon, it seemed. I took it up.

"Sire. . . ." It was my young squire who spoke. "It was caught in your helmet . . . I did not know if I should bring it. One of those ribbons the folk had hung from the trees at Charenton, when we landed there—" His voice failed him. He loved me well, it seemed. So many did; I was glad of it but wondered why.

I turned the ribbon about in my hands; I still could not read what was writ upon it. "What does it say?" I asked.

A voice spoke, reading. I do not know whose. "It says, 'Henry conquers all.' "

I shook my head, thinking, dimly, "No—not all. . . ."

It grew dark, though I know there were candles all about; I could feel their heat. Out of the dark a hand came, my confessor's, holding a crucifix. I put it to my lips; the wood was cool. And then I heard the Latin of my shriving. I followed it, mouthing the words. *"In manus tuas, Domine. . . ."*

EPILOGUE—1429

*(Told by Morgan ab Owen,
wife of Rhisiart ab Owen,
of Dolgelly in Wales)*

Men say that in Wales time stands still. It has never seemed so to me; the changes wrought here are like mountains rising up or sinking into the sea, devastating, heart-stopping. It is true that little happens here of moment in the rest of the world, and events swirl around us without changing our life. Still, we hear everything somehow.

It is that which has set me to writing this. Word has come of a young girl in armor, that they call the Maid of France. And she has led an anointed king to his crowning. Long ago, in the last great days of Owen, this was prophesied, only then we all thought it would be a Welsh girl and that Owen would be the crowned one! I had forgot the name of the prophet, though he was made much of all over Wales; my husband, Rhisiart, though, remembers everything—he is a great scholar. He said the man was called Hopkin ap Thomas, and that also men named him the Bard of Gower; I had not known he was a bard— he was got up like a magician when I saw him, in a Merlin hat, cone-shaped, and robes all covered with magical signs, the moon and the stars and strange letters, too, in an unknown language. I remember he had no teeth at all in his head, and his words hissed; we even laughed at him, Catherine and I, for she was alive still then, and we two not much more than girls, though she was wed. Sweet Catherine; I grieve for her still, as I do for so many of us. Though, truth to tell, there is not really enough time for grieving; we are always so busy, just in order that we may live.

There were other things said then, of the future, by this same prophet or seer or bard—this Hopkin, the Divine Hopkin, some call him, now that he is long in his grave. He prophesied that a Tudor of Mona would sit some day on the throne of England. This has not happened either—though a strange coincidence has occurred. For Harry's widow, the French Katharine, has married Owen Tudor! Or some say not married at all; at any rate, scarce two years after my Harry's death, she bore a child to this same

Owen Tudor. And now they have three; and true it is he is of
Mona in Wales! He is my kin, though distant and I never knew
him. It is a botched-up prophecy, like the other of the Maid, but
mayhap there is something in it, for all that. For who knows, his
Tudor child, or grandchild, perhaps, may unseat the lawful king
someday and usurp the throne, as Harry's father did with poor
Richard!

Hopkin foretold war to last a hundred years, there in England;
for sure war has been awaging now for a long, long time, already
half a hundred years, if you count the Black Prince's times. At
least the French wars keep the English busy, too busy for us here
in our Welsh valley. At least they leave us alone—with the little
we have left.

It set me to thinking, though, remembering old Hopkin. There
is a curtain somewhere that they almost pierce, those prophets.
For sure there are sciences not yet invented and mysteries of the
mind not yet solved. In these things we are like the old folk who
ran upon all fours, time out of mind ago. And these seers, perhaps, are like the first who stood tall, not able to do it for long or
without faltering. Ah, well, it is a foolish fancy of mine, perhaps.
Rhisiart, at least, would say so; all thought, to him, must be
proven or it is valueless.

I remember, too, that other seer, or seeress, the Lady of Dinas
Brân. She, also, is famous and much revered, now that she is
dead; in some places she is even worshiped as a saint! And *that*
she surely never was; she was a pure pagan, priestess of some old
forgotten cult.

People are more superstitious now than ever, here in Wales;
one cannot blame them, they are sore oppressed by hunger and
privation, and there is no learning, no colleges or schools even,
except our little one here in Dolgelly. But I am getting ahead of
my story, which happens often; I am getting old, for a woman—
forty-two!

I was telling of more prophecies. That Lady, when I was in
Dinas Brân, foretold that I would "know pain—and sorrow too
great for tears—and the bright wings of love . . ." All nebulous
words, that could mean anything, but true, in their dim way; the
words come back to me, for they had a bardic ring to them. She
said, too, that I would come to ruin, in the end, that Owen would
bring me to ruin. This is not so; unless, of course, you might call

it ruin, a high-born damsel (though bastard!) brought low to walk behind a plow. For this I do often, still, when the land's needs are upon us, and we are short-handed. We all can turn our hands to everything, here in our valley. A thing I take some pride in.

She told truth, though, that Lady, when she spoke of poor Alice. Though not quite in the way that Alice feared. Flames, she said; she saw flames only, for Alice. And that is how she died— not burned as a witch, like her mother, or burned for the New Learning which she embraced, but in a stable fire. She had been a byremaid as a young girl, Alice, and had much love always for the gentle cows and their pretty calves. When the barn was light-ning-struck and all was flaming, the creatures trapped and ter-rified within, she dashed inside to bring them out, and perished there. Her husband, Walter Brut, bears the marks of that night still, for he went after her, beating out the flames among her clothes with his bare hands. When he had dragged her out, she was hardly burned at all, but she was dead anyway, overcome by the smoke. His hair and eyebrows were all burned away, and his hands raw and bleeding. He has still not much use of them, and they are dreadful to look at, scarred and shriveled. I miss her, too, Alice; we all do.

So the prophecies are half true, or something less. Maybe they are accidents only, and meaningless, for all my musing; I was never used to put any credence in any superstitions, but I am growing old now, as I have said.

Rhisiart says I do not show age at all; he has been a kind hus-band and friend. When I look at him I see that he, who once looked like a Norman sparrow-hawk, resembles now a Roman eagle. His thin face is thicker and blunter, all the lines coarsened; his mouth has now a sensual curve, and there are deep pouches under his eyes, as though he debauched. It is comical, almost, for we live, all, as austere as monks; sometimes we do not even taste a drop of wine from one year to the next, and often there is not much to eat. Walter, too, looks a very Silenus, with his face that was always round, and his bald head, for the hair never grew back after the fire; he has a little round belly, too, from sitting too much at books (he cannot use his hands for farming or other labor).

I have always been tall and have not grown stout (we work too

hard for that), so from a distance I resemble still my young self;
my colors have faded, though, hair and eyes, as though they had
been left out in the rain, and my skin is sun-darkened. What
would you? I have seven children living, besides the twins that
died; my eldest is a man already, twenty-one, and has learned
medicine at Oxford. He will come home soon; we all wait him
eagerly, for we need a doctor here—there has been none all these
years. We called that first son Rhys, a Welshing of Rhisiart; in
England they call him Dick Richards. No one knows that he is
half-brother to the little King Henry, though Owen guessed, before he died.

I carried my son inside me, those days long ago, all the way
across England and Wales, on horseback, and walking, too, till I
came to this place where my father lay hidden, Rhug Hall, in
Dolgelly. My husband Rhisiart was here too, he that I had given
up for dead. And Alice's husband, Walter. All that was left of
Owen's people came to him here, Meredith and Elliw, his wife,
and the twins, Gwynneth and Gwenllian, with their babes. My
son was born here, too; he was big for a seven months' child.
None thought it strange, though; all Owen's race are large of
bone, and this son was the image of Owen, even in his cradle. Except for his dark coloring that he gets from his father. But then
Rhisiart is black of hair and eye, too, so no one wondered.

I had never thought to tell the little Rhys of his royal lineage;
the people roundabout pull their forelocks at him already, in
homage to his Owen-looks. He can do without a hero-image on
the other side! For he is a big, peace-loving creature, my son,
gentle and wise beyond his years; from his earliest days he sought
to mend a broken bird wing or nurse a sick fox cub till it lived.
The little king's own physician, Nicholas Colnet, tutors Rhys
there at Oxford; he is a master there. I knew that man long ago;
he tended me after the siege of Harlech, and my sister, Catherine, too. I sent Rhys with a letter to him; I do not know, truly, if
Master Colnet remembered me, or if the boy's own quality won
him, but he accepted him as student. Not many Welsh are admitted there at Oxford nowadays; we Welsh are despised all over
England, since the rebellion.

Several times, through the years, I have sought to tell Rhisiart
the truth about the boy, but each time he has not listened, seeming to skirt the subject. I have thought, sometimes—perhaps he

knows! For Rhisiart and I have agreed well all these years, and have much fond accord—yet did he, Rhisiart, love Catherine first. And my heart was given, once and for all, to Harry. We have made do, the two of us, with what was left.

And it is good—what we have. Our children, and our home—it is good. Even our sorrows, they have brought us together; the death of our twins, still-born, that came after Rhys, the tragedy of Alice, and Owen's long death-in-life.

There are many, all over Wales, that do not believe that Owen has died at all; they say that he is waiting in the hills somewhere and at Welsh need will rise again, like Arthur. And there are some who think he did die there, in the Snowdon fastnesses, hunted like a beast, living in caves underground. But it is not so; he is buried here at Rhug Hall, the home of his earliest youth.

It was a goodly holding once, Rhug Hall; Owen had given it for dower to his oldest daughter, Janet. One can still see the foundations of the great manor house; we have never rebuilt it—there is never enough time, or men either, to do the work. The English burned it years ago in the war, or some say the Nannau people did it, who followed Lancaster. They slew all who lived here, too, or carried them off; not a trace has been found of Janet or her husband or children. Even the serving folk were long gone when we came here; the place was a ruin. The enemy had not bothered to fire the outbuildings though, or perhaps they were in a hurry; it is in these little places that we have settled, Owen's people. Meredith and Elliw have the gate cottage, for they have no children; it is tiny and thatched, all covered with climbing roses in summer. Rhisiart and I live with our great brood in what was once the minstrels' house; it is long and low, and we have added on to it as we needed, so we are comfortable enough. There were several barns on the land, besides the one that burned, that we had kept our few beasts in; the others are dwellings, now, for our people. The church, or chapel, is our school; the same lightning bolt that destroyed the barn and killed Alice struck the steeple, and it is gone. Walter said that was a judgment, for the house of Christ should be a plain house, not set apart; he has taken away the cross that was there, also, but the people come there every Sunday anyway, and he speaks to them of Scripture and the New Learning. So, in a way, it is a church still. During the week, the little children come to learn their letters, and Rhisiart teaches some Latin, too, to those who are clever enough.

Rhisiart and Walter brought Owen south to Dolgelly after they were released from their own English prison; they brought him all the way in disguise, for there was a high price on his head. He had been hiding in the hills with the Savage Gethin's band; the years of his exile and the hardships he had suffered aged him greatly, and the mark of death was on him when I saw him, finally. He had a dreadful deep hollow cough, and the skin was stretched tight over his cheeks; he looked transparent. We made a home for him here, with us, Rhisiart and I; after the first months he did not leave his bed. Sometimes, only, he was conscious. Mostly he lay in a coma. Once I saw him watching my little Rhys, where he played with a litter of new puppies on the floor; a small smile played about Owen's lips, and he spoke, I bending close to catch his words. "His hands—they are like the Lancaster boy's. . . ."

I stared at him, feigning stupidity, and he said, pressing my hand, "You do not mean to tell him then?"

I answered him, saying, "No, Father . . . I want him to be a—quiet man. . . ."

"Un-sung . . ." He nodded. "Yes . . . it is good. . . ." And so I knew he knew, Owen.

He died soon after, and we buried him in an unmarked grave at the bottom of the orchard. Rhisiart, though, recorded it, in a secret place, so that those who come after will know where he lies, the great Owen of Wales.

We live quietly here, working hard, as I have said. All are equal, each owning the land he can farm and care for, even the lowly folk. They call themselves, all, Owen. Such as, it might be, a David ap Griffith Owen. So it will be a Welsh surname forever, Owen.

I have thought long about Harry, especially since he died, some seven years ago. They say he grew very hard in his last years; when I knew him he was tender and of a sweet reason. But war is not a gentle school, and killing is not done kindly. Perhaps, if I had stayed—but that is a presumptuous thought, and besides, I could not. I had seen already what way he was shaping his fate, Harry.

He has left his son two crowns to wear. But he has left a France ruined by war and a beggared England, though there are those in both kingdoms who worship Harry as a very St. George.

There is another thought I have, which I must tell. When first I came back to Wales to live in Owen's house, under the Argyllwyddes' care, I took great pleasure in all the marvelous treasures he had collected there, rare and costly things from all over the world. One I remember well, for it was a kind of puzzle and fascinated me. It was a beautiful, smooth, perfect box, from Chinese parts, Owen said. It was perhaps six inches all around, on each side, of a black so shiny to hurt your eyes. When one opened it, there was another inside, a little smaller. And, inside that, another, and another, and another—almost to infinity. But at the last, a box no bigger than a fingertip remained, and inside that, there gleamed a perfect pearl. Those boxes, in my fancy, are like the inner parts of people, to be opened and opened painstakingly—until one comes to the hidden thing. I am old enough now to be myself named, in these parts, the Argyllwyddes; I know that it is difficult to do, to come upon these treasures of the soul. One glimpses them sometimes in moments of love, or under the stress of pain or fear. Walter Brut wears his looking out of his eyes, he is so candid, but most men are not like that. Rhisiart is complex and hard to fathom, but still, over the years, I have now and then known him at his core. But Harry, that I loved to break my heart . . . though I searched all the time I knew him, and gently, too, and with care, I never came to know him. I never found the Orient pearl. I wonder if anyone ever did.

Author's Note

Of the five narrators of this story, only Morgan is invented. A daughter of that name is listed as one of the many illegitimate offspring of Owen Glendower, another daughter is listed as being in the train of Isabelle of France, and there are references to "the Welsh girl, Owen's by-blow" in Henry's tavern days. I have put them all together.

The fool is listed in many sources, though not by name.

John Page did serve for many years under Henry V and wrote an account of the siege of Rouen. Nothing is known of his origins.

For a battle fought nearly six hundred years ago, Agincourt is extremely well documented. There are four eyewitness accounts on the English side, and several on the French.

It can be clearly seen, now, that the period of this novel was one of transition. Reforming of ideas—political, religious, economic—was on the way. The Crusades, which had united Christendom, were giving way to a new spirit of nationalism, to reach its peak a few years later in Joan of Arc. There were two Popes, and religious dissent was beginning to rise all over Europe; peasant revolts, too, had broken out in many places. Everyday life was still medieval; the great bulk of the populace moved, all unknowing, as I suspect we do today, through seething and turmoil. Change was coming, but it had not yet arrived. Henry V was one of the last great medieval kings; he was, at the same time, one of the first great national heroes.

Elizabethan sentiment made a kind of warrior-saint of Henry; present-day historians, possibly as a reaction to this empty patriotism, have a tendency to downgrade him. I think the truth lies somewhere between.